"Anything you want to tell me?" asked Helm.

"That nymphomaniac act of mine," she said. "Do you know how many men I've really slept with? Two, just two, in my whole life. My husband and . . . and a mystery man who calls himself Felton because that's not his name. What is your real name?"

"Helm," I said. It could do no harm for her to know it now. "Matthew Helm."

"Did I fool you Matthew Helm? Did I convince you that I was a very wanton woman?" She laughed softly. "It was . . . rather fun, pretending to be a person like that. Every faithful wife should have one little fling at being a whore; but what happens when the mark she picks up on a street corner turns out to be much nicer than she expected? What does the faithful wife do then?"

Fawcett Gold Medal Books
by Donald Hamilton

The Mona Intercept

MATT HELM SERIES

Death of a Citizen

The Wrecking Crew

The Removers

Murderers' Row

The Ambushers

The Shadowers

The Betrayers

The Interlopers

The Poisoners

The Intriguers

The Intimidators

The Retaliators

The Terrorizers

The Revengers

THE
ANNIHILATORS

Donald
Hamilton

FAWCETT GOLD MEDAL · NEW YORK

THE airlines lost or misplaced a plane in New York, the one that was supposed to take me on to Chicago. It took them four hours to find it, maintaining the breathless suspense by announcing its imminent arrival every half hour. One of these days I'm going to invent a transportation device that runs on rails and call it a railroad. It may not operate on time, either, but at least I won't have to worry about what made it late that might cause it to fall out of the sky after I'm on board.

During the delay I managed to phone Eleanor Brand at her Chicago apartment and let her know that there was really no way of predicting how long it would take them to get the big bird to flap its wings properly so she'd better not try to meet me at that sprawling insane asylum known as O'Hare Field. I'd just take a taxi up to the Near North Side, as Chicagoans call it, whenever I finally got in.

She said that she'd be waiting with something nice for me to drink, eat, and screw. As a lady reporter—journalist —she didn't always talk like a lady was supposed to talk. Come to think of it, I never did meet a real lady, even the certified aristocratic variety, who talked like a lady was supposed to talk; supposed to by people who weren't ladies.

It was past eleven at night when I walked through the door of the building. The doorman knew me by this time, of course; but his attitude still said that, while he wouldn't presume to approve or disapprove morally, he thought that a bright and attractive young career person like Miss Brand in 504 should have been able to do better for herself than a tall, skinny nonentity like me, occupation unspecified. Well, he had a point. When I got out of the elevator and rang the doorbell, to save myself the trouble of digging out the key she'd given me, nobody answered.

I hadn't expected that. She'd said she'd be there; and

1

when she said so, she usually was. It was like being in a sports car, caught in the wrong gear by a sudden grade; the temperamental machinery lugged and bucked a bit before I could get it shifted down into the proper working ratio. I mean, I'd just finished a job. I'd left it all behind me, I thought, way over there in Europe. I was tired after the long flight. I was out of the spook business for a while. I was a human being again, well, as human as we ever let ourselves get. All I wanted was to relax and pick up where Elly and I had left off a couple of months earlier in this apartment, when she'd handed me the phone and told me Washington was on the line.

There had been no reproach in her voice. That was part of the unspoken, unwritten deal we had. We had a good time together, a very good time together. Then the phone rang and she had an assignment or I did—in our different fields of endeavor—and we didn't see each other for a while. So far, for over a year, it had worked quite well on an unofficial (some stuffy people might prefer the word illicit) basis.

It was understood between us that it could go either way eventually. Marriage wasn't outside the realm of possibility, although we were neither of us particularly good matrimonial material. On the other hand, for the time being, either party was free to terminate the relationship at will, no explanations required, no questions asked. But if she hadn't wanted me to come to her now, she'd have said so. She wouldn't have left me standing outside her door fumbling for the key, particularly not after answering the phone with every indication of pleasure at hearing my voice, and after promising to be waiting to welcome me appropriately whenever I managed to get here. I heard the telephone start to ring behind the closed door. Nobody answered it.

I swallowed something in my throat and, having found the elusive key, hesitated, wishing I had a gun—but the airport X-ray machines make a secret agent's life very difficult these days. It hadn't seemed worthwhile to have somebody waiting at O'Hare to slip me a weapon, not in a city I was just visiting to see my girl. I told myself not to be paranoid; she was probably just in the bathroom with the water running or in the kitchen with the dishwasher running. But the phone was still ringing in there, nobody was

2

doing anything about it; and you do not disregard the unexpected in my line of work.

I unlocked and opened the door and went through it fast, the way they teach us in the spook-factory-and-repair-shop we maintain out in Arizona, known as the Ranch—although they do keep changing those ballet routines on us from time to time, and I wasn't quite certain that I was employing the latest, improved door-penetration technique. As it turned out, it didn't matter, since there was nobody hostile waiting inside. There was nobody waiting inside. The phone had stopped ringing. I picked myself up and made my way cautiously into the bedroom and got out the snubnosed .38 Special revolver I'd left with her—for a spare, and because I don't feel that a woman living alone should be unarmed these violent days, particularly when she has a close friend, if you want to call it that, with as many enemies as I have. I checked the loads: full house.

Then I brought in my suitcase and closed the hall door. The apartment felt very still and empty. I looked through it carefully. It was small and very neat and not particularly feminine; she wasn't a frilly-curtains girl. The electric typewriter in the corner was tidily covered; and the pages on the table, an article she'd been working on, were precisely stacked, weighted down with an ashtray containing one crushed-out last-minute cigarette. She was a very terrible little person by modern standards; she smoked. The faint residual odor of tobacco did funny things to my throat. I wished to God she were there turning the air blue with her lousy carcinogenic fumes, just so she was there.

Drink materials were set up on the little bar in the living room. There was stuff on the stove in the diminutive kitchen; but all the burners had been turned off and no residual warmth remained. The bathroom was clean, and the big double bed in the single bedroom had been turned back for immediate occupancy, but there was no occupant. I knew a limited sense of relief. It wasn't too many years ago that I had entered an apartment in another country to find the champagne ready to be popped, the roast ready to be carved, and the lady of the place lying dead by the window in her prettiest negligee.

At least here the clock was still running, or could still be running. I wished I knew how much time was left on it, if any. I could be drawing falsely optimistic conclusions from

3

the lack of blood. Or I could, of course, be jumping to falsely pessimistic conclusions because of Eleanor's simple absence. In my line of work we do tend to expect the worst, always. I told myself that she could have run out on a last-minute errand and been delayed by some quite innocent and innocuous circumstance. She might come through the door at any moment, flustered and apologetic because she hadn't been here to greet me. Or she could call to tell me that she was stuck somewhere with a flat tire. . . .

As if in answer to my thought, the telephone started to ring again. I let it jangle three times and picked it up with a small prayer, which was not answered. The voice that spoke in my ear, although feminine, was not Elly's. It was a younger voice and strongly accented.

"Señor Helm?"

"This is Matthew Helm," I said.

The girlish voice said, "You are about to have a visitor, señor. You have the reputation of being a hasty man. If you value a certain lady's life, please restrain yourself. Negotiations are only possible in an atmosphere of restraint. Violence will be met with violence, do you understand?"

"Send in your boy, or girl, señorita," I said. "Just remember what you said: Violence will be met with violence. And I've probably been dealing in that merchandise a hell of a lot longer than you have, whoever you are."

"We are quite aware of that," the assured young voice said. "In fact that is why we are approaching you. We require an expert in violence and we have reason to believe that you are the best. The messenger will explain, señor."

"Give me his name so I can tell the doorman to let him come up."

"Her name is Dolores Anaya, señor."

The girl at the other end of the line replaced the telephone gently, severing the connection. I called downstairs; then I sat frowning grimly at the undeserving instrument. Not Cuban, I thought. Not really Mexican, although that was closer. Farther south. Guatemala wasn't quite right and neither was Colombia; but I'd heard that particular Latin-American accent before, although not that particular voice. But educated, no wetback she. Elly, what the hell have you got yourself into? What have I got you into?

But that was a stupid question. I knew exactly what

4

we were into, and I was coldly aware of the standing orders governing this particular situation. They were not very pleasant orders. But I was given no time to consider how unpleasant they really were. Somebody was knocking on the door.

I went over and let her in. She was of medium height and quite young, perhaps in her early twenties. She could have been even younger. They mature early down there. She was wearing high-heeled shoes, very snug black slacks that were a little wider below than current fashion indicated—flamenco-dancer pants—and a crisp white wedding shirt with a lot of elaborate ruffles. Her long black hair flowed down her back smooth and glossy and unadorned, but there were small silver earrings and a silver bracelet or two. She looked very slim in those black trousers, and not a bit boyish. Her face, with its smooth olive skin, was very pretty; it would be beautiful when she'd done a little more living, if she managed that. But she was going about it the wrong way.

There were big dark eyes that could have been irresistible —until she narrowed them slightly, seeing the gun in my waistband, and let me know that she could turn snake-mean, given the provocation.

"The weapon will not be necessary, señor," she said coldly. It was the voice I'd heard over the phone, of course; she'd been preparing the way for her own appearance. She must have made the call from a nearby booth to get here so fast. "Lay it aside, please."

I said, "Go out that door, baby, turn around, come back in, and start over. If I'm the man you want, the violent gent you need, I don't lay aside my gun for the first little girl who asks."

She did not like being called "baby," or being told she was a little girl. Her young face hardened. "We have the señorita!"

It was no time for displays of rage, or even concern. I said, "You're wasting my time and yours, Miss Anaya. Of course you have the señorita, so what else is new? Speak your piece and stop throwing your weight around." When she didn't respond at once, I said, "Just give me the name."

She frowned quickly. "What?"

"You want somebody killed, right?" I said, watching her. Her eyes flickered, letting me know I'd guessed correctly. I went on: "You've swung, you and whoever you're working for, but you've struck out. He's a tough proposition and you haven't got anybody on your team who's good enough, so you picked me. I suppose I should be flattered. So tell me: Who are you and who do you want dead?"

She studied me suspiciously. "Who has talked, señor?"

They're as bad as certain government agencies, these wild-eyed action groups. They never give you credit for having brains enough to figure out their dirty little secrets. If you know something you shouldn't, there must have been a leak, and somebody must be punished.

I said irritably, "Hell, I'm in a certain line of work. Sometimes I'm called upon to do a little bodyguarding when the subject is important enough. Sometimes I'm called upon to penetrate to a little intelligence material others have been unable to reach because they weren't willing to get rough enough or didn't know how. But those aren't my normal assignments. I won't ask how you learned, but you know what they are or you wouldn't be here. So give me the name and I'll tell you if I'll do it for you."

"You will do it! We have——"

I grimaced. "You have the señorita. You have the señorita. So you have the señorita. It's something, but it's not a blank check. I need the name. I need to make a telephone call to find out if that name is available or unavailable. If it's available, I'll erase it for you."

This was pure distilled bullshit, of course. It's the one game we never play. Technically I was breaking the rules by even pretending to consider the girl's demands; but I do have a certain amount of seniority in the outfit, and I thought I'd be forgiven if I went along with these creeps a little way, far enough to find out what we had to deal with.

When Dolores Anaya still stood there frowning, I said sharply: "Do you think this has never happened before? Do you think you're the first bunch of bloodthirsty characters who ever had the idea of employing a government guy like me for your private purposes, using a little pressure? Well, you hold something I value. To preserve it, I'm willing to make a deal if I can. It goes like this, señorita: You pick up that phone and let me talk with her so I know for sure you really have her and didn't hurt her too badly grabbing her. Then you let me make my call. Then I'll tell you where we stand. Okay?"

CHAPTER 2

COSTA Verde, I thought, waiting. Not everybody knows what we do for Uncle Sam, particularly not everybody down in Latin America. But certain people in Costa Verde knew because we'd done it for them once—I'd done it for them once—upon request.

There had been a bandit or revolutionary patriot, depending upon your point of view, named Jorge Santos, who'd called himself *El Fuerte*, The Strong One. He had not been a very nice man, but his unniceness had been, of course, strictly irrelevant. Political affiliations are seldom based on nice or not-nice. *El Fuerte's* real mistake was that he'd caused embarrassment to President Avila of Costa Verde and, through President Avila, to certain people in Washington who'd considered Avila to be a stable and friendly influence in the region, although, objectively speaking, he really wasn't a very nice man, either. So I'd been sent down there with a big rifle to remove this revolutionary annoyance to our good friend President Avila, with the help of a small military detachment commanded by a competent Costa Verde army colonel named Hector Jimenez.

Unfortunately for Washington, it became obvious shortly thereafter that Colonel Jimenez had certain political plans of his own when he used the same accurate rifle, which I had left with him as a token of the friendship between our countries—had it used, actually, since he wasn't much of a marksman himself—to remove Avila and earn himself a promotion to president, after which he'd shipped the big gun back to me with his thanks. . . .

Dolores Anaya had her connection. She was speaking

into the phone. "Oso? Leona here. Let me speak with Lobo." She waited; then she said, "Lobo? Is it permissible for the man to speak with the woman? He will not proceed without . . . *Bueno.*" She extended the instrument to me.

"Elly," I said. Her voice said something in my ear, but it wasn't clear. "Elly?"

"Matt? I'm sorry, they had me gagged and my lips don't seem to . . . Matt, I'm sorry. Stupid me. After you called to say you'd be late I drove out to get some vermouth before the liquor store closed. I saw it was getting low, and they . . ."

I had a mental picture of her, small and angry and unafraid, but probably a little disheveled from being captured and gagged and perhaps bound; and she would hate that. She had the idea that she was a very ugly little girl, with her mobile monkey-face and straight brown hair; and that the only way to deal with this dreadful handicap was to take special pains with her appearance.

We'd happily overcome, in the past months, some of the inferiority feelings that had been hammered into her by, I gathered, a lovely and unloving mother who'd wanted a pretty doll to play with, not a bright but somewhat less than beautiful child to bring up. But she still had some distance to go; and it was unbearable to think that she might not be allowed to make it all the way now and become the person she was meant to be, the person she would have enjoyed being, just because of some hot-blooded political screwballs and a cold-blooded fish of a so-called lover who couldn't forget his idiot notions of duty and discipline, or could he? I listened to her telling me how they had grabbed her and how dumb she'd been to let them. . . .

"Are you all right?" I asked when she stopped.

"Yes, so far, but . . . Matt."

"Yes?"

There was sudden, breathless urgency in her voice: "Matt, I couldn't stand it if you . . . It would never be any good again. Nothing would ever be any good again. Please don't let them make you do anything because of me. . . ." Her voice was cut off abruptly, presumably by a hand over her mouth.

"Enough." It was a man's voice, a young man's voice, presumably the voice of the man called Lobo, the Wolf, who seemed to be running the show. At least the girl had shown him a certain deference. He continued: "You heard her say she was all right, señor. It is up to you whether or not she will continue to be all right. Consider it very carefully. For our cause, we will kill if we must, even a pretty lady like her."

The phone went dead, leaving Elly alone somewhere with Lobo the Wolf and Oso the Bear, while I got Leona the Lioness for company. Kid stuff. But they all have causes. It's getting to the point, I reflected, where it's like a ray of sunshine after a long dark winter to meet some splendid mercenary creep who simply murders for money, or a fine sadistic jerk who merely likes to see the agonized wiggles and hear the tormented screams and smell the blood. Those are natural impulses I can understand; but I'm getting pretty damn sick of these incomprehensible high-minded ladies and gentlemen who kidnap and slaughter innocent people with the purest and most idealistic motives in the world.

I started to give the phone back to Dolores Anaya and caught myself and glanced at her questioningly. She made a gesture of rejecting the instrument, nodding.

"Make your call, señor."

I dialed the Washington number and identified myself. "Condition Blue," I said. When the girl looked disturbed and made a move to break the connection, I said, "That means there's a gun at my head, or somebody's head. Is it supposed to be a secret?" The outstretched hand was withdrawn.

"I'll put you through," said the girl in Washington. Almost immediately, Mac's voice came on the line.

"Matt here, sir," I said. "Condition Blue."

The fact that I used my real name instead of my code name—which happens to be Eric—warned my superior that the conversation was being overheard at my end.

"Yes, Matt," he said, acknowledging the signal. "What's the problem?"

At this hour of the night he wouldn't be sitting at the familiar beat-up office desk in front of the bright window he liked to make us squint at. It was well past midnight in Washington, and I'd never entered his home, so I couldn't visualize him at the phone in pajamas and dressing gown. To me he was always the lean, ageless gray-haired man in a gray suit with whom I'd worked longer than I cared to remember.

I looked at Dolores Anaya. "The name," I said. She hesitated but gave it to me. I said into the phone: "Name check, please. Rael, Armando Rael. Is that name on the available list?"

Well, it was what the kid expected, wasn't it? She was sitting there obviously impressed by all the undercover nonsense and even more impressed by the thought that we seemed to have the world's population classified, presumably by computer, into available people we could blow away at will, and those few lucky folks who were unavailable to our grim assassination teams, at least for the moment.

There was a little pause, as Mac digested the request and its implications, and marshaled his facts a thousand miles away. He spoke precisely at last: "Armando Rael is the current president of Costa Verde—dictator, actually—having thrown out the former incumbent a few years ago in a sudden coup. That was Col. Hector Jimenez, whom you may remember, who replaced President Avila rather forcibly. Jimenez, although a military man, was a little too liberal, particularly on the subject of land reform; he was therefore overthrown by a junta of reactionary landowners and conservative army officers headed by Rael. Jimenez was fortunate to escape with his life—and of course some money. They never escape poor, do they? The current president of Costa Verde is not exactly a firm believer in human rights and democracy, I'm told. There have been two known attempts on his life already, both unsuccessful."

"Yes, sir," I said. "The question is, would anybody besides Rael object to a successful attempt?"

"By whom?"

"By me," I said. "I repeat, Condition Blue."

"Yes, I see," he said, and I thought it very likely that he did by this time. He wasn't a man for whom you needed to draw detailed pictures. He said, "Very well, I'll check."

I spoke to Leona, the young black-maned lioness. "He's consulting the oracle. Be patient."

Dolores Anaya did not speak. We waited. I tried not to think of a small, brave, intelligent girl with whom I'd shared some very pleasant experiences and some not so pleasant—we'd met under rather strained and violent cir-

10

cumstances. What she'd gone through then had not been my fault, but this obviously was. I should have remembered that a man in my peculiar line of work draws violence the way a lone tree on a hilltop draws lightning. Well, actually I had remembered, and warned her, and she had laughed and said that she'd long since given up expecting anything good to come to her safely and free of charge. . . .

"Matt?" The phone spoke in my ear.

"Yes, sir."

"Unavailable," Mac said, playing the game on my terms, which was nice of him. He could simply have ordered me to cut out the stalling and, for a start, send the pretty messenger—of course I hadn't told him she was pretty—back to her friends with a neatly slit throat the way I was supposed to, the way we were all supposed to, in any situation like this. As I said, the hostage game is one we simply do not play. Mac went on: "I checked the classification with State, just to be certain. I was informed that President Armando Rael of Costa Verde is not expendable; and that there must not be the slightest suggestion that we consider him so, since he is a very sensitive person in a very sensitive area and we must not jeopardize this valuable relationship in any way." When I didn't respond to this immediately, Mac asked, "You are in Chicago?"

"Yes, sir."

"I think I understand the problem, but that solution must not be used, not even as a feint or distraction. No move whatever must be made in that direction. I am truly sorry."

He sounded sincere, and I got the impression that under other circumstances he might have been willing to make an exception to the standing orders; but national policy made it impossible for him to free my hands. Check to the tall, skinny gent with the gun in his belt and the stupid look on his face. And to the tough little lady who, with her life at stake, had in effect given me my orders, telling me that nothing would ever be any good again if I allowed her to be used against me in this fashion.

"Sorry," I said. "Yes, sir. Don't hang up. Hold the line."

I looked at Dolores Anaya, whose beautiful dark eyes were watching me steadily. It was too bad. You hate to see them waste themselves, the young ones. She was a pretty thing;

11

she could have become a lovely thing; but she'd never make it now. Not unless she had more sense than I thought. I said, "My chief says the name you gave me is unavailable."

"It is too bad, señor. Then the señorita must die."

I made the expected, reasonable, useless noises: "What's the point? It won't get your dictator killed." I could see that this made absolutely no impression on her—she was locked into her predetermined course of action—and I went on: "And it could get some people killed you'd rather keep living."

She bristled fiercely. "Are you threatening me, señor?"

"Don't be corny," I said. "Of course I'm threatening you. But let's try something else first. Will you let me talk with your daddy?"

She looked startled; then she frowned suspiciously. "Who has told you? I did not give you my full name."

I said. "Hell, I once spent several days in the jungle with Col. Hector Jimenez. I got to know him pretty well; do you think I don't know a daughter of his when I see her?" This wasn't quite true, of course. I hadn't realized who Dolores Anaya must be until I asked myself why Costa Verde had popped into my head like that; then I'd looked again and seen the unmistakable resemblance. I said, "Your male parent was a sensible man when I saw him last. He wouldn't pull a fool stunt like this; and even if he did let somebody talk him into it, he wouldn't persist with it after it had gone sour. Get him on the phone and let me talk some sense into him."

Dolores Anaya, whose family name was Jimenez—they weight down babies with great long strings of names down there—shook her pretty dark head. "It will do no good, señor. You are wrong, the idea was altogether my father's. He has always remembered the very expert and professional manner in which you dealt with the bandit *El Fuerte*. He said we must have you now, since others have failed. Two others, one of whom was"—she hesitated—"was my older brother Ricardo. My father said it was too bad, and he regretted the necessity for coercion, but the people of Costa Verde must be saved from the butcher Rael regardless of cost. Their freedom is more important than the respect and friendship he feels for you, and perhaps you for him."

12

Well, it made sense. It's the old Savior-Of-Your-Country syndrome. And of course no conspirator, particularly no Latin-American conspirator, would ever dream of simply picking up the phone and asking me if I'd shoot somebody for him, please. It has to be done complicated, with kidnaping and intimidation, or it doesn't count.

There was, of course, another consideration that the girl hadn't mentioned, either because she hadn't been taken wholly into her father's confidence or because they'd agreed not to call it to my attention, since it might influence my decision unfavorably. It seemed very unlikely that if they did obtain the services of an agent of the U.S. Government against Rael, by whatever means, they'd keep it a secret from Rael, even if it made the job harder.

Mac had already hinted that the present dictator of Costa Verde was a sensitive person—read: paranoid bastard—who'd blow his stack at any suggestion of treachery on the part of his gringo allies. Even if I should fail, the fact that I had tried could be used to sow a great deal of discord between Rael and his Americano supporters, to Jimenez's advantage.

I said, "Aren't you forgetting something? Isn't your daddy forgetting something?"

"What, señor?"

"He may have Eleanor Brand, but I have you."

The girl tossed her head haughtily and gave a scornful little laugh that an aristocratic lady of revolutionary France might have used when threatened with the guillotine. "So kill me now!" She made a sharp gesture. "I claimed the right to speak with you. I was not good for managing the abduction, that was work for the men, but I could do this. I could speak just as convincingly for my father as my brother Emilio, who calls himself Lobo. And the fact that I would put myself into your hands, and that my father would allow it, should prove to you how seriously we take this matter. So if you wish to kill me, kill. It will do your lady no good, I assure you. There will certainly be no trade, if that is what you are thinking. I would take my own life, first."

She was very impressive, so young and so dedicated; but they are always slightly incredible in their arrogance, these baby martyrs. They are so ready to sacrifice themselves for their beliefs, but it never occurs to them that they may not

13

be unique; that there may be other folks around ready for sacrifice, too.

"Sure," I said. "It was just a thought."

Dolores Jimenez glanced at her watch. "There is a time limit. If I am not back soon . . ."

It was time to play the last card, even though I had no faith in it, dealing with youthful fanatics like this one. "All right, listen closely. . . . Sir," I said into the phone.

Mac's voice said, "Yes, Matt?"

"The classification on Jimenez?"

"Available. I thought you might need to know, so I also asked that question. Although of course they do not condone violence over there in the halls of diplomacy—at least not publicly—nevertheless if violence should occur, I gather they would not be displeased to have it occur to Colonel Jimenez. Well, at least as long as the act cannot in any way be attributed to the present regime. There are softhearted elements of the administration, not to mention of the liberal press, who disapprove of our support of Armando Rael and would use any terrorist act of his in this country to discredit this policy and those who favor it. But if it can be accomplished discreetly, they will not be unhappy. The colonel's repeated loud condemnation of their man, Rael, and his constant efforts to return to power, are becoming very annoying to certain of our policy makers."

"I see," I said, and looked at the girl as I spoke. "The colonel is available. Very good. Then I request a complete cover on the whole Jimenez menage. In particular I want to know when Hector himself gets up in the morning and when he goes to bed at night. I want to know when he sleeps with his wife and if they both have satisfactory orgasms. . . ."

Mac broke in: "Señora Jimenez died about a year after escaping from Costa Verde, perhaps due to the hardships she suffered getting out of there. As far as the rest of the family is concerned, the older son Ricardo was captured while making an attempt on Rael's life and disappeared into the political prison known as La Fortaleza. It is believed that he died there, not pleasantly. There is a younger son Emilio and a daughter Dolores."

"I have just had the pleasure of meeting Dolores," I said.

"I have even spoken with Emilio, unfortunately under rather unfavorable circumstances. But that's beside the point. I want to know when the colonel goes to the can in the morning and whether his bowel movement is soft or hard. I particularly want to know his whereabouts at any hour of the day or night. And of course his security arrangements."

"We have a lot of that information, or we can obtain it," Mac said. "As I indicated, his political activities have aroused some unfavorable interest. Surveillance will be arranged."

"Around-the-clock surveillance, excellent," I said for Dolores's benefit. "Next item: Please send somebody to my Washington apartment with the spare key they keep down in the office. At the back of the bedroom closet is a long plastic case containing a .300 Holland and Holland Magnum rifle with a heavy target barrel and a twenty-power telescopic sight. You may remember the gun. I'd appreciate it if you'd have it delivered to the armorer. Ask him to check it out carefully. It's been sitting idle for several years."

"Yes, I remember the rifle quite well," Mac said.

I said, "Ask the armorer, when he's overhauled it, to make me up a hundred rounds of fresh ammunition. His records will show the load we worked up for the gun—the hundred-eighty-grain bullet. The particular bullet we used isn't manufactured any longer, so unless he still has a stock of them, he'll have to find another with the same expansion characteristics. Remind him that I do not want an armor-plated grizzly-bear bullet that won't open up on lighter game. The primary target will be a not-very-big human male at extreme range, where the bullet will have lost a great deal of its velocity. I want a slug with a light jacket that'll expand reliably under those conditions and tear a nice big lethal hole through the sonofabitch. There will be some other targets, but let's set it up for this one. What with the current rules for interstate shipment of firearms, you'll have to get the weapon to me by courier. I'll call later and let you know where."

"Very well. Anything else?"

"That'll do it for now," I said. "Thank you, sir. Matt out."

I passed the instrument to the girl, who replaced it firmly in its cradle. There was a little silence; then she said, "Do you really think you can frighten us?"

"Not really," I said. "Some people are too stupid to be scared. But tell your friends, tell your daddy, that unless Eleanor Brand is returned unharmed, I go hunting. Colonel Jimenez has seen me at work. Ask him if he really wants to be at the wrong end of the rifle that finished *El Fuerte* half a valley away. Tell him that if anything happens to my girl, he can just forget about saving the poor suffering people of Costa Verde. They'll have to make it on their own because he won't be around to help them. And neither will you, Miss Lioness, or your brother Mister Wolf, or your friend Mister Bear. Don't start this thing going, señorita. You can stop it right here. Send back Eleanor Brand, unharmed, and we'll just forget the whole thing. Hurt her and you're dead."

She looked at me for a moment with those lustrous brown Spanish eyes; and I saw that I had failed. She, a Costa Verde patriot, was not to be intimidated by a little secret-agent foolishness, some menacing ballistic jargon, and a few threats. I had hoped—well, just a little—that she might be bright enough to realize that the last thing their lousy revolution, or counterrevolution, needed was a vengeful sniper in attendance; but she was hypnotized by the pure bright image of Costa Verde freedom that now required a human sacrifice. . . .

"Good night, Señor Helm," she said politely, turning toward the door. "I regret that we could not come to an agreement. I regret it very much. And I think you will, too."

I watched her go; I gave her a small lead; I went after her. If they had any sense at all, any technique at all, any caution at all, it was useless, but I couldn't pass up the slightest chance of a break, even if it was no chance at all.

I made it down four flights of stairs in time to see her go out the front door of the building. I followed the slim figure in the plain black trousers and the elaborate white blouse at a suitable distance. There was a filling station on the corner, closed at this late hour. She stopped at the public telephone there that she'd probably used to call me earlier. I prayed, if you want to call it that, that she was not as impervious to reason as I'd thought, as proud and dedicated and intractable. Maybe she could accept failure. Maybe, standing there at the phone, she was now advising delay, reconsideration. Maybe there would at least be a consultation before anything was done. Maybe somebody sensible would prevail.

Waiting, I thought about one possible course of action I'd passed up: I could have tried to beat the location out of her while she was still within my reach. The fact that she was a girl and quite attractive had not, of course, figured in my decision on the subject: Hell, they ask for equal treatment these days. Who am I to deny it to them? But that kind of interrogation is a long, slow process and doesn't always work with the patriots and fanatics. Well, anybody can be broken eventually, but sometimes it takes days, even weeks. And even if I'd learned where Elly was being held, the odds would have been very great against my getting her away unharmed. . . .

Dolores Anaya Jimenez was hanging up the phone. I could tell nothing from her attitude, at the distance. She started walking again, in her crisp high-heeled way, and I followed; but when we came to a larger, better-lighted street and she flagged down a late-cruising taxi, I let her go. She probably knew I was behind her. It was my obvious move because it was my only move. She would lead me nowhere useful; and the word had now been passed, one way or the other.

I walked back to the apartment building. Their timing was very good; or maybe they'd been waiting for my appearance. I saw the big old sedan turn the corner ahead very fast and brake hard in front of the building. I saw the door open. Something fell out and rolled along the pavement. Then they were roaring past me, accelerating violently. There were two of them. The street lights caught them briefly: a heavy-faced, darkly moustached young man in front, with massive shoulders, driving: and in the rear, struggling to get the car door closed again after discharging his cargo, a smaller, slighter young man, clean-shaven, whose features were quite familiar. I was getting so I could spot a Jimenez at a glance. Brother Emilio, and his friend the Bear. I suppose I could have shot at them, but what was the point? That would come, but there was no hurry now. There would be plenty of time for all that, later.

The doorman was hurrying out to look, drawn by the screech of rubber, but I was the first to reach her. You learn how to shut yourself off at times like that. You button up the emotional armor like a tank going into battle. But the defenses are never perfect; and I stood there thinking how small she looked, lying there. I thought of how it would have hurt her to know she'd be seen like that, with a shoe missing and her stockings torn by the fall and her dress dirty and disordered, darkly stained in front around the small tear under the breast where the knife had penetrated.

Elly's face was very pale. Her eyes were open and unseeing. There was an ugly scrape along one cheek, but it had not bled significantly. They do not bleed much after the heart stops beating. I knew a sickening sense of loss and guilt. I reached down to tidy her dress a bit, but stopped. That was just me catering to my lousy conscience. The police wouldn't like it; and it didn't really matter to her now. . . .

The police gave me a hard time, of course. They don't like to find a man with a gun, even a man with an unfired gun, standing over a dead body. In fact they simply don't like to find a man with a gun, period. They want the firearms concession all to themselves.

But I finally managed to get my ID looked at by a plainclothes supercop of some kind named Bannon, to whom they'd turned me over at last like a curious specimen of butterfly they'd netted and stuck on a pin for careful scientific classification. Bannon was large and red-faced and sloppy-looking; and I'd met them before, those sloppy-looking law-enforcement gents who hope you'll assume that their brains are as dull as the creases in their pants. His small greenish eyes studied the fancy little leather folder with its impressively official-looking contents that we carry to intimidate the peasants when we're not pretending to be somebody we aren't and secrecy isn't mandatory. His chest heaved in a sigh under his rumpled vest, one button of which needed his wife's immediate attention if he wasn't going to lose it. If he had a wife.

"Three o'clock in the morning," he said, "and I don't just have an old-fashioned gangland-type killing and a dead reporter-girl, I've got you, Mr. Helm. Well, give me the number." I gave him the Washington number and he made the call. There was a brief conversation; then I got to talk a little. Finished, I gave the instrument back to him and he returned it to its cradle. He sat for a full minute, looking at me across his scarred desk. At last he said, "I don't have to, you know, Mr. Helm. This is my city, not yours."

I shrugged. "It's my country, and yours."

"And what's that got to do with a young lady journalist getting herself killed?" He grinned abruptly. "Okay, we'll do it your way. Washington's way. I've got troubles enough right here without getting myself or the department involved in international politics."

So by four in the morning we were all good friends and I had my gun back. We all agreed, for newspaper purposes, that the poor girl shouldn't have poked her pretty little nose into the local drug business like that; the boys played rough and didn't appreciate reporters, male or female, snooping around. This theory of the case was, of course, as I'd known it would be when I proposed it, confirmed or at least supported by the half-finished draft of the magazine article that had been found on her typewriter table.

CHAPTER 3

THERE were fourteen people in the small classroom in the new building on the south side of Chicago's Midway that is known as the Ransome Institute, more formally the William Putnam Ransome Institute for Pan-American Studies. As a foreigner originally hailing from the distant and ignorant state of New Mexico—people living east of the Mississippi sometimes think we need passports to enter the U.S.—I'd been patronizingly informed that the two surnames involved were real big in Chicago. The Putnams were old railroad money, and the Ransomes were right up there in the meat-packing business with the Swifts and Armours.

It was two days since Elly Brand had died. Although I'd been functioning after a fashion throughout those two

19

days, they were not entirely clear in my mind. Now, sitting in a chair at the rear of the little room, I felt oddly fragile, as though I were convalescing from a serious illness or a bad wound; and in a sense I suppose I was. The lady at the front of the room didn't seem quite real—well, hell, the whole room was a little unreal—although I knew exactly who she was and why she was there and why I was there. But it was an intellectual sort of knowledge only. I was an observer of the scene, not a true participant.

The lady was named Frances Dillman—Associate Professor Frances Ransome Dillman, Ph.D., to you. And to me. She was some indeterminate age between an old twenty-five and a young forty; a tall female beanpole who somehow managed a faint air of upperclass elegance while wearing a brown tweed suit that had the comfortably threadbare look the British love and some Americans like to copy, with leather patches where she'd gone through the elbows of the jacket at last. Even the best Harris tweed, and this was the very best, doesn't last quite forever.

Mrs. Dillman, Dr. Dillman, Associate Professor Dillman, was wearing a high-necked beige cashmere sweater with her comfortable tweeds. It was obviously expensive, very fine and soft, but she didn't really have the frontal development to do a sweater justice. Her narrow legs were encased in knee-length wool stockings, her feet in well-worn but well-polished brogues suitable for tramping a Scottish moor, if you had a Scottish moor handy.

But the lady was not unhandsome in her way. She had a fine blade of a nose, strong cheekbones, a firm jaw, and a wide if thin-lipped mouth. Her gray eyes were rather striking under her dark, unplucked eyebrows. Her brown hair was cut quite short but neatly and becomingly arranged about her well-shaped head. She stood sternly at the blackboard with a pointer in her hand, indicating the areas of interest on the map she'd drawn in chalk—not a bad job of freehand map making, I had to admit.

"For the benefit of those who've joined us late," she said, with a cold look in my direction, "I will repeat that we'll be visiting the cradle of the ancient Melmec civilization, recently discovered in the Costa Verde jungle, here." The pointer tapped a stylized little flat-topped pyramid that she'd drawn in an otherwise particularly empty space on her map. "The existence of this lost civilization was de-

20

duced quite recently by my husband, Dr. Archibald Dillman, in much the same manner in which the existence of the planet Neptune was deduced back in 1846 by its effect upon the orbit of the neighboring planet, Uranus. . . ."

The unseasonably warm weather in which I'd arrived had broken, and the view out the window was typically winter-in-Chicago. Big snowflakes were drifting past the windows. The sky was bleak and gray. Good funeral weather, totally miserable, I reflected; but Elly had been hastily adopted, in death, by some family members she'd had little use for alive. She'd be buried in the family plot in the small New England town from which she'd come, which she'd left as soon as she could scrape up the fare out. Well, I'd said my good-byes, such as they were. Or maybe I was still saying them and would be for some time to come.

The tall lady at the blackboard had returned from her brief interplanetary excursion. "In other words," she said, "down here in Central America, the behavior of the Olmecs on the one hand, and of the Mayas on the other, as revealed by their surviving artifacts and records, the ones we've been able to decipher, indicated clearly that they had been subjected to certain influences, linguistic and otherwise, that *must* have originated in this previously unexplored area. My husband and I were able to make the first scientific penetration of the area, with the assistance of this institute, and with the full cooperation of the Costa Verde government."

She had been regarding the blackboard map as she spoke. Now she turned abruptly to face us, slapping the pointer against the palm of her hand. "One thing we must have very clear before we start," she said. "You've presumably joined this tour for strictly archaeological purposes. The present politics of the area do not concern you, must not concern you. Our work is totally dependent upon the good will of the current regime down there. They can close the site to us any time they wish. Therefore, I must insist: Whatever you think of conditions in Costa Verde, please keep your opinions to yourselves. Please, no public criticism of their institutions, political or economic or social. Please, no photographs that may reflect unfavorably upon the present government. Understood?"

There was a small murmur of protest, but she stared us

down, waiting for the hostile sounds to stop. At last she nodded minutely as if satisfied, and spoke in milder tones:

"Now let's get to the practical aspects of our journey. To review what's in the printed instructions you were given: You should have stout shoes and some durable clothes. Unlike Chichen Itza and Tikal, this area has not yet been fully developed for tourism; and if you've visited those older sites—older in terms of the length of time we've known about them—you'll know that even there a considerable amount of hiking and climbing is required. On the other hand, let me also remind you that while the flight home is direct, on the way down we'll be staying in good hotels in Mexico City and in Santa Rosalia, the capital of Costa Verde. You'll want to have some reasonably presentable clothes to wear there. Having already threatened your freedom of speech, I won't attack your sartorial principles; but if the gentlemen can bear to wear jackets and neckties, and if the ladies can bring themselves to appear in dresses and stockings, I think they'll feel more comfortable. Sports shirts and pantsuits have not yet taken Latin America by storm, at least not for polite evening wear. . . ."

When we emerged from the building, the snow had stopped, but the sidewalk was slushy. I made my way to my rental car without paying much attention to my fellow tour-members; I'd have plenty of time to get to know them later. I drove directly to the nearby motel where I'd taken a room. I hadn't gone back to stay in Eleanor's apartment, of course. Not only was it a place of too many memories, it wasn't safe. I hadn't even returned there to pick up my suitcase. Somebody in the organization would retrieve it for me and hold it for me until I returned.

I mean, my threats would have been reported to Hector Jimenez by his daughter, and while the girl might discount them, I knew that the colonel himself, knowing me, would take them seriously. He might even get the bright idea of striking first—a preemptive strike, in military terms. So I'd broken clean; and even though circumstances had made it necessary for me to remain in Chicago a few days longer, it's a big city, and I didn't think the homicidal Costa Verde patriots, self-styled, were likely to stumble upon me way down here at the other end of town, the south end, the university end. I parked the car in front of my room and went inside to call Washington.

"I'll put you through," the girl said after I'd identified myself properly.

"Just a minute," I said. "Note this down, please. Information required: Frances Dillman, Ph.D., Archibald Dillman, Ph.D., both on the faculty of the University of Chicago. I'd like everything I can get on them, including the husband's current whereabouts. And brace yourself; here are some more names for Research to play with. Ready?" I got out the mimeographed stuff I'd been given when I signed up for the tour—pulling a good many strings to get myself admitted so long after the official deadline—and read off the list of participants, and had her read it back to me for accuracy. I said, "All these people are taking an archaeological safari to the newly discovered Copalque ruins in Central America, sponsored by the Ransome Institute of Pan-American Studies. What I particularly want to know is if any of them could be using this tour to get them into Costa Verde for purposes totally unscientific. As I just found out, what with the unsettled political conditions down there, there are no regular pleasure tours available, and individual tourists are apparently eyed with considerable suspicion. That's why I joined the group, and I'm wondering if any of my fellow explorers could have had the same idea. So please have Research find out for me if any of them has ever been associated with Costa Verde in any way that might give them a motive for sneaking back unobtrusively. I'll try to phone in for the preliminary data tomorrow before we take off; but we're leaving here at the crack of dawn, so somebody'll have to get the full report to me later, either at the Hotel El Paseo in Mexico City, or at the Hotel Gobernador, Santa Rosalia, Costa Verde. Now put me through, please."

Mac was apparently already on the line, listening, because his voice came immediately: "Yes, Eric?"

"How are they doing with my new passport and my camera gear, sir? There'll be a bus at the institute to take us to O'Hare at seven-thirty tomorrow morning; and the bosslady was very definite about us having all necessary documents before takeoff."

"The courier should be knocking on your door," Mac said. "In addition to the items mentioned, he has the rifle you requested, with ammunition."

I said, "The armorer must have worked around the

23

clock. Thank him for me, and apologize, please. Actually, I ordered it made ready mainly to impress somebody who didn't impress; and while I'm glad to have it handy, I don't think I'll be using it immediately."

There was a little pause. At last Mac said, "You have not told me the reason for the delay, Eric. I have acceded to your various requests since time was too short for argument—besides, you were not in a highly rational condition—but now I think you had better explain yourself. Why wait? Instant retribution is essential as a deterrent to others with similar notions."

It's the one crime that, after all his years in the business, is still capable of arousing him to a state of cold, unreasoning fury. He once told me that if it were left to him, he would solve the skyjacking problem very simply: He'd merely send up a couple of fighter planes to blast any hijacked airliner out of the sky and to hell with the passengers and crew. To be sure, he'd said, it would cost, maybe a few hundred innocent lives; but it wouldn't take more than one or two such object lessons to discourage this vicious type of extortion permanently, probably saving more lives in the long run.

I said, "Jimenez and his family and his political hangers-on are pretty well forted up in that estate he's got out in Lake Park. Maybe we could blast them out, but a gory massacre attributed to this agency, with whatever justification, isn't the kind of publicity we need, sir. When it happens, the people who count will know who was behind it and why; but give me time to set it up discreetly."

"How?"

I said honestly, "I don't know yet, sir."

He said coldly, "Let me remind you that we have always operated on the principle of quick retaliation. They *must* learn that this kind of blackmail will earn them nothing but instant death. That is the basis for the instructions I have formulated to deal with such contingencies."

"Yes, sir," I said, and took a big chance: "But with all due respect, sir, you're not giving the orders here. She is."

There was a dangerous pause; but when he spoke his voice was less harsh. "I see. A sentimental gesture, Eric?"

"Call it that, sir. I've had a couple of days to think it

24

over. It will be done, I promise you that; but it's going to be done the way she'd want it done, sir."

When you're bucking him, it's always well to go heavy on the "sirs." He's not fool enough not to see through the phony respectful smokescreen; but it kind of amuses him and he's somewhat easier to influence when he's amused. It was an odd reversal of our usual relationship, I reflected wryly, for me to be acting as the advocate of caution and restraint.

When he didn't speak, I went on: "As we both know, Elly wasn't a turn-the-other-cheek girl. She believed in giving as good as she got, or as bad as she got. But I don't think she'd have wanted us to indulge in a mindless vendetta on her behalf. She was, well, concerned about the state of the world. She wouldn't have wanted to be avenged to the last drop of blood if total vengeance could only be achieved at the expense of innocent people."

"The innocent people of Costa Verde, you mean," Mac said dryly.

"That's right."

"So you do not think Miss Brand would have favored the obvious: instant and complete annihilation of the organization by whose members she was murdered?"

I said, "What's the real hurry, sir? I'm going to wipe out that goddamn junior-grade zoo of Jimenez's: the lioness, the wolf, and the bear. Don't worry. They'll be taken care of. But as for the colonel himself, we don't really know the extent of his responsibility. Maybe those bloodthirsty kids got out of hand and exceeded their orders. I've got to remember that Jimenez was a good man once. I fought beside him, remember: a very tough little gent, a highly competent soldier with all the guts in the world and lots of compassion for his people."

Mac said, "But he's older now, and he's known what real power is. Even good men, elevated to high political office, tend to start thinking that they are so indispensable to their countries that they are justified in using any means whatever, no matter how brutal, to keep their positions, or to regain them if lost. At that point they become the same bloody tyrants we've known since the dawn of history, and the world is better off without them."

It was an echo of my own thoughts of a couple of nights

25

ago. "Yes, sir," I said. "That's exactly what I have to find out, what I'm heading down there to find out. Just how bad a president is this Rael? And how good was Jimenez while he was in? If he's really what his country needs, I think . . . I think Elly would prefer to settle for the three immediately involved in her death, and leave Colonel Jimenez himself alive to ride into Santa Rosalia on his big white horse, the glorious savior of Costa Verde. That way . . . that way, in a sense, she won't have died for nothing."

There was a little silence. At last Mac said, "Remember that official government policy favors Rael."

"I'm not forgetting," I said. "But official government policy can change, or be changed."

Mac said, "I didn't hear that, Eric. There must be something wrong with our connection."

"Yes, sir."

"Very well, I'll authorize the delay. The information you requested will be sent as soon as available. And you can leave the rifle, and whatever arms you're carrying at present that you don't want to take on the plane, with the courier who brings your travel documents; he will know where to store everything until you need it. Anything else?"

"Not at the moment."

"Be careful. The climate of Costa Verde is rumored to be moderately unhealthful at the moment."

"Yes, sir." I hesitated. "Oh, there is one more thing. A wild stab in the dark. Since Jimenez has thought of recruiting a professional like me to deal with Rael, it's just barely possible that Rael may have thought of recruiting a professional like me to deal with Jimenez. Ideas like that are contagious. Could you have somebody check to see if anybody we know, either in the private or public sector, is moving around that part of the world in a purposeful manner?"

"Request noted."

"And please tell the surveillance team out in Lake Park to be careful. People living under the constant threat of a sniper's bullets tend to get slightly desperate; another good reason for delay. Let's let them feel the pressure for a while, until they mess their pants or panties every time a door slams. But the boys should be prepared to deal with the cornered-rat syndrome . . . no, never mind. I'll warn them myself. Eric out."

I sat there for a moment after hanging up, looking around the bleak motel room and, I suppose, comparing it subconsciously with the warm and friendly little North Side apartment in which I would have been staying now, in pleasant company, if certain things hadn't happened.

I picked up the phone again and called the surveillance number and asked a question. The answer was that the subject in question, the male Jimenez senior, was still in residence and had just been seen driving in and, yes, they did have his telephone number. I gave my warning and broke the connection and called the number. I was answered by a very familiar voice, feminine, young, with a strong and unique Spanish accent. I'd wondered how I'd feel if I'd heard that voice again. I felt nothing but a mild regret. Dolores Anaya Jimenez had been a reasonably intelligent and quite good-looking kid with lots of potential. She could have become a happy wife and mother; she could have become the first lady president of Costa Verde. It was too bad that she had chosen to commit suicide two nights ago, a pretty young girl like that.

"Señor Hector Jimenez, please," I said.

"Who ees thees, please?" Then I heard her breath catch. "Señor Helm, I want to tell you——"

I said, "Señorita, I hold no conversations with the dead. Well, I will ask one question. Did I or did I not watch you pass the sentence of execution over the phone the other night?" Her silence was an answer. I said, "Very well. I gave you a choice and you chose the bullet. Now put your daddy on, please."

There was a little pause; then I heard high-heeled shoes recede across a hard floor of some kind. Presently other, heavier, duller footsteps approached and Jimenez's voice spoke in my ear. I was surprised at how familiar it sounded after all the years that had passed.

"Matthew?"

"Long time, Hector," I said. "That was a very stupid thing you just did. If you'd made mistakes like that back when we were stalking *El Fuerte* through the jungle, we wouldn't be here, either of us. A question."

"Ask."

"Did you really give those jackass kids those jackass orders?"

He hesitated. "The basic idea was mine, amigo. The

27

execution of it . . . well, the commander is responsible for the actions of his troops. Matthew?"

"Yes?"

"Your quarrel is with me. My daughter, in particular, is very young——"

"Bullshit!" I said sharply. "Your homicidal daughter is old enough to tell her brother to use a knife, and your homicidal son is old enough to do it. And what's this "amigo" crap, anyway? If we'd really been amigos, you'd have picked up a phone and called me when you needed help, instead of what you did."

"And you would have said no, most regretfully, because it would have been against the policy of the government for which you work, which favors the butcher Rael."

"Correct," I said. "But it would have been handled in a friendly and civilized fashion and nobody would have got hurt." I drew a sharp breath. "Jesus Christ, man, we sneaked through the boonies together with that tough little task force of yours; we stood off the mass attacks of *El Fuerte's* ragged-ass army on that lousy ridge; we ran for the coast together hauling that beat-up agent of ours your people had rescued from the camp; and after all that you still don't know any better than to try me with a stunt like this? If that's the kind of decisions you made in office, your people must have been damn glad to get rid of you. Well, I have orders to see they're not bothered with you much longer."

He was silent for a little; then he said, "It is very unfortunate that we should come to this. Of course, men have tried to kill me before and I am not yet dead."

I said, "I guess I just called up to say good-bye, for old times' sake. However it goes, it seems unlikely that both of us will survive. Adios, Hector."

"*Vaya con dios,* Matthew."

Hanging up, I decided that it had been a mistake to call. He'd sounded exactly like the man I'd known and fought beside all those years ago. The conversation had settled nothing in my mind; it wasn't going to be that easy. I decided that it was a good thing I was going to Costa Verde. Maybe what I learned there would help me find an answer Elly would have approved of.

CHAPTER 4

"BULTMAN," said the voice in the phone.

It was Mac's voice; and I stood in a booth in the airport in Houston, Texas, listening to it. A little distance away the rest of our happy tour group stood around and sat around on the cushioned benches—well, most of the rest of it. I gathered that there was one member of the party still to come, a guy with the good Scandihoovian name of Anderson, according to the list, who'd be joining us here; but he hadn't shown up yet.

However, it was a three-hour connection, and our plane from Chicago had been on time for a change, so the missing would-be archaeologist could still make it, and it wasn't my problem anyway. Our efficient lady tour guide was taking care of everything, including the boarding passes for the next leg of our journey, from Houston to Mexico City, where we were scheduled to spend a couple of educational days improving our minds in the well-known *Museo Anthropologia*, and a couple of enjoyable nights sampling the after-dark entertainment of the great urban sprawl that now occupies the ancient valley of the Aztecs and holds, I believe, the world number-two spot in population, behind New York, but ahead of Tokyo, Los Angeles, and Shanghai.

Then we would fly to Santa Rosalia, the capital city of Costa Verde, which also had a museum that required a day of our attention. The final leg of our journey, from Santa Rosalia to the jungle site of Copalque, where our archaeological education would begin in earnest, would be accomplished by bus.

"Bultman is in Costa Verde?" Lounging in the booth, I was watching hard for surveillance but hadn't spotted any yet. It was beginning to look as if I'd managed to slip away from Chicago without a tail. I said, "So the reports of the

29

Kraut's death in Cuba were slightly exaggerated. Do we know yet what optimist paid him to make the touch on Fidel?"

Popularly it's referred to as a hit, but in our outfit, for some reason, we always call it a touch.

Mac said, "Various sponsors have been suggested, including of course our ever-hopeful friends of the CIA, but there seems to be no firm evidence pointing to any particular individual or organization." He paused, and went on: "To answer your question, Bultman is not in Costa Verde, at least not yet, not as far as we know. But he was seen not too far away in Guatemala City, in earnest consultation with a man identified as Enrique Echeverria, fondly known as Enrique Rojo or Red Henry, the head of the Costa Verde *Servicio Seguridad Nacional*, Armando Rael's secret police force. The subject under discussion could not be determined. You'll be interested to hear that Bultman was seen to favor his left leg, leaving; and that an informant, usually reliable, states that he did not wholly escape from Cuba after his unsuccessful attempt on Castro's life. One foot remained behind, severed in the crash of the getaway vehicle in which he was thought to have died; apparently he has not yet fully mastered the artificial one."

I said, "If that's true, unless it broke him altogether, he's going to be hard to handle. What have we got on him?"

I heard paper rustle half a continent away. Mac read off the dossier: "*Bultman*, given name(s) unknown, aliases employed . . ." He ran through a string of them, with no discernible pattern, and went on: "Forty-three, five-eleven, one-ninety, blond, blue. No distinguishing marks on record, no fingerprints. 1973 passport photo (Minox copy). 1978 telephoto series (five exposures, poor). Competent short, long, expert auto. Adequate edged. Adequate unarmed. No explosives experience on record. Hetero, sadistic tendencies, not compulsive. Alcohol usually in moderation, no tobacco, no record of drugs. Team player, seldom operates alone. Varshavsky 1967. Lindermann 1969. Smith-Watrous 1972. Eladio 1974. Marais 1977. Castro 1980 (failed). Suggested from MOs but unconfirmed: Hernandez 1971, Lagerquist 1975. Unreported since 1980, believed dead." Mac cleared his throat. "The dossier has not yet been updated in the light of our most recent information."

There was a little silence while I digested all this. Five confirmed kills and two possible in ten years. The top of the heap. One of the select few you'd consider for a really tough one, if you could afford him. Then crippling disaster. As I'd indicated, he'd either be a broken man now, or a real tiger eager—perhaps overeager—to wash out his defeat with blood and reestablish himself at the summit of his chosen profession.

According to the dossier, we had only the most general physical characteristics to identify him by; and a small-film copy, probably snapped in haste, of an old passport photo; and some fuzzy long-range tele shots. However, that was not a real problem now. A killer with a brand-new tin foot to which he was still unaccustomed shouldn't be too hard to spot. In other respects the record revealed the man: A man who didn't really favor the face-to-face stuff either bare-handed or with edged implements, who could handle a pistol or rifle okay, but who really excelled with the fully automatic weapons.

Well, that agreed with his description as a team player; more accurately, as I recalled, a team leader. Mostly you don't need a regiment—although I'd used Jimenez's assault group the last time I'd been in Costa Verde—to slip a sniper into position, or sneak a pistolman within range of his target; but if your habit is to blast through the opposition by brute force, a well-trained unit equipped with rata-tat guns can be very useful.

It wasn't really my cup of tea, as the British would say, but it was Bultman's, and I gave him full credit; although he had a reputation for arrogance, he must have something that inspired loyalty or his boys wouldn't have gone to the trouble of getting him away, disabled and bleeding, after the Cuba fiasco. Of course it was also a weakness of sorts and our rules read differently. We're not supposed to jeopardize our important missions, or even our valuable government-trained selves, performing heroic rescues of one-footed comrades (or of small girl hostages either, memory said; and I wished it would shut up and leave me alone).

I asked the important question: "What's the current word on Bultman, sir?"

"Immediate where found."

Interesting. It doesn't mean we blast them in the public

plaza at high noon, of course; however it does mean that unless the mission upon which we're engaged has extreme priority, if we stumble across them—the ones with that designation—in the course of it, we take time out to arrange for a discreet removal before proceeding with our regular business. Apparently Bultman had made somebody very angry, or scared, somewhere up the chain of command. Open season.

"Whose toes did he step on?" I asked; and then I said, "Never mind, sir. I guess I can figure out the answer if I try real hard."

"I should hope so," Mac said.

"What about the person who spotted him in Guatemala?"

"Observation personnel only."

"Who's been sent for action—just in case I should fall over him in the dark somewhere down there?"

"You don't need to know who was sent. He has been recalled."

"I see."

And I did. I couldn't help a rueful grin. I'd thought Mac had yielded a little too easily when I had announced my sentimental pilgrimage to Costa Verde. Hell, I had even asked innocently what homicidal talent might be wandering around that part of Central America. I'd walked right into it. He'd had to make a few arrangements, or rearrangements; but if temperamental superagent Helm insisted on heading down there anyway, why risk another valuable operative in such an uncertain area?

I said, "My baby, sir?"

His voice, when he answered, was cool: "Your baby, Eric. You did express interest, you're visiting the country with a resonably good cover as a magazine photographer, and it seems likely that Bultman's presence in that part of the world is related to your current business. What else would President Rael's dirty-work specialist, Echeverria, have to discuss with a trained and experienced assassin? That makes you the logical man to deal with the problem." Mac hesitated. When he spoke again, his voice was carefully expressionless: "I think you understand the situation, all aspects of the situation. I will leave the final decision to your judgment."

I suppose I should have been flattered. He was giving me

a free hand; but the trouble with that is that if your judgment turns out not to agree with certain other people's judgments, you can wind up in serious difficulties. Definite orders are safer. . . . I looked up as somebody tapped on the glass of the booth. I said into the phone: "Just a minute. Somebody wants me."

It was Dr. Frances Dillman, holding out a boarding pass. When I opened the door to take it, she said, "I wonder if you'd give me a hand with something, Mr. Felton. After you've finished your call, of course."

"I'll be along in a minute," I said. When she'd gone, I spoke to Mac: "My judgment. Yes, sir. Thank you, sir."

Mac said, "Research has asked me to tell you that they'll try to have a full report on your fellow travelers ready for you in Mexico City. You know how to make contact. A weapon will be passed to you in Santa Rosalia; let's hope you'll have no need for one earlier. Unfortunately, we have no resident personnel there, but arrangements are being made." He hesitated, and went on: "Be careful, Eric. The Costa Verde situation is not good, your traveling companions may not all be as innocuous as they seem, and with two feet or one, Herr Bultman is not to be taken lightly."

"Yes, sir," I said. "Careful."

He always tells us that, but he never tells us how. I hung up, picked up my camera case, and went over to where Dr. Dillman was chatting politely with an older couple named Henderson, Austin and Emily. The woman was a formidable dowager type with blue gray hair. The man, tall and gray and rather stooped, had been introduced as a retired contractor; but in spite of the bowed posture I sensed military experience beyond the average. They stopped talking when I came up.

"Private Felton reporting for duty, ma'am," I said, saluting smartly.

Dr. Dillman's unamused glance said that she would have liked to have me for a student. Here I was a paying customer toward whom she had to behave tolerantly; but she knew how to deal with smart alecks in her class.

"This way, please . . . No, you'd better leave that big camera bag. Austin will keep an eye on it for you."

The fact that I might not like leaving my cameras out of my sight in a big busy airport was, of course, irrelevant. I

33

followed in her wake. She had a long explorer's stride in spite of the fact that she was wearing moderately high heels that brought her almost up to my level. Her traveling suit, worn with a white silk blouse, was not a comfortable old friend like the tweed number of yesterday. She was rushing the season a bit in view of the southern latitudes toward which we were heading; and this was a light, tailored costume in businesslike khaki poplin—well, I guess beige is the proper word for that particular shade of tan when the garment in question is very high-class indeed.

The well-fitting skirt was somewhat too narrow for her impatient manner of walking, snapping sharply at her legs; but a little pleat in front prevented the situation from becoming critical. I decided that the neatly nyloned legs weren't quite as thin as I'd thought them at first glance; and that the figure wasn't skinny enough to constitute a real deformity, either. But she certainly was a tall and masterful lady. Mistressful?

"I am going to ask a favor of you, Mr. Felton," she said as we marched briskly through the airport crowds, two long-legged people covering a lot of ground with each stride. "One that I have no right to ask. We have a . . . a slight problem, and, well, you seem to be reasonably able-bodied and not too ancient unlike, for instance, Austin Henderson. I'm fairly strong, myself, and I'll do what I can, but the red tape of the tour will keep me pretty busy and I'll need a little assistance from time to time. I'd like to be able to count on you, Mr. Felton."

I drew a long breath. I kicked myself hard, mentally, for jumping to conclusions; for judging by first impressions. I would have bet a considerable sum that this was a woman who'd be too proud to ask for help; and that if she were forced to do so by circumstances, she wouldn't know how to go about it graciously. Well, I've been wrong before.

"What is the predicament, Dr. Dillman?" I asked.

She glanced at me quickly. "I'm sorry. I've been awfully stiff, haven't I? My name is Frances. I prefer not to be called Fran or Frankie."

"Samuel here," I said, "but I don't mind being called Sam. Okay, Frances, what's your problem?"

"You'll see in a minute. I'm responsible for this tour, and I've let somebody come along who . . . Well, you'll see." She hesitated. "A little personal background may help you

34

to understand. I . . . we have a handicapped child. Never mind the clinical details. She's quite a bright and delightful little girl, she just doesn't get around very well. And I would like to think that when she grows up people will be willing to go to a little trouble to help her lead a reasonably normal life. So when this request was put to me, as tour director, I couldn't help acceding to it even though I knew it would cause some difficulties. . . ." She was looking ahead, frowning. "I told him to stay right here. Ah, there he is!"

I looked ahead to see a young man rolling himself toward us in a wheelchair. It was marked with the name of the airline; presumably his own chair had been checked on through. He brought himself to a stop in front of us.

Frances Dillman said, "Sam, this is Dick Anderson. Mr. Anderson, Mr. Felton. Well, we'd better get you to the gate, Dick; the airport people said for us to be early so they could put you on the plane ahead of everybody else."

He was a blond young man in his late twenties; and there was something a little wrong with one side of his face. I knew what it was, of course; I'd seen burned faces before. The plastic-surgery boys can perform miracles these days, but they're seldom quite perfect miracles. Anderson was wearing jeans and a checked shirt with a gray ski sweater over it; and his legs didn't look quite right, either, thin and shrunken in the blue pants. Obviously they weren't much use to him. Accident, I thought, no birth defect, no polio; they wouldn't have resulted in a badly cooked face. But it wasn't a bad face. It was rather handsome in spite of the repair surgery that had been performed on it. The brown eyes under the heavy brows were steady and intelligent. . . . Brown!

I looked at him more sharply as he sat there in his mobile chair—and I knew him. The straw-colored hair was phony, of course. Anderson, hell! He was about as Scandinavian as I was Spanish, just about exactly; and I'd seen those big soulful brown Latin eyes before, all too recently, in the face of a young and attractive girl. I'd seen them go snake-mean at the sight of a gun. I'd seen them go murder-cold; I'd seen them condemn to death a girl I loved. Well, as much as a man in my line of work can love anybody.

It took me a moment to dredge up the given name, but

only a moment. I was looking at Ricardo Jimenez, Dolores and Emilio's older brother, Hector's older son, who was supposed to have died in the political prison called La Fortaleza after making an attempt on the life of President Armando Rael; an attempt that had failed.

CHAPTER 5

My first thought, after a sick wave of hatred that surprised me—after all, this damaged young man had done nothing to me; and I don't usually blame the sons for the sins of their fathers, or of their sisters and brothers either —was that it seemed to be a great day for resurrected, unsuccessful hitmen. I'd just heard of Bultman's return from the dead after his try at Castro; now here was young Jimenez still more or less alive after his try at Rael. It was an interesting idea, but I couldn't make anything sinister of it. Coincidences do happen after all.

But I knew why I hated the phony-blond fragment of humanity in the wheeled chair: If this stupid little amateur assassin had done his job right, his father would never have felt compelled to try to recruit me for the work, and Eleanor Brand would still be alive. And it was a damn good thing that somebody—maybe that secret-police chief Enrique Echeverria of whom I'd just heard—had broken his lousy incompetent back for him so I didn't have to.

"Don't you think so, Sam?"

I glanced at the tall woman who'd addressed me. "Sure," I said. "Whatever you say, Frances."

"All right, we'll try it over there, it looks easier."

"You don't have to push me," Ricardo Jimenez said. I mean, Dick Anderson. "I'm perfectly all right on level pavement."

He didn't have much of an accent, not nearly as much as his kid sister. I noticed that something had happened to one of his hands also; the nails hadn't grown back quite right. A couple hadn't grown back at all. I drew a long

36

breath, losing that hot feeling of hatred in spite of myself. It was replaced by an odd sense of kinship. After all, this was something we all had to face. This was something that could happen to any of us, and often did.

They'd caught him, burned him, smashed him, mangled him, broken him; but he was going back to Costa Verde. All right. Maybe he didn't know how to shoot worth a damn, if that was the way he'd tried to do it—I remembered that his father had always been a lousy marksman— but he had the courage to return to the country where this had been done to him. And I would wrestle his crummy wheelchair, dammit, in memory of the good men I knew who'd tried what he'd tried and wound up sitting where he was sitting, as Frances Dillman would make the same effort for the sake of her handicapped child. Besides, I had to find out why. Why was he going back? What could he hope to accomplish in that condition?

As we wrestled the heavy chair down some steps, I glanced at the woman beside me, wondering if she knew that she was helping to smuggle into Costa Verde the son of an exiled political figure, a wanted man in his own right as a failed assassin and escaped prisoner, a man whose presence in the group could get us thrown into what was by all reports a particularly unpleasant prison. I decided, looking at her severely handsome face, that she'd happily sacrifice us all for her science, but that was just the point. It seemed highly unlikely that she'd risk having her work stopped and her precious ruins placed out of bounds by Armando Rael's government because she'd meddled in local politics exactly as she'd warned us not to. I decided that she couldn't know.

And I wasn't about to tell her. After all, I'd embarked upon this crazy semiscientific expedition to learn about the political situation in Costa Verde, and it seemed very likely that this crippled young man was a significant part of it. And I didn't really owe any Dillmans anything. I'd do what I could to see that the lady and her tour group escaped unharmed if the blowup came, but I couldn't afford to interfere by speaking now.

We delivered the warm body to the shipping point, where the airlines personnel took over; they'd load him aboard the plane, I gathered, and take back their wheelchair.

"Thanks a lot, fellas," he said with a jaunty wave, as we left him. It wasn't exactly authentic Yankee slang, addressing a lady Ph.D. as a fella, but it was a good enough try for a Spanish-speaking amateur.

"Any time," I said, replying for both of us.

As we moved away I couldn't help thinking that it was very nice to walk with a woman who could just about match my ridiculous stride, even in a tailored skirt. In pants she'd probably walk me into the ground.

I said idly, "It's too bad your husband couldn't come along on this trip, Frances. But on second thought I don't suppose it would be any great treat for him, helping you play nursemaid to a bunch of Sunday archaeologists."

"Archie's in Arizona, attending a conference at Canyon de Chelly. He was involved in that dig for several years, you know." She glanced at me quickly. "Isn't that a terrible name? But the poor man can't help it. And is Archibald any better? Archibald Dillman, archaeologist, for God's sake! But he's really rather a nice person. Anyway, I happen to like him." She stopped abruptly and turned to face me, putting a hand on my arm to halt me. "Dammit, I was going to work up to it very cleverly, but I'm just not built to be subtle, Felton. I'm about as subtle as a hippopotamus. But, please, you *will* be nice to us, won't you?"

I was a little startled by the request. "Nice how?"

She said rather breathlessly, "It's terribly important, you know. You could spoil everything for us down there, you and your cameras and your magazine connections. I really didn't want to let you come along—I guess you sensed that—but the institute insisted that we needed all the publicity we could get. What they meant, of course, was all the *good* publicity. But I saw you in that room when I was talking yesterday, sneering at me like the rest because I was willing to go down there with blinders on, disregarding all the human suffering just so I'd be allowed to dig up a few moldering old artifacts. . . . But this is *significant* material we're uncovering, Felton. I can't begin to tell you how significant!"

"You could try," I said.

She shook her head sharply, dismissing that. "Look," she said, "look, I don't mind a bit if you make fun of the stuffy professor-lady or take pictures that make her look ridiculous. You can even, if you want to be mean, use your cameras to make a . . . a cruel joke of a bunch of mostly older people who are childishly eager to absorb beautiful culture in romantic jungle surroundings. Go ahead, if you're that kind of a man and want to do it. But please, please, don't publish anything—please, no starving children with flies on their faces; no overbearing policemen with submachineguns pushing people around; no trigger-happy soldiers getting a big kick out of delaying every vehicle with an endless, pointless search, just showing off their petty authority; no sneak shots of arrogant officials accepting a little *mordida* to look the other way from the way they're supposed to be looking. It's there, of course it's there, it's always been there, and we can hope that some-day maybe it won't be, but don't destroy an important—you can't possibly understand how important!—scientific project for your damn social consciousness. Please." She drew a long, shaky breath. "Oh, God! One secondhand soapbox, never driven over thirty-five, prefer cash."

She was becoming quite human in her desperate concern, and I was liking her better all the time; but I said as if unimpressed: "What's so important about a few rock carvings?"

She stared at me bleakly. "All right. I suppose you'll go snooping around, and maybe you're a good enough investigator to find out for yourself, now I've said this much. What do you know about Central American history?"

"Not much, yet," I said. "You're supposed to tell me."

She gave that shake of her fine head that indicated annoyance at my stupidity. "You must have heard of the Mayas, and you must know that they died out very suddenly and mysteriously, leaving their magnificent cities to fall into ruins. Well, the Olmecs before them went through exactly the same gradual rise and the same abrupt fall. And now we're discovering the same strange cycle among the even earlier Melmecs; but there's a difference. We have some clues. Certain records have thrown a new light. . . . Well, anyway, we hope that some-day, if we're allowed to search long enough in this new area, if we handle the political situation very carefully and don't get ourselves booted out, we'll find the answer. We're quite sure it's there."

"What answer?"

She didn't reply directly. She said, "You'll hear all kinds

of theories. The latest, very comfortable indeed for those who can believe in it, is that none of these people *really* died out, there was no great catastrophe, no sudden exodus, no panicky flight from the great cities; there was only a gradual erosion of the old religious beliefs, a slow degeneration of the old social structures, that finally made the temples and palaces superfluous; and we've still got the direct descendants of the Mayas, at least, if not of their predecessors, living humbly and happily in their wattle-and-daub huts in the land of their glorious pyramid-building ancestors. Well, of course we have. *Everybody* didn't die. But Archie and I don't believe in the theory of gradual decline. We're convinced, like many archaeologists before us, that these civilizations, and maybe others on this continent—maybe even elsewhere—met with sudden overwhelming disasters from which only a few pitiful stragglers escaped to form the basis of the present-day native populations of the area."

When she stopped, I asked in my dumb way, "So what, to put it crudely? What makes all this of such earthshaking significance, doctor?"

She sighed. "You're really an impossible man, aren't you? I don't know why I'm fool enough to try to . . . *Think*, damn you! Three very advanced and complex civilizations on this continent destroyed, each in a matter of a few years! Aren't you a bit curious about what did it? Do you think it has absolutely no application to our own time, our own civilization? Do you feel that you live in a society that's so beautifully safe and stable that nothing can touch it except, perhaps, the nuclear bomb? What if I should tell you that we've uncovered some very interesting, potentially very disturbing, religious records from the end of the Melmec reign foreshadowing the disaster to come?—"

I frowned. "You mean, they knew they were going to die?"

She said sharply, "The Sleeping Beauty wakes. Yes, Mr. Felton, they knew their doom, they knew what shape it would take. At least the priests did. We're trying very hard to decipher the records now, but we need a great deal more material before we can even begin to read all the glyphs . . . No, that's enough! And you'll probably run right out and make a wonderful laugh-piece of it, won't you? The crazy scientific dame who thinks our world is going to be destroyed tomorrow, as the Mayas' world was destroyed yesterday, by little pink men from Canopus who've also visited America on a couple of earlier occasions with their little rayguns and signed their stellar names in beautiful Melmec hieroglyphs! Shades of Erich von Daniken, correct?" She licked her lips. "I don't suppose it's any use my asking you to keep this in confidence."

"You might try," I said.

"Please, Mr. Felton, will you keep . . . no, will you *try* to keep what I've told you off the record until we've had a chance to carry our research a little further? Just try, that's all I ask."

"Yes," I said.

CHAPTER 6

THE two great snowcapped volcanic peaks—Popocatapetl, the smoking mountain, and Ixtlachuatl, the sleeping woman—slid past the plane windows, and the Anahuac plateau was below us, ringed by lower mountains to form the high Valley of Mexico in which the city of the same name was supposed to lie. I could only hope the rumors were correct, because there was absolutely nothing to be seen down there but a brown cloud of smog that made a bad day in Los Angeles look like a light morning mist by comparison. Trapped by the surrounding mountain ranges, the grungy pollution-cover filled the entire valley, so that the sprawling metropolis below us, the former city of Tenochtitlan, Montezuma's pride and joy until Cortez, the spoiler, came along, was totally invisible from the air. As we descended through it bravely, civilization appeared with startling suddenness only a few thousand feet below.

Then we were on the ground. Our competent leader got us past customs and immigration in record time. Since she was busy seeing to our luggage and organizing our transportation, it was up to me to do the wheelchair bit, coming to the assistance of the son of a man I was probably going to kill—as soon as I determined that his country could spare him, since I wouldn't want to distress the small ghost that haunted me.

A chartered bus took us away through the mad Mexican traffic. Please understand, I like people who drive as if they mean it; but after the timid road behavior of the American drivers with whom I'd been associating the past couple of days, the determined aggressiveness of the Mexicans, while theoretically admirable by my own driving standards, took a little getting used to, even on a bus.

But it's a fine city, if you don't mind viewing it through eyes smarting from the acrid air; and our hotel was located on the Reforma, the handsome main boulevard. More wheelchair-juggling got us inside the lobby, where rooms and luggage were dealt out with admirable efficiency under Frances Dillman's stern supervision. I escorted Ricardo Jimenez as far as the fourth floor and worked the elevator doors for him although he protested that he was an old elevator hand by now and could manage by himself—it was just those lousy steps and stairs that people kept putting in his way that he found insurmountable. I didn't risk offending his pride by insisting on taking him to his door and helping him inside. He made it clear that he'd rather do that on his own.

"See you tomorrow, Dick," I said.

"Thanks much, fella," he said.

"*De nada*, as we say in our fluent Spanish."

He grinned. "At least you know a couple of words, which is more than I can say."

Standing over him, looking down at his fake blond hair, I reflected grimly that he'd never make it. He wasn't much of an actor; and concealing your knowledge of the language to which you were born is one of the hardest cover jobs you can tackle. However, there is one harder: actually mangling that language clumsily without betraying how well you actually know it. He'd made the best choice available to him.

I said, "If you know *cerveza* and *baño*, you've got it made. The intake and outgo are all taken care of. Be good."

"Hell, not much else I can do, is there?"

But he grinned again as he said it; he wasn't complaining. Well, I'd never kidded myself that cowardice ran in that family. I took my camera bag from young Jimenez's lap, where he'd been nursing it for me, nodded good-night to him, stepped back into the elevator, rode up one more floor, and headed for my own room. It was marked by my suitcase, which had already been brought up and set outside the door.

"Mr. Felton. Sam."

It was the scientific tour-guide lady herself, in the open doorway of the adjoining room. She had dispensed with her suit jacket, but she still looked tall and smart in her moderately high-heeled shoes and her severely tailored blouse and skirt, which had survived the long journey from Chicago reasonably unmussed and unwrinkled. Any travel damage to her hairdo had been neatly repaired; and her firm mouth had been lightly touched with fresh lipstick, which made her less forbidding and more feminine.

"May I reward your labors with a drink, Sam?" she asked. "I happen to have a little Scotch, a luxury that's practically unknown in this part of the world. It'll cost you well over thirty dollars a bottle if you try to buy it."

I laughed. "I hate to consume such a priceless commodity when my tastes are not terribly refined." Then I saw the carefully lipsticked mouth tighten a bit at the hint of rejection. There was no need to hurt her feelings, and I hadn't really looked forward to having a lonely drink in the bar or, as an alternative, discussing the finer aspects of Central American archaeology, which I hadn't yet had time to read up on, with other members of the tour who happened to have gravitated there. I said quickly, "Sure, I'd love a drink. Just let me shove this ten-ton photographic outfit, and my suitcase, into my room, and make a quick inspection of the facilities. I'll be right back."

When I returned, the door to her room was ajar and her voice said, "Come in and tell me how you like this . . . Oh, close it, unless you're afraid of being compromised. I'd rather not have any of the others wandering in casually. I've had enough of playing the jolly housemother for the day. Being a managing woman is kind of a strain." She turned, holding out a glass. "Taste that and see if it's to your liking."

"Satisfactory," I reported. After a moment, I said, "You're very good at it."

She didn't answer at once. She moved to the windows and looked out. It was dark now and the lights of the city were spread out below, with endless streams of cars moving both ways along the Reforma. Frances Dillman turned abruptly and pulled the cord that closed the drapes. She went back to pick up the drink she'd made for herself, and gestured to me to sit down in one of the big chairs in the corner. She took the other.

"Good at it?" she murmured. "Being a managing woman, you mean? Well, I've had lots of practice, Sam. My husband is, well, kind of a vague genius type. You know, the kind who forgets where he put his glasses when they're right on his nose. Somebody's got to keep things organized around the place. But thanks for the compliment. And thank you for watching over Dick Anderson for me. When you start working with your cameras, I'll see if I can't recruit some of the less decrepit male members of the group to help him around so you can get on with your job."

"I'll let you know," I said. "In the meantime, it's not really much trouble, and he's a pleasant enough guy."

"Yes, it's too bad, isn't it, a nice young man like that."

I grinned at her, so superior and condescending about her half-dozen years'—maybe—advantage over Ricardo Jimenez.

"Yes, grandma," I said.

It startled her. It was the first really personal thing that had been said between us. We'd conversed politely as scientist and photojournalist, as efficient tour director and helpful client; but we'd said absolutely nothing as person to person or man to woman, as Samuel Felton to Frances Ransome Dillman or vice versa.

Now she glanced at me with sudden awareness in her eyes, as if realizing abruptly that she, a married woman with a reputation to cherish, a career to protect, and the responsibilities of this tour to consider, was actually entertaining in her hotel room a lone male who was not her husband. She was also, her eyes said, becoming very much aware of the fact that she was not really old enough to refer to Dick Anderson as a nice young man; and that I, while no chicken, wasn't exactly in the final, safe stages of senility, either.

In fact, her eyes said, there was absolutely no excuse for

44

the two of us to be having a cozy drink in her room like this, alone and with the door closed, even if the Victorian niceties were not always scrupulously observed, not even by perfectly decent and respectable people of the opposite gender, these relaxed modern days. Her eyes said that she couldn't understand how she, of all people, could possibly have got herself into such an awkward predicament and she hoped to God I wouldn't embarrass both of us by misconstruing the situation.

That was what her fine gray eyes told me now, or tried to tell me; but her fine gray eyes were, of course, goddamn liars. Suddenly we were both fully conscious of the fact that she'd set it up like this quite deliberately and that we both knew it; the difference between us being that only she knew why. I found it very puzzling and rather shocking. She didn't look like a sex-starved woman. In fact, when I'd first seen her I wouldn't have been surprised to learn that she and her fellow-genius husband lived and loved only on a purely intellectual level scorning all passions of the flesh —of course, that had been before I'd learned about the handicapped child that presumably had not resulted from immaculate conception.

On the other hand, if she hoped to influence my photographic activities by these tawdry bedroom tactics, well, it seemed like a hell of a thing for a proud and well-educated lady to be doing merely to promote a favorable picture story about her and her husband's scientific endeavors in Costa Verde. I'd already developed considerable respect for her. I couldn't believe this of her.

The silence ran on tautly for several seconds. Abruptly she gave a kind of a shudder and rose and walked quickly back to the window and parted the draperies and looked out for a second or two. She let them fall together again and took a deep swallow from the glass she still held. I had risen and moved to stand behind her, but I didn't touch her.

"I'm ashamed." Her voice was an almost inaudible whisper. "I'm so ashamed, Sam."

I didn't help her out by saying anything. After another sip from her glass, she turned to face me.

" 'Come in for a drink, Sam. Close the door unless you're afraid of being compromised, Sam.' My God, how cheap can you . get?" Her voice was ragged with self-contempt. When I still didn't speak, she went on: "Would you be a real gentleman? Would you just withdraw very quietly and leave the lady, who's no real lady, to her humiliation? And in the morning please try not to look at her and make her blush at remembering the shabby tramp she was, or tried to be!"

I said, "That's all very touching, sweetheart."

She stiffened and stared up at me, her face pale. She started to speak angrily and stopped herself, licking her lips.

I said, "You do it very well. But I don't know whom you're trying to kid, me or yourself, Dillman."

She drew a sharp breath and let it out. A pale smile stirred her carefully made-up mouth. "I can't be doing it too well, or you wouldn't be seeing right through it, Felton." She sighed in a resigned way. "No, you're perfectly right. I don't really want you to go."

I studied her, perplexed. "Why me?" I asked. "I mean, I know I've got the face of Adonis and the body of Hercules and the brain of Einstein and the balls of a rampant bull. There's no doubt whatever that I'm totally irresistible on every level from the intellectual to the horizontal, but you still look to me like a lady who'd put up a good fight against infidelity, even under the most tempting circumstances. So why me, and on our first night out of Chicago, yet?"

Her smile grew; and now there was a little malice in it. "Who else was there, my dear? One of those elderly gentlemen with their battle-axe wives? That legless boy who may very well be missing something more than his legs? Anyway . . . anyway, I wouldn't want him, even if he were intact. He's too young. He wouldn't know how to do it. He wouldn't be . . . careful of me. He'd get all passionate and excited and, God help us, he might even fall in love with me, enchanting older woman that I am. I might have a hard time getting rid of him afterward."

"Whereas I look like I shed easily?" I said dryly.

"You're adult and I suspect you're fairly experienced, Sam. I don't think you feel obliged to make a grand passion out of every one-night stand." She drew a long breath. "I'm glad you think I look . . . looked like an ever-faithful wife, a very reserved and respectable and sexless sort of person. I've worked very hard to preserve that image. And if I hadn't done it tonight, my dear, well, I was afraid we were going to be friends in another day or two. And it's very hard to seduce a man who's become a good friend. I mean, he gets so terribly shocked when he discovers what the lady *really* wants from him. I have plenty of friends; I don't need you for another. I need you for . . ." She stopped, and gave a tiny shrug. "I need you," she whispered.

I didn't believe a word of it, of course. This handsome woman might well be more passionate than she allowed herself to appear; but that she'd be totally at the mercy of her passions was not credible. And while I like to think I'm as charming as the next guy in my rough-hewn way, I always remember that a lot of good, and more not-so-good, men have died from overestimating the attraction they exerted upon the opposite sex. No, I didn't buy it for a moment. But the lady was committed now. She'd offered herself to me without reservation. There was no gentle way of refusing her. However I put it, I would be saying crudely: *Sorry, babe, tonight's my night to be virtuous, and anyway you're really not all that desirable.*

I said, "Sure. Need. Well, you're the managing lady. Tell me how you'd like this managed, lady." When she hesitated, I asked baldly, "Do you want to be kissed, for a start?"

She shook her head minutely. "No. I think we can dispense with the phony kisses." Her voice was very calm. "But you may undress me if you wish. Just be . . . be careful, please. Aside from a rather dressy dress, these are the only civilized clothes I brought along."

"Careful Felton is my middle name."

I set my glass aside. I took hers from her hand and put it beside mine. I stepped forward deliberately and started to unbutton her silk shirt, aware that she was wearing some kind of a faint but pleasant fragrance. Being a cynical bastard, I had a vision of her dabbing it on with grim resignation, preparing herself for the disgusting seduction scene she was being compelled to stage. Compelled how?

"Sam." When I looked at her, having unfastened three small pearly buttons to reveal a rather pretty white slip with lace on it, she said, "Please. You're looking so . . . so

47

goddamned cynical. You're making me feel cheap and dirty. Can't you see I wouldn't be doing this if I could help myself?"

I wanted to ask why she couldn't help herself; but I knew that all I'd get would be the same phony nympho routine. I straightened up to face her. She was rather disheveled-looking now, with her blouse gaping to reveal her underwear; and I felt very sorry for both of us, trapped in this lousy sex production.

I said, "You're the one who specified this crummy cold-blooded approach, Frances."

Then I reached out and tipped her chin up a little—she was tall enough that it didn't take much—and bent forward to kiss her. Her lips were cool and unresponsive at first, hardly the lips of a compulsive sex-freak, but after a little they remembered how this was done, and after a little longer they began to enjoy it. Her body relaxed gradually and allowed itself to be brought into contact with mine; soon she was helping to draw us together fiercely, her fingers digging into my back. When we parted at last we were both breathing hard and no questions or reservations remained.

I said, "That takes care of that ladylike lipstick. Now you'd better get your own damn clothes off if you want to be able to wear them again."

I turned away, fumbling with the buttons of my shirt. When I turned back, stripped, she was standing there with her garments neatly arranged on a nearby chair. She awaited me nude with a certain regal and at the same time rather touching pride that was quite justified. She was even more striking, naked, than she had been dressed.

It had been a long time since I'd seen a truly white lady. They're all so healthy and brown these days, with cute little bikini-marks, and it's very nice, no doubt; but this one gleamed like pale marble or, since it was a warm glow, finely polished ivory. I'd kind of expected a lean, strong, rawboned body, but she looked almost fragile, all white like that; a long, slim lovely shape with everything perfectly formed, just slightly attenuated to make a tall woman out of a limited amount of material.

She waited, unmoving, as I approached, and we kissed again, rather formally this time, a little self-conscious in our nudity, although we were both adults who'd been here before. We separated briefly so I could turn out the table lamp. In the sudden semidarkness, broken by shafts of light from the city outside, we proceeded to the bed and entered it with careful dignity; but that dignity did not endure beyond the first tentative contacts between our unclothed bodies. It's not really a very dignified act.

CHAPTER 7

IN the morning I woke up early in my own room next door, having slipped out of the lady's warm bed, regretfully, in the middle of the night after the hotel was asleep. I found that I was feeling very hungry and not particularly guilty about taking advantage of the situation —whatever the situation might be—to help a troubled woman break her sacred marriage vows. It did occur to me that my period of mourning hadn't lasted very long; but Elly would have told me not to be silly. She wouldn't have expected or wanted me to honor her memory with everlasting continence.

The small fourth-floor dining room or coffee shop— according to the placard posted in the elevator, there was a big formal restaurant on the roof, but it functioned only in the evening—had glass walls facing a sheltered patio open to the sky, with a good-sized swimming pool; but at our present altitude of seven thousand feet, in the middle of winter, the green wind-ruffled water held no attraction for me or, apparently, for anybody else. A couple of doves were foraging, undisturbed, in the tiled pool area. I was a little surprised to see them in the center of a city of fourteen million people. Unlike its big cousin, the pigeon, the dove is usually a country bird at heart.

The place had just opened, and there wasn't much breakfast business being transacted yet; but one couple from the tour was established at a table by the wall. I'd noticed them before, not only because they were the youngest members of the group except for Ricardo Jimenez—somewhere in their thirties—but because they were dressed to be noticed. The girl was wearing big yellow boots, a wide, flounced, flowered peasant skirt, and a man's striped shirt with the tails out, bound around the middle by a handsome silver concha belt. Her dark brown hair was frizzed all over her head, dandelion fashion. I wondered if it was still called an Afro if the wearer wasn't African. If you looked hard you could see that, in spite of the wild getup, she was really rather an attractive young woman, in a sturdy, healthy way.

The man, lean and dark and a few years older, was imitating a Navajo chief or his own idea of a bearded Navajo chief—to the best of my knowledge the only one in captivity. He wore jeans and a blue velvet tunic of some kind; and he was hung all over with silver, some of it wrapped around massive gobs of turquoise. It was presumably the genuine stuff, no Japanese imitations need apply, since he could afford it. His name was James Wallace Putnam, of the Chicago Putnams; and he could probably even afford to let his wife (the relationship was legal and her name was Gloria) get her hairs bent one by one, by the best hair-benders in the business, if she so desired.

I couldn't help wondering, as one does, what they were trying to prove by their unconventional getups. Well, it was her hair and his jewelry, and if they simply thought they looked great that way, it was a fairly innocent self-deception compared to some.

"May I join you, Mr. Felton?"

I looked up, and there she was in her nice beige suit, looking neat and intellectual and totally untouched, even a little old-maidish; but I had an impulse to kiss her good-morning that was strong enough to scare me. It was a very simple psychological phenomenon, of course. Whatever her motives, she had caught me at a bad time and made it good, very good. Now the orderly psyche wanted to make the whole untidy, confusing business nice and neat and call it love. I was going to have to watch that psyche.

I rose in gentlemanly fashion and held the chair for her. "Good morning, Dr. Dillman."

"We're going to have to stop this, darling," she said softly after I'd seated myself again. Then she laughed at my expression. "No, silly, not *that*. I think we can figure

50

out safe ways of doing *that,* two clever people like us. I just meant tête-à-têtes like this. We've got to remember that I hauled you off on that wheelchair mission yesterday, perfectly innocent but just the two of us, and now I'm having breakfast with you; and that's all we can possibly get away with. You must stay completely away from me now, my dear, until . . . It can't be this evening; we're all having dinner together, and afterward you can visit anybody's room you like, except mine. I'll ask some others in for drinks, but you'll stay away. I'll tell you when. I may be a . . . a nymphomaniac, but I don't have to be a stupid nymphomaniac."

"Crap," I said.

"Don't be crude, Sam."

"It's time for a little crudity," I said. "For God's sake, this is a guy who just made love to you, remember? You're a sweet, sexy lady, sure; but don't try to convince me you're a female weirdo compulsively grabbing at anything in pants to help her scratch an itch her intellectual husband isn't man enough to satisfy."

She said stiffly, "That's a very ugly way to put it, a very cruel way, darling; but it happens to be the unfortunate truth."

I shook my head. "Last night, you were far from pathologically eager to haul me into bed. Oh, you talked a good fight, but you were tense, apprehensive, in fact scared shitless to keep up the crudity—until I kissed you. You'd heard things about me. Not nice things. You didn't know what I was going to do, a dreadful, dangerous character like me. You had a vision of being forced to perform ghastly perversions, or of simply winding up horribly battered and disfigured, hurt and bleeding, after I'd worked my violent will on you. And then I kissed you just like an ordinary human being, male variety, and you sensed it wasn't going to be such a tough chore after all, making love to me; and in relief and gratitude you . . . well, you made it very nice and I thank you. But let's just forget that sickie-sexy bit. You're a very nice, perfectly normal lady who's in some kind of a bind; and of course you don't dare to tell me about it because you've been ordered not to, so let me tell you."

"Sam, your imagination is running away with you. And I'm disturbed by what you're saying about yourself. You sound as if . . . as if you aren't really a magazine photographer. . . ."

I said, "Cut it out, Frances. You've been told who I am, what I am, by the people who aimed you my way and told you to get me into your bed earliest. Maybe the picture they gave you of me isn't flattering, it may not even be true in some respects, but as you say, we'd better not spend too much time talking like this, so let it stand. The question is, What do we do now? Well, the people who are running you——"

She drew a sharp breath of annoyance. "My dear man, nobody's *running* me! What a disgusting idea, as if I were a horse or a greyhound being galloped around a track! How could you think anybody could possibly coerce me into doing what . . . what I did last night?"

"You're a very conscientious, very dedicated person, Frances; and you take this dig of yours very seriously," I said. "The fate of the whole world is at stake, you implied. If your right to keep on digging were threatened, you might just possibly decide even to let yourself be soiled by intimate contact with an awful character like me, if it would allow you to continue your scientific researches and, eventually, learn enough to save the human race from destruction. That's one scenario. I can think of others."

She shook her head. "You're a very stubborn man. And a very wrong one."

I said, "Yes, you have to say that. Keep on saying it. But in the meantime let's throw your friends—enemies—a couple of bones. First of all, they probably want to know if I'm armed. Well, you know I don't have a gun in my clothes; you watched me getting undressed and dressed last night. And I'll tell you I don't have one in my luggage either; but of course that won't do. So next time we'll use my room, and you'll put a sleeping pill in my drink, and search the place while I'm pounding my ear, afterward. That should impress them with your loyalty and obedience. Okay?"

She licked her lips. "Sam, I don't understand. Suppose . . . suppose I were the helpless female victim you think, being blackmailed into doing dreadful things by some sinister villains—which of course I'm not. Why would you want to help me?"

I grinned. "Well, you can take your pick of motives.

Either I'm a sucker for your lovely face, not to mention your lovely body. . . ." I stopped. "May I ask an intimate question regarding your lovely body, Dr. Dillman?"

She laughed abruptly. "Why no tan, you mean? My dear man, I spend endless hours in the glaring sun in the course of my work; lying on a beach getting broiled is no treat at all. Besides, medically speaking, it's supposed to be bad for you. And your other possible motive for helping me, Mr. Felton?"

"Maybe I, too, have sinister plans for making use of you, for my own wicked purposes. Your choice, *querida*." The fact was that I simply didn't know why I was doing it. I did like her, but affection is not supposed to figure in our calculations, as I had recently demonstrated, in my grim and well-disciplined way, in Chicago. I just had a hunch, the kind you get, that this was the way to play it. When she didn't speak, I went on: "Next, your friends will want to know what fall-back story I have rigged for when my photojournalistic cover is blown. They may have their own ideas about why I'm heading for Costa Verde, but they'll be interested in knowing what I put out for public consumption. We'll have to work this carefully; but the basic idea is that, having fallen for you like a susceptible schoolboy, I couldn't bear to keep on making love to you under false pretenses. I confessed guiltily that I really wasn't Samuel Felton, boy photographer, although I'd worked with cameras in the past and there was a perfectly legitimate magazine connection set up to print the story, so that you and your institute will get your publicity. I told you I was a government agent on a mission, using your tour to slip into Costa Verde inconspicuously; but there was really nothing to worry about. If I were exposed, well, relations between the U.S. and Rael's government are very close, and a word from Washington would clear things up immediately. You didn't have to worry about my causing trouble for you or your charges."

"And your real mission in Costa Verde?"

"I'm hunting a man named Bultman," I said. I spelled it for her.

"Bultman." She tasted the name and didn't like it. She looked at me across the table. "I never heard of him."

I said, "No reason you should, unless you have somebody you want dead and plenty of money, *plenty* of

53

money, to pay for the job. This one is good, but he ran into a little bad luck recently, so now he has an artificial foot. He's killed five people certainly, two more perhaps."

"A master assassin with a false foot." Her voice was dry. "I suppose he calls himself Dr. Goldfoot or Professor Silvertoe or something. It sounds like a movie I've seen, a couple of movies I've seen. And what are you supposed to do with this criminal genius when you catch him?"

"Well," I said carefully, "certain people in Washington would be very happy to learn that Bultman was dead."

She nodded slowly. She licked her lips and said, "As a respectable professional woman, I find all this very confusing, not to say shocking and frightening, darling. It's scary what an innocent girl can get mixed up in simply by going to bed with a man, isn't it? Sam."

"Yes?"

Her eyes were steady on my face. "It's odd, but even after what you've told me, I don't feel a bit soiled by what you call our intimate contact. I'll let you know when it's safe for us to . . . to meet again." She had finished her breakfast and was gathering up her purse and the attache case she carried for the tour records. She stood up. I rose to face her. She said crisply, "The bus leaves for the museum at eight-thirty, Mr. Felton. In front of the hotel. Please don't make us wait for you."

I watched her march away, the tailored poplin skirt snapping at her long fine legs. I remembered that I'd once thought those legs a bit too thin. It seemed a long time ago.

CHAPTER 8

I'M not a museum freak, but I have spent some time in those impressive institutions, sometimes dragged there by intellectual female acquaintances yearning for knowledge, sometimes meeting people or following people or trying to shake off people who were following me.

The *Museo Anthropologia* was quite a splendid example of the breed. For one thing, the Mexicans have a fine freewheeling sense of architecture; and for another the exhibits were breathtaking even to a guy who didn't know an Aztec from a Toltec. There was, for instance, an enormous stone Aztec calendar wheel, magnificently carved. There was also—as far as I was concerned, the star of the show —a great, brooding, wicked Olmec head, tons of it, too big to be exhibited inside, so it glowered at you blackly from a grassy knoll in the patio, huge, neckless, bodiless, frightening, reminding you that the fearsome ideas of the human race are not all of recent origin.

I hadn't known where contact would be made, but when a slim, well-dressed young Mexican gentleman paused near our group to adjust the buckle of his well-polished shoe—I guess laces are obsolete in certain circles—and made a certain signal, I cut out of formation with a word of apology to my wheelchair patient, who grinned and said he could make it fine by himself while I answered nature's urgent summons.

I ducked into the nearby male-type *sanitario,* a fancy word they've just invented down there to match our dainty restroom doubletalk. We can't bear to mention the nasty word toilet, and I was discovering that they've got too delicate to refer to *baño* any longer, even though it really means bath and not crapper. I took my time at the urinal, and after a while he came in and stood beside me. I won't bother you with the recognition nonsense, it was as ridiculous as ever.

"You are very clean, señor," the contact said. "If you are being watched, it is being done from within your own group."

"Gracias."

"Bultman has been observed in Santa Rosalia, again in the company of Enrique Echeverria, *El Rojo*, The Red One, the head of the infamous *Servicio Seguridad Nacional,* commonly known as SSN. It is thought that Bultman has also made contact with *El Presidente* Rael."

"Check."

"I am asked to inform you that there is other activity in the area. Kronbeck, Marschak, and Rutterfeld have all been reported in Costa Verde recently. No contact observed with Bultman."

55

I frowned at the news and, after a moment, shook my head. "There won't be. Bultman runs his own shows; he'll be setting up his own team for the job, whatever it is Rael wants of him, presumably Hector Jimenez. He picks them smart and disciplined; he wouldn't touch a muscular meathead like Marschak, or a vicious little snake like Kronbeck; and Rutterfeld wouldn't touch him. Rutterfeld wants his underlings brainwashed and brainless so he can do all the thinking and grab all the credit, not to mention the money." I grimaced. "Obviously somebody's got another project going down there that doesn't necessarily impinge on Bultman's operation. I wonder. Rutterfeld likes the scientific stuff. Somebody could be interested in the rise and fall of civilizations. . . ."

I stopped as a stout Latin gentleman I didn't know came in to use the facilities. Stalling, I spent my time washing my hands thoroughly while my contact made quite a project of combing his thick black hair. When we had the place to ourselves once more, I said:

"Somebody could be interested in the rise and fall of civilizations, wanting to know, perhaps, if there was some special technique or gadget that made them fall that might be adapted to modern conditions. Which could make it awkward for the people who're trying to dig up just those answers around Copalque."

My companion said, "Rutterfeld has been established in Santa Rosalia for several months under a quite respectable cover. He had actually been seen there by somebody attached to the embassy, but the information was not considered important enough for general dissemination, so we didn't learn about it until your request came through. You know how those people are, if it doesn't involve an immediate declaration of World War III, it is of no importance. Rutterfeld is still in place. Kronbeck and Marschak, after being spotted in Santa Rosalia some weeks ago, seem either to have departed or gone underground."

"The Unholy Three," I said grimly. "I wonder who Rutterfeld's principal is. He's been known to work for Moscow on contract, when they didn't want to betray interest by using their own people."

My contact gave me one of those inimitable shrugs that can never be mastered by anyone whose ancestors, like mine, come from more northern climes.

56

"I cannot help you, señor. Everything that is known, and that is very little as yet, is written here, along with the other information you requested from Washington." He glanced around, but we still had the *Caballeros* to ourselves, so he took a thick envelope from the inside pocket of his jacket and passed it over. "You know the number to telephone if you require further assistance here. Because of unsettled conditions, there is no safe number in Santa Rosalia. Arrangements are being made, and contact will be made as soon as possible after you arrive. Use Lewis Carroll for identification. One word. Any messages or instructions?"

"None at the moment," I said. "Many thanks."

"*De nada*. It has been a pleasure to meet you, señor. *Vaya con dios*."

Outside, I found Frances Dillman lecturing on a significant exhibit in the Maya Room that, she said, showed definite Melmec influence. She gave me a reproving schoolteacher glance when she saw me rejoin the class; obviously I should have held up my hand and asked permission to go peepee. Afterward, we broke up. I saw Frances go off with the gaudy Putnams, looking very civilized in that hippie company. They took Dick Anderson with them, freeing me from wheelchair duty. I went back to the hotel to do my homework.

There was plenty of it. I glanced through various background reports on Costa Verde's history, economics, and politics, past and present. Then I settled down to learn about the people with whom I was traveling. The first dossier that appeared was that of Dick Anderson, but it was quite thick, and I wanted to give it special study, so I laid it aside. The report on Frances Dillman was unsurprising: An only child from a wealthy family, she'd gone to good schools and done well in all of them, finally getting her Ph.D. in archaeology and joining the faculty of the University of Chicago, where she'd already worked as a graduate assistant while getting her degree. Her husband's history was very similar: another academic success story.

I read about Howard Gardenschwartz (I visualized him: plump, dark, baldish, remote), professor of history at Northwestern University, and his wife Edith (small, gray-haired, friendly). There were two gray-haired schoolteachers traveling together, Patricia ("call me Pat") Tolson and

Margaret ("call me Peggy") McElder. None of these seemed to have had any connection with Costa Verde before taking this tour, nor did the Wilders, Marshall (red-faced, loud-mouthed) and Betty (thin, shrill). He was in insurance. Paul Hammond Olcott (heavy, blond) was a little more interesting, since he did some big game hunting on the side and I like to keep track of people around me who know firearms. Furthermore he had a rather handsome wife, Elspeth (statuesque, blond). He was an advertising man; but there was no hint of any Costa Verde connection there, either.

The stooped gray ex-contractor, Austin Henderson, with the formidable blue-haired wife Emily, was as I'd thought a former military man; in fact he'd been a general with quite a distinguished World War II record. But the big surprise was that the brooding dark gent with all the Navajo silver had been a combat officer in Vietnam where he'd earned practically every decoration they had to give, plus, in the end, a court-martial for shooting up a village that, somebody thought, shouldn't have been shot up. He'd been acquitted, but he'd left the service shortly thereafter. His conspicuous hippie getup was clearly some kind of a protest, but it was a little hard for me to figure out what kind. His sturdy frizzy-haired young wife was a girl he'd met in Hawaii, where she'd been working as a secretary. There were indications that the Chicago Putnams hadn't been too eager to welcome into the family a nobody-girl out of some government office. Maybe she was another form of protest, this time against Putnam's stuffy railroad-money ancestors.

Okay. Ricardo Jimenez, alias Dick Anderson. The medical record was brutal. Red Henry Echeverria's wreckers had really taken the boy apart in La Fortaleza, judging by the repair work listed on the clinical records: extensive plastic surgery for facial burns, function largely restored to left hand, very limited function restored to lower limbs with further improvement unlikely, operation to correct urogenital injuries partially successful but sexual function found to be irreversibly destroyed.

I drew a long breath and turned the page, wondering how Frances Dillman had known or guessed the full extent of the damage. Maybe it was something a woman, at least a passionate woman, could tell at a glance. For some reason the possibility hadn't occurred to me until she suggested it, although it is of course an area they always like to go for. The poor damn guy, I thought; it shouldn't even happen to a Jimenez.

CHAPTER 9

SANTA Rosalia welcomed us with open arms, which was a considerable relief. I'd been reasonably confident that my own cover would hold up under any ordinary inspection—they usually do a pretty good job in Washington—but I hadn't really been able to convince myself that the grim police state of Costa Verde would admit unsuspectingly a fugitive from its notorious prison sitting conspicuously in a wheelchair with the facial surgery obvious to anyone who really looked, with nothing going for him but a phony passport and a bleach job on the hair that wasn't really very convincing.

But it all went very smoothly. The customs people even waived luggage inspection and passed us through cheerfully to the big bus waiting outside; but it was not really a relaxing country to be in. The airport was heavily patrolled by armed soldiers, and every street corner seemed to be a guard post. Santa Rosalia was fairly dirty, at least around the edges. A lot of Latin American cities aren't exactly model communities by U.S. standards; but I've never got too upset at the sight of cheerful barefoot urchins with grubby faces and fat brown tummies showing through their torn shirts—as a kid I wasn't all that sold on shoes and cleanliness, either, and my jeans were often fairly well ventilated at the knees and sometimes even in the seat. But these grimy street children weren't either fat or cheerful; and their parents had a wary, hunted-animal look.

"I didn't say it was nice," Frances said a little defensively, pausing by my seat. "Don't use your camera, please. Our guide undoubtedly reports to the SSN."

"Science marches on," I said. "I won't stop it."

I watched her move away along the aisle, very business-like, very different from the warm, willing woman who'd visited my room last night in Mexico City—the rest of the group had gone to a performance of the Ballet Folklorica, but she'd passed me a signal to abstain. Now she spoke to the guide, a stocky dark man in a white suit, bracing himself on the platform beside the driver. He nodded and, as Frances returned to her seat somewhere behind me, he picked up the microphone, whistled into it once to check the sound, and went into his spiel.

"My name is Ramiro," he said, "and I am happy to welcome you to our beautiful country, Costa Verde, and our beautiful capital city of Santa Rosalia. Santa Rosalia has an elevation of five hundred and fifty meters above the sea, that is about one thousand eight hundred feet; and a population of four hundred and eighty thousand people, almost half a million. Tomorrow I will be pleased to show you the fine museum constructed by our progressive government to preserve our people's ancient heritage. You will also visit the fine Palace of the Governors and a new sisal plant, one of the many fine industries encouraged by the forward-looking policies of . . . Yes, señora?"

It was Mrs. Henderson, the wife of the ex-general. "What's that enormous building over there?" she asked. "It looks very old."

Leaning over to look across the bus, I saw it looming over the surrounding slums: a great block of ancient masonry with bars at the windows and a weathered cross over the impressive entrance gates. The dark face of our guide showed momentary confusion, but quickly recovered its impassivity.

"Señora, that is the *Mision Santa Rosalia*, established in sixteen hundred and fifty-three by the Society of Jesus. As you can see, it was built for defense, like a fortress—in fact sometimes it is known as La Fortaleza, the fortress—and in times of trouble people came for many miles to take shelter within the walls. The stone is our local limestone of which you will see a great deal at the ruins we will be visiting soon. Once the mission stood in a small native village; now as you can see a great city has grown up around it. There is a very fine little chapel; unfortunately it can not be visited because the mission is now used as an official state building. . . ."

An official state building. I watched it go by the bus windows, and even at the distance of several blocks I thought I could smell the prison filth and hear the screams from the interrogation cells.

"And on the other side of the bus," said the smooth voice of the guide, "you will see the new facilities of our national oil company, Petroverde. Costa Verde has many fine resources and more oil is being discovered frequently. . . ."

Then we were through the ugly perimeter of the city and driving down a handsome tree-lined boulevard, with the guide pointing out to us banks and office buildings. Even here there were soldiers; but there were also important-looking businessmen marching down the sidewalks in dark suits, white shirts, and expensive neckties; and pretty secretaries in smart dresses or pantsuits and provocatively high heels. The bus turned into a maze of smaller one-way streets and brought up in front of our hotel, where I went into my wheelchair drill. Frances did her stuff with the luggage and room keys. It was really getting to be a well-disciplined operation.

"Thanks, Sam," Ricardo Jimenez said as I delivered him to his floor, the third floor here. He glanced down the corridor. "I see my suitcase has already made it; come in for a drink." He paused significantly. "I think we both need one, don't you, amigo?"

I studied him for a moment. "Sure. Best offer I've had all day."

When we reached the room, he worked the key, saying, "If you don't mind bringing my bag inside . . . There's a bottle of bourbon wrapped in a shirt. Just set the combination lock to zeros and it will open." While I put the suitcase on the luggage stand and dug out the whiskey, he got the door closed and rolled himself over to the dresser and peeled the Saran Wrap or whatever the local equivalent was called, off the plastic glasses, holding one out to me as I approached with the bottle. He looked me in the eye. "Pour your own poison, Mr. Helm."

I grinned at him. "As you wish, Señor Jimenez, but I think we'd better stick to the cover names for the time being," I said. "How long have you known?"

He shrugged. "Since Houston, I think. A tall man who is very good with a rifle—it is a story I have heard many times. A tall man who knows much about cameras and often uses them for disguise. A tall man who works for the United States Government. A tall man whose lady friend was recently murdered by my stupid young brother and my stupid young sister and their stupid friend on instructions, or perhaps not on instructions, from my still-so-ambitious father." He looked up at me curiously. "I thought you would certainly betray me at the airport, amigo. I had thought of having you killed, as a preventive measure; but that would have destroyed our plans just as effectively as anything you could do against us. The murder or unexplained disappearance of a member of this tour would have brought everything to a halt; it would have caused an investigation that Mr. Dick Anderson would not have survived. So . . ." He shrugged and raised his glass to me. "So here we are."

I said, "At least you've learned not to go off half-cocked, unlike the rest of your lousy family. Do they know you're alive and out of prison? I got the impression from Dolores———"

"They do not know," Ricardo said. "They really have very few reliable contacts with the land they still hope to liberate; and it was not considered safe for them to know, so the information was not allowed to reach them." He frowned up at me. "Why didn't you, amigo?"

"Finger you at the airport?" I shrugged. "Why the hell should I? You haven't done anything to me, at least not yet. You weren't even in Chicago when it happened."

"So I am to believe that your presence on this tour is pure coincidence?"

I said, "Two people wanted to slip into a country without attracting attention, and there was only one inconspicuous way of going at the time, and they both went that way. If that's a coincidence, you can have it." I studied him for a moment. "Who's running your revolution, anyway? Not you, not from the U.S., not from that chair. And not your daddy, apparently, since you haven't even bothered to let him know you're still alive."

There was some guilt in Ricardo's voice when he said, "I have much respect for my father; but he is very old-fashioned now with his military ways."

"You're going to need some old-fashioned military ways if you have any notion of taking over this country, considering all the firepower I saw on the streets today."

"Actually, the army's loyalty to Rael is very doubtful, now that a Jimenez is on the other side. That is the reason I am here." He hesitated. "It would be very good if we could have my father to advise us in the fighting. He was a great fighter, but he was a terrible president, Sam. Like your General Grant. He could not believe that his old army friends would betray his trust and use for their own profit the positions to which he had raised them without any thought for the people of Costa Verde. It was all army, and all corrupt army, while he was president; otherwise Armando Rael with his reactionary friends could never have come to power. Yet the army has always loved my father, and there are many people who are not military who remember the name Jimenez not so badly, now that they have experienced Rael. As I say, that is why I am here. A Jimenez, a son of a well-remembered officer, but no army man himself, with no cronies in the officer corps. A Jimenez, who has suffered much, sacrificed much, fighting against Rael and for his country. A figurehead, if you like, crippled in this chair; but a figurehead that can, perhaps, lead the revolution to victory and a better life for the people of Costa Verde."

"So you are cutting daddy out, is that it?"

Jimenez shrugged, a little self-consciously. "It cannot be helped. He has never really been in, recently. His time is past. Even if I had succeeded in the mission on which he sent me, and eliminated Rael, he would not have reaped the benefit. There were others on the ground ready to take advantage of the opportunity if it came. I could see at once that they were assisting me for their own good, not for my father's. But there was nothing to do but take advantage of their help, since there was no other help available. The death of Rael was the important thing. Who benefited did not matter greatly. The people would have benefited in any case."

"But you goofed," I said.

The word threw him for a moment; then he nodded. "Yes. I missed with the first shot and they gave me no time for another."

"Well, it happens," I said. "If you're the figurehead, who's behind you?"

He hesitated, and shrugged again. "It is no big secret.

63

The man's name is Lupe de Montano, Lupe of the Mountain. He has the name of *bandido,* of course; here if you are against the government, you are always a bandit. Lupe himself will not claim that he is altogether a patriotic saint. My father scorned him as a swashbuckling outlaw in a big hat, very much like that *El Fuerte* you may remember; but he was willing to make use of Lupe, not knowing that Lupe was instead making use of him, and of me. Lupe is ready to move out of the hills now; and he needs respectability for his political movement and a lever to turn the army from Rael. With the name of Jimenez I am that respectability and that lever. That is why he got me out of La Fortaleza and shipped me to the United States to be repaired and reconstructed as far as possible, looking ahead to the time when he could make good use of me."

"How did he manage to spring you?" I asked curiously.

"Spring?" Again the slang word confused him for a moment. "Oh. I think we can say that he got me out of prison in much the same way he just got us into this country, by influence and threats and some bribery. Rael and his butcher Echeverria have made many enemies who are willing to help anyone working against them, particularly if there is a little profit and not too much risk." There was an old cynicism in the young voice. Ricardo went on: "I cannot tell you much about my escape. I was not really there. I had resigned myself to dying; I wished for death. What did I have left to live for, to live with? I think by this time you have learned what was done to me." He shook his head. "As for my liberation, I have been told that forged release papers were presented to someone who had agreed not to scrutinize them too closely; but I remember only the pain of being carried, and jolted in a truck, and jounced around in a small, fast boat. At the time I was merely annoyed, as far as I had any feelings at all. They would not let me die in peace. And then the American hospital and the doctors and the operations; and gradually . . . Well, I was not good for much, the way Echeverria and his torturers had left me. I was no good for a woman and not much good for myself. But if I could still be of some good for my country, then I was not entirely a useless hulk, you understand. So here I am, to do what I can for my people with what remains to me: my heart and my brain and my name."

It was a little on the heroic side, but they do like their drama down there; and he was obviously sincere. In fact I sensed something a bit obsessive about his patriotic fervor. Well, after what had been done to him it would have been strange if he were totally normal. I thought it possible that Rael and Echeverria might one day come to regret what they'd created here.

I said, "Well, you're going to have to make up your mind, Ricardo. I have nothing against you, or your revolution, or your man of the mountain. On the other hand, there's an account to be settled with some other members of your family; and it will be settled, I assure you. If that makes us enemies, it's just too damn bad. Your decision, amigo."

"Aren't you being a little overconfident, Sam? My father has been taking care of himself for quite a while."

I said, "We're not discussing army maneuvers now. Any competent professional with a few resources could take that bunch of wild-eyed amateurs he's collected out in that Chicago suburb, like that General Grant you just mentioned took Richmond. And I'm a pro."

Ricardo Jimenez drew a long breath. "If my family is hurt, I will undoubtedly hate you, Sam. But they did what they did, and I will not feel obliged to avenge them. Is that satisfactory?"

I nodded. "Thanks for the drink. Anything I can get you before I go?" When he shook his head, I said, "Be good."

He grinned. "I've got a choice?"

CHAPTER 10

LATER in the day the telephone rang, catching me on my hotel bed with my shoes off pretending to myself that I was thinking deep and important thoughts involving my various duties and obligations. Actually, I was taking a nap. It hadn't been a very restful night—in fact it had been a very pleasantly unrestful night—and it had been a mod-

65

erately tense morning, and I couldn't think of anything better to do, after my late lunch, with what was left of the afternoon. Anyway, there was a contact to be made, and I figured I might as well start making it by staying put for a little, where our man in Santa Rosalia, whoever he might be, could find me easily. If he made no move to get in touch with me here, I could try putting the body into motion and letting him intercept it at his pleasure.

When I picked up the jangling instrument, a harsh voice spoke in my ear. "Am I addressing Flashbulb Felton, boy photojournalist?"

I said, "Who the hell? . . . Oh, Christ, it's Miranda!"

"It is indeed Marvelous Miranda Matson," said the raspy female voice. "I saw your name on a press release from the *Palacio de los Gobernadores*—noted scientists and eminent camera artist to tour ancient ruins of beautiful Costa Verde—and I thought I'd see if it was the same Sam Felton. I couldn't bear the thought that there might be two. Remember that crazy trip we took on that ancient tub of a freighter we called the *Snark*?"

Lewis Carroll, the Mexico City contact had said. One word. I said, "Yeah, that sure was a jabberwocky operation, wasn't it? Let's hope we don't hit any more fouled-up stories like that one. Can I buy you a drink?"

"Cheapskate. I was hoping to get at least a free lunch out of you."

"Gold digger," I said. "Okay, where? You know the town better than I do."

"*Restaurante Tolteca*," she said. "The Toltec Restaurant, on the plaza. Any cab driver knows it. I'll meet you there. Tomorrow at one o'clock, okay?"

"Check." I hesitated, but if there were bugs on the line, somebody already knew too much and a little more wouldn't matter. "Miranda."

"Yes?"

"I need everything you can get hold of on a guy called Lupe Montano."

"So does everybody else in Santa Rosalia, including *El Presidente* himself. But you've come to the right girl. I've been doing a little research on the would-be liberator of Costa Verde; and my advice is if you ever happen to meet Mr. Lupe of the Mountain, don't turn your back on him. That's the trouble with these Latin American horse operas:

66

The guys in the white hats are hard to find. I'll put together what I've got and what I can find out between now and tomorrow and have it for you at lunch."

"Miranda, you're a jewel."

"It took you this long to find out?"

I put the phone down; and so much for our man in Santa Rosalia. I wondered how Mac had managed to recruit Miranda Matson, a perfectly genuine news-gatherer of the old hard-drinking variety, with all the brains and guts in the world, and about as much sex appeal as a backhoe, to run our errands for us.

I'd met her under my own name in the days when I was carrying a camera for real, a hell of a long time ago; and I'd run up against her a couple of times since I'd switched to a less peaceful profession, in my boy-photographer disguise, which seemed to be about as much of a secret these days as Ronald Reagan's former occupation. Well, maybe Miranda was hoping to get a scoop out of it; she'd been around long enough to still think in those old-fashioned Front-Page terms. . . .

In the evening before dinner—they feed you late in that part of the world—we had an informal introductory lecture in one of the hotel's small conference rooms on the ground floor. There was the usual confusion while everybody got drink orders in and got settled around the big table and got served and paid or signed for refreshments received. Then Frances, at the head of the table, tapped on her glass to get our attention.

"I'm just going to give you a quick historical survey of this part of Latin America," she said. "It will give you a background for the museum exhibits you'll see tomorrow, and the Melmec ruins from which those exhibits came, where we'll be spending the rest of our time. I'll start with the advent of the Spaniards and work back. The Aztecs are not really relevant to our tale, but since you saw all those beautiful exhibits in Mexico City, I might as well tell you that they were kind of an outcast tribe, banished to an island nobody else wanted in Lake Tenochtitlan, where they multiplied like rabbits for some reason and soon overran all the older civilizations around the lake. They established their own elaborate society which came to an end, pretty much, with the arrival of Mr. Cortez on his big horse. Just about the same thing happened out on the

Yucatan Peninsula, where the Toltecs, another migrant tribe from the high country of Mexico, combined with the remnants of the old Maya peoples to found the civilization centered around Chichen Itza. That culture, we call it the Postclassic, was already declining when the Spaniards landed, but just as in Mexico City they gave it the coup de grace. Earlier, we had the Classic Maya civilization, as represented by the great cities of the Peten. . . ."

I found myself watching her long slim hands as she talked to us easily. Browner than her body, since they could not so readily be shielded from the hot sun under which she often worked, they were beautiful hands, but they were not as relaxed as her voice. She was still a lady under pressure and I wondered who was exerting it and how. I'd been tempted to discuss her predicament, whatever it was, with Ricardo Jimenez, but I'd been afraid I might be giving him information he didn't already have, to her detriment.

I found myself wishing that the lady would take a deep breath and trust me; but that's the trouble with very bright people, particularly very bright female people who've fought their way up in what is still essentially a male world. They're too damn bright to trust anybody.

Before the Mayas came the Olmecs, she said, the carvers of those great brooding heads; and before the Olmecs came the Melmecs. Somewhere in the still unraveled tangle of Melmec history had appeared the two great inventions that had placed these New World civilizations on a level with their Old World counterparts. These inventions had formerly been attributed to the Olmecs; but the Copalque discoveries had already shown that the archaeology books would have to be rewritten in this respect. Somewhere much further back in history than previously thought, the Melmecs had constructed, and so been able to pass on to subsequent civilizations in the area, a perfectly viable numerical system—something the Romans with their idiot capital letters had never accomplished—and an accurate calendar.

As a matter of fact, Frances said, it was well known that the Mayas had inherited not just one, but two, calendars from their predecessors. One had a three-hundred-sixty-day year to keep track of ordinary secular events like the planting and the harvest, with a five-day limbo period at the end to make it come out even with the astronomical year. The second calendar was a religious one with a two-hundred-sixty-day year, by which they scheduled all their religious ceremonies and festivals.

One theory that had been advanced, not altogether jokingly, she said, was that this dual system had been set up deliberately to make things so complicated that only the priests could figure out on what days which gods had to be propitiated, adding to the mystery and power of the priesthood. Naturally, the short religious year came around faster than the long secular year; but the mathematics of it insured that once every fifty-two years the two moved into synchronization briefly; and this was a very important year in the lives of these people.

The lady was good, I reflected; she had us listening to all this dull history and arithmetic as if we were watching our favorite TV shows. Perhaps it was her own enthusiasm that gripped us. When she paused and reached for her drink and sipped from it briefly, there was a stir of movement around the table as her listeners took advantage of the opportunity to change the positions they'd held while she was talking.

"Well, you saw the great Aztec calendar wheel in Mexico City," Frances went on, "with its two concentric calendars, the ones I've just described. It represents the previously accepted thinking on the subject. But there have been a few clues found, a few glyphs discovered in various sites, Olmec and Maya both, that seem to indicate that these theories are, if not inaccurate, at least not quite complete. My husband, after studying these anomalies carefully, came to the conclusion that there had to be something missing, and that it might be found in the area to which we'll be driving tomorrow. Well, I've told you about our discovery of the previously unsuspected Copalque site. And we've already uncovered there clear evidence that his tentative hypothesis was correct: The Melmecs used and passed on to the later civilizations in the area a system involving not just two calendars, but three. The third one was apparently very secret, indeed, and was known only to the very highest of the high priests. It was too secret, too sacred, too dangerous, to be shown on the ordinary calendar wheels; however, we've discovered a large cavern—those limestone formations are riddled with caves and *cenotes*, or water holes—in which was established a so-far unique three-calendar wheel. Apparently some very special mysteries were celebrated in this cave according to this calendar; ceremonies we're still trying to understand."

Her voice stopped. After a moment she gave a deprecating little laugh, as if embarrassed, and tasted her drink, and looked at us.

"I don't suppose this seems very important to you," she said in a lighter voice, "any more than the medieval question of how many angels could dance on the point of a pin. Two calendars or three, what's the difference? I must admit that we archaeologists get carried away by our pretty theories; but I do think you'll find our museum tour tomorrow morning very interesting. The bus leaves the hotel at eight-thirty sharp. Thank you."

Leaving, I made no effort to approach her, mindful of her warning that we must not spend much time together in public; but somehow I found myself walking beside her, anyway, as we crossed the lobby toward the dining room, now open.

"Dr. Dillman?" I said, playing safe in case we had an interested audience.

"Yes?"

I put on my face the look of an eager student in search of knowledge. "That five-day limbo period, as you called it, at the end of each year of the secular calendar. What was the significance of that, besides making the year come out with three hundred and sixty-five days, as it should?"

"It was a bad-luck time," she said. "You had to watch yourself during those five days and perform all the right religious rites, or the next year would be shot to hell."

"And how about that fifty-two-year period? What happened when those two calendars got together every half century and a little?"

She glanced at me oddly, as if she hadn't expected these questions from a nonarchaeological dope like me. She said carefully, "It was a time of doom, Mr. Felton; a time when the gods had to be propitiated with extreme care; a time of change and nobody knew in what direction, good or bad. But it was damn well going to be bad if you didn't do exactly the right things, the things the priests told you to do."

"Next question," I said. "On this three-calendar system you and your husband discovered, what happened when all

70

three calendars came into sync, once every few hundred or thousand years, or whatever?"

She drew a long breath and glanced around; but there was nobody within hearing. "Samuel," she said softly, "I think we're going to make an archaeologist of you yet. That *is* the question, isn't it?" She licked her lips and spoke precisely. "Since you're so interested, I'll tell you that the periods between the critical times of three-calendar synchronization, as far as we can determine with our present data and our present methods of dating, coincide with reasonable accuracy with the life spans of each of the three civilizations we are considering. Interesting, don't you think?" She shivered abruptly and said in a totally different tone, "Well, I'd better go see how Dick Anderson is making out. Until I started wrestling that damned wheelchair, I didn't realize how many stupid, unnecessary steps people built in how many stupid, unnecessary places."

In the morning, the bus took us to the museum, housed in a magnificent old mansion that had been beautifully restored for the purpose but was already deteriorating rapidly, since they had apparently spent money on everything except the roof. We'd been told that the rainy season down there is a real duck-drowner; and it's just as well, since it's otherwise a very dry country, on the surface at least. When it doesn't rain, the only water comes from underground rivers and the *cenotes* Frances had mentioned: places where limestone caverns have collapsed to expose underground pools, very important to the ancients unable to drill for their water. The *cenotes* had largely determined the locations of the great cities.

Anyway, the walls of the fine museum were disfigured by ugly watermarks, and some of the exhibits had had to be moved out of the way of drips from above; which I suppose said something about the administration of Armando Rael, although I could think of worse things against his regime than a casual attitude toward ceiling leaks. The exhibits were not as dramatic as those of the *Museo Anthropologia* in Mexico City; nor had the Melmecs, as far as I could make out, produced any sculpture as spectacular as that of their successors, the Olmecs. However, Frances loved her Melmecs dearly; and her I-was-there account of the discovery of the various pieces was worth the price of admission.

Then we were released for lunch; and I took a taxi to the plaza and the *Restaurante Tolteca,* which turned out to be a rather formal establishmènt, as many of them are down there. I was glad I'd thought to put on a necktie in spite of the warmth of the day—we'd come down five thousand feet from Mexico City and the weather was quite tropical. Since I was moderately respectable in appearance, in spite of the camera bag I was lugging, the maitre d' condescended to indicate to me the table of the señorita Matson.

Miranda was one or two ahead of me already; she always had been. A big woman with white untidy hair and a square brown face, she was wearing a seersucker pantsuit —well, I couldn't quite make out the pants as she sat at the table, but I knew they were there because Miranda had never, to the best of my knowledge, been seen in a skirt.

"Hey, do you know what they charge for Scotch down here?" was her greeting to me. "Forty dollars a fifth! Forty bucks!"

I said, "What do you care? You've always been a bourbon baby. How are you, Miranda?"

"About the way I look, and that isn't good," she said.

"Hell, you don't look much worse than the last time I saw you," I said, sitting down. "What are you doing in this hole, anyway?"

She shrugged. "Somebody thinks something's going to break wide open here and they want a man on the spot when it happens and the closest thing they could get was me."

"That's pretty close," I said.

"You bastard. What do you want to drink?"

"Whatever you're having. If it hasn't killed you yet, it probably won't kill me."

"Don't count on it. Years of heavy exposure tend to build up the immunity, dearie."

She gave the order. Apparently she already had the waiters trained to jump; the man was back in double-quick time. We saluted each other, drank; and then we looked at each other across the table for a moment, kind of catching up with the time that had passed since we'd last met.

The trouble with Miranda Matson was that she was a big ugly competent sophisticated woman who'd seen everything; but when she looked at you with her surprisingly—

72

considering the amount she drank—clear brown eyes you felt sure that somewhere behind them was a pretty, innocent little girl begging to be let out. There were rumors about her sexual proclivities; I guess there always are when the lady is built like a horse. I was in no position to confirm or deny them and didn't care. She was a hell of a reporter and a good friend when one was needed; but I didn't think friendship had brought her here. As it turned out, I was more or less wrong.

"In case you're wondering," she said, "I owe you people one. One of your guys bailed me out of one of those half-ass African countries where they're always killing each other and anybody else who happens to be handy. I said if there was ever anything I could do; and when your big man in Washington found there was nobody in Costa Verde he could use but Miranda, he told me what I could do. Get it out of my purse, will you? I don't even like to touch the damn things."

I reached under the table and dug into the enormous leather bag she had sitting there and found the gun—a two-inch-barreled job by the feel, in a tricky little holster—and the small plastic bag of cartridges. I judged fifteen rounds or three cylindersful. Not enough to fight a war, but I might manage a small battle if I was careful. I tucked the stuff away in my camera bag.

"Whew, it's a relief to be rid of that!" Miranda said. "And here's the material on Montano you asked for. Don't read it here; they don't like to have people puking all over their nice white tablecloths." She waited until I'd slipped the envelope into my jacket pocket, and went on: "Next, I'm supposed to tell you that Bultman's gone underground, whatever that means. Got it?"

"Bultman underground. Check."

"Now look around and see if there's somebody you recognize, maybe from a photograph or description."

I glanced around casually. It was a big, high-ceilinged room with elaborate lighting fixtures. There were, as Miranda had indicated, tablecloths on the tables, and linen napkins. There seemed to be other dining rooms, perhaps more intimate, behind the main one in which we were seated. On the street side, big windows gave a good view of the main plaza of Santa Rosalia, and of the impressive cathedral on the far side. It was of stone construction, but

73

the religious architecture was lighter and more graceful than that of the massive fortress-mission we'd seen yesterday. I noted two groups of armed and uniformed men out there, keeping watch over the tree-shaded square. . . .

My glance stopped abruptly at a table by the window. Red-haired and red-bearded Latins do exist, but they aren't common; and I had no doubt of the identity of the man I was looking at. Red Henry. Enrique Rojo. He was sitting at a table with three army officers in uniform; and in his dark business suit he looked more dangerous than all three military men put together. He was in his late thirties or early forties. He had a hawklike Spanish face. Mephistopheles with a henna rinse, I thought; but instinct told me this was nobody I really wanted to make jokes about.

"Pretty, ain't he?" Miranda shivered slightly. "The Lord High Executioner of Costa Verde. I need another drink."

CHAPTER 11

IT took us most of the following day to drive to Copalque. The bus was air-conditioned, which was just as well, since we were heading down into the real lowlands now, and the temperature increased significantly as the altitude diminished. For a while we ran between large sisal fields hacked out of the jungle and not very carefully cultivated. Maybe they don't need to be, since the plant is kind of an overgrown agave cactus: a great sunburst of thick fleshy leaves with spiny points and edges. It looks like a tough, self-reliant desert plant that shouldn't require much cultivation. They use the fibers for cordage. It's not up to modern nylon and dacron, or even old-fashioned manila; but it's still a thriving industry down here.

The road got progressively worse as we left the capital city of Costa Verde behind; but what really slowed us was being stopped at one roadblock and checkpoint after another. It was apparently the great local sport: Make the lousy rich Americanos climb out of their cool vehicle and stand in the hot sun while their papers are examined, and discussed with the guide, in minute and endless detail. Then on to the next bunch of sloppy, uniformed gun-toters —ironically, the weapons being waved at us were good old American M16s—and the next arrogant bantam rooster of an officer, who hadn't had his hassle-the-gringos jollies for the day and was very happy to see us.

The Hotel Copalque, when we finally reached it, turned out to be a sprawling new tourist resort complete with swimming pool, gardens, and fountains, a real oasis in the strange, low, dry jungle they have down there. There was a main building with desk, bar, restaurant, and curio shop; behind it were the guest cabins, built in the oval native style with heavy whitewashed walls and thatched roofs. But it had been a long, dry drive with just a brief break for a picnic lunch in a village along the way, and most of the party made straight for the bar and to hell with luggage and accommodations. I got Ricardo a drink.

"Save a little time for me this evening, amigo," I said. "I've got something to show you, but in private."

He glanced at me curiously. "Sure, Sam. Whenever you say. I'm not planning on one of my long jungle hikes tonight."

I went looking for Frances and found her by the hotel desk being her usual efficient self.

"Oh, there you are," she said. She handed me a room key. "Oh, and here's Dick's too; you can give it to him. They've taken the suitcases out already. It's the two single cabins right over there, no steps to negotiate. I'm just down the hill from you." She glanced at me. The slight blush that came to her face was very becoming and made her look much less formidable and businesslike. "That's information-information, not action-information, darling. We can't . . . risk anything here; everybody knows Archie and me."

I said, "Sure. But if I should decide that I desperately need pictures of the Temple of the Sun by moonlight, you wouldn't let me go wandering around out there at night all alone, would you? I might get lost."

She said, "There is no Temple of the Sun. Be good, Sam. . . . When we first came here we slept in tents," she said in a totally different tone, looking around the elaborate tiled lobby. "There was nothing here but the jungle and the past.

But the government decided that if the Guatemalans could coin money at Tikal, and the Mexicans could cash in on Uxmal and Chichen Itza, Costa Verde had to have its little tourist goldmine, too."

"Well, they'd better clean up their act," I said. "They're not going to get many tourists here if they subject them to the kind of stupid harassment we got today."

"Shhh," she said uneasily, with a glance toward where our guide was chatting with the desk clerk. "Please, not so loud!"

I said, "For a big, brave Americano lady you sure pick up the police-state mentality fast. What's his name, anyway?"

"Ramiro. Ramiro Sanchez."

"What can he do to you?"

She shrugged helplessly. "Well, he can report that I allowed to come along on our tour a representative of the press who was heard making loud derogatory remarks about certain government policies. He can recommend that, since we seem to use no discretion in our choice of participants, no more institute-sponsored expeditions be allowed; and perhaps our permit to dig here should be reviewed. Please, Sam. I don't want to talk about it. Just call me a coward and forget it. . . . Oh, there they are." She was looking toward the archway leading to the main road, where three men had just appeared. "I'm going to take a quick run over to the dig to see what's being done, so I'll know where to bring everybody in the morning. The college-boy type is our resident supervisor, Marty Ellender, a Texas boy with a degree from Tulane. The other two . . ."

But the trio was upon us. I was introduced to Ellender, a lean, sandy young man in jeans and cowboy boots and a big hat; and the crew foreman, a chunky, middle-aged man with a dark Spanish-Indian face, named Porfirio Gonzaga. There was a little pause.

"Oh, and this is Cortez," Frances said.

I hadn't really had time to look at the third man before. He was short and sturdy, as most of them are down there, and very brown, and very old. He was dressed like Gonzaga, in a straw hat and white cotton pajamas, not particularly clean; but there the resemblance ended. There was nothing Spanish about this face. It was right off one of the old bas-reliefs we'd been seeing in the museums.

76

They had some weird ideas of beauty back in those days—well, weird to us. They thought a flat, sloping forehead was charming and strapped boards on their babies' heads to achieve it; and they considered the loveliest eyes to be the ones that were slightly crossed. A bead mounted on the nose, which the infant tried to look at, helped to make the eyes turn inward permanently.

But it's possible that this standard of beauty had originally been formed in accordance with existing hereditary factors and that artificial means had later been used merely to return to an appearance that had once come naturally. It seemed hardly likely that in the twentieth century, or even in the very late nineteenth when this Cortez would have been born, local kids were still being boarded and beaded; yet this old man had all the ancient features including the bold curved predatory nose. He did not offer his hand and I made no attempt to take it. I gave him a slight bow instead, which he acknowledged in kind.

"Señor Cortez," I said.

He shook his head. *"Yo soy Cortez solamente, Señor Felton."*

He was only Cortez. The name of the conqueror, worn proudly by the elderly descendant of the conquered—except that this man's ancestors had lost their elaborate civilization, for reasons unknown, long before the white-winged ships appeared along these low jungle coasts. Our eyes met and held for a long moment; then Cortez smiled faintly as if he had seen something that pleased and satisfied him, and I had to admit that I was relieved. I wouldn't have wanted to think I displeased this old man, although I didn't know why.

"We will meet again, Señor Felton. Be careful."

"It has been a pleasure to make your acquaintance, Cortez."

Frances said to me, "If I'm not back in time, tell everybody the dining room opens at seven-thirty. . . . All right, Marty, let's go."

I watched them leave; and for once I wasn't appreciating the nice controlled movement of the lady's taut derriere under her well-fitting skirt. I did note that she'd dispensed with her suit jacket and changed to sturdy low-heeled shoes; but I was really watching the old man and wondering exactly what he had seen, and approved of, when he looked at me. There was a whisper of sound behind me, and I turned to see the wheelchair roll up.

"*Dios,* isn't that *viejo* a beautiful specimen!" Ricardo said, watching the group go out of sight. "I tell you, we could use a few hundred like that old one, about a third the age, of course. Or a few thousand. Once they were the best guerilla fighters on the continent, maybe in the world; and to hell with your Plains Indians, amigo. Those were just light cavalry, good only for hit-and-run raids; but down in Yucatan people like that old man defended their jungles stubbornly and held the invaders at bay for decades after the rest of Central America had been conquered. Hell, they rose again in 1847 and just missed booting the Spanish off the whole peninsula; they fought again in 1860; and they were still giving Porfirio Diaz fits in 1910."

"Says proudly a man named Jimenez," I said dryly. "Whose side are you on, anyway, Buster? Personally, I'd have picked the Spanish side. They got to ride horseback."

"But think of having to wear those cast-iron hats and vests in this climate!" He grinned at me. "Have you got my key? You wanted a conference, you said."

Reaching his cabin, I let him unlock the door and open it, since doing this seemed to be a matter of pride with him. I picked up his suitcase and followed the wheelchair into the pseudoethnic structure, which was very picturesque. You could look up into the depths of, or maybe I should say the heights of, the peaked thatched roof—the thatch was either plastic or sprayed with something—and there was mosquito netting hung like a fragile tent over the bed, a romantic tropical antibug device I'd never encountered before, having always put my faith in window screens and smelly chemicals.

"You'd better take it down for me, if you don't mind," Ricardo said. "I can't fight my way through all that cheesecloth when I go to bed. I've got some spray and roll-on stuff to use if they get bad; and I'm taking my malaria pills. . . . Thanks. You know where the bottle is. Can I prevail upon you to do the honors, señor?" When I'd fixed us up with drinks and settled in a chair, he rolled himself up to comfortable talking distance and said, "Something serious, Sam?"

I tossed an envelope into his lap. "It depends upon what you consider serious, amigo. There's what my agency knows about your friend and associate, Lupe of the Mountain. If you were already aware of his larcenous and treacherous propensities, forgive me for wasting your time."

He regarded me for a moment, frowning; then he opened the envelope and began to read the lengthy dossier Miranda had prepared for me. I'd read it myself, earlier. An impressive gent, Lupe Montano. A ruthless gent who'd sacrifice his mother, friends, or girlfriend without turning a hair if his interests required it. Well, who was I to talk? The only real difference between us, I reflected sourly, was that Lupe's interests almost invariably turned out to be financial, whereas I'm not all that concerned about money. Ricardo folded the dossier carefully and returned it to the envelope and looked at me.

"So?"

"That's the man you want running your precious country?"

He shrugged, a little defiantly. "Is there a choice?"

I said, "You could go back where you came from and leave Rael where he is. On the record, there's not a hell of a lot of difference between him and your *bandido* friend. Not enough to kill for. Or die for." After a moment, when he didn't speak, I went on: "Anyway, I thought you ought to know the kind of company you were getting yourself into."

"Why?" he demanded. "Why did you go to this trouble, Sam?"

"A small matter of conscience," I said.

"I see." His eyes were cold. "Act helpful toward one Jimenez so you can feel free to act vengeful toward the others."

It was a fairly shrewd observation. I reminded myself that there were a few brains in the family, even though they were not always employed to best advantage.

"Something like that," I said. "Also there was a lady who had a thing about liberty and human rights and sentimental stuff like that. I didn't get to put flowers on her grave, so I thought I'd make a slightly different kind of gesture—in memoriam, so to speak."

He was watching me carefully. "By sending me back to the U.S.?"

"Are you going?"

He shook his head. "No. What's there for me? Should

I spend the rest of my life sitting in this miserable chair watching your stupid TV? This is my home. Here I stay. One way or another." He studied me thoughtfully. "But I fail to understand your gesture, amigo. How can showing me this record of Montano's villainy, if you want to call it that, serve as a suitable memorial to your lost lady."

I said, "Well, that rather depends upon what you do about it, doesn't it?"

He frowned. "What can I do? I said I'm not going back."

"I never expected you to."

"And if I stay here and refuse to behave as the figurehead Lupe wants, I will undoubtedly wind up back in La Fortaleza where Echeverria will finish the job he left uncompleted. I don't have many choices, my friend."

"There's one you haven't mentioned."

"What's that?"

I spoke carefully: "You don't have to be a figurehead just because Lupe says so."

He nodded thoughtfully. "Yes. The idea had occurred to me. I think I would like to play a somewhat more important role here than was originally intended for me, but Lupe would never share the power. . . ."

I spoke as carefully as before: "Men like Lupe don't live forever, amigo. They've even been known to die rather suddenly."

He stared at me, shocked. "I owe my life to Lupe Montano!"

"Sure," I said. "And you'll owe your death to him the minute he doesn't need you any more. Or the minute it begins to look as if you're getting too popular and powerful in the revolutionary movement. Have you got a gun?"

He licked his lips. "I will have. It is being arranged."

"Not by Lupe, I'll bet. He'll want to keep you as helpless as possible."

"How can you know Lupe's motives? You have never met him."

I gestured toward the fat envelope still lying on his lap. "He's in there, isn't he? And in my business I've known a hundred Montanos; and one characteristic all these outlaw Napoleons have in common is that they cherish their status tenderly, whether they're heading a cell of spies, a gang of bank robbers, or a whole damn revolutionary army. Sure, Montano wants the name Jimenez on his side because with his record he can't win without it; but he'll be real careful to see that it doesn't backfire on him. He'll keep you as isolated and helpless and dependent as he can, amigo. Have you got anybody you can trust, really trust? These people who are arranging for you to get a gun—are they really yours and not Lupe's?"

"They are mine," Ricardo said firmly. "They are soldiers who fought with my father, outlawed by Rael. They joined Lupe of the Mountain because there was no other place for them. But they will fight for me."

"Sure." I regarded him for a moment, rather grimly. "Final question, Señor Jimenez. Can you manage a revolution all by yourself if you have to?"

He said, "I am my father's son. He trained me well, I think."

I said, "Well, there's your answer. If it comes to that, and if you think the people will follow you."

"They will follow a Jimenez," he said. "But——"

"But what? Do I have to spell it out?" When he didn't speak, I said, "Sooner or later there will be a confrontation, Ricardo. Maybe you can swallow what he did in the past as a bandit; but don't kid yourself he's going to change. Sooner or later he'll do something you won't want attributed to your name or your revolution. My advice is: Be just as sweet and docile as you can until it happens, but be ready for it. When you're forced to challenge him, put it to him hard, and be sure you have plenty of firepower in the bushes when you do it, and your own gun in your hand. If he backs down, fine. Make him eat shit but good and he'll be your boy instead of you being his. But if he just gets mad and arrogant—*I am El Jefe and I do as I please!*—and tries to slap you down like a kid, which is probably what will happen, just cut him down on the spot, bang. No more Montano. If you're not up to that, you've got no business in the revolution business."

There was a lengthy silence. Ricardo's eyes had a shocked look; he licked his lips uncertainly. "I do not know if I am capable of killing. . . ." He stopped. I didn't speak. I saw a hard expression come to his face that reminded me of a certain military gent beside whom I'd fought many years ago. He nodded slowly. "I see. Yes. I will not plot against him, but if he defiles the revolution. . . . Yes, it is good advice. I will be ready. After all,

Lupe Montano is not really the man this country needs."

I felt like a latter-day Machiavelli; and I hoped he could pull it off when the time came.

"Now you're talking," I said a bit sourly. "Pretty soon you'll convince yourself that you were sent from heaven to save your suffering people, and you'll have it made."

He didn't smile. His young face was grim. "Not from heaven, amigo." He touched the too-smoothly-repaired burn scar on his cheek. "From hell!"

CHAPTER 12

ONE thing you learn in the business is how to sleep anywhere, on any reasonably horizontal surface, at any time, but somehow it didn't work that night; and instinct warned me it wasn't a safe place for me to dope myself with sedatives, although I keep some around for nights like that. So I lay in the dark looking up into the black recesses of the thatched roof of my pseudorustic cabin—like Ricardo I'd decided to dispense with the fancy mosquito-tent, and so far there had been no insects to bother me. Lying there, I was strongly aware of the long miles of tangled jungle just outside the newly landscaped hotel grounds and, strangely, of the brooding presence of the ancient pyramids and temples and caverns nearby, even though I hadn't seen them yet. Somehow the face of the old man called Cortez was mixed up with these feelings; although I couldn't have said how if anybody had asked.

But that was vague emotional-mystical nonsense. Since I had to lie awake, I told myself firmly, I might as well get a few things straight in my head, in particular the fact that the major question I'd come here to ask had been answered: *He was a great fighter, but he was a terrible president, Sam.* Ricardo had said it, letting me know that I could declare open season on Hector Jimenez at any time with no worry about depriving the poor people of Costa

Verde of an irreplaceable liberator, or offending the small gentle wraith that still pursued me. . . .

The sound of approaching footsteps drove the drifting thoughts from my mind. They were wrong footsteps, stumbling and uncertain; and I reached for the gun lying alongside my leg—under the pillow is too standard a hiding place. I eased back the sheet that covered me. There was a light rap on the door, and a whisper:

"Sam! Sam, please! Oh, God, let me in, I . . ."

When I reached the door, and got it unlocked and opened, she was leaning against the jamb with her forehead pressed hard against the painted wood, panting as if she'd run a hard race, and perhaps she had. She flinched when I put my arm around her shoulder, but allowed herself to be led inside. I locked the door behind us and reached for the light switch.

"No, not the light!" she gasped. "Please, I must look so . . .!"

"Don't be girlish, Frances."

I pressed the switch. She covered her face, frightening me for a moment into expecting something truly dreadful; but when I reached out to take her hands away she let them fall and let me look. It was only a bruise, but a pretty good one, reddening her left cheek from the corner of the eye to the corner of her mouth. She stood there in a slack way I'd never seen, allowing me to take it all in: the rumpled silk shirt coming out at the waist, the dusty and awry poplin skirt, and the laddered nylon stockings bloody at the knees. She'd also hurt her right hand. But what really concerned me was the shattered look in her eyes.

I said, "I hope you got the number of the truck."

"Haha," she said. Her voice was suddenly steadier, reassuring me. "When you're *quite* through being funny, you might break out some Band-Aids. If you haven't got any, there are some down in my—"

"I've got them. What happened?"

She licked her lips. "It was . . . it was really utterly ridiculous. I got lost. Down there at the dig. The new excavations have changed things. I took an old shortcut back here alone after my tour of inspection, and it was all changed and I got lost. And . . . and there were *things* . . . I mean, you'd think after all these years as an archaeologist I wouldn't be susceptible to . . . to *emanations* from ancient tombs, would you? But, well, goddamn it, I could just *feel* the presence of the Lords of the Night. . . ."

"The what?"

"Ah Puch, the God of Death, and the others . . . You'll think I'm crazy, but it was something cold and black coming out of . . . Strange that their hell is a place of cold, not of heat like ours, isn't it? Damn it, Sam, I panicked like a little girl, lost among all those broken temples, and I started running in the dark and took a bad fall and hit my face and almost knocked myself out. . . ." She drew a long breath and looked down at herself ruefully. "God, I really made a mess of myself, didn't I? My poor stockings! Well, I've got plenty of pantyhose along; but I hope I didn't ruin my only skirt, or I'll have to spend the rest of the trip either in jeans or a jersey dinner dress. Incidentally, Ah Puch is the Mayan name; the Melmecs called him Ixchal. . . . What are you doing?"

I reached out to hold the back of her head with one hand; and moved her jaw around gently with the other. "Okay?"

"It hurts a little but . . ."

"Nothing grating, nothing loose? All teeth present or accounted for?"

She nodded. "Fix my hand first, so I don't get any more blood on my clothes; it's all over the bottom of my skirt already. God, how ridiculous can you get? I've never done anything like this before in my life! Fleeing from ghosts at my age!"

She had a real jag on now, and she was still talking as I guided her into the bathroom and washed off her hand and sloshed a bit of peroxide over the shallow lacerations on the heel of it, obviously caused by stone or gravel as she tried to break her fall. A medium-sized Band-Aid finished the job.

"Now," I said, "slither out of those tights and sit down on the john so I can fix your knees."

She was studying her face in the bathroom mirror. "Will it get worse?" she asked.

"It'll probably color up a bit more by morning. But he missed the eye by enough; at least you won't have a shiner to worry about. I think you can cover most of it with makeup . . . ."

"Sam!"

"What?"

She was staring at me indignantly. "I just told you what happened!"

"Sure, baby, sure," I said. "Now get those crazy-looking nylons off, what's left of them, unless you'd rather have me take them off for you. . . ."

"But Sam!"

I drew a long breath. "Damn you, Dillman, why do you keep trying this kind of nonsense on me? I've been moderately frank with you. I've more or less told you I'm a professional; I've even let you know pretty much what kind of a pro I am. And in the exercise of my nefarious profession I've been slugged in the face more than once. I've seen others smacked, men and women both; I've even smacked a few myself. And you've ripped the skin of your hand and scraped some of it off your knees. If you'd really fallen on your face, which isn't easy to do, you'd have some bad scrapes there, too, wouldn't you, instead of just a bruise? Somebody took a good swing at you and knocked you spinning, and you landed on hands and knees—hand and knees. Now let me see about those knees, will you, and just shut up altogether if you can't talk without treating me like the village idiot."

She started to speak angrily and stopped. I put my arms around her and led her, stiff and hostile, back out into the bedroom where I'd have more maneuvering space. I knelt before her and untied and removed her sturdy walking shoes. She lifted her feet on command, like a robot. I reached far up under her skirt and worked the nylon wreckage down her hips and thighs and legs; and whether or not the operation affected me sexually is none of your damn business. She stepped out of the stuff when I asked her to; but when I told her to sit down in a nearby chair she didn't move.

I rose and looked at her hurt, handsome face. The shattered look was in her eyes again. Her mouth was trembling. It shocked me deeply. She was not a woman I'd ever expected to see weeping. Then she was in my arms, shaken by great wrenching sobs. I held her and rode out the storm with her; presently it began to subside.

"It's silly!" she gasped at last. "I'm just being a silly woman, but nobody . . . *nobody* has ever laid a hand on me before. So casual, so contemptuous, slapping me down and leaving me sitting in the dirt with my face all numb and my clothes all dusty and untidy and my stockings ruined. . . ." She drew a long ragged breath and tried to laugh. "I'm sorry, darling, I didn't mean to . . . It was just such a . . . such a terribly *humiliating* experience!"

After a moment, I said, "Knees. We were going to do something about those knees, remember?"

"All right, I'm all right now, but please bring me a Kleenex so I can blow my nose."

I pulled one of the big basket chairs closer for her—the other had my clothes draped over it, and I'd surreptitiously tucked my gun under them after recognizing her voice at the door. Returning from the bathroom with the requested Kleenex and the proper medical equipment, I washed and peroxided and Band-Aided the skinned knees. Then I covered them with a towel and spread the stained skirt over that and, with cold water, sponged the blood smears from the hem, where it had brushed against her lacerations.

"It should be all right when it dries," I said. "Who was it, Frances?"

There was a little pause. "I can't tell you," she said at last.

I said, "That's pretty stupid. If one of our party had suddenly gone haywire and belted you one, you'd have got up and broken a chair over his head. It has to be somebody you couldn't afford to fight; somebody who could slap you around like this and make you take it without striking back." I watched her closely. "Somebody like, for instance, that government fink who calls himself a guide, the one you didn't like me talking so loudly in front of because he might make official trouble for you. Ramiro Sanchez."

She hesitated, and said too quickly, "All right. Yes, it was Ramiro. He thought his position entitled him to . . . certain privileges. I guess I was rather tactless, rejecting his advances. Maybe I lost my temper and made some personal remarks I shouldn't have. So . . . he got a bit rough."

I nodded slowly; but I was suddenly sick inside. She was lying to me, but that was nothing new; she'd always lied to me. But the realization had suddenly come to me that she was faking here. Not that the bruised cheek and damaged stockings weren't real, or the blow that had caused them, or the resulting emotional upheaval . . . but was I truly the kind of guy on whose shoulder strong and independent ladies chose to cry? This strong and independent lady?

Suddenly I understood that Dr. Frances Ransome Dillman would never of her own accord have come to me or any man, not even her husband, for reassurance after such a crushingly humiliating experience. She was a very private individual, and she would never voluntarily have let me or any man see her like that, bruised and torn, disheveled and half-hysterical. Given a choice, she'd have found a secret place and fought it out with herself in the dark, alone. But she'd been given no choice. She'd been brutally struck, and then ordered to seek sympathy from me by somebody she felt compelled to obey; and I'd been flattered enough by her trust to accept her presence as natural, until now.

I looked at her for a long moment. Then I grinned wolfishly and said, "That's the way you get people killed, Dillman."

Her eyes widened. "What do you mean?"

I reached under my discarded clothes and brought out the Smith and Wesson. "Well, obviously, being a gentleman, I'm obliged to go out and teach this bastard Sanchez how to treat a lady. . . . You did say Sanchez, didn't you?"

She was staring at the weapon in my hand. They'd slipped me a tricky one this time: a standard snubby in .38 Special caliber, the chief's Special with the small, rounded, child-sized butt; but some quick-draw genius had been at it, grinding off the hammer spur so it wouldn't catch in the clothing, and removing the front of the trigger guard for easier access. He'd also smoothed the action considerably, but there's only so much you can do with that double-action mechanism, since it has to cock the hammer first before dropping it on the primer.

It still takes a long, strong, steady pull on the trigger; and personally I'm old-fashioned enough to thumb-cock the hammer and then use the crisp, light, hair-trigger mechanism to fire the piece—two separate operations—when real accuracy is required. But I'd have to live without that option for a while, since that smooth, spurless hammer would be slippery and dangerous to cock.

"Oh, God, you have a gun!" Frances breathed, and looked at me accusingly. "You told me——"

"I told you I didn't have a gun in Mexico. I didn't have a gun in Mexico. I never told you I didn't have, or wouldn't have, a gun in Costa Verde." I swung out the cylinder to check the loads and snapped it back into place. "Well, you can sit right there while I pull on my pants and go take care of this lousy woman-beater Sanchez. You did say Sanchez, didn't you? Yes, I remember clearly, Sanchez was the name. Say good-bye to Señor Sanchez, Dillman."

She made a sound of annoyance. "Oh, stop being silly," she said. "You're not really going to kill anybody; and you know perfectly well it wasn't Ramiro, anyway. He's much too vain to make a play for a woman a foot taller than he is; he knows he'd look ridiculous. But I'm not going to tell you who . . ."

I held up my hand. She fell silent and it came again: the rattle of metal outside the locked door as somebody was careless with a weapon out there and let it brush against a belt-buckle, perhaps.

"Oh, goody," I said cheerfully. "The lady inside to keep me busy with her hysterics, and the guard outside to make sure I stay put if she fails to keep me properly entertained . . . while *what* is happening out there, Dillman!" Then I shook my head quickly. "No, never mind. For a scientific lady you have a very strange attitude toward the truth; I'd better go find out for myself. Just sit tight and keep quiet, please."

"Sam, please, you mustn't——"

Tossing aside my pajamas, I turned on her, and the fact that I didn't have any clothes on didn't bother me a bit; we'd never been particularly modest with each other. I said, "I should think you'd have had enough of being leaned on for one evening, Frances. Please don't make *me* get rough with you, too. Gags and bonds are very uncomfortable."

She drew a sharp breath, but let it out soundlessly. I hauled on pants, stuck my feet into shoes, and got a black turtleneck—practically mandatory equipment for night operations—out of my suitcase and pulled that on. I clipped on the tricky little waistband holster and put the loaded gun into it and pulled the shirt down over it. I turned to the woman still sitting stiffly in the basket chair.

"You have a choice," I said. "You can open the door and warn the guard and he'll raise the alarm and his friends—I assume he's got some—will come running, and a lot of people will get shot, probably including me. Or you can sit right there and wait for me to come back, and the chances are that nobody'll be hurt because all I'm after is information; I haven't the slightest intention of interfering with anybody's plans. Suit yourself."

She didn't speak. I moved to the window and opened the jalousie-shutter very quietly.

"Sam." Her voice was almost inaudible. When I looked back, she whispered, "Be careful, darling."

Then I was outside. A moment later I was far enough away from the illuminated walks and buildings to make a careful scouting trip to a point from which I could see the door of the cabin from which I'd just departed. There was a man stationed there, all right: a real *bandido* type complete with hat, serape, weapon, and reserve ammo; but those boys lost something when they switched to automatic firepower fed by clips. A webbing ammunition carrier equipped with a series of snap-closed pockets, three magazines to a pocket, isn't nearly as dramatic-looking as one of those fine, picturesque old bandoliers full of shiny brass cartridges. His weapon was the same M16 as I'd seen carried by the roadblock troops. Well, that figured. Most revolutionary forces seem to have little trouble in liberating enough government equipment to stay in business.

Making like a snake, and hoping I wouldn't meet one, I made my way through the landscaping, taking advantage of the ornate bushes and shrubs, some of which were better equipped to defend themselves than I was. I turned the corner of the main building and crawled forward through the broad-leafed planting there until I could see the parking area out front.

Several beat-up Jeeps and a husky, battered six-by-six vehicle were parked there. The red cross on the side of the truck body did not look too permanent or too professionally applied; it was already peeling. The man I'd come to look at—I couldn't see her accepting a blow from anybody else; and I was still waiting to learn why, proud as she was, she'd take it from him—was standing in front of the ambulance.

There was no doubt of his identity. The picture was so classic I wanted to laugh: a Pancho Villa group shot updated. There were the humble Jeep drivers and assault-rifle toters lounging casually in the background; and there was the arrogant and heavily armed three-man bodyguard standing wary and alert. Posed in front of them all was the *generalisimo* himself, a real Latin-Patton with two ivory-handled single-action Colts sagging on crossed gunbelts in the old-fashioned way; no trick quick-draw belts or fancy *buscadero* outfits for Lupe of the Mountain.

He was a big man for this part of the world, with a good belly on him, and a great black drooping moustache that could have made him look like a comic bandit but didn't. He was dressed in stained and wrinkled khakis. The swarthy, jowly, unshaved face under the greasy uniform cap with the gold insignia was shrewd and cruel; you knew that the shadowed little eyes had seen everything twice; and remembered it all from the first time, anyway.

Then he stepped forward, since there was movement at the front of the hotel to my right. A small man came down the steps there carrying a folded wheelchair which he opened at the foot of the stairway. Ricardo Jimenez appeared above on his aluminum arm-crutches. He gave them to a taller man to carry and made his way down the stone stairs, slowly and painfully, with the aid of the wrought-iron banister. He retrieved the crutches from the man who had followed him down, and stood leaning on them as Lupe Montano came striding up to him, followed at a discreet distance by the fearsome threesome. Montano threw his arms wide in a flamboyant gesture of greeting, and embraced the younger man heartily.

Stepping back, he said in Spanish clear enough for me to understand, "You look somewhat better than the last time we met, outside La Fortaleza. It is a pleasure to see you again, amigo."

Ricardo laughed. "I cannot say that about you, General, since I was not conscious enough to see you the first time. But I am happy to be here."

"General? What is this stupidity? I am Lupe and you are Ricardo. Come, we have much to discuss. . . ."

More men came down the stairs behind Ricardo, keeping a wary lookout behind them. Among them I recognized the well-armed *bandido* type who'd guarded my door. Montano snapped his fingers, and the wheelchair was brought forward. Ricardo sat down and was rolled to the massive truck and lifted inside, chair and all. Montano snapped his fingers again, and the men all piled into the

Jeeps. Motors roared and the whole cavalcade disappeared into the night.

When I got back to my cabin and slipped inside, the place was dark. I couldn't see Frances, and I knew a pang of disappointment. Then, in the faint illumination from the window, I saw the skirt and shirt neatly arranged on the chair in which she'd sat; and the pale slender figure awaiting me on the bed. . . .

CHAPTER 13

IN the morning, with pyramid-prowling in mind, I got out a pair of jeans, bought new in Chicago. I did a bit of swearing while working my belt through the loops. It's a rather special belt, of necessity a bit wider than some; and while it used to fit all normal pants, currently the cheapo manufacturers of clothing, and even some not so cheapo, are saving a few mils here and a few mils there by making belt loops smaller and smaller, even on outdoors clothes where substantial support is essential. It seems like a hell of a niggling kind of economy.

After finally threading it through, I checked out the belt and the little last-ditch weapon it contained, supposedly an improvement over the trick buckles we used to be issued, which were good only for cutting yourself loose if somebody tied you up. I couldn't help remembering that the last time they'd "improved" that particular piece of equipment they'd almost got me killed when the new model hadn't worked quite the way it was supposed to. After pulling on the jeans, I got into a short-sleeved *guyabera* shirt—the kind with the epaulets—that hung loose enough around the middle to conceal the little revolver I tucked away in its clip holster inside the waistband of the pants. Soft rubber-soled desert boots completed the working costume of the archaeologically minded photojournalist.

Properly robed and armed for whatever the day might

bring, I hoped, I shouldered my camera bag and set out to track down some breakfast, passing the swimming pool where a hotel employee, male, was using a small net with a long handle to fish out the leaves that had blown into the water overnight. He didn't seem to be taking his work too seriously. In the dining room, the only members of our group present this early were the elderly Hendersons, also dressed for jungle exploration. They were well along with their meal, but they waved me over to join them.

"Maybe you can tell us, Sam," said the formidable Mrs. Henderson, after I'd seated myself and given my order. "We were wondering what the disturbance was in the middle of the night; but the waitress just shrugs and says *quien sabe.*"

I pushed my camera bag under the table where nobody'd trip over it. "Well, it's too bad," I said, "but Dick Anderson had some kind of an attack, epileptic seizure—I guess he must have sustained a bit of brain damage in the auto accident that crippled him—and I just happened to hear him knock over a chair as he fell; I was in my cabin next door. I got hold of Frances and we routed out some of the hotel staff. Happily the phone was working—I gather it doesn't always—and they got an ambulance down from the nearest town with a clinic, some eighty kilometers away. Dick had come around all right by the time it got here, thank God, but he was pretty weak, and the doctor who'd come along said he'd better go into the hospital for observation." I laughed ruefully. "It got to be quite a production, actually. They'd even got together an unofficial escort, armed to the teeth. There had apparently been some reports of *bandidos* locally, and the government doesn't want to take any chances of having one of us millionaire Americanos kidnaped while driving around these jungle roads at night, even in an ambulance."

Henderson frowned, his old eyes thoughtful. "*Bandido*, that's a local euphemism for rebel or revolutionary, isn't it? Damn it, Sam, I've got a bad feeling in my old-soldier bones. I hope we haven't landed in a hornets' nest. If I'm any judge of troops, those sloppy conscripts we saw along the road yesterday would be no use at all against a determined guerilla force, for all that they're weighted down with U.S. equipment until they walk bowlegged."

Mrs. Henderson was gathering up her belongings. "Well,

you can stay here and make military talk, Austin; I'm going back to our little thatched hut and load my camera. . . . Oh, hello, Frances. Sam just told us about Dick Anderson. It's too bad; he was so looking forward to seeing the ruins. Do you know how he is this morning?"

"I just had the hospital on the phone, and he's doing fine," Frances said. She looked lean and competent and picturesque in slim, well-fitting jeans and a long-sleeved silk shirt or blouse, open at the throat. The silk was a particularly bright, flaming shade of red. She'd done a good camouflage job on her bruised cheek, but makeup couldn't quite conceal the slight swelling. She laughed. "Did Sam also tell you how he knocked me down, the brute? Actually, he was carrying Dick's crutches over his shoulder, making sure they got into the ambulance; and I walked right into them just as he started to swing around, stupid me. It was a rather hectic midnight crisis, and I guess we were all a bit rattled."

Austin Henderson decided to accompany his wife back to their cabin. When we were alone, I grinned at the handsome woman settling herself on the far side of the table.

"Well, it's an improvement over the old I-ran-into-a-door-in-the-dark routine. But with that shirt on you hardly have to worry about people looking at your face. That is one loud garment."

She laughed. "It's my guide blouse. I just climb up on a high place and the stragglers all rally to the red standard to hear my next boring lecture." She shifted position in her chair and winced. "I feel rather like a kid who took a bad spill on a bicycle; I seem to have little hurts all over me."

I said, "Curiosity is rearing its ugly head. You still haven't told me *why* Lupe Montano hit you." When she started to speak, I held up my hand and said, "Just a minute, let's clear the decks first. I'm getting a little tired of all the deceit and disinformation, as the boys out in Langley like to call it. Can we now start operating on the assumption that we both know that Dick Anderson is really Ricardo Jimenez, son of an exiled former president of Costa Verde, imported into this country for revolutionary public relations purposes by Lupe Montano, who feels that his own outlaw image isn't quite immaculate enough to be used as a shining symbol of national liberation? Can we also assume that you were slugged by Lupe, not by Ramiro

Sanchez or a stray Melmec ghost? Although that was quite a convincing spook story you gave me first, I will admit."

Frances said, a little stiffly, "Yes, Mr. Felton or whatever your real name is, I think we can commence acting upon those elaborate assumptions."

"So both you and Ricardo are working with Montano," I said. "Well, it's a relief to know that; it's a question that's been bothering me. And now let's get back to Montano's reason for hitting you last night. What did he ask you to do that was so bad that you balked at last? Even worse than using your official position to smuggle an escaped political criminal into Costa Verde; even worse than crawling into the sack with one Samuel Felton to gain said revolting Felton's trust and confidence?"

Frances started to speak and stopped as the waitress, a handsome, compact, brown lady in a crisp, white, beautifully embroidered native smock and petticoat—they call them *huipiles*—put my breakfast before me and asked for Frances's order.

When we were alone again, Frances said, "Go ahead and eat; don't let it get cold." Then she laughed rather bitterly. "But don't you see, darling, that's exactly what he did order me to do last night, crawl into the sack with you so you wouldn't get inquisitive and interfere with Dick's—Ricardo's—departure."

I frowned. "But why the argument? Whence the necessity for harsh disciplinary action? I realize that sleeping with me is a terrible ordeal for any girl to have to endure; but you'd managed to suffer through it a couple of times already. Why did you rebel last night?"

She shook her head quickly. "It wasn't what he asked me to do, Sam, it was the way he asked it. You must have seen what kind of a man he is. He not only ordered me to keep you . . . amused, distracted, he told me exactly how I should do it, in obscene detail, with some very dirty, sneering, and degrading comments about our relationship that . . . Well, I was stupid and lost my temper. I got on my dignified high horse: *How dare you speak to me like that, you varlet, you?* But you don't use that arrogant-aristocrat act on a peasant-revolutionary like Montano—as I found out at the expense of my dignity and my stockings." She shuddered reminiscently. "So the battered lady picked herself up humbly and stumbled off to carry out her instructions, to the accompaniment of loud male laughter." She swallowed hard, and I saw that her eyes were wet and shiny. "Oh, God, darling, it's such a mess!"

It was very touching, but it still left the main question unanswered. "I'm still asking why," I said.

"What?"

"Why does the proud and respectable and respected Frances Ransome Dillman, Ph.D., obey the dirty and dangerous instructions of a greasy hill bandit? Why does she allow him to slap her down as if she were a streetcorner *puta*?" I stared at her grimly across the table. "What does this two-bit, two-gun desperado have on you, Dillman?"

She hesitated, and drew a long breath. "Copalque," she said.

The waitress came with her food; and we were both silent until we were alone once more. The dining room was filling up now. I saw the insurance Wilders and the advertising Olcotts having breakfast together in a corner. The Putnams were at a table for two by themselves. Jim Putnam was wearing less jewelry than usual, and instead of his fancy tunic he was wearing a plain blue work shirt—tails out—over his jeans; but his wife clearly intended to tackle the Melmec ruins in her regular costume of wide cotton skirt and big boots.

"Copalque?" I said at last.

Frances nodded. "We hacked our way in here with machetes," she said softly. There was a fond, reminiscent note in her voice. "We thought it was a totally lost and forgotten city—forgotten, at least, by everyone but a few natives like the old shaman, or medicine man, Cortez. Actually, of course, he's a high priest of one of the oldest religions in the world. We were very careful to look him up, when we heard about him. We let him carry out his purification rites on every tomb and temple we opened. Let him, hell! We were delighted to be allowed to watch him, Sam. We'd thought all the old traditions and ceremonies were dead, and here they were being performed—in a somewhat degenerate and bastardized form, of course—by a living descendant of the ancient people we wanted to learn to understand. It was wonderful, and rather frightening sometimes. When I made up that nonsense about being scared by emanations from ancient tombs I wasn't altogether kidding. We had some rather weird experiences, pseudopsychic experiences, I guess you'd call them, while that old man was . . . Well, never mind *that*."

There was something a little shamefaced about her attitude, the look of a scientist who's encountered something that can't be explained by her science, but who is trying to convince herself that there must be a rational explanation somewhere. Clearly she didn't want to discuss it, and I was more interested in other aspects of her story than in some ancient religious mumbo jumbo, no matter how impressive she'd found it.

"Go on," I said.

She drew a long breath. "As I said, we tried to make friends with all the local natives; but we had a feeling that there were people around we never saw as we were opening up the dig. And the workmen we hired from the nearby village were very nervous about something that seemed to have nothing to do with religion or superstition. But the discoveries we were making were wonderful. We were writing bright new pages in archaeological history and getting closer and closer to confirming Archie's theories about the rise and fall of these civilizations, the basic rhythm of Meso-american history. And then we found the cave and the magnificent triple-calendar wheel, the answer, Sam, the proof! Because, as I've already told you, the times of conjunction of those three calendars, once I'd deciphered the number system—it's not quite the same as the dot-and-dash system later used by the Mayas—and Archie had worked out the mathematics of it on his calculator, coincided almost exactly, as I said, with the sudden downfalls of the three great civilizations that had in turn dominated this part of the world. But of course that still left us with the truly important question to answer, the obvious question."

"Obvious?"

Frances made an impatient, professorial gesture. "Well, it should be obvious! We now knew that the Melmecs had been able to predict the date of their own annihilation, and presumably so had the Olmecs and Mayas after them—but what had destroyed them? We still didn't know that. But *they* knew, Sam. The finds we were making showed beyond a doubt that they knew what they were facing. They knew how their deaths would appear, as well as when. And we kept getting hints as we uncovered more and more tablets and murals and bas-relief wall-carvings, hints of something terrible to come. There were scenes of mass destruction, temple courts carpeted with dead and dying, images of men and women writhing in their final agonies. . . ." She drew a long breath. "And then, as we worked in that cave, we found the most dreadful thing of all. As we pulled away a barrier of loose rubble, surprisingly loose in fact, not compacted at all, we came upon a new arm of the cave behind it. Stacked there in the darkness was case after neat wooden case strapped with metal, each box carefully marked. I had no trouble at all in deciphering those hieroglyphics, Sam. None whatever!"

I said, "The suspense is terrific."

She licked her lips. "The stencils were perfectly clear in the beam of Archie's flashlight. The nearest one read: SMALL ARMS AMMUNITION 5.56 MM BALL 1000 RDS WT 37 LB."

CHAPTER 14

OUT of the corner of my eye I saw our two gray-haired schoolteachers approaching, clearly intending to settle in the two vacant chairs so they could impress Frances with intelligent questions demonstrating how carefully they'd been doing the suggested reading. They did it every day. Without letting on that I'd seen them, I hoisted the big camera bag onto the table, pretty well preempting that side of it, and took out of it a small notebook.

"I'd better write that down, Dr. Dillman," I said. "You say this temple faces east and west? Which is the better side of it?"

"The west side of the Temple of Ixchal faces the Great Court and is really quite remarkable. . . . All right, Sam. They've gone. You're a brute to spoil their fun, the poor old dears."

"Poor old dears, hell. That Tolson woman has a tongue like a Borgia dagger." I regarded her for a moment. "So what you found was a nice modern ammunition dump some fifty feet underground—5.56 mm, that's the .223 stuff they use in the M16s."

She nodded soberly. "And not just ammunition. There were larger crates, too, and long nasty-looking things wrapped in plastic—rocket launchers or something. We learned later that there was another entrance to the cave. You just climbed straight down into a deep sinkhole and came across through the rock about a hundred feet—they'd enlarged the narrow tunnel they'd found there, originally just a crack in the limestone, to the point where they could actually use carts and dollies and wheelbarrows to trundle the stuff inside after it was lowered into the sinkhole by a truck winch. Of course they camouflaged their tunnel entrance carefully with brush and vines and smoothed away the tire tracks above and covered the trail they'd made through the jungle as well as they could after every use. It was a lot shorter and easier way of getting to the ceremonial chamber than the long slanting underground passage we'd used, and the Melmec priests before us."

I asked, "How did you manage to find the cave in the first place?"

She hesitated. "Well, there had to be a *cenote,* a source of water; they wouldn't build a city without plenty of water. We found a couple of nice big ones in the jungle near here, and another at the subsidiary center of Labal about fifteen miles away—we'll visit that later—and they all showed use, but not as much ceremonial use as you'd expect, considering the size of the city. Archie, who has a feeling for that kind of thing, as I told you, was sure that there had to be a hidden *cenote* considered much more sacred. He kept poking into every little hole and depression until he finally—" She stopped, and gave an odd little laugh. "No, dammit, I'll be honest. I told you about those pseudopsychic phenomena, remember? Well, Archie had a dream one night. In it he saw a file of Melmec priests disappearing into the ground. The face of the high priest was the face of Cortez. Archie recognized the place; he'd looked there and found nothing. So he went back and *really* looked; and there it was, a passage leading underground so overgrown with brush and thorns he'd never have found it if he hadn't known exactly where to make his search. And how the hell are we going to put *that* into a scientific paper, Sam?"

I looked at her for a moment. "You're proposing the idea that Cortez sent that dream to your husband?" She gave an embarrassed little shrug. I said, "Accepting that theory as a working hypothesis, just why would Cortez want you to find the cave?"

"It had already been found by Lupe Montano and his men, remember? Maybe Cortez didn't like the sacreligious use to which they were putting his underground temple. Maybe he thought we could help him put a stop to it in some way." She made a little face. "But of course we're talking nonsense, Sam. We're sensible people; we don't believe in dreams that are sent around like telegrams. If I put such foolishness into a serious archaeological report, I'd be laughed out of my profession."

"Sure," I said. "But the people who'd hidden those munitions were presumably keeping an eye on them. They must have known you'd learn their secret once they saw you find the cave."

She hesitated. "They'd apparently thrown up that concealing wall of rubble when we started work in the area, hoping that even if we found our way down there, we wouldn't look behind it; but of course, being so oddly new, it attracted our attention immediately—well, as soon as we started looking around a bit. At first we were simply stunned by the magnitude of the find: the calendar wheel and all the ceremonial artifacts and the *cenote* itself, the underground pool that we just knew would yield all kinds of treasures. They used to throw their sacrifices into those pools, you know—sacrifices human and otherwise. Many of the great archaeological discoveries in this part of the world have been made by divers working the *cenotes*. . . ."

She sipped from her coffee cup thoughtfully, remembering the moment of discovery. She went on, smiling faintly: "At first we were just like kids on Christmas morning, running from one marvelous object to the next, but after a while we got organized—and there was that peculiar wall. Naturally we couldn't be satisfied with what we had, we wanted more. So we had the men clear away some of the rubble. As soon as they'd made an opening, Archie crawled

99

through and then called to me in an odd voice not to come. Well, I knew what he'd found, of course, some nasty-looking skeletons or mummified bodies—something like that—and he was protecting his tender little wife from the horrible sight, and to hell with him. So I crawled right in after him, and got to my feet beside him, and we stood there with our flashlights, staring in a sick way at all those lousy weapons and crates of ammunition that, we both realized, were going to spoil our wonderful discovery."

"Did you ever learn where the stuff came from?" I asked when she paused.

Frances nodded. "We knew right away. There had been a bandit raid on a government arsenal just before we came. Of course the official word was that the subversive gang of vicious criminals had met with no success and had been slaughtered to the last man. . . . The possibility of danger didn't really occur to me at first, although I guess it had been in Archie's mind when he told me to stay back. I was simply grief-stricken and furious at having that beautiful ceremonial cave—*our* cave—tarnished, contaminated, spoiled, by the presence of all this ugly modern murder equipment." She swallowed hard. "Then a couple of powerful lights blinded us and a voice told us to put our hands up and suddenly there were armed men all around us. What's the time?"

I said, "A quarter of eight. Sanchez will get the bus driver here on time. And today neither of us has to worry about Dick Anderson. *Mas cafe?*"

She nodded. The little girl stationed at the nearby coffee-maker—her white *huipile* was prettily embroidered in blue —was alert and eager for business; she filled both cups and gave us a gentle smile and went back to her post.

"Go on," I said.

"That was how I first met Lupe of the Mountain," Frances said. "He searched me for weapons as well as Archie. Ugh. Then there was a long debate, in Spanish, of course. I couldn't follow all of it, it went too fast; but I gathered that the question wasn't whether or not to kill us. It was merely how we could best be killed without attracting too much official attention. An accident was indicated; but it would not be well to have the inquisitive gringos caught by a rock-fall inside the cave, so close to the hidden munitions. A collapsing ruin a respectable distance away,

100

however, could be made to appear quite convincing; and somebody knew just the right precarious ruin. And then of course there was the question of whether or not the woman should be utilized, in proper communal fashion of course, before being killed. Unfortunately, it was decided, such a thing could probably be determined by the medical people even on a badly crushed female body, so proper prior utilization would have to be foregone. *Que lastima,* what a pity."

Her voice was quite steady; but I noticed that she sipped her coffee a little too fast, forgetting that her cup had just been refilled. She winced as the hot stuff burned her mouth, and set the cup down hastily.

"Fun and games," I said.

"Yes, indeed," she said. "I don't mind admitting that I was . . . rather frightened. But just as they were about to take us away, there was a kind of gravelly rattling sound in the hole through which we'd come; and there was Cortez. Later we heard that when our workmen fled, hearing us taken prisoner like that, they'd run straight to him with the news. As he stood up and put his hat back on and brushed himself off, Montano gave the order to seize him, but nobody moved. He just looked at Lupe, and Lupe didn't repeat the order. Cortez started to speak. It was a long speech, and his Spanish is strongly flavored by the ancient language, so I couldn't really follow it, fast as he was talking, haranguing them. Then there was a question-and-answer period. At last Lupe came forward. . . . What's the time now, darling? After all the things I've said about being punctual, I don't want to be the one to keep the bus waiting."

"Still not quite eight o'clock," I said. "You don't have to build up the suspense artificially, Frances."

"Is that what I'm doing?" She smiled faintly. "Anyway, Lupe said that he understood from Cortez that we honored the ancient people and their gods and their places of worship, particularly this sacred cave. Most particularly this cave. This cave was very important to us gringos, to our scientific work, was it not? We would seriously like to preserve it, would we not? So there might be an alternative to killing, if we could be trusted. He would like to show us something. . . . He took us around and showed us." She swallowed. "It was booby-trapped, Sam. That whole gallery was mined, loaded with explosives ready to be fired. If the government forces learned about the place and tried to take back their materiel, they'd be blown sky-high. And of course, when the charges went, all that ammunition and stuff would go, too; and those limestone caverns aren't very solid. The explosion would almost certainly bring the whole thing down, the entire roof of the cave, obliterating the underground chamber and the *cenote* and destroying everything we'd found. . . . We couldn't bear to think of it, Sam. After all our work, after coming so-*close*, to have it all wiped out before we could record it, study it. . . . And of course there was the fact, the very minor fact, that if we didn't come to an agreement with Lupe, he would undoubtedly have us killed."

"So you made a deal?"

Frances nodded. "It was the only thing we could do. Of course it was really a very good deal for Lupe, as Cortez had pointed out to him. Killing us would have been risky, no matter how well the 'accident' was staged. It would have brought all kinds of government investigators snooping around. Having us simply keep our mouths shut and continue our work made everything look respectable. Lupe didn't have to worry about somebody discovering the tracks of modern vehicles, for instance, in unexpected places in the jungle, because we had our own vehicles in there by then and everybody knew those foolish gringos were chopping trails and snooping everywhere. *Loco, muy loco.*" She drew a long breath. "He couldn't have asked for better camouflage for his secret weapons cache; and of course once we'd agreed, we were stuck with him and his damned revolution. We *had* to do everything possible to help him keep his secret. If it were discovered now, we'd be in terrible trouble for not having reported it earlier." She grimaced. "I know you're remembering the speech I made in Chicago about not offending the local authorities. It's all right to laugh, Sam. I laugh myself, sometimes. But rather bitterly, and not very often."

I watched her closely. "I see. So that's why you were willing to go so far to obey his orders, and to hell with pride and honor, if there still is such a thing in this dishonorable world."

"Yes, Sam," she said, meeting my eyes very steadily.

"That's why. That's the whole story. I knew you'd understand."

And she was lying again, at least to some extent. I knew those too-candid, too-honest, too-steady gray eyes by now. Well, I told myself grimly, if she ever told the truth, all the truth, she wouldn't be my Frances and I'd miss her.

"Understand?" I said. "Sure, I understand. So let's talk about these calendar conjunctions. When is the next one due? Have you figured it out?"

"Yes, of course." She spoke quickly, obviously happy to change the subject. "But first there's an interesting coincidence you should know about. Perhaps you could call it a confirmation. A totally different line of research seems to indicate that the Mayas, who came much later of course, believed that the decadent peoples of the world would be destroyed in their sins once every thirteen *baktuns*, a *baktun* being their longest measure of time. A *tun* was a year, a *katun* was twenty years, and a *baktun* was four hundred years. Thirteen *baktuns* works out to fifty-two hundred years. So according to them, Armageddon or Götterdämmerung or what have you, would come around cyclically every five thousand years and a little, sweeping the world clean for a fresh start. However, at the end of the thirteenth Great Cycle of the Long Count Calendar, the whole world and all creation would cease to exist, period."

"Don't tell me, let me guess," I said. "We're in this thirteenth Great Cycle now." When she nodded soberly, I asked, "And it ends when?"

"If you follow the Thompson correlation, the year of total annihilation will be 2013 A.D."

I drew a long breath and took a sip of my cooling coffee. I cleared my throat. "And what do you and your husband come up with, working it out from your three-calendar business?"

"We come up with almost the same length for the Great Cycle, well, actually a hair less than five thousand years. Close enough, considering that we're still working from very rough preliminary data. And the Melmecs ran their chronology from a different base date from the one used by the Mayas, determined by Thompson—and I must say I would never stick my neck out as far as he did by trying to pinpoint it with such precision. Not within a single year. You've got to remember that all these calendars supposedly run back to dates almost contemporary with the dinosaurs. Those old priests played their religious calendar games with very large numbers, probably for astrological reasons, not historical ones. And we know the time intervals they used, all right, but the problem is trying to figure out the dates they started counting from. Like our calendar runs forward and backward from the birth of Christ. If we didn't know exactly when the star shone over Bethlehem, and if it all took place tens of thousands of years ago, we'd have some trouble writing down an exact date for the Declaration of Independence, wouldn't we?"

I grinned briefly. "Okay, professor. That's enough scientific background. When's the end of the world going to be?"

She licked her lips, unsmiling. "We give ourselves fifty years' leeway. Well, twenty-five either way. In round numbers, according to the Melmec calendar, the world should be due for cleansing again—unlike the Mayas, they do not predict total cosmic annihilation, merely the end of existing civilizations—some time between 1980 and 2030."

After a little, I signaled the girl again, and she filled our cups again. I said, "I'm going to have the caffeine jitters."

Frances said, "I've really got to go and see that things are properly organized."

But she didn't move, and I said, "So we've just come into the danger zone. The world has. If your theories mean anything. If your Melmecs actually knew something."

"Yes, Sam."

"But you don't know what's going to kill us, assuming that the curse, or whatever you want to call it, is still operative."

"No. But the answer is here, somewhere; and we have to find it while there's still time to do something about it."

"Assuming something can be done." I frowned thoughtfully. "Would you say it involved a weapon or something that can be used as a weapon?"

"To destroy an entire civilization?" She shook her head dubiously. "I don't know, Sam. The Mayas apparently thought the job would be done by earthquakes; but there's no archaeological or geological evidence that it ever hap-

104

pened that way. There are no indications of seismic cataclysms coinciding with the Great Cycle; we've checked that out carefully. Nor can we find any suggestions of pl: gues or other diseases, although that would be harder to determine after thousands of years. Nor does the evidence to date indicate that the Melmecs expected to be wiped out by overwhelming enemy attacks; although of course these were all warlike peoples." Frances frowned thoughtfully. "I don't know about a weapon, but whatever it was, they expected it to be quick and thorough. Their wall paintings, their carvings, their records as far as we can decipher them, all indicate that the Great Court would be knee-deep in dead bodies on that final day. Nobody would be left alive except a few priests and priestesses sheltered underground—selected to keep the ancient knowledge alive—and a few peasants trembling in the more distant fields."

"I suppose Cortez is a descendant of those selected survivors," I said. Frances nodded. I asked, "Have you published any of your findings yet?"

She shook her head. "Not really. We wanted to wait until the . . . the problem here was solved. The Montano problem. If it ever is. Archie did make a speech at the Center for Mesoamerican Studies a few months ago that outlined the general nature of our discoveries. . . ." She stopped and looked at me sharply. "Why did you ask that?"

"Because there seem to be some gents snooping around who are sometimes employed by Moscow to investigate scientific rumors that could indicate discoveries with possible military applications. These boys aren't the first team or even the second, just a freelance operator named Rutterfeld presumably working under contract with a couple of helpers, whose job in Costa Verde could be to determine if you're picking up anything here that might be of practical military value."

She grimaced. "Oh, God, the commie menace rears its ugly head!"

I said grimly, "If you dig up an ancient Melmec cosmic-death-ray machine, commies aren't the only ones who'll be snooping around. Hell, anything that kills lots of people interests lots of people. And the trouble is that those interested people, like the unpleasant trio I have in mind, often use some fairly crude methods to find things out. So keep your eyes open." After a moment I went on: "You seem to've been in touch with Lupe Montano, or his people, all through this trip. How did they make contact with you?"

"There does seem to be quite a bit of support for his revolution," Frances said. "He's got people working for him just about everywhere, particularly in the hotels. . . . Oh, oh, here comes Ramiro to tell us we're late and everybody's waiting for us."

She started picking up her things, while I closed my camera case. The stocky guide had eschewed his formal white guide-suit for today's expedition; he was wearing white sailcloth slacks and a blue knit sports shirt.

"Do not hurry yourself, señora," he said. "I merely wished to confirm our plans so I can tell the driver: You do wish to start at the Temple of the Jaguar today?"

"Yes, let them get the impact of the Great Court first. We'll spend this morning on that, and plan to pay it another visit the last day before we leave, to kind of pull it all together for them. Tomorrow we'll pick up the minor temples around here and the big *cenote* and the Ball Court; by that time they should be ready to appreciate the Sacred Cave, those who aren't afflicted with claustrophobia. Then we'll spend a day looking over Labal, and maybe a couple of other outlying centers if there's time, whenever you can round up enough Jeeps, to show them how big this ancient urban complex really was." She gave him an odd sideways glance. "Did you sleep well, Ramiro?"

He met her look with a meaningful one of his own. "After midnight I slept very well indeed, señora. It is always a relief to see the goods properly delivered, as you say in America." He went on in a dry voice, deliberately mimicking the political jargon he'd been using on us: "As a loyal agent of my fine progressive government I must, of course, consider it regrettable that the patriotic forces of right and justice were not available to apprehend the anti-administration criminals before they could join forces to conspire further against the free people of Costa Verde." He smiled thinly, looking at me. "I am glad you chose not to interfere, Señor Felton."

Watching him move away, I said, "So Ramiro Sanchez is one of Lupe's people, too. The guy I wasn't supposed to talk too loudly in front of yesterday because you were afraid, oh, so afraid, that he'd report my subversive utterances to the government!" I looked at Frances grimly.

"One of these days you're going to start trusting me, Dillman, and I'll die of shock."

She smiled nicely. "If that's the only thing that can kill you, Sam, you'll live a long time."

CHAPTER 15

IT was a long, hot, hardworking morning. I used the 24 mm wide-angle lens for the overall shots and the 70-140 mm zoom for the details; each lens on a separate camera body, of course. That gave me enough optical equipment hanging around my neck to look nice and professional and fool the people.

Actually, I'm still a little uncomfortable with those zooms. They're convenient, of course, letting you frame each shot—near or far—with a twist of the wrist; but the early ones had all the crisp definition of an operable cataract. This was a new one, and I'd checked it out and it had seemed sharp enough, but I still didn't have the total faith in it that I had in my old-fashioned one-focal-length lenses. But you can't play pro nowadays without at least one long, fat zoom lens on display.

Whoever had laid out the tour—and I suspected Frances was largely responsible—had planned the approach for a maximum of drama. We hiked half a mile along a trail through the tangled jungle, single file, between odd overgrown rocky mounds that were pointed out to us as ruins that had not yet been excavated and perhaps never would be. Unless a certain site promised new information, Frances said, it was left untouched because the old friezes and bas-reliefs tended to deteriorate quite rapidly once they were exposed to air and rain and sunlight, unless they were carefully stabilized, an expensive and not always totally successful process.

Then we scrambled up a steep slope and found the Great Court lying open before us, very impressive, table-flat and several football fields long. It was flanked by two massive temple-crowned pyramids. At the end of the long court the enormous bulk of the Great Pyramid loomed ominously, black against the sun. A ray of light shone directly through the temple at the top, the Temple of Death, apparently open from east to west.

"As you can see," Frances said after giving us time to catch our breaths and admire the view, "as you can see, this whole ceremonial area is a tremendous level platform raised about twenty feet above the jungle floor; the pyramids rise from that. When you climb them, please be careful. You'll note that the steps themselves are quite narrow and the risers are quite high. The best method is to go up and down in a crabwise fashion. Anybody who's subject to vertigo had better not try it. It's a good deal steeper than it looks."

One of the lady schoolteachers, Pat Tolson, looked up at the shadowed temple silhouette surmounting the forbidding mass of the Great Pyramid. She asked, "Up there, isn't that where they sacrificed the virgins by opening their chests with an obsidian knife and tearing their hearts out?"

Frances said, "That sacrificial technique was more popular with the later Aztecs over in Mexico. However, the Melmecs did have their human sacrifices; you'll see various methods illustrated in the temple decorations. But that particular death, as far as we can determine, was usually reserved for prisoners taken in war. Bones indicating female sacrifices have been found; but unfortunately after a few thousand years it's a little hard to determine just how pure the lady was at the time of her death."

After that, as far as I was concerned, it was Pyramid Day; and as I started up the first one I realized that I'd never make an archaeologist. The damned thing had looked reasonably negotiable at a distance, but close up it loomed above me like the United Nations Building with a few inadequate notches in it. Each step, as Frances had indicated, while almost two feet high, wasn't even wide enough to plant your shoe on properly. . . . The simple fact is that I get dizzy, dammit. Vertigo, like the lady said. And not only do I not like places high in the air, I do not like them deep in the ground—and I still had a cave to look forward to. Scratch archaeology as a possible career alternative.

Fortunately, the big camera bag gave me a good excuse to be clumsy and cautious about it, hauling myself up ignominiously on all fours, more or less, while Gloria Jean Putnam, for one, in her wide skirts and heavy boots, bounced up and down the giant stairs like a frisky chamois; and Frances herself strolled casually about those murderous steps while explaining that the Melmec priests probably didn't want their pyramids to be too easy for ordinary mortals to climb; there was also the theory that the pitch had been scientifically calculated so that a dead sacrificed body dumped from the top would roll all the way down without hanging up halfway in embarrassing fashion, which would be a very bad omen. I was glad to know that if I started to roll, I wouldn't become a bad omen.

But the temple carvings were spectacular, once you got to the top and recovered enough to appreciate them, carefully blocking from your mind the fact that you still had to get back down. We learned about the corbeled arch, which isn't really an arch. We were shown scenes of bloody battle and bloodier sacrifice in a world tormented by strange demonic beasts ruled by the jaguar, Death. We came to understand a little about a tough, lusty, cruel fighting people who'd had intelligence enough to discover systems of mathematics and astronomy that were not to be surpassed for thousands of years, but who had left odd little gaps in their civilized knowledge.

They had built some fine paved roads, but they'd never invented wheels to run on them—not even the later Mayas had made use of the wheel. They'd had shields and obsidian knives and stone-studded clubs and stone-tipped spears, but the *atlatl,* or throwing stick, was still to come, and that dreadful implement of long-range homicide, the bow, was not yet—as far as this part of the world was concerned—even a gleam in its inventor's eyes. And intelligent as they were, they had never discovered a way, perhaps they'd never even discovered the desire, to escape from the total, absolute domination of their priests. . . .

It was well past noon when we all got together up where the great menacing two-headed stone jaguar at the top of the Great Pyramid looked both ways out of his open temple, scowling fiercely toward the Land of Morning and the Land of Night as if he didn't like either very well. When she'd finished explaining the elaborate carvings on the temple façade and turned everybody loose to look around, Frances beckoned me to follow her.

"Over here," she said. "Let me show you something, Sam. Have you got a flashlight?"

It was a dark alcove—in a Christian church it might have been called a small chapel. I dug a little flashlight out of my camera bag and turned it on. The mural leaped out at me from the stone wall opposite, faded of course, chipped here and there where the lime plaster had flaked away with the centuries, but magnificent and terrifying. It was Picasso's *Guernica* set back in time and style a few millennia and done without the dying horse; but everything else in the picture was dying, priests and priestesses, armed and plumed warriors, richly dressed citizens, even a few children, all gasping their last in the Great Court below us, and on the ceremonial platforms before the three elevated temples, including the one in which we now stood, the Temple of Death.

"But what's killing them?" Frances whispered. "What's *killing* them, Sam?"

There was no indication of what was killing them. There were no spear wounds or knife slashes or club fractures; there was no blood except around the altar where, obviously, elaborate sacrifices had been made just before *it* happened, whatever *it* was. They were simply dying, all of them.

"I'd rather you wouldn't photograph that," Frances said. "We've made careful record shots of it, of course; but we'd rather it wasn't publicized until we've found some kind of explanation to go with it."

"Sure."

Outside, the sunshine seemed very bright. Although I'd only been in there a few minutes, I felt as disoriented as if I were coming out of a long and scary movie. Frances left me; she wanted to find Sanchez and ask him when he'd scheduled the bus to take us back to the hotel. I worked my way around to the west side of the temple where the early-afternoon light now threw the carvings into sharp relief. As I turned the corner of the building, I almost bumped into the old man named Cortez. He gave me his formal little bow, and I answered it.

"Iglesia hermosa," he said.

"Yes, it is a beautiful church," I said.

"But for you," he said, "better *Templo Guerrero*." He pointed. "For me, priest, better *Templo Sacerdote*." He pointed again. Then he looked at me hard. "When I call, you come. Soon now."

He had those strange brown in-turned Maya-Melmec eyes; and I reminded myself that as a good transplanted Scandinavian, I allow myself to be slightly prejudiced against the brown-eyed variety of human animals, simply because as a rule I find them less comprehensible than the blue-eyed variety to which I belong; but somehow the prejudice did not apply here. I realized that, despite some minor differences in pigmentation, we knew each other very well in a strange and disturbing way, this old man and I. Uncomfortably well.

I heard myself say, "I will come."

"Be careful. *Vaya con dios*, señor."

"What was that all about?" It was Frances's voice behind me.

I watched the old man move down the steep pyramid with a strange floating gait; well, climbing pyramids was in his blood. Maybe if my ancestors had been climbing pyramids all those centuries, I'd be good at it, too. *When I call, you come*. Who the hell did he think he was, anyway? Who did he think I was?

But that was a foolish question. He knew who I was; he'd known ever since he'd looked at me in the hotel lobby. One day he'd tell me, and then I'd know, too.

"What was he saying to you?" Frances asked.

"He was saying that this is a beautiful church," I said, "but that as a warrior, I'd do better over in the Temple of the Warriors; and as a priest, he'd do better in the Temple of the Priests. I think he was making a joke, in his own obscure fashion. What's the bus story?"

The bus story was that the bus was already waiting to transport us back—well, forward—a few thousand years to modern civilization as represented by the Hotel Copalque. When I came into the lounge for a much-needed drink, Miranda Matson, in her usual baggy seersucker pantsuit, was perched at the bar with a tall one in front of her, obviously not her first.

"Hey, Flash, how are you making it?" she asked.

"They got the wrong guy," I said, sitting down beside her wearily. "Sir Edmund Hillary would have loved it;

111

although Everest was never like this. Anything I can do for you, Miranda?"

"Introduce me to the professor lady in charge, will you? She's supposed to be digging up all kinds of strange and wonderful things around here, revolutionizing Mesoamerican history. What's a Melmec, anyway?"

"Ask her; she'll tell you," I said, and beckoned to Frances, who'd just come in. "Dr. Dillman, Miss Matson, and vice versa. Watch out for this one, Frances. Unlike some polite journalistic types you've been dealing with, she's no gentleman."

I went over and had a drink with Paul Olcott, whom I'd seen negotiating the giant pyramid steps in a very relaxed fashion. Well, I suppose after chasing mountain sheep and goats—his hunting specialty—up thousand-foot cliffs, it had seemed easy. We were joined by his handsome blond wife Elspeth; but after a little they said that after all that climbing they wanted to shower before lunch, and left me to nurse my glass alone. Presently Miranda joined me.

"Get what you wanted from Dr. Dillman?" I asked.

"Bright lady," Miranda said, and looked at me shrewdly. "Good-looking, too. Just about the right size for you, you damn beanpole, you. Too bad she's married."

"Go to hell," I said. "Let's get something to eat."

We carried our glasses into the dining room and found a table overlooking the pool. The Putnams were swimming; and she really did have a nice, sturdy, well-proportioned young body, although she made it hard to appreciate, the way she usually dressed. He was in good shape, too. He had a long, slashing scar under the right shoulder-blade where something warlike had gone by very close, but not quite close enough to do the job.

"Voss, Schmidt, and Roybal-Saiz," Miranda said. "It's supposed to mean something to you."

It meant something to me. It was the surviving remnant of the team that Bultman, the Kraut, had used for his ill-fated Cuba operation; the trio that had finally got him out of there alive in spite of a severed foot.

"Where?" I asked.

"They were all seen together in Mexico City, but the report came in too late, it says here, for anybody to get on them before they disappeared again."

"Great," I said sourly. "Who's holding down the fort in Santa Rosalia while you're here?"

"A young fellow came in, but I wasn't allowed to know his name; I'm just the volunteer errand girl. But if your man appears, with or without friends, he'll get word to me and I'll pass it on to you."

I said thoughtfully, "It depends upon whether Bultman's supposed to check back with Rael for final instructions after getting his manpower organized, or whether he'll just head straight up north to do his job, if I've got the right job in mind." I shook my head ruefully. "Wherever he goes, it's going to get rough. That is one tough and competent and ruthless little crew of high-priced mercenaries."

"I suppose you know what you're talking about," Miranda said. She went on casually: "Incidentally, I heard rumors that the *insurgentes* had some kind of a head-quarters down this way. Would you know anything about that? An exclusive interview with this elusive Lupe of the Mountain would help polish up the journalistic image."

I regarded her for a moment. "Scoop Matson, girl reporter!"

"The tall, handsome professor-lady is a lousy liar," Miranda said without expression. "She knows something about it, even if you don't. She jumped like a goosed virgin at the name."

"So you didn't come here just because of your burning interest in archaeology."

She gave me her rusty, scornful laugh. "I'm a working girl, dearie. Sure, I pay my obligations; but I won't get rich running friendship errands for your crummy outfit. And things are getting ready to blow around here, and Montano is one of the explosive factors. I'd be a damn poor reporter if I didn't make an effort to interview him for my loyal readers before the fireworks starts."

I hesitated, and said, "If they shoot you and throw you to the *zopilotes*, don't blame me. . . . You'll be here over-night?"

"As long as it takes, love." She smiled. "I thought you might have an angle. Once a newspaperman, always a newspaperman."

"I can't guarantee a thing; and I've never spoken to Montano. But you're right, there is a possible angle. Let me try for it. I'll let you know."

Leaving her there to wash down her lunch with another tall one, I found Frances in the lobby talking to Howard Gardenschwartz, the quiet professor from Northwestern, and his pleasant wife. Presently they went off and she turned to me with a certain amount of hostility.

"That reporter friend of yours is a very rude and inquisitive person," she said.

"Most reporters are when they have to be," I said. "She says you're a lousy liar—well, I could have told her that. But she wants to have a little chat with Lupe Montano."

"Oh, my God! I never said anything to indicate——"

"You've got honest eyes, sweetheart. I've noticed that myself. The mouth tells all those lies, and the eyes get terribly embarrassed. Anyway, one way or another, you kind of confirmed some rumors she'd heard and some guesses she'd made; so now a problem exists. Do you trust Ramiro Sanchez?" I shook my head quickly. "Never mind that. The real question is, does Montano trust Ramiro Sanchez?"

After a moment, Frances nodded. "I think Ramiro is fairly high up in the councils of the revolution, when he isn't playing tour guide and spouting the Rael party line." She hesitated. "Actually I think that, given a choice, there's another party line he'd rather spout."

"Oh, one of those," I said. "Well, let's talk to him. Ostensibly, we're just arranging for me to have a Jeep and driver to take me back to the Great Court later this evening for some sunset shots. . . ."

We found Ramiro down by the pool, chatting with the attendant. We sent the man for drinks and sat down at one of the umbrella-shaded poolside tables. Ramiro said he would be happy to arrange my transportation for later in the afternoon.

"But you say there is another problem, señor?"

I looked at him: a stocky brown gent, rather handsome in his Latin way, with thick black hair and hostile brown eyes that confirmed all my anti-brown-eyes prejudices. There was no empathy between us. He had me classified as a lousy gringo, and there was nothing I could ever do to change that, so I disliked him cordially right back, the goddamned racist. I explained our problem, and my solution.

Ramiro was incredulous that I would even consider

making such a stupid suggestion. "It is out of the question, señor!"

"Why?" I asked. "Hell, isn't that exactly why you went to all this trouble to get Ricardo Jimenez here? Wasn't the whole point to use him to make good public relations for your liberation movement? Well, here's your public, why not start relating? Let Señorita Matson talk with General Montano. Show her young Jimenez, the crippled victim of Rael's tyranny and Echeverria's terror, fighting for his country's freedom from his lousy wheelchair. The lady is good; she'll give your revolution favorable publicity you couldn't buy for a million bucks. If you're careful setting up the interview, what harm can she do?"

He hesitated. "You are persuasive, Señor Felton. Very well. Let me consult . . . my principal. I will let you know." He rose. "The Jeep will be waiting for you in front of the hotel at five-thirty."

In the evening, returning to my thatched cabin at dusk, I felt pretty good; there's always something satisfying about doing something that scares you shitless. Correction: about having done it.

I'd ridden back out to the Great Court and I'd gone up and down those lousy stair-stepped rockpiles in the fading light; and I'd got all the low-sun shots I'd wanted without skipping a single one because it involved climbing where I didn't want to climb. I guess I'd been doing penance for my easy entry into a certain married lady's bed by doing something difficult for a change. Well, difficult for me. I felt pleasantly tired when I turned in at last, expecting a sound night's sleep after all the exercise.

The call came shortly after midnight.

CHAPTER 16

I awoke sweating with the sound of the sharp command ringing in my ears: COMECOMECOMEVEN-GOCAVERNACOME.

115

Correction: not in my ears, only in my mind. I knew there had been no sound in the room. It took me a moment to disassemble the run-together words; but they remained clearly imprinted on my brain, so I could separate them and study them without difficulty.

My Spanish is far from good, and *vengo caverna* left something to be desired as a complete grammatical sentence, but Frances had indicated that the old man's Spanish wasn't all that great, either. Once I had pulled those two words out of the jumble the meaning was clear enough. I got up and put on shorts and jeans and turtleneck and socks and shoes and gun, operating in the dark because it seemed indicated, although I couldn't really have said why. The habit of secrecy, I suppose.

I groped around in my camera bag until I found the diminutive flashlight and stuck that into my hip pocket. Then I slipped out the door very cautiously—exit procedure Mark VII—and moved softly past Ricardo Jimenez's former cabin, and down the steep path toward Frances's rustic hut at the foot of the hill. The windows down there were illuminated; then they went dark. I stopped and stepped off the concrete into the nearest flowerbed and crouched by a low bush, watching a wavering light come up the hill toward me.

"Pssst," I whispered, straightening up.

"Oh, God, you scared me!" Frances turned off her light, one of those husky hand-held spotlights employing a square hotshot battery. She watched me step back onto the path. She was dressed as she had been earlier in the day, a tall slim shape in her jeans; but the bright red shirt looked black in the darkness. We faced each other for a moment. "You received it, too?" she asked.

"Loud and clear," I said. "Full gain on the transmitter."

"I don't believe this, you understand!" she protested with sudden anger. "Even if Archie did have a very useful dream, it's got to be extrasensory bunk. I'm a trained, skeptical scientist and I don't believe a word of it!"

"I didn't believe in flying saucers either, until I saw one," I said. "If you care to look it up in my hometown paper, I'll give you the date. Everybody saw the green thing go across town; it was written up on the front page the next day."

"Oh, the green fireballs."

116

"Calling them that doesn't explain them," I said. "I saw another one off Mazatlan later. Nobody ever did tell me *what* I saw, but I damn well saw it; and I'm not going to say it didn't exist simply because nobody'll explain it to me. And I know what I heard—felt, sensed—tonight. Maybe the old gent hypnotized us both with a glance this afternoon, and left a posthypnotic suggestion to be triggered by the phase of the moon or an accomplice tossing rocks at our windows. I don't know how the hell it was done, but I damn well know it was done. COME TO THE CAVERN. The question isn't whether or not we received it, because we did. The question is: Do we go?"

She hesitated. "Do we have a choice?"

I grinned. "I guess not. How far is it? Should we try to promote a vehicle?"

"No, it's well this side of the Great Court, only about half a mile from here. We have to go through the site that's currently being restored. I was over there the first night we were here. They've got it pretty well cleared; once we're on the Jeep road it's plain sailing. This way . . ."

Even with discreet use of the lights, it was difficult to follow the winding concrete paths through the picturesque gardens; but once we emerged from the hotel grounds and found the proper Jeep track, progress was somewhat easier, since it was a fairly wide slash between the dark trees. The jungle was eerily silent; there were no gibbering monkeys or chattering parrots or slithering boa constrictors that I could hear.

Then the cleared site she'd mentioned opened before us; and ragged black silhouettes of ruins loomed against the sky on both sides of the trail. I caught glimpses of trestles and scaffolding in a couple of places, but even with those modern touches it was a disturbing place, the one where she'd claimed to have been panicked by cold emanations from ancient tombs. That had been another of her numerous falsehoods; but at least she'd picked the right shooting-location for her phony script. I stopped at the touch of her hand on my arm.

"Listen!"

Standing still, I heard it, too; a distant thumping sound. "Hell, that's a motor."

"Somebody's started the gasoline generator for the cave lights!"

117

"How modern can you get? I thought we'd have to do it all by torchlight."

"I just wonder who . . ." She shrugged. "Well, watch your head when we start inside; they didn't build this cave for people your height. Or mine. There are several places where we'll have to crawl."

I faked a shiver that wasn't entirely playacting. "Lady, you've got an unerring instinct for my worst phobias."

She laughed softly in the darkness. "I know. I saw you on those pyramids; but you went up anyway, didn't you?"

"That doesn't necessarily mean I can go down. If I freeze and start weeping helplessly, just take my gun and go on without me."

She shuddered in the dark. "You and your nasty gun! Now you're talking about one of *my* worst phobias, darling. . . . Why do you think he wants us?"

"Cortez? He's your friend; I've barely met him."

"Hardly a friend," she said, "but of course I have known him for a while. Consulted him; worked with him. I think he likes me, or at least respects my feeling for these ancient places. But, nothing derogatory intended, darling, why would he pick you?"

I said, "I've been picked before. By people who were looking for a man who had a gun, knew how to use it, and was willing to use it."

She nodded in the dark. "It could be that. I guess the selection makes sense if . . . if there's real trouble. Your gun, and my knowledge of this place to guide you."

"In that case," I said, "we'd better stop stalling and get moving. People who need men with guns generally need them now. . . . Just a minute. One question."

"Yes?"

"Talking about guns, if I do have to use mine in there, will it bring the whole damn cave down on top of us?"

She hesitated. "I shouldn't think so. It's been here thousands of years, remember. A major explosion deliberately set to shatter the rock walls would be one thing; but I don't believe just the noise of a little handgun fired in the open cave . . ."

"It would be nice if you were sure," I said sourly, when she left the sentence incomplete. "Well, you lead the way and tell me when to duck. And if you spot anything suspicious, fall flat and roll behind a rock and *stay* there."

It was just about as bad as I'd expected it to be. We passed the shack that housed the pounding generating machinery; and the trail dipped down into a depression in the earth where the underlying limestone had collapsed centuries ago. There was a low cliff ahead, and in the cliff was a hole, and in the hole some lights were burning. We ducked into the opening. The illumination system was not reassuring; just a pair of cheap insulated wires lying alongside the trail, running from one dimestore light socket holding a dirty naked bulb to the next; and not all the bulbs were burning. I was glad of the flashlight in my pocket and the spotlight in Frances's hand. I wouldn't have wanted to trust myself in the bowels of the earth with nothing between me and total blackness but that jury-rigged lighting system.

The passage was low, as Frances had warned; but fortunately for my claustrophobic tendencies it was not narrow. Apparently certain strata had been leached out extensively here, and the path simply followed the deepest part of this considerable horizontal crack in the earth's crust. Dark passages branched off on either hand; and we began to see ghostly stalactites and stalagmites gleaming in the weak light—I remembered that the *tites* were the ones working their way down from the top, while the *mites* were the ones growing up from the bottom.

As we went deeper, we encountered water seepage both below and above; my hands and the knees of my pants were soon wet and muddy as I went under one low bridge after another on all fours. Dark stains and smudges appeared on the shoulders and back of Frances' bright blouse as she failed to scrunch down far enough occasionally. I tried not to think of all those tons of dirt and rock above us. . . .

Frances signaled a stop. "Only about fifty yards farther," she whispered. "Listen."

I heard a distant murmur of voices ahead. "Tell me what's there," I said.

"It's a rather large underground chamber, quite high, kind of domed. There are four pillars: stalactites and stalagmites that have met and fused together. They look as if they'd been deliberately put there to support the ceiling, as in a cathedral. The sacred calendar wheel is mounted on the large central one. It has been lightly glazed with silicate deposits from ground water running over it, but the inscriptions are still readily decipherable. In front of it is the jaguar altar. . . ."

"The what?"

"Like you saw in the Temple of Ixchal, the two-faced god, Life-and-Death, but flattened to form a large sacrificial altar with a blood hole in the middle. There's also a fire pit. Around the other pillars are many sacred urns and other vessels all coated and frozen in place by mineral deposits from centuries of seepage. Rather eerie, like one of those ghost movies where everything is shrouded with cobwebs, but this is semitransparent stone. Far to the right is the rubble wall concealing Lupe's revolutionary arsenal; of course he built it back up again after we made our little deal. And straight ahead as you approach, beyond the pillars, is the sacred *cenote*, a large clear bottomless pool. . . ."

"Bottomless?"

"It slants back down under the distant wall of the chamber, we don't know how far. We've picked up a great deal of valuable material from the sloping bottom nearby, but the scuba diver who tried to see how deep it was beyond the dropoff never came back up. It was . . . rather unpleasant; and the government forbade any further attempts to sound the rear of the pool. We believe that it simply taps into an underground river—there are many in this area— and that the diver was swept away by a current too strong for him to swim against, poor man." She shuddered, and went on: "Of course there's also the local theory that the old gods simply punished him, vanished him—poof!—for trespassing on their forbidden domain."

"Sure." I looked around and grimaced. "Do you really plan to bring our whole tour group into this dismal hole?"

She grinned maliciously. "Darling, they'll love it. A return to the womb. You forget, there are people who simply dote on exploring underground, and make a hobby of it. For a dangerous secret agent, you certainly have some odd hangups."

"Well, at least I'm not scared of a funny-looking little piece of steel with a hole in the end," I said. I looked at her for a moment. "You realize of course that you've done your part now. You've served your purpose; you've brought me here with my gun. Now you're entitled to bug out if you want to."

"Don't be silly," she said.

I shrugged. "Not my fault if people insist on being stupid. But stay right here until I call you. I mean that. We don't know what's down ahead there, who's down there. If there should be shooting, I want to be able to blast instantly at anything that moves; I don't want to have to wait until I'm sure it's not wearing a red shirt and a superior smirk on its face."

"And . . . if you don't call?"

"Go back to the hotel and have them open up the bar and have a drink to a pleasant memory. At least I hope it was pleasant." I kissed her on the nose. "Remember, stay here until it's over. Keep your head down if there's any shooting. In here, God knows where the ricochets will go."

I moved away cautiously, just keeping low at first, then resorting to the hands-and-knees bit, and finally the belly-and-elbows crawl. Leaving the trail, I worked my way left to a kind of rocky ridge where the floor of the cave rose to within three feet of the roof. Slowly, with the modified Chief's Special in my hand, I wiggled up to where I could peek between two limestone boulders that had fallen from above sometime within the past few hundred or thousand years, not a nice thought.

It was, as Frances had described it, a rather impressive underground cathedral. The stalactite-stalagmite columns did look like ornately sculptured architectural features deliberately designed for both structural support and religious decoration. The calendar wheel was a disappointment, however; it wasn't nearly as large and impressive as the one in the *Museo Anthropologia* in Mexico City. This was just an eight-foot disc of stone that had been set into the great central pillar in some way—I couldn't help thinking, disrespectfully, that it looked a bit like a large archery target.

Facing it was Cortez, lashed to the slimmest of the three subsidiary pillars that surrounded the massive central column. He was bareheaded; and I noticed that his hair was a lot thicker than I expect mine to be if I ever reach that age; it showed very little gray. He was dressed in his customary white pajamas. They were spotted in front with blood that had run down his chin as the result of a couple of preparatory softening-up blows to the face. Even as I watched, the man in front of him slugged him hard in the body.

121

This was a big blond man and he liked his work. I could tell by the happy way he went about it; but of course I already knew him by name and reputation. He was Marschak, Rutterfeld's meatheaded muscle specialist. But Marschak's happiness wasn't perfect. Beating on people was fun, but beating on people who moaned and wept and pleaded for mercy was more fun; and the old man made no sound except for an inadvertent gasp as the breath was driven out of him.

Rutterfeld was supervising the proceedings, standing back a little, as tall as Marschak but much thinner; emaciated and dark and, according to his dossier, very, very mean.

"Again!" he said, and Marschak struck again. Rutterfeld spoke to Cortez, pointing to the round calendar disc. "This stone, what means it? In a recent speech, the man who found it is reported to have claimed that it holds the secret of the destruction of the civilization by which it was made, a secret passed down by generations of native priests. What is this secret? You are the latest of these priests, you must know, you will tell us. . . . Ach, put it into Spanish, Pedro."

Pedro Marschak, a nice combination of names for a blond giant, started translating. I looked around for the missing Kronbeck, Rutterfeld's weapons expert. I found him where a weapons expert should have been, in the rocks below me where he could cover the path and anybody who came along it. He was a small, dark, moustached weasel of a man. Marschak had finished speaking. There was no answer from the old man. I heard Rutterfeld's sharp command and the sound of another blow.

ANDALE!

It was a silent cry for help blasting into my brain: *Hurry!* It didn't mean that the old man was afraid; it merely meant, I knew, that his old body had taken about as much as it could, and he had things to do before he died, and I was there to see that he got to do them. What he had to do and why I had to help him were things I didn't know; but I've had blind assignments before. In fact, the times when I know exactly what I'm doing and why are in the minority. I threw a message back: DON'T HONK, I'M PEDALING AS FAST AS I CAN. Whether it

122

went anywhere I didn't know; that telepathy stuff is not my bag.

"You will tell us," I heard Rutterfeld say, seating himself on the sacrificial altar with its two snarling heads. "You will tell us how your ancestors died, old man. It is on that stone, no? They all died, something killed them very fast without a mark on them, I have seen the mural in the Jaguar Temple. You will tell us how they were killed or you will die, too, but there will be many marks on you. My clients, my masters, are very interested in things that kill quickly and efficiently. What was used, what weapon? Is it something ancient that our modern scientists have overlooked? Tell!"

He gestured to Marschak, who went into his translation act once more, giving the old man a little more time to rest. His voice helped to cover my movements. Actually, the stalk was easy. This was a city team; they should never have let themselves be sent out into the boonies. Kronbeck never knew I was there until I chopped him down from behind; but as he went down he dropped the Browning Hi-Power he was holding and, while it didn't discharge, thank God, it did make a lot of noise on the rocks. I crouched and took aim as Marschak whirled, producing a Browning of his own with reasonable celerity.

It was not time for fancy marksmanship, at thirty yards, with a short-barreled weapon I'd never fired before. I simply centered the blunt front sight on the blocky body and worked the squishy double-action mechanism twice. The double report was impressive in that vaulted rock-chamber; it seemed to echo and reecho from all sides. I heard some small stones clatter down from the ceiling of the cave, jarred loose by the crashes of sound, but the ceiling itself stayed up. A great relief.

Marschak dropped his gun and hunched over and hugged himself, the typical gut-shot reaction. Okay, so the piece threw low at thirty, that was something to remember. Rutterfeld had his hand inside his dark windbreaker, but he was a pro after all, he knew he was covered, had to be covered, and would be dead in a moment if he persisted in that dangerous project. The hand came out very slowly, empty. I bent down and picked up Kronbeck's Browning and slammed it across its owner's skull, just in case he was entertaining any subversive thoughts about waking up. I stood up.

"All right, Frances, you can come out now," I said.

CHAPTER 17

It seemed disrespectful, if not actually sacreligious, for Frances to rinse my bloody handkerchief—she'd requisitioned it after using up the one tattered Kleenex she'd found in her own pocket—in the sacred waters of the sacred *cenote*. When I said as much, she laughed.

"I don't think they took its sanctity all that seriously," she said. "Anyway, it's sacred priest's blood, isn't it? And I somehow don't think this pool is any stranger to blood." She wrung out the handkerchief and glanced at me over her shoulder. "You're a bit weird, aren't you, darling?"

"Just careful," I said. "No sense insulting anybody's gods unnecessarily, particularly in view of the funny things going on around here. I've got enough enemies without making more on any level, here or above or below. How is the old gent?"

"I don't know. That last blow slammed his head against the stone pretty hard. And there may be internal injuries."

"He should have yelled for help a little sooner."

"Maybe he didn't know a little sooner," Frances said.

"Well, he knew they were coming for him," I said. "He told me this afternoon to be waiting for his call."

She'd got the gore off the old man's face and was cleaning it off his coarse cotton shirt. She didn't look up at me when she spoke again, her neat brown head bent over her work. "You don't *really* believe it, do you, Sam? We didn't *really* hear him, did we? 'Hear', or whatever you want to call it."

"Hell, no," I said. "It never happened. We just imagined the whole thing. But if they could do that, the old ones, what else would they do?"

"Of course, ESP and telepathy have been studied in

some fairly respectable institutions of higher learning by some fairly respectable academic investigators." Frances grimaced, sitting back on her heels. "Rather inconclusively, as I recall. . . . Now, shouldn't we be doing something about that one?"

I glanced toward big blond Pedro Marschak who, hands and feet tied with pieces of the long rope that had been wound around Cortez, was slumped against the nearest pillar, moaning. On either side of him, also bound, sat his friends—if the concept of friendship had any meaning in that company. Marschak's eyes were closed and his face was greenish. There was a sheen of blood on his dark trousers, but not as much as you'd expect; the real bleeding is almost always internal when they're shot down there.

"Whatever you like," I said. "Pull down his pants and stick some Band-Aids on his tummy, if it'll make you feel better and you've got some Band-Aids."

Marschak heard me and opened his eyes and whispered: "You sonofabitch!"

"But he could be dying!" Frances protested.

I said, "Lady, I keep telling you, but it doesn't seem to penetrate: I'm a pro. I don't go around shooting people just to turn right around and start unshooting them. But as I say, if it'll ease your mind, go ahead and play Florence Nightingale to your heart's content. Maybe he'll make a grab for you and give me an excuse to put the next one right between his ugly eyes."

"*No mate!* No kill!" It was Cortez's voice. The old man was trying to sit up, a disturbed look on his bruised face. "Please no kill, señor. No dead."

There was a brief silence; then Rutterfeld spoke for the first time since his capture, if you disregard a few derogatory terms he'd applied to me while I was disarming and binding him.

"The old savage has the correct idea," he said rather smugly. "He knows what his government will do if white foreigners are found murdered by these primitives. The army will seize the excuse to exterminate them all; it has happened elsewhere in these jungles. So you had better get my associate to a hospital rapidly and hope you have not injured him too badly."

I said, "Friend Rutterfeld, the only trouble with that reasoning is that I'm the one who'll be doing the murdering, very cheerfully considering who the murderees are; and I'm no downtrodden primitive. In fact I think you know what my real name is and whom I work for; and the government of Costa Verde treasures its friendly relations with Washington—as well they should, considering the way the U.S. supplies and dollars keep rolling in—so I don't think anybody in Santa Rosalia is going to object very strenuously to my knocking off a few cheap Marxist spies I find abusing respectable Costa Verde citizens, primitive or otherwise." I looked down at him grimly. "Moscow must be pretty hard up for weapons, reaching for a prehistoric death ray, or whatever, five thousand years old. Of course, if they really took it seriously, they wouldn't have sent you and your clowns after it. . . ."

But Rutterfeld was looking past me. I saw a quick flicker of hope in his narrow eyes; in his position he'd consider any new development hopeful. I sidestepped and turned, gun ready; but the man who stood there had his empty hands outspread in a gesture of peace. He was a young native man, short and brown and stocky as they all are, dressed in loose white like Cortez, with a sisal bag like a large, heavily-reloaded lady-type purse slung over his shoulder. I didn't like to think that he'd got that close without my hearing him.

"I am Epifanio," he said. "I have come to attend *El Viejo*."

"How did you know the Old One needed attention?" I asked; a stupid question because I knew damn well how he'd known. Well, it beat carrying around walkie-talkies, I guess. I saw that this one had the same classic Melmec-Maya face, although much younger, with the same bold beaked nose, and slanting forehead, and inward-turning eyes. Epifanio. I'd thought that living in the U.S. Southwest most of my youth I'd heard all the Spanish names, but that was a new one for my collection. I wondered what his real name was. Something full of x's and ch's no doubt. Like Ixchal, the God of Death. "I think we should get him to a doctor as soon as possible," I said. "He got slugged pretty hard. I was a little slow getting down here."

"It was foreseen," Epifanio said. "There is no blame. *Con permiso?*"

He moved past me and crouched beside the old man. There was a dreamlike quality to the night that was partly due, of course, to the fact that I had to keep closing my mind to the thought of all that rock above me: Subterranean operations are very hard on my nerves. Also there was the fact that, like Frances, I didn't really believe some of the things that were happening and would have preferred to dismiss them as a lot of psychic bullshit—and probably would so dismiss them, try to forget them because I found them disturbing, as soon as I got the hell out of this miserable hole in the ground and breathed fresh air again. *It was foreseen,* indeed!

Epifanio had taken a small cloth pouch from his sisal bag. He loosened the drawstring and reached inside for a pinch of some kind of leaves, which he fed to Cortez, who began to chew deliberately. Gradually the grayness faded from his weathered old skin. He spoke softly to Epifanio in a language I didn't recognize at all; and the young disciple, if that was what he was, nodded and moved over to Marschak and gave him a quick examination and tried to feed him some of the magic leaves, but the blond man spat them out.

Frances said, "Don't be stupid. He's just offering you some coca leaves for the pain. . . ."

I didn't follow the rest of that, because I'd suddenly become aware that there were more people in the cave now: white-clad figures standing silently at the edge of the light, mostly men but some women. When I looked back to Marschak, he was chewing obediently, and his color had also improved. Epifanio approached me.

"*El Viejo* wishes to speak with you. And the lady also."

"Sure."

We moved over to where Cortez was sitting. A couple of men had come forward carrying between them a large square of canvaslike cloth full of firewood; they were laying a fire in the pit before the jaguar altar with its two snarling heads.

"*Gracias, guerrero,*" the old man whispered, looking up at me. "It was well done."

I wasn't too sure of that. He still didn't look very good. It could have been done better, or at least faster. But I said modestly, "*Por nada.*"

"And thank you, too, señora." Cortez started to say more, but changed his mind and gestured to Epifanio to take over instead.

127

The younger man said, "The Old One finds your language difficult to speak. He asks me to explain to you, señor, why you were chosen to help. He says that the old warrior in your party, the former general, was too old and might not have believed; the elderly do not accept unfamiliar ideas readily. He says that the young warrior, the *capitan*, was troubled in his mind and might not have heard; it is difficult to reach those with heavy troubles. The others . . ." Epifanio shrugged. "They were not *guerreros*. One *cazador*, perhaps, a hunter, the others, *nada*. So you were chosen." He smiled faintly. "Besides, only you had a gun, señor."

I said dryly, "Yes, I can see that might have made a difference. But what about your own people?"

He smiled his thin young smile again. "With all due respect, señor, it was felt better that gringos should fight gringos. Now the Old One would request of you a great favor."

I said in their formal way, "It is granted."

"The captives, the prisoners. Your prisoners."

"They are his," I said. "He earned them. I was only the weapon in his hands."

Epifanio looked at me sharply. "I am sorry. I may have spoken badly. I did not realize that you understood. . . ."

But Rutterfeld, who'd been listening to every word, spoke sharply: "What is this? What do they want with us? What will be done to us?"

And Frances had touched my arm. "I don't get it, Sam. What's going on?"

I said, "Hell, you're the archaeologist; you're supposed to know their customs. What does it look like is going on? They're lighting the sacred fire. They're reconsecrating the ancient altar—look at them—and they have here three lousy gringo criminals who'll never be missed, whom they carefully baited and trapped in their sacred cave beside their sacred underground lake. Well, Cortez did, using himself as bait and me as the trap. If they'd grabbed three respectable American tourists, out of our group, say, they'd have had endless official troubles. Three of their own? I don't know if their religion permits the use of their own; anyway, prisoners of war were the customary subjects for this kind of ceremony, I think you told us; and here are three very suitable POWs. Armed, they invaded Copalque with hostile intentions, didn't they? And they were taken in fierce combat by that great warrior ally of the ancient Melmec people, Sam Felton, who has just waived all rights to the warm bodies." I grimaced. *"That's* why the old man didn't want any of them killed. He wasn't being humanitarian, just practical. You can't sacrifice a dead man properly."

"Sacrifice!" Frances gasped; and Rutterfeld was protesting shrilly; and Marschak was cursing rather repetitiously. Frances grasped my arm: "But, Sam, we can't let them—"

"Let?" I said. "Look around, sweetheart. Count noses. Even if I wanted to shoot down a bunch of nice local citizens for the sake of these three creeps, the pistol's only got five chambers. Besides, I'm a firm believer in freedom of religion. And I must say I'm a little surprised at your attitude, professor."

"What do you . . . Oh." I saw her face change, and a speculative gleam came into her eyes.

"That's better, Dr. Dillman," I said. "How many of your professional colleagues have actually *seen* this ritual performed?"

She licked her lips. "Of course . . . of course I'll never dare to publish. . . . And it will be a totally degenerate form of the old ceremony after all these years, but still . . ."

"That's my girl."

Rutterfeld shouted at me wildly, "It is insane! You are a white man, you cannot allow these little brown niggers to—"

"Oh, shut up!" That was Kronbeck, the diminutive gunman, opening his mouth for the first time since his capture. "I told you we had no business in the fucking jungle messing with a bunch of Indians; now shut up about brown niggers. Felton, or whatever your name is . . ."

"Yes?" I said.

"You did a slick job of sneaking up on me. Okay, no hard feelings. As between one lousy manhunter and another, how about asking that high priest j.g. to pass those painkiller leaves around. Tell him I have a hell of a headache and that's no lie."

"Sure."

But when I started to speak, Epifanio raised his hand. "I heard. It would have been done in any case. *Un momentito.*"

I asked him, "Will we be permitted to remain?"

Epifanio said, "It is the wish of the Old One that you should do so. He thinks the lady will find answers to some of the questions she has been asking. And you, señor, I think you will find it interesting, also."

Some men were untying the prisoners and leading them away, Rutterfeld and Marschak still protesting loudly. Cortez was moving off, helped by two women in white *huipiles.* Elaborate courtesy was still the order of the day, and I said to Epifanio, "Inform the Old One that we are grateful for the privilege he has accorded us."

The young man bowed ceremoniously. "You honor us all by your attendance, señor, señora. Over here, if you please."

Moments later we were seated in the semidarkness on a flat rock some distance from the lighted altar, aware of others in the gloom all around us. I felt Frances search for my hand and grasp it tightly.

"Privilege!" she breathed. "I'm not so sure . . ."

But the drums were starting now, just a faint, whispering, throbbing sound at first, gradually becoming louder. I'd heard drums before, all kinds of drums, from the full U.S. Naval Academy Band giving Sousa hell as the midshipmen passed in review on the banks of the Severn where I'd been sent for boat training once, to a couple of old gents with tomtoms beating out the rhythm for a harvest dance at one of the smaller pueblos near my boyhood home in Santa Fe, New Mexico; but it was very different hearing them reverberating and reechoing hypnotically in this underground temple. Epifanio had thrown something on the fire that was filling the cave with a strange, thin sweet-smelling smoke.

They didn't hoke it up. They used the electric lights they had instead of going in for flaming torches. They wore their own clothes instead of cobbling up tawdry imitations of the elaborate costumes of their ancestors. This was not an artificial revival, a nostalgic restoration, of an ancient rite, meaningless today; this was their living religion and their living ceremony—but I couldn't help wondering how many of them also turned up at the local Catholic Church on Sunday, keeping on the good side of the Christian god as well.

Even the knife Epifanio produced from his sisal bag and unwrapped and presented with deliberate ceremony to Cortez as he appeared in the lighted area was no exercise in nostalgia. Obsidian was out, steel was in. It was a thick, brutal, businesslike blade apparently ground down from a heavy machete. But the grip was lovely, all gold and jade, their one concession to the glorious past.

They took Marschak first, perhaps afraid that he'd die on them if he had to wait. They had stripped him and washed him and disguised his wounds somehow. He looked enormous among all those short people, and soft and white and flabby, as he was led naked to the altar and made to lie down across it, obviously drugged, while the old priest—showing no signs of his recent beating—stood back gripping the great sacrificial knife. The drums were louder now and the scented mist was heavier. Cortez stepped forward and struck skillfully and powerfully. The body on the altar arched itself in blind agony; there was a formless bellow of sound above the rhythmic sound of the drums.

Cortez passed the bloody knife to Epifanio, standing behind him. The old man leaned over and reached with both hands into the gaping incision he'd made. Distantly I was aware of Frances's nails biting into my skin as she gripped my hand fiercely. I heard her make a small gagging sound as she watched the disposal of the now incomplete body in the sacred *cenote*, which accepted it and caused it to vanish in a manner inconsistent with the normal laws of hydraulics, I thought; but I didn't seem to be thinking very clearly any longer.

The disembodied heart lay, dripping, in the old priest's hands. They had another way of dealing with that, we learned, that Frances also found unpleasant. I was a bit annoyed by her queasy reactions, in a vague sort of way. For a tough scientist she was really pretty sensitive; but I reminded myself that after all, while I had encountered a few fresh corpses in the line of business, in her profession the poor girl was accustomed to dealing only with dead people who'd been dead for thousands of years.

Then the young priest was passing among us with the receptacle containing the first blood of the evening's first offering, making the purifying mark on the face of each worshipper; but the smoke seemed to be getting thicker and the cave was becoming very hazy. Another picture was breaking through; another scene quite near in place but incredibly distant in time, of a great wide sunlit area crowded with people and dominated by three great pyramids. . . .

CHAPTER 18

ACHUAC was having a good day, I reflected after the second sacrifice as I stood at attention in the hot sunshine before my squadron, Dog Squadron, in the place of honor, the place of greatest danger, at the end of the Great Court, the way to the King's Road and the jungle, the way they would probably break and flee if panic should strike. Fox Squadron on my left held the open space between the Pyramid of the Priests and the Great Pyramid. Wolf Squadron, on my right, closed the last opening, between the Great Pyramid and the Pyramid of the Warriors.

I hoped the people would not break. Not that we could not hold them; the King's Axes would not be overrun by an unarmed mob, even one as large as this, a whole nation gathered for a final day of worship and sacrifice. Enemy armies had attempted it and had died under the great stone weapons wielded by us, the axemen of the king, somewhat assisted by the darting spearmen, who are useful for harassing the attack and harrying the retreat although the Spears are, of course, never required to endure the full shock of battle.

But I hoped very much that our people would stand firm on this great day, this last day, the Day of Ixchal. There must be no shame today; and Achuac, the High Priest, had started well, although he was no longer young and his wrist did not have its former strength and cunning. He had been known, sometimes of late, to need more than one stroke of the knife to reach the heart, a dreadful portent of disaster

—in fact there was often betting in the ranks on the day's performance, although the penalty for such sacrilege, if discovered, was death, of course.

Normally we would have had a new high priest by now, a younger and stronger man who could be relied upon at the altar; but with the Day of Ixchal in sight the priesthood had closed ranks behind the old man who had guided us and our king, Becal Xia, spiritually through these last difficult years and who therefore deserved, they said, the honor of officiating to the very end. And at the very end. Today.

We—the highly placed men and women of my generation—had always known. We had known that the honor would be ours; that we would be the ones to lead our people into the Place of Night to meet the Lords of the Night, going not as before singly at the call of Ixchal, but all making the deliberate dark pilgrimage together to complete with courage and dignity this Great Cycle, allowing the sun to rise tomorrow on the beginning of the next, as the gods required.

We had served our purpose. We had made our contribution; but perhaps over the centuries sin and evil had grown among us that could only be eradicated in this way; perhaps the time had come for the world to see a shining new people, starting afresh where we had once begun when our own Great Cycle was clean and new. So the gods said, or were said to have said—but doubt was blasphemy and I was in no position to indulge in further sacrilege after flouting the commandments of my gods and the edicts of my priests in the most awful and wonderful way possible. . . .

But old Achuac was doing very well indeed. He had now completed the third and final offering with a fine stroke and was holding the heart aloft for the crowd to see—and behind me, I knew, the men of Dog Squadron were nudging each other in unmilitary fashion, reminding each other of bets won and lost. Even on the Day of Ixchal, even with no hope of ever collecting on a successful wager, a soldier will gamble; and it is better for an officer to look straight ahead and feign total ignorance.

Looking over the heads of the great crowd, I could see her now with the others—her equals in rank and all their maidens—up there behind the high jaguar altar, with the plumes of her rank on her dark head, and the priestess-

robes half-concealing her strong smooth body but open in front to reveal the fine breasts with which I was well acquainted; and the elaborate waistcloth; and the gleaming jewels.

It had been madness, of course; but when one knows the day of one's death, even the hour, one does not look quite the same way upon the rules that have bound men of all previous generations, to whom lying with a virgin Priestess of the Jaguar would have been quite inconceivable. They would probably have been rendered impotent by the mere idea of such sacrilege and would have deemed that a just punishment from the gods for even entertaining the thought of such wickedness. But I had not been rendered impotent, knowing that there were only a few months left; if the gods required punishment, I would be with them soon enough, for them to deal with as they pleased.

Nor had she been rendered unresponsive by the disrespect she was showing for her holy position among the god's attendants, by the sacred oaths she was breaking, by the risk we were both taking. Not that the risk was not considerable. The punishment prescribed, as is well known, is cutting and maiming in certain ways for both the man and the woman who must then—no longer recognizable as man, no longer recognizable as woman—be exposed to the populace in all their bloody naked mutilated shame to be pelted with rocks and filth for the specified time after which, if still living, they must be put to death in the manner reserved for the lowest criminals, and those who deliberately spit upon the gods.

But with the Day of Ixchal so close, after which there would be no more such pleasure ever, at least not for us, we had not counted the risk, my priestess and I; if anything, it had made our illicit lyings-together more desperately satisfying, helped by the knowledge that we had to make a few months take the place of the lifetime we would never have. . . .

But now the time of the king had come; and Becal Xia was stepping forward up there to perform his part of the ceremony, a handsome figure of imposing dignity in his plumes and cloak but, some said, not as much his own man as some kings who had ruled us in times past, more a puppet moving at the wishes of the priests. But those who said this did not say it aloud. And the priestesses were now descending the tall steps of all the pyramids with the graceful gliding motion that, my priestess had told me, took years to master and yearly cost them several novices because a fall was not only dangerous in itself but was a sign of the gods' displeasure, so even if you survived falling, you were instantly put to death where you fell.

The king had ceased his ritual of farewell. Old Achuac stepped forward; and the horns blew; and it was time for me to make certain that Dog Squadron was ready to stand firm if the crowd broke; but my people did not break. They did the directed thing with the material that had been given them, the little cakes that, my priestess had told me, had been prepared from a certain root. Like their king they took the bitter medicine that had been prescribed for them. Then Becal Xia was falling, dead, along the path of death that had been painted for him down the front of the Great Pyramid with the blood of the sacrifices that had preceded him; and the crowd before me was no longer before me. They were going down, all of them; and I watched my nation die.

The horns blew once more. I gave the opening command and the Axes separated to let the Spears come through. I gave the closing command, and we waited and watched as the spearmen of the now-dead king swept along the Great Court searching and probing while we stood ready to receive with the axes any who had betrayed their faith, our faith, but they shamed our doubts; they had faithfully taken the death that had been given to them. Not one of the thousands now lying there required the thrust of a spear; not one rose and fled alive to be dealt with by an axe. I was proud of them all, and I asked their forgiveness for the precautions we had taken that their faith and courage had rendered foolish.

It was the time of the Spears; and they formed and the priestesses passed among them with the cups of death—no death-cakes now—and they were soon down. Then it was our time, the time of the Axes, the time of Ixchal; and high on the Great Pyramid Achuac had a cup in his own hand; and my priestess was coming to me. There were no horns now; the blowers had gone before us. We were the last.

I watched her come and behind me her maidens were sharing their final cups with the men of the Axe. She held out the cup to me, and the thought was in my mind and in

135

that moment I knew it was in hers as well: the thought that it would be very easy now. There were no eyes left to see, there were no spears left to probe. We could drink without drinking and die without dying and rise again; together we could leave this place of death. Together and alive.

But the gods would see and we would see. And it was not fitting for a Priestess of the Jaguar and a Warrior of the Axe to cravenly betray their people and sneak away into the jungle to live like animals with a great nation, their great nation, lying dead behind them.

I took the cup and drank and gave it back. I felt my death come quickly, but not before I had seen her drink deeply in her turn, smiling at me as she drank. . . .

CHAPTER 19

I came awake uneasily, feeling dazed and lost, not knowing where I was or where I had been; knowing only that it had been a long and harrowing journey. Then Frances moved beside me in the dark and turned toward me, sleepily indicating her wish to be held, as always in bed a trusting and vulnerable woman very different from the tall, cool, competent person I knew by daylight. But in the act of snuggling closer she came fully awake and sat up with a start.

"Oh, my God! Darling, I had the damndest dream! . . ."

We were in my bed in my hotel cottage without any clothes on. How we had got there I had no idea.

"It *was* a dream, wasn't it?" Frances said uncertainly.

I rolled over and turned on the light. Our clothes were scattered untidily between the door and the bed as if we had fumbled our way out of them drunkenly—but of course it had not been drink, it had been that damned smoke. And perhaps a little hypnosis on the side? When I turned toward Frances, she looked suddenly a little sick.

"Your face! . . . I guess it wasn't really a dream, that part of it anyway. The cave part. Do I have . . . something on me, too?"

She turned her face to the light; and a neat band of dried blood ran from her hairline down her nose and across her lips to the point of her chin. She saw the answer in my eyes and, quite pale, started to get out of bed hastily. I grabbed her arm.

"Easy," I said.

"Damn it, I have to get it *off* before I . . ."

"It's not fuming nitric acid, sweetheart. Take it easy. Just sit right there and relax."

I got up and went into the bathroom and wet a washcloth, wrung it out partially, and brought it back. I turned her face to the light again and gently removed the red brown stripe. I took the cloth back, rinsed it out, and returned and knelt before her so she could do the same for me.

"And why is that any better than what I was going to do?" she asked a bit sulkily as I returned after disposing of the wet cloth.

I stopped by the dresser and peeled the usual protective plastic film off the glasses, also plastic—after the strange places we'd been this night, the familiar modern motel-hotel junk was kind of reassuring—and poured out a couple of drinks, one of which I put into her hand. I sat down beside her on the edge of the bed.

"Respect, doll," I said. "Respect is the watchword."

"Respect for what? Are you still afraid of offending their damn old gods?"

"I wasn't thinking of the gods," I said. "I was thinking of the people. They did us a considerable honor, remember; allowing us to participate in their secret ceremony. I wouldn't want to give them the idea I didn't appreciate that honor by removing the sacred mark in a hasty and disrespectful manner."

She looked at me for a moment; then she grinned. "You are without a doubt the *weirdest* man. . . . All right. As an archaeologist I have to agree with you. I was being childish; I was forgetting my scientific objectivity. But in this room? How would they know when they can't see us?"

"Are you sure of that?" I asked. "We've had some very peculiar things happen. I'm not making any wild assumptions about what that old priest can and can't see. Or the young one, either, for that matter. And I wouldn't want to hurt their feelings for the world, if you know what I mean."

She took a gulp of her drink. "I know."

I hesitated. "How authentic was the sacrifice we saw?" I asked. "I'd always assumed they did it by hacking open the rib cage lengthwise, instead of just making that great transverse incision under the sternum and reaching up from below."

"Ugh," she said, "it was very authentic, judging by the friezes and murals I've seen, but do we have to talk about it?"

I grinned. "For a dedicated scientist who spends her life digging up dead bones, you are the most squeamish lady I have ever met. How the hell have you got as far as you have in your profession without realizing that those old bones were once surrounded by flesh and blood, lots of blood, and that a lot of them probably didn't get to be old bones in an entirely peaceful manner?"

She looked at me and smiled a bit uncertainly. "Criticism acknowledged," she said softly. "I *have* thought of it. But the crude gory reality was . . . was just a little much for a sheltered Ph.D. who got most of her education out of books and museums. I'm sure it was a very valuable experience, but I need a little time to assimilate it." She hesitated. "We both saw the sacrifice, didn't we? That was real. The blood we just washed off was real blood. I presume they went ahead and . . . and did it to the other two prisoners; but I wasn't, well, really there after the first one. Were you? Or did you have a very strange and vivid dream instead?" When I nodded, she said, "To be scientific about it, we should both write down what we remember, independently, and then compare our dreams, if they really were dreams and not some kind of hypnotic suggestions. But I don't think I'm up to the scientific method right now. Was I in your dream?"

"Yes," I said. "In a manner of speaking. You were shorter and browner, you had lovely coal-black hair and beautiful brown eyes, and you were one of the high priestesses of Ixchal; but in some way I knew it was you. Was I in yours?" When she nodded, I asked, "What was I?"

"You were the handsome captain of the Dog Squadron of the King's Axes. And you had no business at all, you wicked man, seducing a virgin priestess of the royal blood."

She was not looking at me; and there was color in her face. She spoke dryly: "Apparently I'm just a pushover in every incarnation. But anyway, we seem to have shared pretty much the same dream experience, wouldn't you say?" She drew a long breath and turned to look at me. "Give me a critique of our joint dream, Sam. I know what I think of it as an archaeologist; what do you think of it as a layman? Did you believe what you were dreaming?"

I said, "If you put it that way, yes. While I was dreaming it, I believed in it completely. I could hardly bear to drink the poison out of the cup you gave me, not because I feared death, but because it would part me from you, my true love, my only love. I even considered betraying my people, and my honor as a warrior, for your sweet sake."

She was smiling a little. "And now that you're awake?"

I said bluntly, "I think most of it was a lot of Hollywood crap."

She didn't seem startled. She was watching me steadily. "Tell me why."

I said, "Jesus, that one about the virile warrior and the virgin priestess has whiskers on it! The doomed lovers and the love that endures beyond the grave! Do you really think they entertained such romantic notions back in those early days? You know more about primitive people than I do, but I have a hunch they fucked when they felt like fucking, and maybe sometimes they felt like it enough to break a sacred taboo or two, but they didn't make a tender production of it the way we like to. They didn't lead that kind of sheltered dreamy live or think that kind of mushy thoughts. Or, dammit read that kind of slushy novel. Correct me if I'm wrong."

"You're not wrong. Anything else?"

I said, "Again, you're the expert, but the military business was nonsense, in my opinion. Regiments of soldiers standing rigidly at attention three thousand years B.C.? Opening and closing their formations smartly? One unit trained to let another pass through, and then reform on command? I'm not even sure an experienced Roman legion could have pulled off that evolution successfully; and the disciplined legions came a good many dozen centuries later. I'm just guessing, but I'm willing to bet a small sum that the Melmecs never even thought in terms of that kind of rigid military discipline. Judging by what I've seen and read on this trip, they dressed their wars up with very fancy costumes, and maybe even with their own ideas of martial music, and certainly with a lot of religious ceremonies; but basically their battles were just one disorganized bunch of guys clubbing and knifing and spearing another bunch until somebody'd had enough and ran away. Or somebody saw an omen in the sky saying his side had lost and it was time to quit. As jungle fighters go, they may have been terrific with sneak attacks and ambushes; but when it came to close-order drill, forget it." I looked at her for a moment. "Your turn," I said.

Frances drew a long breath. "The priestesses," she said. "We've found evidence indicating that women did take some part in their ceremonies; but that chorus line of lovely bare-breasted maidens gliding seductively down the pyramid steps! . . ." She shook her head quickly. "Do you know what it reminded me of? Not when I was dreaming it, of course; like you I believed in it completely at the time; but now that I think back on it, well, you remember the Ballet Folklorica in Mexico City that I advised you not to see; and we found . . . something else to do that night instead." There was color in her face again, but she went on steadily: "Well, I saw the performance the previous time I was there, and they had a supposedly authentic Aztec dance that looked just like that, about as genuinely ancient and ethnic as Radio City Music Hall."

"Yes, I agree that the death dance of the virgins was a bit much," I said when she paused. "And then there was that business of the axes. I'm kind of weapons-oriented, and I've been looking carefully at the stuff you've been showing us. I haven't seen a single war axe of any kind, either as an artifact or carved on a wall. Up in what is now the U.S. they used the tomahawk, sure, but that was a little one-hand job for throwing and close-quarters hacking. What my Melmec warriors and I were armed with, in my dream, was a king-sized battle-chopper such as the Vikings sometimes used, except that the head was stone instead of steel."

There was a little silence in the room; and no sound came from outside. There were no cars driving on the single road leading into this hotel; there were no birds or animals communicating in the surrounding jungle. Frances gave an abrupt laugh, looking down at herself.

"Do you realize that we're indulging in this scholarly

discussion without a stitch on? You'd better toss me my shirt; and make me another drink, please. And you put something on, please, and don't sit quite so close, and look straight ahead, because I'm going to tell you something that embarrasses me dreadfully and I don't want you looking at me."

I followed her instructions, pulling on my shorts and refilling our glasses. When I was seated at the indicated distance, facing in the indicated direction, I said, "Carry on."

"You must bear with me, Sam," she said. "This is all going to be very personal, but it connects. . . . I was a tall, shy child, darling, and I grew up to be a tall, shy schoolgirl. And bright, dammit, bright enough that I could hide my shyness by acting very snooty and superior. I was the smartest kid in class, wasn't I? A totally unpleasant little monster, well, big monster. Taller than practically all the boys. And being so smart and so superior, being so tall, how could I learn about . . . about certain things like the pretty little dumb girls around me? I mean, how could I let a boy much smaller than I, and stupider, smear my lipstick and muss my dress and . . . and fumble with my undies? I'd have been making myself totally ridiculous; or I thought I would. So I stuck with my snooty act, and I became terribly afraid that somebody would learn what a fraud I was; that some night I'd find myself wrestling with a boy all sweaty and untidy and half-undressed and suddenly he would realize that the tall, self-possessed young lady who'd condescended to . . . to cooperate graciously out of the kindness of her heart was really a very frightened and inexperienced girl who didn't know a damn thing about anything. And he would laugh and laugh and laugh and tell all his friends, and I would simply die of shame and humiliation."

She took a swallow from her glass and stared down into it for a moment. I did not speak or look at her directly.

Presently she went on: "So I rationalized it. I told myself that sex was really a very undignified and disgusting business and to hell with it. But in secret I read endless mushy novels about unrequited love, and Elaine the Lily Maid of Astolat, and Lancelot and Guinevere—well, I guess their love wasn't exactly unrequited—and I waited for the handsome, understanding prince who would liberate me from my dark prison tower and appreciate my unblemished purity." She made a face. "I don't suppose this is very interesting to anybody but me."

"I'm not bored," I said.

She glanced at me warily and went on: "It's funny how one can be very tough and smart and hardheaded on one level—I got my degrees in record time with all kinds of honors—and still be a totally mixed-up mess on another. Of course, around the universities I attended, I was known as the original ice maiden. And by this time I'd really painted myself into a corner, to scramble a metaphor. I mean, I was twenty-six years old, apparently a very sophisticated and competent and successful young woman; how the hell could I tell a man who took me out that I'd never done it and the very idea frightened me silly, even made me a little sick, but . . . but that I was perfectly willing to try it, well, reluctantly willing to try it, because I was beginning to realize that the way I was just wasn't any good. But please, Mister, be gentle, be kind and understanding. How could I bare my soul and my fears, not to mention my body, to a stray male character who'd bargained only for a pleasant evening with the lady, not a session of psychiatric therapy?"

She was silent again, and I said, "But your prince came along."

She nodded. "Yes, Archie came along. We met professionally on an expedition into . . . Well, it doesn't matter where. There were other people, of course, the men sleeping in one tent and the women in another, so there was no question of . . . Anyway, we just talked. And talked. And talked. Whenever we had a chance to be together. I don't know what we talked about. Everything. And when we got back he asked me to marry him." She paused to clear her throat. "I said . . . I said that I was perfectly willing, but he should know he'd be getting a frozen twenty-six-year-old female freak who'd hardly been kissed, let alone . . . bedded. It was as easy as that, telling *him*. He said, well, we could take care of the kissing right now; and the rest would undoubtedly take care of itself. Of course it didn't. It was . . . rather difficult for a while, I was *really* a mess, but he was endlessly gentle, endlessly patient, and in the end it worked very well indeed. I was very lucky, Sam. If it had been another man, just a little overeager and impatient, just a little rough and demanding, I'd probably have spent the rest of my life as an emotional cripple. I owe my husband a great deal. He's a wonderful person. I really . . . really love him very much in spite of the way I . . ."

Her voice trailed off. We were getting pretty far from the subject originally under discussion; but I sensed that she had motives for telling me this quite apart from the problems of the night. I sensed also that I wouldn't like those motives very much when I understood them. In the meantime I wasn't all that impressed with Professor Archibald Dillman's shining nobility. Being granted the privilege of introducing a woman like this one belatedly to the joys of love shouldn't really, I reflected sourly, qualify a man for hardship pay, or a saint's halo. But it didn't seem advisable for me to say it; anyway, I was probably a bit jealous of Bonnie Prince Archie.

Frances laughed sharply, with sudden self-contempt. "And owing him a great deal, loving him very much, I'm sitting on another man's bed without any pants on! I guess perhaps he overdid the treatment a little; or maybe I'm just compulsively making up for all the lost, loveless years. But the point is, Sam, don't you recognize the basic elements of our dream scenario? The awakened virgin scientist-lady—read priestess. The romantic notion of star-crossed love, out of all those mushy books I read. The pretty ballet on the pyramids, from the show I saw. Dammit, Sam, that lousy old man just picked my brains—our brains—and fed us back our own sentimental TV notions in that so-called dream he sent us! I'll bet if you scrounge around in your mind, you'll find an axe in there somewhere. Obviously he did. What about those Vikings you mentioned?"

I nodded slowly. "You may be right. My parents were Scandinavian, you know; and I was a red-hot Viking aficionado as a kid. I read every gory old Norse saga I could get my hands on. And the battle-axe was certainly one of their weapons, but . . . Wait a minute! I've got it. H. Rider Haggard."

"Who?"

"Not your type of escape literature, doll. African adventure was his bag. His best-known book is probably *King Solomon's Mines*, but I read them all; and the one I remember best was called *Allan Quartermain*. Allan was the wise white hunter, and his native sidekick was the great

143

Zulu warrior Umslopogaas, one of my favorite fictional characters at that youthful time. Umslopogaas carried an outsized battle-axe and died nobly, shattered axe in hand, holding a palace stairway against overwhelming odds. And the inhabitants of Umslopogaas's home village were known as the People of the Axe."

Frances drained her glass and set it carefully on the bedside table; then she drew the thin red shirt around her and shivered slightly.

"The idea of people rummaging around in my mind gives me the creeps," she said. "But I guess I've got to accept the fact that there are things that can't be explained scientifically, at least not yet." She looked at me sideways and spoke in a different tone. "Well, Sam?"

"Well, what?" She waited without speaking, and I said, "Oh, you mean about the dream?"

"Yes. We've pretty well picked it apart, haven't we? All except . . ."

"That's right, except," I said when she hesitated. I grimaced. "What you want to know is, do we assume that because the frosting is phony, the whole damn cake is a fake?"

She smiled briefly. "You put it so picturesquely. But we do have to decide if, just because we know it didn't happen the way Cortez showed it to us in our dream, it didn't happen at all."

"And what is your considered decision, Dr. Dillman?"

"I can't possibly come to a firm conclusion without checking back through all our findings and studying the temple decorations and that terrible mural with this possibility in mind. But I don't think the fact that the old priest dressed it up with a lot of colorful trappings for our benefit necessarily means . . ." She stopped, frowning thoughtfully. "There are obviously limits to Cortez's knowledge, Sam. I mean, he doesn't really seem to know much about archaeology, or the day-by-day customs of the ancient people from whom he came. Not as much as we know from studying the materials we've found in the ruins —and remember, those ruins weren't uncovered until quite recently. He probably has only an incomplete idea of what they reveal. His knowledge comes from a totally different source. What he knows isn't what's carved on the stones out there, it's what's been handed down from high priest to high priest over uncounted generations: the meaning of the calendar wheel, for instance, and the ritual of the sacrifice." She glanced at me. "I wonder how often, how many . . ."

"Probably not often and not many," I said. "If people started disappearing weekly into the sacred *cenote* with their hearts missing, three at a time, somebody would notice. It could be, even, that the ceremony was revived tonight for the first time in years, maybe even centuries, because the three sacred calendars are approaching that major conjunction we know about, and the people have to start getting ready for it in the old ways, with the old offerings to the gods."

She was watching me oddly. "You seem to be . . . totally unconcerned about having been present at three murders, even if they were ritual murders."

I said, "For God's sake! I'm supposed to weep for Rutterfeld and his creeps, after watching them beat up on that old man?"

"They were human beings, Sam."

"That's debatable," I said. "And even if you're right, we have a recognized oversupply of those; we can spare a few of the less desirable specimens."

She said, "Isn't that a rather dangerous philosophy? What if somebody should decide that you're one of the undesirables?"

"Lots of people have," I said. "But somehow they never quite managed to do anything effective about it."

She sighed. "Well, at least you're a consistent monster. What were we talking about when I got all moral? Oh." She drew a long breath. "The fact is that these priests, regardless of the psychological or psychic tricks they can play, don't really have a direct pipeline to the past. What Cortez has is a large body of Melmec tradition, passed on from generation to generation by word of mouth. And in that tradition is the answer to a question he knows concerns us deeply: the question of how his ancestors came to vanish from their great city of Copalque, of how their elaborate civilization came to die. So tonight, in gratitude for the help we'd given him, he passed us that answer; but the old gentleman is a showman accustomed to catering to the tastes of his audience. Not knowing all the details of life back in those far-off days, he just gave us the package in the kind of Hollywood wrappings he thought we were accustomed to. But I think the answer was still there." She paused and licked her lips and went on: "And the answer isn't death rays from outer space, or lethal plagues, or violent earthquakes, or secret weapons that the hopeful Russians might be able to adapt to modern use. That's not what killed off the Melmecs, and presumably the Olmecs and Mayas after them. The answer is . . . Jonestown."

After a little, I said, "That's the answer Cortez gives. But do you believe him?"

She hesitated. "A few years back I probably wouldn't have. But if one modern zealot can persuade nine hundred fairly recent converts to kill themselves on command, which we've now seen happen, why shouldn't an ancient Melmec priest, who's dominated his people spiritually all their lives and their parents before them, give the same command to nine thousand and have it obeyed?"

I said thoughtfully, "Back to Haggard's Africa, the story goes that the Zulu emperor Chaka once ordered a whole *impi*—regiment—to commit suicide merely to impress some visitors with his power. The order was obeyed."

Frances drew a long breath. "It would explain a great deal. How they knew *how* the end was coming, as indicated by that graphic mural in the Temple of the Jaguar. They didn't have to be able to predict the future to paint that; because they knew that was exactly the way they were going to do it when the calendar, and the priests, told them to. We've wondered why the great cities were left standing, untouched and deserted, as if the inhabitants had all marched out in a body. Well, according to this theory, they did march out—as far as the Great Court here, and its equivalent elsewhere. At least it's a better explanation than many that have been proposed; it gives us a new viewpoint from which to review the material in our possession. It tells us what to look for in future digging. And it's a possibility that hasn't, to the best of my knowledge, been considered by anybody else. If we find enough confirmation to publish, it should create quite a stir."

"In fact," I said, "it would be a real professional triumph, wouldn't it? But you don't seem very happy about it. Why?"

She turned her gray eyes on me again; and I saw that

there was pain in them. "You know why," she said. "You know why I told you . . . that about my husband."

"I see," I said slowly. I swallowed something in my throat. "The time has come?"

She nodded. "We've . . . shared a little too much already, Sam. There's a little too much . . . involvement already. There wasn't supposed to be any. Make it easy for me, please. Tell me to go now. Treat me like, well, a tour guide for the rest of the trip. Please?"

I said, "Yes, that was the original deal, wasn't it? Hit and run. A one-night stand." I looked at her sitting there barelegged and bare-assed and beautiful in her rumpled red shirt, a very different woman from the severe and unapproachable academic female I'd first seen in Chicago. I drew a long breath and said very carefully, "Well, it's been nice and I'll miss you. I'll miss you very much. But you must do what you feel you have to."

"Don't hate me, Sam. Don't ever hate me."

I regarded her for a moment longer, rather grimly. "Don't be stupid, Dillman. If I hated you, there'd be no problem, would there? Now just pull on your damn jeans and go, will you, please?"

She did.

CHAPTER 20

WHEN I awoke to daylight, I found that most of the events of the night had lost all reality, assuming that they'd ever had any. With sunshine at the window I couldn't really believe that I'd experienced miracles of telepathic communication, watched a human sacrifice, and solved by means of an induced dream—if you'll buy that, I told myself, you'll buy anything—a problem that had baffled generations of trained archaeologists.

It all seemed very unlikely and really very unimportant beside the one event of the night I did believe. I was aware

147

of an empty sense of loss; and the fact that what I'd lost was another man's wife didn't make it any more bearable. She'd been perfectly right about the involvement. I was discovering that it had gone considerably deeper than I'd suspected—strange in a way, because I still remembered very clearly a small girl who'd died, whose memory I could be said to have betrayed, although Elly Brand herself would have laughed at the sentimental notion of being faithful after death.

I got into yesterday's grubby jeans, my .38 revolver, and my desert boots; and I found a clean but suitcase-wrinkled *guyabera* shirt to top off my costume respectably. Frances was already at breakfast with the Putnams when I reached the dining room. All three gave me the same kind of casually cheerful good-mornings as I found an empty table overlooking the pool and tucked the big camera bag under it. I gave my order to a pretty waitress, in a crisp *huipile*. She reminded me of the lovely priestesses who, in my dream, had brought my Melmec axemen their cups of death.

"Do you want company or do you prefer to brood alone?"

It was Miranda Matson looking bulky and shapeless in a short-sleeved green jumpsuit that, I realized, was actually a faded military coverall with the sleeves partially amputated. The washed-out black-stenciled name and unit of the original owner could still be deciphered, if anybody wanted to take the trouble.

"I've just decided that the last thing in the world I want to do is climb another goddamn pyramid," I said. "Sit down, sit down."

She sat down. "Well, we've all got something," she said easily. "With me it's horses. Honest. Every so often I have to climb on one of the brutes out in the boonies because it's the only way to get to the damn story; and every time I tell myself it's a perfectly friendly and harmless animal, a docile servant of mankind, and every time I'm in a total helpless panic the whole time I'm aboard the crummy beast." Her pale blue eyes studied me shrewdly out of her wide red face. "Why don't we ever tell the bastards to shove their lousy nags and pyramids, hey?"

"*Machismo?*" I suggested.

"That may be the answer for you, but what the hell have

I got to be *macho* with? No, *cojones* aren't the answer, Flash, but I'm damned if I know what the answer is. Incidentally, nothing's come in for you since last night. Apparently the Santa Rosalia *status* is still *quo*." She hesitated. "I'm told our target for today is a place called Labal about fifteen miles from here. A change of plan, I gather, but apparently they've got some Jeeps available today and might not be able to get them later."

I frowned. "You're coming with us?"

"That Ramiro character is trying to set something up for me out there. He said if it worked, somebody would spirit me away to meet Lupe Montano some time during the day while you're all drooling over old ruins; but I'd better be dressed for a pretty rough trip." She grimaced. "I hope the trip is the only thing that's rough, if you know what I mean. Nothing I love like interviewing a bunch of nervous revolutionaries bristling with machine guns."

Across the room, I saw Ramiro Sanchez come up to speak to Frances. She excused herself from the table and went off with him, looking businesslike and competent in her expensive jeans, now a bit creased and stained like my lower-class pants, but that's what jeans are for. Like me, she'd put on a fresh shirt, a blue gingham number dressed up by a blue bandana handkerchief tied around her neck cowboy-fashion. No matter what she wore, threadbare tweeds or soiled jeans, there was always that faint air of elegance about her. To hell with Associate Professor Frances Ransome Dillman, Ph.D.

Then we were all wandering out toward the front of the hotel where we found six Jeeps waiting. Miranda, who'd put a straw hat the size of a cocktail table on top of her wild white hair, was asked by Sanchez to join him in the lead vehicle. I wound up with the Putnams; and I saw Frances waiting with the Wilders to bring up the rear of the caravan. We took off, soon turning into a rudimentary track chopped through the jungle. It was a long, rough ride and, Miranda or no Miranda, I thought I'd have preferred a horse; they have slightly better springs and shock absorbers for this kind of work. We passed some overgrown temples and small pyramids that had not yet been excavated or restored.

At last we broke out of the jungle into a large clearing decorated by still another goddamn pyramid, but it was the

149

only one there, thank God; and although surmounted by a rather imposing ruin, it was considerably lower than any of the three I'd already conquered bravely. After we'd milled around a bit getting organized, I got up and down it without either distinguishing myself or disgracing myself, bringing back some pictures and a rather disturbing impression of the scrubby, low, dry jungle surrounding us, a green barbed-wire entanglement of vines and thorns extending clear to the horizon, unbroken by any sign of civilization except for the rudimentary track that had brought us here and a foot trail taking off at a slight angle to it.

We scrambled back into the Jeeps for a short ride across the clearing to the local *cenote,* a very different kind of water hole from the sinister black underground pond I'd visited last night. This was a lovely blue jungle pool with a shelving stone shore on one side, our side, and a perpendicular rock wall on the other. It was really an odd geological area, I reflected, with no surface water to amount to anything, except for these sudden holes scattered arbitrarily through the jungle.

In addition to the six Jeep-drivers, already having lunch by their vehicles, there were four nonswimmers in the party including me—I didn't particularly care to leave my clothes, with the revolver, unattended; and imitating a fish isn't my favorite pastime anyway, perhaps because I do it so unconvincingly. Ramiro Sanchez was not among the swimmers, either; he had disappeared somewhere, perhaps on Miranda's business. Miranda hadn't brought a bathing suit. She said she had no desire to make a spectacle of herself, and anybody who wanted to see a walrus could visit a zoo. And Frances was making a big deal of setting out our picnic. I moved over that way casually while the aquatic members of the party splashed and shrieked in the clear blue water like a bunch of kids.

"Need any help?" I asked.

Frances jumped nervously and looked around. "Oh, God, don't sneak up on me like that! No, thank you, Mr. Felton, I think everything's under"—she licked her lips—"under control."

I looked at her and saw the fear and tension inside her. I realized with a shock that she was a woman expecting something terrible to happen, very soon.

I drew a long breath and said carefully, "Sir Samuel

150

Felton at your service, milady. Problems solved upon request. It's not too late to start trusting people, Dillman."

She licked her dry lips. "But it *is* too late. . . . Please go away, darling. Please!" Her voice changed abruptly. "Thanks, there's nothing left to be done, Sam, but you can start eating now if you like. Ham or cheese. Fruit for dessert. Beer in that cooler and soft drinks in that one. . . ."

"Beer sounds good," said Miranda, who'd come u) behind me.

"I'll get a couple," I said.

When I returned, Frances had moved off. Miranda was looking after her, frowning a little. "That intellectual lady takes her tour duties seriously," she said. "You'd think she was catering a grand society banquet instead of just supervising a lousy little picnic."

I said, "I think we have trouble coming up, Matson. Keep your eyes open, will you?"

"Drunk or sober, I always do," she said. "Drunk if I can manage. You like her, don't you?"

"Nobody's wife is safe when I'm around," I said sourly. "Swill your damn beer and shut up."

But in spite of my premonitions of disaster, it turned out to be quite a pleasant picnic on the bank of the *cenote,* and if there were any virgins' bones at the bottom of it, their owners did not arise to haunt us.

Frances said that, actually, this pool had been a disappointment to the divers. Apparently it had not served any serious sacrificial purposes. For important religious festivals, she said, the local residents had apparently made the pilgrimage to the central ceremonial area of Copalque. A paved road had been built for them to travel on even though, she reminded us, the wheel had not yet been invented in this hemisphere, and the horse would not arrive until the Spaniards came a few thousand years later. A small part of the road had now been cleared and restored to give visitors an idea of its construction, she said, and there was a rather interesting arch through which ceremonial processions used to pass. For those who cared to settle their lunches with a short hike, it was about a mile. . . .

Leaving behind Miranda, who was waiting for word from the vanished Ramiro Sanchez, and the elderly Hendersons, who said they'd rather nap under a tree, the rest of us set off, pausing to be shown a ruin called the Monastery set upon a small hillock, and an underground watercistern with a catch-basin that funneled the rain into it during the wet season. There were several such around, Frances said, to supplement the community's main water supply, the *cenote*.

The arch itself was a large rectangular monument vaguely resembling the Arch of Triumph; but the opening in it was the customary corbeled arch, meaning that it was a blunt inverted V kept from collapsing simply by the sheer weight of rubble and stone holding the masonry in place, with no tricky engineering principles involved. It was, however, handsomely decorated, and it looked quite spectacular all alone out there in the jungle, straddling the wide stone road. The foot trail to it was the one I'd seen before lunch from the top of the pyramid.

"Where did all these names come from?" I asked Frances as we retraced our steps, heading back toward the Labal clearing and the waiting Jeeps. "The Citadel, the Monastery, the Arch of the Emperors. Is that what the Melmecs called them?"

Frances shook her head. "We don't really know what the Melmecs called them. In many cases we just adopted the names used by the locals who knew about these ruins. Otherwise, well, we just made them up for purposes of reference."

Her voice was steady enough, but her pale face was damp and shiny, although the day was not very hot. She was clearly under terrible strain, and her eyes would not look at me. Okay, it was getting close, whatever it was.

As we once more approached the ruin called the Monastery, I fell back, letting one of the schoolteachers, McElder, take over the place of honor beside Frances. Making like a photographer, camera at the ready, I scrambled up the man-made hill to the ruin; but that was not high enough. I found a place near the rear, where the heavy wall of the building had crumbled, leaving a nasty slope of rubble which I didn't trust a bit; but it let me gain six or eight feet of additional elevation, enough to see over the surrounding jungle.

I looked toward the Citadel and ducked hastily. A man was up there with binoculars, staring my way expectantly, obviously stationed there to warn somebody the moment he saw us returning. He had a weapon slung over his shoulder. Crouching low against the ruined wall, I studied the rest of the visible terrain. They'd put an armed guard at the Jeeps—actually he was one of our original drivers, but he was now holding another U.S.-type firearm in his hands. As I watched he took cover hastily. So did the man on the pyramid high above him. . . .

Frances and her entourage were obviously approaching the clearing. Frances would be chatting brightly and knowledgeably, I reflected, to keep her charges from sensing the trap into which she was leading them. *Don't ever hate me,* she'd said; and I realized that she'd known this was coming when she said it. I drew a long breath and slid down from there, considering the alternatives, but there were no alternatives.

Warning the group to flee was useless; where would a bunch of mostly middle-aged people flee to? Even if we were willing to leave Miranda and the Hendersons, we were not equipped for either defense or jungle survival. And the chances of my getting clear alone to summon assistance were also minimal. Escape along the single road was unlikely if they'd taken any precautions at all. I didn't particularly fear the jungle, but I knew damn well that without a machete I'd never make my way through fifteen-odd miles of the tangled, thorny stuff to help, even assuming that there was help to be found back at the hotel. Besides, when they counted their catch they'd know I was missing; and it was their jungle, not mine. With strong machete-men out ahead to clear the way, they'd run me down within a mile.

I had to assume that an immediate wholesale massacre was not intended. Better to walk into the trap, then, apparently dumb and unaware, hoping for a break later, than to be dragged back by the scruff of the neck of perhaps shot in flight. I looked around and found a hole under a fallen block of dressed stone and shoved the revolver and holster into it, thankful for the clip arrangement that let me slip it all off without having to pull the belt through the undersized loops of my bargain jeans. I remembered the bag of spare cartridges and laid that with the weapon. I shouldered the camera bag again, spent a moment memorizing the spot, and slid down the little hill, but stopped and turned my back to the path and opened my fly as footsteps hurried toward me. When Jim Putnam came into sight, looking annoyed and impatient, I was just zipping myself up again.

"Frances sent me back to see if you'd broken a leg," he said accusingly.

I said, "Hell, can't a man stop to take a picture and a leak if he wants to?"

It must have startled and frightened her to find me missing. Knowing that I was armed, she'd be terribly afraid that I'd louse things up for her by some drastic action, even though it could hardly be successful against the firepower that probably awaited us. I followed Putnam along the path, wondering if I should warn him, but I didn't know him that well. With all those Vietnam war medals, he could be a compulsive hero who, with a little advance notice, would dream up something that would get him killed and others with him. Besides, he was an ex-combat-type, dammit; he should have sensed the ambush himself, without being warned.

I just hiked along behind him briskly therefore, and we rejoined the waiting group. Frances was very careful not to meet my eyes. She set off again; and we emerged from the shadowy jungle path into the sunlit clearing and strolled innocently toward the waiting Jeeps. Miranda and the Hendersons were no longer visible by the pool, but nobody seemed to notice.

"If anybody needs a Coke or a beer or something after that walk, we can take a little break," Frances said. Her voice was admirably controlled. "No? In that case, let's take a look at the two buildings over here. The massive temple out in the middle of the plaza is called the Chapel; but let's first examine the long low building on this side, on that raised platform beyond the *cenote*. It's a series of small chambers, and we don't really know what they were used for; but above each doorway you'll find a well-preserved carving of a different stylized animal. There's even one we suspect of being a forerunner of the Feathered Serpent of the Aztecs, although the cult of Quetzalcoatl didn't really appear until much later." She was speaking rapidly and tonelessly, like a talking doll. "We call the building the Nunnery; but as I was just telling Sam, you shouldn't take all these names too seriously, most of them have no historical significance. . . ." She looked back to check on us as she walked. A puzzled frown came to her face and she stopped and turned. "Ramiro, what in the world? . . ."

Half a dozen men had stepped out of the brush at the side of the clearing as we passed. Their leader, Sanchez, was no longer our natty, rather pompous civilian guide; he was a full colonel in the revolutionary army. The eagles on the collar of his khaki shirt said so; but the fact that he'd taken time to change his clothes for this big moment indicated that his officer act would probably be just as pompous as his guide act. He was wearing a Sam Browne belt supporting a husky Browning 9 mm automatic pistol.

The slender young man beside him, handsome and delicately moustached in the way that usually indicated a would-be lady-killer—he could have been a Latin stand-in for Errol Flynn—was also more or less uniformed in khaki and also carried the thirteen-shot Browning status symbol. It seemed to be a popular weapon in these parts. The other four men were armed with plebeian M16s and less formally dressed.

Six here, I thought, and the six Jeep drivers, and the man on the pyramid if he's still there, and probably a sentry or two to block the road and the trail. It was just as well that I hadn't tried to take them on with a five-shot .38. Even with a few spare cartridges, I'd have run out of ammo before I could finish them all off.

Ramiro Sanchez cleared his throat. "I regret this very much, Señora Dillman, but you and your friends are all under arrest as enemies of the revolution," he said. "You should not have allowed yourselves to become pawns of the reactionary American criminals of the CIA who support the fascist murderer Armando Rael. Please stand very still and hold your hands up. Resistance will have very unfortunate consequences, I assure you."

Like I'd expected, pompous.

CHAPTER 21

THERE followed, of course, the usual you-can't-do-this-to-me nonsense session. In such a situation, there are always people in any group who feel compelled to announce loudly that nobody's going to push *them* around, no sirree, even while it's happening. Particularly while it's happening.

White-haired, red-faced Marshall Wilder, the insurance man, said they couldn't do this to him; and his rather handsome black-haired wife Betty agreed shrilly that they couldn't do it to her, either. Thin, intense, gray-haired Pat Tolson, highschool teacher, informed everybody that she was an American citizen and our ambassador would have something to say about it, which showed, I thought, a touching faith in the U.S. Foreign Service. Her stouter, calmer friend Peggy McElder, made of less stern—or less stupid—material, pleaded with her to be quiet, couldn't she see that those men had *guns?*

Big blond Paul Olcott, advertising man and sportsman, knowing firearms and very much aware of the multiple gun-muzzles looking our way, silenced his statuesque blond wife Elspeth when she started to voice her angry objections to the proceedings. Plump, dark Howard Gardenschwartz, the college professor, looked mildly apprehensive and kept his mouth shut. I saw his peasant gray-haired wife Edith, also commendably silent, find his hand and grasp it tightly. Dark Jim Putnam, wealthy disturbed war vet, like Olcott very much aware of the M16s he knew better than any one else in our party, had a protective arm about his sturdy young wife, who'd glanced toward him for guidance and, like him, said nothing.

But the Wilders and the Tolson woman were making enough outraged noises to go around, until a shattering burst of sound silenced them briefly. The thin-moustached young officer beside Sanchez, at Ramiro's command, had grabbed an automatic weapon from the man beside him and let off a burst, aiming high but not too high. I thought I could hear the cracking sound of the speedy little .223 projectiles passing overhead, although you usually don't, so close; the muzzle blast drowns it out.

"*Silencio!*" Ramiro snapped. "You are my prisoners; you will obey! I order you to be quiet and raise your hands!"

Wilder shouted, "Who the hell do you think you are, anyway?"

They always ask them who the hell they think they are, anyway, and how the hell they think they can get away with it, anyway; and they almost always earn themselves a bullet in the guts, a sap across the head, or a gun butt in the teeth—the last being the reward won by Marshall Wilder for his heroic defense of the principle of free speech. The officer who'd fired the warning burst stepped forward; and Wilder went down with a broken, bloody mouth. His wife dropped to her knees beside him and screamed hysterical abuse at Sanchez until the young man with the M16, at his colonel's nod, stepped forward again. His body blocked the view, but a dull thunk let us know that she'd taken the gun butt alongside the head.

That took care of the protest movement. Even the Tolson woman, displaying a little sense at last, fell silent. If I seem unsympathetic, it's because that kind of loud-mouthed bravery always seems so damn pointless to me; even if you've got courage to burn, why not save it until it counts? Frances had gone to her knees beside Wilder, producing Kleenexes to wipe his blood-dripping chin. She seemed to be getting into a rut of cleaning up the gory wounded, but at least she'd come better supplied today; she had a whole little packet of the stuff.

Nearby, Mrs. Wilder sat up dazedly, her dark hair—suddenly it was quite obvious that she dyed it—straggling about a face that had suddenly gone old and ugly with pain. She held the side of her head and rocked back and forth, moaning. The young Latin Errol Flynn type who'd done the damage handed the M16 back to the man from whom he'd taken it and stationed him to watch the casualties.

"Line up!" Ramiro snapped at the rest of us, indicating where he wanted us. "Right there. Hands remaining in the air while Lt. Julio Barbera, here, my second in command, examines for weapons. The ladies will excuse that we have no matron." His anger was interfering with his tour-guide English. He turned his look on me. "Señor Felton."

"Yes, Colonel?" I said respectfully.

Respect is cheap and, particularly when they belong to armies without official standing, they do love to hear their titles spoken.

Sanchez said harshly, "We know who you are, a dangerous man, si? So you will come over to this spot, here, and this man, here, will have you as his personal responsibility. . . . Shoot him if he moves, Eugenio!"

"Si, mi colonel!" The soldier, a chunky brown man with a badly scarred cheek, seemed enthusiastic about the idea.

The special treatment was causing my fellow tour-members to eye me oddly, wondering just what kind of a dangerous man I was. Handsome young Lieutenant Barbera, under the eyes of his colonel, did an elaborate job of searching me, doing the armpits, waist, crotch, and ankles, but missing the funny belt buckle. He was really more concerned with humiliation than exploration; he'd have missed a neck-knife, too, if I'd been wearing one. But hardly a gun.

Pronouncing me clean, after a quick and questioning glance toward his superior officer that let me know he'd been expected to find something, he went on to deal with the rest of the party. I noted that Frances was subjected to the same treatment as the rest of us; of course they wouldn't want to point suspicion her way by leaving her out. Colonel Sanchez gave an order, and a man ran off in the direction of the *cenote*. Presently the Hendersons and Miranda emerged from the brush over there and came to join us, guarded by several of the Jeep drivers, now all armed. Sanchez waited while Barbera did a final, lingering, hands-on job on Gloria Jean Putnam that made her husband's fists close tightly and the little muscles work along his jaw; then Sanchez summoned his lieutenant back to his side.

"Now you will listen, all of you," Sanchez said. "Serious crimes have been committed against the people of Costa Verde. As American citizens whose government supports the brutal dictatorship that oppresses us, you are all guilty of these crimes. But here we are not concerned with your general responsibility, and that of your government, for the evils of the present regime. We have specific charges to make against you, as accomplices of two CIA criminals sent to sabotage and destroy the work of the revolution. Those criminals stand there!"

Barbera had come up to Miranda; now he gave her a sudden shove that sent her stumbling toward me. I had to catch her and steady her, while Ramiro Sanchez pointed at us accusingly.

"This man who calls himself Felton and pretends to be a photographer is actually a CIA agent—a CIA murderer— sent by your government to assist the criminal Armando Rael by eliminating one of the leaders of the liberation movement, Ricardo Jimenez, whom you knew as Dick Anderson. And the woman beside him, Matson, who pretends to be a journalist, is actually his associate who has been supplying him with the information necessary to his campaign of assassination." He glared at me. "Well, Señor Felton, or whatever you call yourself truly, what have you to say?"

I said, "Colonel, if I am an expert assassin, I must be the slowest and most inefficient one on record. I've had the best part of a week to deal with a helpless, handicapped young man and he's still alive."

"Do you deny working for the CIA?"

"Yes."

"We have evidence——"

"I didn't say I didn't work for the United States Government."

"You are quibbling, señor!" Outside the U.S., if you do anything for the government, if it's sneaky and unpleasant, you're automatically considered CIA, since it's the only undercover agency they've heard of. "Do you deny that the woman beside you is your government accomplice, sent to assist you?"

I said, "Miss Matson is an old friend and fellow journalist, that's all. She got in touch with me in Santa Rosalia when she saw my name on a publicity release. . . ."

"And followed you here to Copalque for old times' sake, no doubt! And is now trying to use her position as a reporter to locate our revolutionary headquarters for you —and Ricardo Jimenez, the man you have come to kill!" He didn't wait for my response, but turned slightly to address the others: "As I have demonstrated, whether

159

knowingly or unknowingly, you have allowed yourselves to become involved in criminal counterrevolutionary activities. For this you could be put to death, all of you. However, since it is possible that you were merely unwitting pawns of this man and his vicious agency, you will not be executed if certain fines are paid." Sanchez stared at them bleakly for a moment, and went on: "The penalty for your offenses against the revolution is one million dollars to be paid into our treasury by Señor James Putnam, since we know he has adequate funds available. How he chooses to be reimbursed by the rest of you is his concern, not ours."

There was a long silence. I could hardly keep from bursting out laughing; it was a ridiculous anticlimax. He'd had me scared for a while. Fanatics frighten me, and I'd thought him the genuine, dedicated, patriotic, revolutionary article. But old *bandidos* die hard; and his master, Lupe of the Mountain, was still as much outlaw as liberator, just as I'd warned Ricardo. Old Million-Buck Montano; and how much of the ransom would really go to the revolutionary cause?

Looking back, I understood better some of the things that had happened on this trip. It was clear that, somehow, Frances had let Sanchez or Montano or a go-between know that there was a very wealthy individual taking the tour; or perhaps all the conspicuous jewelry had led them to inquire about Jim Putnam. It had probably not seemed important to Frances at the time. She'd always been reasonably well off herself, and other people's money didn't impress her. Smuggling Ricardo into the country and keeping an eye on me, according to instructions, had presumably been her major concerns. Under duress, she'd cooperated with the revolutionaries to this extent; but I was willing to bet that kidnaping and extortion had not been in the original bargain she'd made with them.

My guess was that the night she'd come to my cottage bruised and half-hysterical had been the night she'd learned that our whole party was to be held for ransom. She'd been slapped down so humiliatingly, not as she'd claimed for reacting arrogantly to Lupe's insulting comments, but for protesting against the betrayal that was now being required of her. . . .

"A million dollars!" That was the irrepressible Miss Tolson. "You've got to be out of your mind! After I pay for this trip I'll have exactly three hundred in the bank until my next . . ." She fell silent abruptly as Barbera took a step in her direction.

"Well, Señor Putnam?" Sanchez said. "I believe your finances are handled by the Putnam Management Corporation, a Chicago firm. Will you be sensible and write them voluntarily, or do you insist on being coerced?" Deliberately, Sanchez pulled the 9 mm pistol out of its army-type holster. "Need I remind you that you are very vulnerable, señor? It would be a pity if your pretty wife, such a healthy and attractive young lady, were to spend the rest of her life limping badly as the result of a bullet-smashed knee."

Whoever started this kneecapping business—I've heard he was an IRA Irishman—should have patented it and got rich; it's getting as popular as the Frisbee. Gloria Jean started to speak quickly, obviously to plead with her husband, but checked herself and stood stiff and silent. Putnam tightened the arm he'd placed about her shoulders; and spoke to Sanchez.

"It will take time. A week, ten days, maybe more. Chicago is a long ways off, and we don't keep a million dollars in the ready cash. You'll probably want it in particular kinds of currency, anyway."

"We have the time. And you are—how do you put it?— stalling, señor. Perhaps this will persuade you that I am serious about this matter!"

He lifted the pistol, and I saw Putnam pull his wife to him and turn sharply to interpose his body between her and the weapon; but Sanchez wheeled and fired twice. Beside me, Miranda gave a surprised little gasp as the bullets struck. She slumped to the ground. I went to my knees beside her, seeing the two small reddening holes just below the washed-out stencil that gave the name and unit of the previous owner of her worn military coverall. Her faded blue eyes looked up at me, hurting, knowing, dying.

She licked her lips and started to speak, but I never heard her last words, if any. My chunky watchdog, who'd been told what to do if I moved, went into action. Something exploded against my head and I went out, not really knowing whether I'd been shot or clubbed.

CHAPTER 22

I awoke in a shadowed place remembering sunshine. The change was startling enough to make me sit up abruptly, very much afraid that it was my vision that was clouded, not my surroundings.

The movement sent agony through my head, but the view was reassuring. I was in a shallow cave of sorts—a man-made cave for a change, I realized after a moment. It was a small stone chamber with a high wedge-shaped ceiling; another of the Melmec corbeled-arch jobs. There was a similarly shaped doorway with sunlight outside. I was not alone in the place.

"Careful, you got a bad knock on the head." I was aware of the big yellow boots and the flounced yellow skirt; then Gloria Jean Putnam was kneeling beside me, dabbing at the side of my neck. Something had changed about her and after a moment I realized what it was: the patriotic liberation movement had relieved her of her necklace and silver bracelets; they'd also taken her concha belt, leaving her shirt hanging loose outside her skirt. All done with the highest ideological motives, no doubt, I reflected grimly. Gloria Jean said, "The scalp cut isn't serious, it's almost stopped bleeding, but you could have a bit of concussion."

I tried to speak but my mouth was too dry. I licked my lips and got something out: "Where? . . . "

"You're in our cell, cell number four, in the Labal Detention Center, formerly known as the Nunnery. The ventilation is swell, but the facilities are kind of lousy and I think we've got a couple of good-sized lizards for company." The girl's voice was humorously resigned. "Just in case you're wondering, we got you because nobody else wanted you, and Jim was too softhearted to leave you lying there. You're not very popular right now, Sam Felton, or whatever your real name is."

I tried to assimilate all that, finding it a bit puzzling in view of the fact that softheartedness was not a characteristic I would have attributed to James Wallace Putnam.

I remembered something. "Miranda?" I whispered.

"I'm sorry, your friend is dead."

"I know, but . . ."

"Jim and some of the others are burying her right now, under military escort." She licked her lips, studying my face. "Mr. Felton, or whoever you are?"

"Yes?"

"I understand how you feel. But please don't get Jim mixed up in any wild get-even schemes."

"Forty percent," I said.

"What?"

"You read the papers. Down here in Latin America holding people for ransom is the great local sport, like drug-smuggling around Florida. And how many of those kidnaped are never seen again, alive, even if the money is paid? Somebody told me that the hostage-recovery rate is about forty percent. I wouldn't have put it that high myself."

The girl licked her lips again. "You mean you think they might actually kill us?"

"The killing's already started. My bet is that Miranda was shot deliberately, not only as an object lesson, but because she was the most dangerous of us in one respect: She was the one who could really blacken the name of the liberation movement, with her press connections, by letting the whole world know about their little sideline in kidnaping for money. Which seems to indicate that it's unlikely the rest of us will be turned loose to talk once Lupe has his million bucks. Unknown bandits from the hills did the dastardly deed; and anybody who says different is simply parroting the foul slanders invented by the Rael dictatorship to discredit the revolution." I shook my head. "At the moment we're being preserved because they may need Jim's further cooperation; but in the long run . . . well, even if Frances is right and the *cenote* wasn't used as a depository for dead bodies before, there's always a first time. It's a nice deep pool. So I think a little enterprise on our part is indicated, Mrs. Putnam, risky though it may be. . . ."

A shadow darkened the doorway. "What's risky?" Jim

Putnam asked. "Here, grab one of these mattress pads, honey, before I lose my grip on it. I think that corner back there, don't you? We're going to wish we had a mosquito bar like at the hotel before we're through. . . . Incidentally, they've gone through our bags and grabbed all the rest of the jewelry, the larcenous bastards—your cameras, too, Felton—but thank God they didn't steal the 'Off.' "

"We have our luggage?" I asked. "Here?"

Putnam nodded. "Yes, your bag's outside. Apparently we're all checked out of the hotel and our tour bus was seen taking us away—well, a load of people unidentifiable behind all that dark glass—in a totally different direction. But at least they're providing a roof and something to sleep on; they may even break down and feed us occasionally before they shoot us. After the money gets here, of course." He looked at me hard. "That's why I hauled you in here; I thought we'd better talk the situation over. Maybe it would even be a good idea if you moved in with us."

"And maybe not," I said.

He frowned and nodded. "On second thought, you could be right. In that case we'd better get our talking done right now." Stripped of his metallic adornments, like his wife, he looked like a lean, dark stranger. There was more animation in his face than I'd seen on the trip so far. He squatted beside me. "Okay, we'd better make it quick, Sam. We don't want them thinking we're holding a council of war in here, even if we are. Let's have your thoughts on getting away. Is that what you were telling Glory was risky?"

I looked at him for a moment and spoke carefully: "Getting away is no problem, amigo. Hell, it's only fifteen-some miles back to the hotel, with a passable road all the way. Even if they take away all the Jeeps, we can walk it. It's not as if we were on a desert island, or as if they'd dropped us by helicopter a hundred miles out in the jungle."

He was studying me, frowning. "But——"

I said, "You're worrying about the wrong thing. To hell with getting away. That will take care of itself, once certain preliminaries are disposed of."

Gloria Jean was puzzled. "I don't understand, Sam. What preliminaries?"

I waited and saw what I'd been waiting for. Jim Putnam's dark face broke into a crooked smile; not a very nice crooked smile.

"Where have you been all my life, friend?" he asked softly. "I could have used a few characters like you in a certain war, not to mention at a certain court-martial."

"Hell, they turned you loose, didn't they?" I said deliberately. "What did you expect, daddy, a medal?"

He looked a little startled; then he grinned ruefully, the first time I could recall seeing him smile. He said, "Well, actually I did, kind of. We'd performed very well, militarily speaking. I was naive back in those days. As company commander, I thought my job was to bring my company back alive and to hell with the enemy. I didn't realize I was supposed to bring the enemy back alive and to hell with my company."

I said, "So the dead Vietnamese lady had a baby under her garment instead of the grenade somebody thought she had when they blasted her. And there was a sentimental war correspondent handy."

He made a face. "Well, not quite like that, but something like that." After a moment he went on, "I'd seen too damn many men in my outfit hesitate and die—good men —but they'd been ordered to be careful. There had been too much adverse publicity back home. . . . Well, you remember. I was sick of it. Hell, it was a war, wasn't it, not a Sunday turkey-shoot in the park? So I gave the orders. I told them, when in doubt, shoot, shoot *now*, and I'd take full responsibility for any mistakes. And I did." He frowned at me. "Why the hell am I telling you this?"

I said, "Because it looks as if we might have a little work to do together, and each of us wants to know that he's not going to lose his life because the other guy got all tangled up in tender humanitarian principles at the wrong moment. . . . What the hell is that?" There was a lot of noise outside.

"Just a minute, I'll look," Putnam said. He moved out of the door of the stone chamber; after a moment he returned to us. "Sanchez is heading out with the Jeeps and drivers; he's left that slimy young bastard Barbera with half a dozen uniformed men to hold the fort."

I said, "I'll be glad when they settle down to a routine so we know what we have to deal with."

Putnam nodded and started to speak, but Gloria Jean interrupted. "I wish you two would let me know what you're talking about. Even though I'm positive I'm not going to like it."

Putnam hesitated and said reluctantly, "What Sam means, honey, is that getting away from here is no problem —once Sanchez and his men are dead."

She got quite pale. "But . . . but that's a horrible idea! You can't just set out to slaughter——"

"Can't you?" I asked harshly. "I can. And if we were to take a vote on it, how do you think Miranda would have cast her ballot?" I looked at Putnam. "Tell me what you'd need, Jim."

"Me?"

But the surprised note in his voice didn't ring quite true; he'd done some thinking about it already. There was an odd gleam in his eyes I hadn't seen before. The man was coming back to life.

"Who the hell else?" I asked. "I'm the lone-wolf type; I couldn't handle an operation like this. Who's the gallant leader of men around here, anyway? It's your baby, Captain Putnam, sir. Now, assuming you had a few moderately competent guys to work with, what would you want to put into their hands, of the stuff you've seen out there. Minimum."

He didn't hesitate. "Minimum? Three of the M16s and three or four of the grenades those characters have pinned all over them. That's assuming surprise, good planning, and lots of luck. And also assuming that Sanchez doesn't come back with a whole revolutionary regiment, in which case all bets are off. I'd like more, but it can be done with that. Any sidearms you can pick up in addition will be greatly appreciated."

I said, "Okay, that's my job, procurement. Midnight requisitions, I believe they used to be called. Your assignment is to study them, right? Learn all their routines and habits. Any time of day or night I bring the guns, you be ready with a suitable plan that'll let us wipe them out without losing too many of our tourists. . . ."

"Jim!"

The interruption annoyed him. He started to speak angrily; then he checked himself and put a hand on his wife's arm. "It's what I was doing on the other side of the

Pacific, honey," he said. "You knew that, you came to terms with it, remember? What makes it so much worse here? Now, please, let Sam and me finish up before somebody comes to see what we're plotting in here." He looked at me. "Who?"

"Henderson and Olcott."

He frowned. "Henderson's pretty old, and not too well."

"Don't send him up any pyramids, then. And you'll have to treat him diplomatically because he outranks hell out of you. But he was a jungle fighter back when you were bruising other kids' fists with your nose in that fancy school they undoubtedly sent you to, if you did such a crude and lower-class thing as fight with the other little rich boys."

"I did," he said with a grin. "Olcott? He hunts, doesn't he?"

"His specialty is mountain sheep, which means that he can climb, he can stalk, and he can shoot. Whether or not he can shoot a man remains to be seen; some of them can't. But I don't think we can afford to pass up an expert marksman."

Putnam said thoughtfully, "I wouldn't want to trust a gun in the hands of that blowhard Wilder. What about Gardenschwartz?"

"The information I have is that he and his wife are members of a couple of Hate-the-Handgun groups. Their privilege; but my experience indicates that people who want to prohibit guns generally don't know much about shooting them."

"Just four of us, then." He glanced at me. "You've been doing your homework, haven't you?"

"Call me Boy Scout for short, always prepared."

"You're mixed up, son, it's the Coast Guard that are *Semper paratus.*"

I grinned. "And now I think you'd both better hate me a little," I said. "Ostracized, that's me, the wicked guy responsible for this whole dreadful predicament. Sanchez deliberately turned you all against me; well, that's great, stay turned. They know what I am, they'll have their eyes on me, so you and Gloria Jean will have to make all the contacts and arrangements. Just pretend that I don't exist and that you wouldn't want to be contaminated by knowing me if I did exist. But have things ready to move when I produce the armaments. I may need some help with that once I've got it figured out. If I do, I'll get in touch. One more thing. Well, two more to be exact."

"Yes?"

I got up carefully, and waited for my head to stop pounding, and looked down at the two of them sitting there. "We're harmless," I said. "Keep that in mind every minute of every day. We're scared like rabbits. After seeing Miranda shot down like that we're broken, browbeaten, docile like sheep. No spunk, no defiance. No matter what happens, repeat, no matter *what* happens, we don't fight back until we have something effective to fight with. Console yourselves with the thought that when the time comes we'll totally eradicate the bastards; but in the meantime we let the others make their grandstand plays all over the place, but the four of us who're going to do the work don't get ourselves beat up so we can't fight, or shot up, or locked up, or tied up, not if we can possibly help it. Pass the word. We eat all the shit they offer us and ask for more: *mas mierda, por favor.* It could be a week, it could be much longer, but that's the way we handle it, no matter how long it takes. Okay?"

They nodded. Gloria Jean, who seemed to have resigned herself to our plans, asked, "And the other thing?"

"Don't trust anybody you don't have to," I said. "If Henderson and Olcott feel they have to tell their wives you can't stop them; but there's no need for anybody else to know what we're hoping to do. That goes for the Wilders, the Gardenschwartzes, the two schoolteachers, and even Frances Dillman. All it takes is one peace-loving character who starts a big loud argument with one of us about the virtues of patience and nonviolence, and all our work to maintain a low profile is shot to hell." I thought I'd done it pretty well, throwing Frances's name casually into the pot like that. "Well, we'd better break this up."

Jim said, "I think there's an empty apartment a few doors down; let me give you a hand with . . . No, that's right, we hate you, you sneaky CIA sonofabitch. Haul your ass to hell out of here and I hope next time they knock your lousy brains out."

"Please, Mister, I didn't mean to make no trouble for all you nice people. . . ."

I saw Gloria Jean, watching us, stop smiling and look

quickly toward the door as the light was suddenly diminished by a human body—four human bodies, as it turned out. Lt. Errol Flynn, otherwise known as Julio Barbera, was there with three armed men.

"You!" he said to me. "You can walk now, si? You will pick up your belongings outside and go with this man, here. He will show you where you must stay. And this time, if you move too rapidly, he *will* shoot you."

I saw that it was the same scarred, chunky man, Eugenio, who'd clobbered me earlier. I moved forward as he gestured with his weapon; but I heard Julio Barbera's voice behind me:

"And you, beautiful señora, you will come with me. . . . Tell your husband to stand still unless you wish him to die!"

Eugenio poked me in the back as I hesitated. The sunlight was very bright outside. We emerged on the long raised platform, a dozen feet above the clearing, that held the Nunnery we'd never got around to exploring, that was now our home away from home. It was simply a long, low, narrow stone building consisting of a series of cubicles like the one from which I'd just emerged: kind of a tourist court thousands of years old. From up here you got a good view of the blue water of the *cenote*, at the edge of the jungle; and you could look down a little on the ground-level Chapel, in the center of the clearing; and up at the Citadel on the far side, on its much higher pyramid. A sentry lounged carelessly against one of the ancient stone pillars up there.

"No, Jim, no!"

It was Gloria Jean's voice, breathless and pleading. I waited for shots, but none came. Eugenio poked me with his M16, and I picked up my suitcase and the thin ragged mattress-pad that had apparently been issued to me *in absentia.* I was aware of the girl emerging from the chamber behind me as I moved away, her arm gripped firmly by Lieutenant Barbera, although she was offering no resistance. In fact she was walking quite steadily beside him, holding herself very straight. She didn't look back at all.

After a moment, the other two soldiers who'd come with Barbera backed out of the chamber warily, guns ready, and took up stations from which they could cover the doorway. I drew a breath of relief. The precautions seemed to indicate that Jim Putnam was still alive in there. . . . Eugenio poked me again, indicating the last little doorway down the line. I crouched and started inside, but stopped as somebody moved in the shadows ahead of me.

"Oh, it's you," said Frances Dillman.

CHAPTER 23

GLORIA Jean Putnam returned to us just as the sun was setting behind the high Citadel ruins. She had to run the ghoul gauntlet, of course. They had all been waiting—okay, we had all been waiting—to receive her, solicitously ready for the worst, to cover up the poor outraged body revealed by the torn clothing, to minister to the poor battered face, to steady her as she stumbled, carry her when she could walk no further, sympathize fulsomely with her shame and suffering. . . .

She was a big disappointment to everybody. She simply came marching up the steep rubble slope to the Nunnery, holding herself as erect as when she'd left with Barbera, a strong, sturdy young woman getting along perfectly well under her own power, thanks. Her costume was intact and neatly buttoned and zipped. The dark frizzy hair was no wilder than usual.

Perhaps the face looked a bit pale and shiny, perhaps the mouth looked a bit swollen, perhaps there was a bruise on the temple, but in the fading light, with all that hair, it was hard to be sure. Perhaps she moved just a bit awkwardly, as if there were places that hurt, and certainly there was a stony look in her eyes as she passed without acknowledging our presence in any way; but it was clear from the undamaged condition of her clothes and her own lack of conspicuous injuries that she had undressed for the man obediently and done what was required, and allowed to be done to her what was required. She'd satisfied Barbera's demands well enough that he had not felt compelled to

170

abuse her further. Then, given permission, she'd cleaned herself up and dressed herself with care; and anybody who wanted a poor whimpering little rape victim for a pet could just go look elsewhere.

We watched the guards step back to let her go by. She disappeared into the fourth little doorway from the far end. I drew a long breath and moved back into my assigned chamber, the seventh and last, without looking at my assigned roommate. I sat down on my thin sleeping-pad with my back to the wall and wished, for the first time in a long time, that I had a pipe to smoke. After all, there were worse things than emphysema.

After a while I said, "Ten pieces of silver was the going rate two thousand years ago, but I hope you allowed for inflation."

Frances was hardly visible at the other side of the little room. She didn't react to my needling. She said, "You knew at the *cenote*, at lunch, what I was going to do. What was going to happen."

"Yes, sweetheart. As an actress, you're a hell of an archaeologist. And I'm not going to tell you."

"Tell me what?"

"Where I hid the gun. That's why they put you in here with me, isn't it? To keep an eye on me as before; and to find out where I hid the revolver and ammo you'd told them I had. A missing firearm can make people awfully nervous in a situation like this."

"You were in there with the Putnams for quite a while." Her voice even. "Did you tell them about me, about what I'd done?"

"No," I said. "I warned them against trusting certain people around here including you, that's all. One thing we don't need is a lynching party. What the hell do you think you're doing, Dillman? What does Montano have on you that gives him the power to order you around and slap you around as he pleases? Your passion for archaeology can't be all that compulsive; you can't be doing all this just to preserve your lousy dig."

She said, "You're really a pretty stupid man, aren't you, darling?"

I said, "Goody, does the fact that she's got around to insulting me indicate that she's going to break down and tell me the truth I've been pleading for for a week?"

She said, "Goddamn you, Sam, look at me! Don't you have any respect for me at all? Don't you know me well enough by now to know there's only one thing that could have forced me to do the things I've done? Can you really see me acting like this for money, or for a political cause, or even for my career—the Copalque excavations are important to me, certainly, but not *that* important! Not important enough for me to betray a lot of people who trusted me. . . ." She drew a deep and uneven breath. "Sam, when a married woman does strange and desperate and inexplicable things, what's the usual answer?"

I looked at the pale shape of her face in the growing dusk and realized how obtuse I'd been. "Your little girl, the one in the wheelchair?"

"I don't have any little girl, in or out of a wheelchair. That was just another of my lousy lies, to explain my concern for Ricardo Jimenez."

So much for the great detective. I guess when I studied the report on Frances Ransome Dillman I'd been looking for things that were there, not for things that weren't there, like a child she'd talked about but never had.

"So what's left, darling?" Her voice was insistent. "You really ought to be able to figure it out by now."

I said carefully, "I thought your husband was attending an important conference at Canyon de Chelly."

"That's what you were supposed to think," Frances said. "That's what everybody was supposed to think. Archie had one of his inspirations, something about the cave and the calendar wheel; and he just had to dash down here—he only planned to take an extended weekend—to recheck some inscriptions we'd only examined superficially. He didn't tell anybody but me because he didn't want to make his brainstorm seem too important in case it turned out to be nonproductive. The next thing I knew, there was an envelope in the mailbox with a little lump in it. I thought it was some kind of advertising, you know, where they send you a tiny pencil or something as a gesture of good will. When I opened it, I found a note." She was silent for a moment, clearly projecting the memorized message on the screen of her mind. She licked her lips and said, "It read: I AM BEING HELD PRISONER. TELL NOBODY. YOU WILL RECEIVE INSTRUCTIONS. PLEASE OBEY EXACTLY, REPEAT, *EXACTLY*, OR THEY WILL

172

KILL ME. MY LIFE IS IN YOUR HANDS. I LOVE YOU. ARCHIE."

Again there was silence in our little artificial cave. I found myself trying to assemble in my mind the jigsaw puzzle that was the unseen Archibald Dillman: the absent-minded professor who couldn't find his glasses on his nose, the gentle lover, the coward. Because only a coward would put "I love you" in a ransom note. Or "My life is in your hands." Those sentences had not been dictated by Montano, although he'd undoubtedly been glad to have them. They were the frightened husband reminding the loyal, loving wife of the duty she owed him, giving her no choice whatever because he was terrified for his life and wanted her to take no chances at all, no matter what the cost to her. They left her no alternative but total obedience to the kidnapers' demands.

"And the enclosure?" I asked.

She licked her lips. "A small plastic bag. There was a little scrap of . . . of flesh in it, all bloody. Dried, of course. I had to wash it off before I could identify it." She swallowed hard. "It was a human earlobe."

Outside I heard a Jeep drive up. I was glad of the excuse to move to the chamber opening. Looking down from our minor elevation, I saw the vehicle come to a halt in front of the Chapel, in which our captors had now established their headquarters. I recognized Colonel Ramiro Sanchez in the bounce of the headlights before they were turned off. There were four uniformed men with him.

That made it ten men and two officers total, I reflected, wondering if that was more than Putnam was prepared to handle with the armaments he'd requested. The trouble was, the way he was feeling at the moment, after what had been done to Gloria Jean, he'd probably be willing to charge the hordes of Attila the Hun with an aerosol can of roach killer. I had to hope he was professional enough not to let his military judgment be influenced by his personal feelings.

"Sanchez is back," I said, returning to sit on my rudimentary bed. Frances didn't speak. I said, "So you covered your husband's continued absence with the story that he was attending an important conference. And you didn't confide the truth to anybody. Then your instructions came: You were to include Ricardo Jimenez in your tour

173

group and make sure he entered Costa Verde unsuspected. Then you got further instructions: Get acquainted with me, seduce me, and find out if I was a danger to their plans. But finally Montano's bandit instincts got the better of him, and he decided to pull a wholesale abduction with your assistance. This time you balked, and he had to knock you around a bit before you'd agree to lead our whole group into the dead-fall. But in the end you did that, too."

She nodded. Her voice was dull when she spoke: "It wasn't . . . wasn't because of the way he hurt and humiliated me, Sam. I could have stood that. But don't you understand—you *must* understand—I'd done so much already. I'd already sacrificed my self-respect and my conscience to keep Archie alive. I just couldn't waste all that by refusing this last request."

"Where's your husband now?"

"With Montano and his so-called Army of Liberation. Somewhere not too far from here, wherever their main hideout is located."

I drew a long breath. "Is there anything you won't do for this Archie of yours, Dillman?"

Her voice came out of the gathering darkness. "No, Sam. Not anything. Not now, after all that's happened. I have to see it through, now. Maybe . . . maybe at the beginning, if I'd known what I'd have to do, what they'd be asking of me, all the awful things they'd be asking of me . . ."

I said dryly, "Awful things like sleeping with me."

I thought I saw her smile faintly in the gloom. "Awful things like sleeping with you, of course." I heard her draw a long breath, like a sigh. "As I just said, maybe if I'd known from the start how it would be, I could have refused and . . . and let it happen, let him die. But not now. I have too big an investment in it now. I've paid too much for it. I couldn't let it all go for nothing, everything I've done to save him. And he is my husband and I do love him dearly. No, Sam, I don't think there's any dirty thing in the world I wouldn't do to get him back unharmed. . . ."

She was interrupted by the sound of a loud voice down at the headquarters temple. Somebody was really catching hell down there in machine-gun Spanish. I couldn't make out the words that were being yelled, but they were ob-

174

viously blasphemous and derogatory and should have scorched the hair and shriveled the testicles of the person at whom they were aimed. Then a man, just a dark shape down there, went hurrying across the clearing to the big pyramid and started scrambling hastily up toward the Citadel on top.

A group of three figures, one with a light, moving more deliberately, started climbing the Nunnery slope toward us. As they came closer, I recognized Sanchez, with escort. He headed directly for the Putnams' cell and, when he reached it, dismissed the two guards stationed there and went inside. Presently he came out and marched along the row of little doorways to our opening and aimed his electric lantern toward me, briefly, and then toward Frances.

He spoke to her in formal tones: "I have come to apologize, señora, for what was done in my absence. I have already presented my profound regrets and apologies to the young lady chiefly concerned, and to her husband. Now I am addressing you as the director of this tour. What was done was not done with my knowledge or by my authority. The so-called officer who perpetrated the atrocity will spend the night on sentry duty on top of the pyramid while I consider what further disciplinary action to take. We are not animals, señora, we are men fighting for the liberation of our country."

Frances said, "Sometimes it's a little hard to tell the difference, Colonel."

"I have made my apology," he said stiffly. "And I assure you there will be no further molestation of the ladies. I apologize further for the fact that food and water have not yet been made available; they are being brought now. Sanitary facilities, unfortunately crude but I hope adequate, will be arranged on the far side of the building. There will be opportunity during the day for bathing and washing clothes. Later I will discuss the details with you, as the representative of the group."

Standing in the doorway, he was speaking loudly enough that his words undoubtedly carried to the other cells down the line, as he skillfully laid the groundwork for future consultations.

"As you wish, Colonel," Frances said.

He went on, "I will let you know the camp rules I expect your people to obey. You will have the opportunity to protest any that you feel will cause undue hardship or inconvenience. We do not intend that you should suffer while we all wait here. If there is anything further I can do for your comfort, please inform me. I am not a harsh man." He glanced at me briefly. "That is to say, I am not a harsh man unless I am provoked. But if you and your people cooperate in a reasonable manner, señora, I think you will find me reasonable also. And again, my apology for the shameful incident that took place in my absence."

He turned smartly and marched away, a clever man. Having earlier isolated me from the group, he was now announcing to the rest that they had nothing whatever to fear if they only behaved themselves, since their camp commandant was a fine, compassionate fellow who only shot people occasionally.

CHAPTER 24

THERE are times in practically every operation when things come to a tired halt and there's nothing to do but wait patiently for them to get moving again. Not that this was an official operation, aside from the Bultman angle that would have to wait until I had more information and was free to act on it, but the principle was the same.

After a few days in Labal it seemed as if we'd always been there, living in our row of doorless cubicles in the ancient ruin raised a little above the clearing and the jungle. There were sunny days and cloudy days and sometimes windy days. There were no rainy days, because this was the dry season. We ate the simple food that was brought to us and went around the ends of the Nunnery to dispose of the byproducts in the primitive fresh-air toilets that had been constructed for us—the toilet paper provided was the usual Latin-American variety noted for its total slick non-absorbency. We bathed (in bathing suits, modestly) in the cool water of the *cenote* and washed our clothes there, under guard, of course.

To my surprise, that liberated modern career woman, Dr. Frances Dillman, insisted on playing the old-fashioned feminine role and doing my laundry as well as her own. Perhaps she was impressing our captors with the intimacy of our relationship, or perhaps it was a simple gesture of defiance: If the other members of the group wanted to assume that we were lovers simply because we'd been stuck into the same cell, she'd wash out my lousy shorts and shirts in loving wifely fashion and give them all a real treat, the mouthy old gossips.

Or perhaps it was a gesture of apology because, as a matter of fact, ironically, we were no longer lovers now that we were sleeping in the same little room and it would have been easy. It was definitely not my idea. After a couple of nights of purity appropriate to the changed circumstances, I found myself having a perfectly normal male reaction to the presence of an attractive and already quite familiar female body in the darkness a mere six feet away from me. I moved that way hopefully to see if something could be done about it; but when she felt my touch she drew away. After a moment she sat up to face me. I could just make her out in the darkness. She was sleeping in a shirt and her legs were bare.

"I can't, Sam," she whispered. "I'm sorry, but I simply can't, not like this, not with everybody watching us all day and wondering how long it took me to take pity on your masculine needs and betray my husband; and how often we're doing it now. I want to be able to wash your dirty laundry and look them all in the eyes, knowing that they're all wrong in their dirty imaginings; and the fact that I'd already been unfaithful to Archie, with you, before we ever got here, is quite irrelevant. I don't know why, but that's the way it is." She reached out and touched my face with her fingertips. "Please? I know you can . . . persuade me if you really try. I'm not an iron woman. But please don't try; and I'll be as unprovocative and unsexy as I can. I know it's a lot to ask, my dear, with the two of us cooped up together like this, but I'd really rather not, if you can stand it." Then she laughed ruefully. "That sounds as if I thought I was irresistible, doesn't it?"

"You are," I said, "but I'll try to resist you anyway, since you ask so nicely."

It was a rather touching example of feminine irrationality, if you wanted to look at it one way. After all, by any logical standard, Professor Archibald Dillman had already been quite thoroughly betrayed by us, so what further harm could we do him now? Of course there were other ways of looking at it that made it seem not quite so touching; but there was nothing to be gained by confronting her with those. It was no time for confrontations. A low profile had been prescribed, by me. If I didn't take my own medicine, who would?

So we lived in chastity, with considerable self-control required on my part if not on hers. We ignored the knowing glances that were sent our way, particularly by the Wilders, who resented me bitterly, considering me—or pretending to consider me—the cause of all their troubles. There's never been a loud-mouth yet who could conceive that he could possibly have got himself slugged in his big loud mouth through any fault of his own. Under other circumstances, I would have felt sorry for the man with his smashed and swollen lips and the gaping emptiness behind them where much of the dental equipment in front had been destroyed. He had a hard time eating and great difficulty in making himself understood, lisping almost unintelligibly; but what he lisped was either obscene or threatening or complaining, so my sympathy soon faded.

His wife also complained, of constant headaches. She was heard to announce that it was a pity that I, responsible for everybody's sufferings, hadn't been shot instead of Miranda Matson. She had further expressed the loud opinion that any decent woman—any *decent* woman, mind you—would have died before allowing herself, as Frances had done in such a docile fashion, to be coerced in accepting such a shamefully compromising situation, particularly one involving a despicable creature like me. It was odd. They'd seemed like perfectly ordinary if not very interesting people until the pressure came on. I couldn't help wondering how many other perfectly ordinary people had that much vitriol—not to mention that much stupidity—penned up inside them.

I didn't take much stock in her headaches. She seemed to negotiate the Nunnery slopes without dizziness, she ate well and had no apparent trouble keeping it all down—the symptoms of concussion were nonexistent. But why should her husband get all the sympathy when she had suffered cruel violence also?

I didn't forget my primary duty; and gradually I worked out a few possible, if rather ambitious, scenarios—all they involved was employing my superhuman strength and diabolical cleverness to dispose of three or four armed men in total silence some convenient night. Nothing to it.

In the meantime, Lieutenant Barbera was undergoing punishment for his offense. It consisted of systematic humiliation. He took turns at sentry duty with the common soldiers and was even required to help them prepare and distribute the food. I suppose it suited the crime in a way, being a form of castration; but I wondered if Gloria Jean Putnam and her husband considered it adequate. They were tragically polite to, and considerate of, each other these days; it was easy to see that they hadn't come to terms with the disaster that had struck their marriage.

"I want to shake those poor damn kids sometimes." It was plump, gray-haired Emily Henderson, the general's wife, wearing a short yellow terrycloth robe over her flowered old-fashioned bathing suit, the kind with a little skirt —no bikinis or tank suits here. It was our bath-and-laundry hour, and we were sitting on the bank of the *cenote* watching the swimming and clothes-washing while a young revolutionary soldier with a thin face and an automatic rifle stood by uncomfortably like a shabby excop guarding the presents at a glittering society wedding. Mrs. Henderson went on crudely: "So somebody else got to put it where he'd been putting it, so what? It's not the end of the world. I'd like to give them a piece of my mind." She gave me a quick, sharp look. "And don't you dare tell me I can't spare it, young man!"

"You said it, I didn't," I said. "And thanks for the compliment."

"From where Austin and I sit, anything under sixty looks positively juvenile."

"Now you went and spoiled it," I said. "You had me feeling like a kid there for a moment. As for the Putnams, they're still in the ball game, so I think they're better left alone."

"What do you mean?"

"They'll make it," I said. "If they haven't said it by now, it'll never get said."

"What?"

"The thing that would finish them. She, hurt and shamed and weeping, blurts out: *Oh, God, why didn't you stop him, what kind of a husband are you?* And he, hurt and angry, snaps back: *Well, it doesn't look as if you put up such a great fight yourself, what kind of a wife are you?* That would have done for the marriage, but good. But even if they thought it, and I really doubt they did, they obviously held it back; they've got a good chance now."

Emily Henderson regarded me thoughtfully for a moment. "You're smarter than you look."

"That's not difficult."

She laughed. "You said it; I didn't." After a moment, and a quick glance around, she said, "Speaking of the Putnams, Jim wants to know when."

"Antsy, is he?"

"He's been ready for days."

"Who hasn't been? But the longer we wait, the more careless they get. It's hard to maintain strict guard discipline with nothing happening. And something could be happening over in Montano's camp to help us, although we can't count on it. Mostly, the weather's been too good the last few days. I'd like a night with a nice noisy wind to cover our operations." I glanced at her. "So the general took you into his confidence."

"Army wives always know everything, Sam. Incidentally, if there's an extra gun, I know how to use it."

"That comes as no surprise to me," I said. "I hope your husband doesn't mind the way we've set up the chain of command. Jim Putnam's military experience is more recent and the problem is more his size, if you know what I mean. We aren't dealing with armies here."

She laughed. "Austin is quite satisfied with the chain of command; he's not one of your rank-happy retired officers." She made a face. "He's . . . looking forward to it. Like an old firehorse. I hope the old fool doesn't kill himself, running around with a gun. His heart isn't all it should be." She glanced at me quickly. "I didn't mean that the way it sounded. And maybe you think I should be worried about his getting killed, instead. Well, the Japs tried it, and he made them wish they hadn't before he was pulled out with all those holes in him. So I'm not worried about a bunch of half-ass greaser revolutionaries, sonny." Her defiant voice said she was worried sick about it.

I nodded. "Tell Jim I'll move as soon as I get the right combination of weather and sentries."

"Yes. There's another thing. Some of the group have been snooping, asking questions. Like why doesn't a trained man like you *do* something instead of just marking time and fucking somebody else's wife. Could it be that you really have something up your sleeve and are acting harmless to dispel suspicion?"

"The Wilders?" I asked.

"And the Tolson woman, and her sidekick, McElder."

I said, "In any camp like this there are always people ready to pay off their grudges by carrying information to the prison authorities."

"I don't see why the Wilders are so mad at you. It wasn't you behind that gun butt."

"Ah, you don't understand the subtlety of it, ma'am. Getting mad at a man who has a gun, or lots of men who have lots of guns, is dangerous. It's much safer getting mad at a man without a gun, telling yourself he's the one *really* at fault." I grimaced. "And then there are the panicky ones who don't want to see the boat rocked the tiniest little bit, figuring we'll drift safely ashore if nobody, but nobody, disturbs the delicate balance. And then there are the real weirdos who undergo some kind of transference phenomenon in a captivity situation and begin to love their captors more than their fellow captives."

She was studying me carefully. "And how do you feel, Sam?"

I shrugged. "I have a very primitive reaction, doctor. Any time anybody points a gun at me and tells me to do something he has no right to tell me to do, I find my mind filled with one simple thought: *How do I kill this son-ofabitch?*"

She laughed softly. "And then there are the Gardenschwartzes," she said. "They keep to themselves pretty much. I'd put them in the don't-rock-the-boat category, but that's just a guess. And of course your attractive cellmate."

We both sat for a moment watching a slender white figure in a white one-piece bathing suit doing a businesslike crawl across the *cenote.*

181

"What about Frances?" I asked.

"She's spending a lot of time with Colonel Sanchez. People are noticing."

I spoke evenly: "She's the camp representative. He keeps sending for her to talk over our problems. And isn't it great that at least one of us has regular access to his HQ? If we didn't have a Frances to go down there regularly, we'd have to invent one to keep track of what's going on, wouldn't we?"

"Well, that's one way of looking at it." Mrs. Henderson was watching me steadily. "Are you, Sam?"

"Am I what?"

"Fucking her?"

I grinned. "At the moment, no, but I wouldn't want to try to get anybody to believe that."

"I believe it. You don't have the smug, self-satisfied look of a man who's getting his ashes hauled regularly."

I said, "My God, I haven't heard that phrase used since I was a boy. And you are a foul-mouthed old lady."

"I'm a smart old lady. I hope you're a smart young man. And I think you know what I mean without my drawing any blueprints for you."

Our eyes met for a moment, and I knew that this stout gray-haired woman knew everything about Frances Dillman she needed to know. She merely wanted to be sure I did, too, since her husband's life, not to mention her own, might depend on my having a clear head undisturbed by irrelevant sexual complications. It was strange, I reflected, just as the Wilders had turned into total human rejects under stress, so Mrs. Austin Henderson had been transformed into a rather intelligent and confidence-inspiring old lady.

The guard was moving our way now—they never liked to see any of us talking together too long—and I excused myself and picked up my towel and toilet kit and strolled away. The afternoon sunshine was warm and pleasant and the *cenote* was a beautiful spot and the people around it and in it looked like happy visitors to an expensive resort in their bright poolside costumes. I had a sense of unreality, knowing that the uneasy dark kid with the automatic weapon, finding the foreigners he was guarding totally incomprehensible and rather frightening, could easily misconstrue a perfectly innocent gesture and cut loose, in an instant turning the pleasant scene into a gory shambles. I heard quick footsteps behind me and paused to let Frances catch up.

"What were you and Emily talking about so earnestly?" she asked as we moved unhurriedly toward the Nunnery.

"She wanted to give the Putnams a piece of her mind," I said. "I told her not to waste it."

Frances hesitated and glanced at me sharply. "Sam, you're not . . . I mean, it would be stupid for a bunch of unarmed prisoners to plot some kind of a, well, jailbreak. When it's just a matter of time. After all, it's not really unbearable here, is it? And you don't know what that jungle is like. Even if a few did manage to get away, they'd just tear themselves to pieces trying to make headway through that stuff, and Ramiro would be bound to catch them and bring them back. And punish them. Particularly you. He's just waiting for you to . . . to make a false move, if you'll excuse the corny phrase. Don't let the others talk you into doing anything stupid, Sam. Just because I won't sleep with you . . . Well, I am fond of you, and I don't want to see you hurt."

I wondered if she really believed that we'd all be turned loose in the end to live happily ever after. But of course she had to believe it; she couldn't have lived with herself, after what she had done, believing anything else. But her warning confirmed what I'd heard from Mrs. Henderson: Somebody had alerted Colonel Sanchez to our plans.

I said, I hoped convincingly, "Sweetheart, I haven't the slightest intention of tackling that goddamned arid jungle out there. It happens that I know very well what it's like. I once carried out an operation through a similar garden of thorns and vines down near the coast not too far from here; but I had plenty of expert machete-type help and I'm quite aware that I wouldn't have got anywhere without it. Hell, it can't take too much longer for them to get their damn money and turn us loose, can it? Any word on the negotiations?"

She said, "I think the money is already in this country; but the intermediary sent down from Chicago doesn't like the specified method of delivery and is creating difficulties. And of course they've got to work very quietly so the authorities don't get wind of what's going on."

"Yes, I can see that Rael might not like to have the

rebels financed to the extent of a million bucks. Well, I hope they get it sorted out soon."

We fell silent as we climbed up to the Nunnery under the eye of the sentry—an eye which, I noted, seemed to be largely concerned with the nice picture made by Frances, who'd apparently, seeing me leaving, terminated her swim and slipped on her thin white robe without pausing to dry herself. Wet from her body, the garment now clung to her in a very interesting manner. We entered our cozy home and she started toweling her hair.

"Tell me about that jungle operation, darling," she said. "I didn't know you'd . . . worked here before."

"The guy's name was Jorge Santos," I said. "He called himself *El Fuerte*, the Strong One. He was the Lupe Montano of his time. I nailed him at a little over five hundred meters after my military escort moved me into position. Not a bad shot, if I do say so myself. We had a bit of a firefight breaking away."

There was a small silence. She'd stopped drying her hair, watching me, frowning slightly. "Why did you tell me that?" she asked.

"Hell, you asked."

She shook her head slightly. "No. You're trying to say something, Sam."

I said deliberately, "Maybe I was trying to remind you who I am, sweetheart. What I am. In case it wasn't clear in your mind already. Maybe I was trying to make sure you won't make any bad mistakes involving me." I looked at her and drew a long, angry breath. "Goddamn it, Frances, why the hell don't you stop playing footsie with these dumb amateur soldiers who can't make up their minds whether they want to get free or rich?"

She licked her lips. "You know the situation. I have no choice." After a moment, she frowned again and said, " 'Playing footsie.' Have people been talking? About me and Ramiro Sanchez?"

"Let's say that your numerous visits to headquarters have not gone unobserved."

Her face was pale. "Hadn't they better make up their foul little minds?" she asked harshly. "They can't have it both ways, or can they? Do they think I'm so insatiable I keep Ramiro for my daytime lover and save you for the night shift?" She was a slim white shape in the dusk of the chamber, in the long robe that was made of the very thin crinkly material that, I'm told, packs very well because it's all prewrinkled so who'll notice an additional crease or two? I saw her sway, and stepped forward to steady her; and she sighed and let herself be drawn into my arms. "It's so lousy," she whispered. "I don't know how much more of it I can stand, darling." I heard her give a strained little laugh that had some hysteria in it. "Do you want to know something very funny, Sam?"

"Anything you want to tell me."

"That nymphomaniac act of mine. Do you know how many men I've really slept with? Two, just two, in my whole life. My husband and . . . and a mystery man who calls himself Felton because that's not his name. What is your real name?"

"Helm," I said. It could do no harm for her to know it now. "Matthew Helm."

"Did I fool you Matthew Helm? Did I convince you that I was a very wanton woman?" She laughed softly. "It was . . . rather fun, pretending to be a person like that. Every faithful wife should have one little fling at being a whore; but what happens when the mark she picks up on a street corner turns out to be much nicer than she expected? What does the faithful wife do then?"

She was silent for a moment. Then she turned her face up to me for the kiss, clinging to me desperately; and her lips were warm and urgent. I untied the single little bow that closed her outer garment at the throat, and slipped the thin, damp stuff off her shoulders, and let it fall; but when I reached around to unfasten the scanty white bathing suit—it tied at the back of the neck—she grasped my wrists.

"No!" she breathed. "Please, no! I can't. We can't."

"Make up your mind," I said.

She shook her head quickly. "I'm sorry. No. Please, no."

I let my hands fall and stepped back. "The lady says no. The lady says please." My voice didn't sound the way it was supposed to.

"I'm sorry, Sam . . . Matt. I'm so sorry. I shouldn't have. . . ."

There were footsteps outside; they stopped at the doorway. A voice said in Spanish: "Señora Dillman. The colonel requests your presence, señora."

185

Frances drew a long breath and answered, also in Spanish: "Inform the colonel that I will attend him as soon as I have changed my costume."

"Si, señora."

I listened to the sound of army boots receding. "Saved by the bell," I said sourly. "Do you know what the hell you're doing, Dillman?"

When she spoke, after a little pause, her voice sounded very tired. "Yes. I know. Now. I'm sorry, darling."

A few minutes later I watched her leave, tall and competent-looking in her well-cut jeans and the bright red shirt I'd seen before. Toward evening the wind came up that I'd been waiting for.

CHAPTER 25

IT was getting dark when Frances returned, but, even so, I could see that her hair wasn't quite as smooth as it had been, nor was her bright silk shirt tucked into her pants quite as neatly as it had been. She gave me a bleak, meaningless look as she entered our stone room—she'd told me earlier that nobody really knew what this series of little chambers had been used for—and sat down on her pad at the other side of it and buried her face in her hands. After a little I realized that she was crying silently; but when I moved over to comfort her she shrugged my hand away.

"Don't touch me, I'm dirty," she gasped. "Dirty, dirty, dirty!"

"Cut it out," I said. "Just because the Putnam kids are acting out that silly soiled-for-life routine doesn't mean we senior citizens have to."

They weren't that young, of course, and we weren't that old. It was a feeble joke of sorts, and after a long moment of silence, she gave me a rather shy, rueful look and a reluctant little grin.

"I guess I was overdramatizing it a bit, wasn't I? After all, it's not as if I'd never dreamt of sleeping with a man who wasn't my husband."

I put my arm around her; this time she let me. I felt very sorry for her, and maybe for myself, too; and I touched my lips to her forehead. Her skin was smooth and cool, and she smelled faintly, sweetly, of the soap and shampoo she'd been using at the *cenote* earlier in the afternoon.

"I'm a little surprised," I said. "I thought Sanchez looked like a man who'd take pride in keeping his word. He promised that no lady would be molested."

"He didn't m—molest me." She swallowed hard. "It isn't molestation when . . . when the lady permits it. Even asks for it."

After a moment I asked, "Why?"

She did not answer directly. She said, "Regardless of what everybody seems to think, Ramiro's been a perfect gentleman. Oh, he made it clear at the start that he found me desirable and wouldn't, well, kick me out of his bed if I cared to climb into it; but it wasn't really much more than the usual Latin gallantry. He actually did enjoy my company; and he said it was pleasant for a change to have somebody cultured and intelligent with whom to converse for an hour or so daily, stuck as he was in this dismal place surrounded by uncouth peasant-types. So we got into the habit of just talking for a while after disposing of the day's problems. He's really rather an interesting man, a theoretical upper-class revolutionary, Marxist of course; I think he's actually been to Moscow for some kind of training. He scorns Lupe Montano as a clownish bandit, and I'm sure he hopes to turn the liberation movement to his own advantage, and that of his political cause, once Lupe has done the heavy work for him. Sometimes Ramiro is kind of scary; I feel he's actually more ruthless in his aristocratic way than the savage downtrodden peons rising up against their oppressors. I wonder how many people have been slaughtered in cold blood by overeducated men and women who got their icy ideologies out of books. But to me he's always been polite and charming."

"Until tonight," I said.

She was finding it difficult to get to the point; but I held her and let her work around to it her way, with just a verbal nudge or two in the right direction.

"Even tonight," she said. "But you've got to understand that I've encouraged him, Matt. I've let him get used to talking to me. I've let him know that I found him interesting and that our daily conversation was also a pleasant break in the dull prison-camp routine for me. I mean, it was the obvious thing to do, wasn't it? For our sakes here, and for Archie's sake, wherever he is, I was bound to take any advantage I could get, wasn't I? Gaining Ramiro's confidence, making him like me, was only sensible. I'd have been a fool to insult him or antagonize him, wouldn't I? And after a while I did begin to overhear moderately useful things, like what I told you this afternoon about the progress of the negotiations. But tonight . . ." She hesitated. "Tonight, he asked me to stay the night."

"Polite and charming," I said dryly.

"That's just the point, he was. And apologetic. He said he sincerely hoped that I wouldn't misconstrue the suggestion. He said that we were friends, as much as a man and woman could be friends, and that he wouldn't dream of doing anything that would cause him to lose my respect and friendship. He merely would like me to stay there until morning, safe, for reasons he was not at liberty to divulge." She drew a long ragged breath. "Of course I couldn't act the least bit curious. I couldn't afford to arouse the slightest suspicion. I had to think very fast. I knew I had to find out what he planned to do, why he wanted me out of the way. I said . . . I said I'd be happy to stay, for a while at least; but wasn't he being just a little *too* gentlemanly and considerate? I said, after all, Ramiro, *querido,* it is not as if I were a sheltered virgin." She swallowed hard. "He looked at me and gave a great laugh and pulled the curtain that hung across the doorway, saying that he had been waiting many days for this moment and he hoped his fine patience was appreciated. . . ."

There was still light in the doorway. It was about the same time of evening that they'd come for Gloria Jean that first night nine days ago, or was it ten? It was hard to keep track of time in a situation like this.

Frances said, "You don't want a pornographic play-by-play account, I hope. Afterward . . . afterward we talked a little. He was relaxed and unguarded then; he let me know that the reason he didn't want me here is that he's coming for you tonight. He has considerable respect for your warlike abilities, darling; and he didn't want me present in case shooting became necessary."

"When?" I asked.

"After midnight some time, when everybody's pretty sure to be asleep."

"Why, after all this time?"

"That Tolson bitch. And that stupid Olcott woman. Olcott confided the main outlines of your plan to his handsome, brainless, blond wife; he thought she had a right to know what he was getting them into. Tolson wheedled it out of Elspeth Olcott somehow and took it straight to Ramiro. Tolson's got that strange hostage fixation and feels that it's wicked and disloyal, not to mention dangerous, for anybody to plot against the camp authorities. Besides, she's of course firmly and self-righteously opposed to violence."

I said grimly, "So was Miranda Matson. She hated guns."

"Don't get mad at me. I'm just passing it along as I heard it," Frances said. "So Ramiro knows you'll probably go on the prowl the first suitable night. He's been letting your conspiracy come to a head, so to speak, so he can lance it brutally. . . . Meaning that he's going to grab you and make a terrible example of you for the rest of the camp, just as he established his authority in the first place by shooting Miss Matson."

"But he let you come back here after all," I said.

She nodded. "I pointed out how it would look if I were seen stumbling out of his quarters, sleepy and disheveled, on the morning after you were taken. All the people who'd been depending on you would assume I'd betrayed you, and they'd tear me into little pieces if they could get their hands on me. At least they'd have nothing more to do with me, and my usefulness to him, Ramiro, would be destroyed. And there was also the fact that if I didn't come back here tonight, you'd get suspicious and might do something drastic and unpredictable before he was ready to deal with you."

"What does he plan now?" I asked.

"We've arranged that when the camp is quiet and I'm sure you're asleep, I'll slip out and give the signal. If you should wake up and see me, I can always say I'm going to the john. Real Samson-and-Delilah stuff." She rubbed her forehead against my cheek. "Matt, what are we going to do?"

189

"What do you suggest?" I asked. Then I looked at her more sharply. "We?"

She said, sounding a little surprised, "Well, if you do escape, Ramiro will know I warned you, won't he? He'll be very angry, justifiably so; and I don't think he's a nice man when he's angry. I don't think I want to stay behind and have my face remodeled with the butt of a gun, like Marshall Wilder. Or worse." When I didn't speak, she went on breathlessly: "It wasn't easy for me, darling. I had to make a choice between playing along with Ramiro for Archie's sake, or trying to save your life; and here I am. I hope you appreciate the . . . the sacrifice I'm making for you!" Then she turned abruptly against me, gasping her words into my shoulder: "Oh, Matt, Matt, darling, I couldn't let you be killed! I just couldn't!" After a while, in a totally different voice, she said, "There's a path back to Copalque. I think I'm the only one here who knows about it."

"Where?"

"We cut it when we were tracing that ancient paved road that, we finally discovered, leads straight from the Great Court at Copalque to the Arch of the Emperors and here to Labal. That's how we found this place. We used the path for a while; but after we started excavating here we did some more exploring and found a better route, the Jeep road we still use today. Our old path to Copalque is probably pretty overgrown by now, but at least it should be considerably better than crashing through the virgin jungle, and there's enough of the old Melmec pavement left to let us know when we go astray. Well, you saw it the day we visited the arch."

I hesitated; then I said, "I can't run out on these people, Frances. As you pointed out yourself, they're depending on me."

She shook her head quickly. "Matt, your fancy escape plan is doomed. It will never work. Certainly not now that it's been betrayed to Ramiro; and most certainly not if you're captured and tortured to death. If we can get away, we can try to get help to free the others."

"Well, maybe you're right." I sighed. "Okay, you'd better get your boots on; you can't flee through the jungle in those sandals. We'll go as soon after dark as the sentries cooperate."

It turned out to be absurdly easy. It was just a matter of timing, picking a moment when the distant sentry up on the pyramid was at the far end of his beat, on the other side of the Citadel ruins from us, and the near one on the Nunnery patio was also at the far end of his, away from our cell, preferably lighting a cigarette and destroying his night vision. But it wasn't much of a wait, and the near man actually did light up conveniently—apparently they'd never heard of lung cancer in these parts—turning his back to the gusty wind to shelter his match.

We were out of our cell and around the end of the building before he straightened up and looked around. We passed the men's toilet, which had already developed the ripe excremental odor of any well-established outdoor facility. Momentarily safe from observation behind the Nunnery, we made our way cautiously down the rubble slope into the adjacent jungle with the wind covering the sound of the occasional pebble we couldn't help dislodging. We followed the edge of the clearing where the thorny vines had been chopped away, but the trees remained to give us cover as we came out from behind the man-made Nunnery hill.

There were, again, two sentries to be considered. There was still the Citadel man with his fine elevated viewpoint; but he was far enough away, now, that I doubted he could distinguish a couple of small dark shadows moving among the trees on the far side of the big open space—jeans don't show up much at night, and I was wearing my black turtleneck; and Frances's red shirt looked black in the dark.

And then there was the man guarding the Jeep road to Copalque. It took me a while to spot him. He was sitting in the lee of a tree trunk, sheltered from the wind, with his weapon across his knees and his cap over his eyes, sound asleep. We slipped into the footpath fifty yards away without arousing him and stumbled along the cleared trail that led to the Arch of the Emperors; but I stopped when I saw the ragged ruin of the Monastery loom black against the sky.

"Stay here," I said. "I'll be back in a minute."

"For God's sake, they could be looking into our room right now and realizing that we're gone!"

"Relax, I won't be long."

It took me a few minutes to find my landmarks in the

dark and get my bearings; then I was reaching under the rock and feeling the butt of the .38, cold and reassuring in my grasp. I tucked away the spare cartridges, clipped the holster into place, and made some adjustments to the buckle of my belt. Frances, standing stiffly in the path, looking back the way we'd come as if expecting the pursuit to charge into sight at any moment, gave a start and an audible gasp when I rejoined her, indicating that she hadn't heard me coming for the sighing, rustling sound of the wind in the jungle all around us.

Then on again down the path that was only a pale track through the trees; and at last we stumbled out onto the cleared portion of the ancient road that had never known a wheel, with the massive *Arc-de-Triomphe* shape of the ancient ceremonial gate black in the darkness ahead. Suddenly I was aware of armed men stepping out of the brush behind us. A familiar voice spoke.

"You will raise your hands, Señor Felton!"

I stopped obediently and raised my hands.

Frances's voice, strained and ugly, spoke quickly: "He picked up the gun, Ramiro. It was hidden near the Monastery, just as we thought."

Colonel Sanchez laughed behind me. "Perhaps we could have found it by searching, but it pleases me to have the clever Yankee secret agent deliver to me his own weapon. At least we no longer have to worry about that missing firearm being used against us. You have done very well, señora; and I will see what can be done about obtaining your husband's release. Trust me. Now you will disarm this man, *por favor.* . . ."

There were three of them, which I suppose was flattering; four including Frances. I couldn't see the colonel, directly behind me; but I assumed he was still wearing his fancy Sam Browne belt and holster—the Browning Hi-Power itself was presumbly in his hand. On my right was my old friend Eugenio, Scarface himself, whose M16 I'd become reasonably well acquainted with on an earlier occasion. On my left was the slim dark boy who'd stood guard at the *cenote* this afternoon, also armed with U.S. artillery, junior grade, 5.56 mm—.223 caliber to you.

Then Frances was in front of me, reaching for the holstered Smith and Wesson at my waist. She paused and met my eyes. "I'm sorry, but I *warned* you!" she breathed.

192

"I *told* you I'd do any dirty thing to get Archie back safely!"

"Well, you really made a project of it, didn't you, Delilah? All you forgot was the haircut!" I said harshly. "What's the matter, can't you even pull a gun out of a holster? No, that's right, you're better with other weapons, aren't you? There's a trick catch, see. . . . Great, and now you've got it, let's see you use it. Or haven't you got the guts to do the job yourself? God, to think I really was sap enough to like and respect . . . Well, finish the job, Frances, dear! Use the gun you betrayed me for; don't leave the dirty work for somebody else! Shit, I'll *make* you shoot me, get a little real blood on your dainty treacherous hands!"

I'd been crowding her, moving against the .38 she was holding inexpertly and trying to keep pointed away from me. Now I lowered my hands to reach for her throat. I was rewarded—and reward is precisely the correct word—with a sharp jab in the kidney.

"Halt! That is enough melodrama!"

I knew a moment of incredulous triumph. I'd gambled on it, of course, but I hadn't really believed it would work; I hadn't quite been able to convince myself there were people that stupid in the world. Against anybody in the business, or even a good cop, I'd never have tried it; but I'd reassured myself—or tried to reassure myself—with the thought that these people were not professionals in the sense that we think of professionals. I'd reminded myself of Eugenio using his M16 like a cattle prod. . . .

Military men are great at a thousand yards and don't do too badly at a hundred, but they don't really expect to have to cope with the enemy at zero range very often. Colonel Ramiro Sanchez of the People's Liberation Army, or whatever they called it, was probably hot stuff when it came to emplacing a heavy machine gun for a good field of fire, but when it came to dealing with a prisoner at gunpoint he was, like his boy Eugenio, a hopeless amateur. Shoving a gun into a trained man's back, for God's sake!

I whirled left while he was still speaking, slamming my left arm through the space between us to knock the weapon aside and, with the other hand, slugging him low as I turned. The Browning fired and I felt a blow against my back, whether a lethal wound or just the muzzle blast I couldn't tell and I wasn't waiting to find out. For the moment the human machinery was still operative, and that was all that counted. The little belt-buckle knife, which I'd slipped under the watchband on my left wrist at the time I'd picked up the hidden revolver and grabbed right-handed when my hands came together just now in my dramatic lady-strangling pose, went into Sanchez to the hilt, edge up—or since it had no real hilt, it went in until my knuckles came up against the cloth of his pants. Crowding him, not letting him back clear, I ripped upward savagely.

It was a schizophrenic moment. I had to have the Browning; and I was groping for it left-handed as I moved against him; and all the time I was aware of the well-sharpened little knife in my right hand slicing upward, parting the clothing and the skin and the fatty layer underneath and the ridged mucles of the abdominal wall. I hoped the weapon was up to the job. In all respects but one it was an ordinary little buckle-and-blade instrument. You simply unfastened the belt, grasped the buckle a certain way, freed it from the leather a certain way, and the blade that was part of it slipped out of its hidden sheath in the end of the belt, leaving you with your pants falling down, unless they were a good snug fit—mine were—and with a mean little three-inch slicer protruding from between your knuckles. Such hideout knives are not uncommon; the special thing about this one was that it was plastic: a special space-age composition with a silvery coating, the blade bonded to just enough steel to take and hold an edge, meaning that you could stroll past the airport metal-detectors all day and they'd never let out a murmur.

Well, I would be able to report that, although I'd had some doubts, the plastic-and-steel composition was strong enough—assuming that I lived to make a report, which was beginning to seem doubtful because I'd lost the Browning. Aghast at what was happening to him, Sanchez had dropped the pistol before my left hand could find it. He was trying now, desperately, to minimize the damage, to keep the dreadful incision from being further enlarged, grappling for my bloody knife-hand with both his hands. But already the air held the nasty stench you get when you dress out a deer or an elk carelessly and damage the intestines, letting the contents of the digestive tract spill out. Stolid Eugenio was standing by as we wrestled, gun ready, waiting for a safe shot; but I realized suddenly from his tense posture that the nervous dark boy wasn't going to wait. He was going to save his colonel, he was going to try for it, for me. . . .

I released the buckle-grip of the knife, befouled and slippery now, and dove for the ground as the M16 opened up. There was no time to locate the fallen pistol in the dark, let alone retrieve it; I simply hit and rolled, and rolled some more. The kid was swinging with me but shooting high where I'd been instead of low where I was. I heard at least three bullets go into Sanchez as the weapon traversed; and farther away Eugenio was hitting the ground to avoid the wild burst of fire. Abruptly the M16 was silent.

Still rolling toward him, I caught a glimpse of the young revolutionary soldier, face gray in the dark, mouth hanging open slackly, gun muzzle sagging, as he realized that he'd shot his commanding officer. Then I hit him hard and brought him down. When I scrambled up I had a weapon —his weapon—solidly in my hands, a lovely feeling.

I beat Eugenio up by a bare fraction of a second. He tried to bring his weapon to bear, but, still on his belly, he had to shift his whole body first. On my feet, I had no trouble pivoting freely to line up my liberated assault rifle by instinct, firing from the hip, although I prefer to use the sights whenever I can. Here there wasn't time enough—nor was there light enough—for such refinements; he was already rolling away. My five-shot burst bracketed him for an instant before he disappeared into a depression on the far side of the prehistoric road; but with that small caliber it was by no means a sure kill.

Ramiro was down. There were dark bloodstains on his khaki shirt where he'd been shot, but he seemed unaware of them, concentrating on the knife-torn mess that was his belly as he sat against a roadside rock, holding himself together with both hands. Frances was still standing where I'd last seen her, frozen with shock but apparently unhurt. I found that even in that moment I was pleased by that, although I could see no reason why I should be. The boy whose weapon I'd liberated was on his knees, vomiting convulsively. I moved to where I could cover him and still keep an eye on the spot where Eugenio had disappeared. The kid soldier wiped his mouth on his sleeve and looked up at me fearfully.

"Ammunition," I said. I tapped the magazine of the weapon I held. *"Municiones por la ametralladora, por favor."*

It wasn't great Spanish, but it got through. Numbly, he fished another of the straight twenty-shot magazines from a pocket of his bandolier—they make a long curved thirty-round magazine as well, and I think there's even a belt-fed version of the weapon that'll shoot until it melts, but all I'd seen here had been the straight twenty-shooters. He left the magazine on the ground on the spot I pointed to, rose at my gesture, and backed away a short distance, moving like a zombie. Then I had the fresh magazine in the gun, just in case Eugenio was in shape to make a real firefight of it. I could hear the painful breathing of Ramiro Sanchez. I knew that the sound would have been a mindless, hopeless whimpering if his pride had allowed it. I looked at the boy in front of me.

"What the hell am I going to do with you?" I asked him in English, and he didn't understand a word, which was just as well because it was not a serious question.

"Matt! Drop the gun! Please, Matt, don't make me shoot!"

It was the single-minded married lady with the .38, of course, behind me; and of course I should have disarmed her, but who would have thought any one woman could be so stubbornly stupid all by herself? Ignoring her command, I hit the trigger of the M16 and practically cut the kid in front of me in two, as the Smith and Wesson blasted behind me and the bullet went over me somewhere.

ONE.

I threw myself to the right, and a bullet passed me on the left.

TWO.

Eugenio was back in the game, a shadowy figure rising painfully at the far side of the road. I sent a quick three-shot burst his way and threw myself flat in the roadside bushes on my side, and rolled to avoid his answering fire. As I came to a stop, dirt sprayed up about five yards to my right and I heard the ringing muzzle-blast of the short-barreled .38 once more.

THREE.

I scrambled farther into the bushes; and Eugenio's burst brought down a shower of leaves and branches where I'd been. I lay there for a ten-count, found a rock, and pitched it farther ahead of me. I rose as it landed, an old trick; but Eugenio fell for it enough to be just slightly out of position when I appeared. I held the hammering M16 steady against the recoil—it didn't have a hell of a lot of kick—and put enough of the lousy little jacketed bullets into the dark shape over there to get the job done at last, aware of a .38 slug screaming off an ancient Melmec paving stone at my feet.

FOUR . . . FIVE.

The last one came as I turned to look at Frances. It missed like the rest, high, if it matters. She clicked the mechanism twice more as I stood watching her, before she realized that the revolver was empty. I raised the M16 to my shoulder and looked at her over the dim sights, and knew that I could never do it, at least not now when it was all over, not just to show how terribly hurt and disillusioned I was. I lowered the weapon, but I had to do something to express my feelings—after all, she'd had five shots at me and there was a certain reaction—so I spat deliberately, ashamed of the crude gesture but a little proud of the fact that I still had something left to spit with. I turned from her and walked over to Ramiro.

He looked up at me, his face greenish gray in the night. "I underestimated you, señor. My humble apologies." His voice was a ghost of a whisper.

"You should have stuck to war and revolution," I said. "Never play another man's game, Colonel. This is my game."

"There is a favor I would ask," he breathed, "although I have of course no right to any favors from you."

I looked down at him. In that moment we were both professional fighting men and the differences in our specialties did not matter. Depending on the seriousness of the bullet wounds, he might have been saved if a well-equipped medical unit had been standing by. Perhaps they could have repaired the knife damage and sewed him up and shot him full of antibiotics—but there was no medical unit, and he would know that even if there had been, with the rest of his command still to be dealt with, I was in no position to indulge in humanitarian gestures.

All he had to look forward to was, at the best, a painful dying. At the worst he would last long enough to lie there helpless watching the *zopilotes* gathering in the dawn sky overhead, and circling down on their great black vulture wings and, when he became too weak to frighten them away, squabbling over his intestines and genitals until, at last, one of them would dig deeply enough to sever an important blood vessel and set him free. . . .

"Of course it is your right," I said. "It is any man's right."

I set the M16 to single fire and shot him through the head.

Chapter 26

I stopped along the dark path to check the hole made by Sanchez's 9 mm Browning, in the soft flesh below the ribs, but although it was well over to the right, it was still far enough back that I couldn't have seen it even if there had been light enough to see much by. My fingers merely told me that a certain amount of bullet erosion existed, and that it was producing a certain amount of hemorrhage, which didn't add much to my previous knowledge.

I was feeling a little weak and dizzy, but any imaginative man will feel weak and dizzy with his blood running down his ass from an injury of undetermined magnitude. Anyway, I told myself, with three dead men and a treacherous tied-up woman behind me, I had every excuse to feel weak and dizzy from reaction—but I wished there had been some less uncomfortable and humiliating way of dealing with her. Of course I could have tried trusting her. Ha!

The sentry by the Jeep road had awakened when I reached the Labal clearing. He was standing up, leaning against the same tree he'd used for sleeping purposes; but he didn't look like a wary man alerted by distant gunfire. The wind was stronger now, not a roaring gale, but a good stiff breeze making plenty of noise in the trees; it would have carried the noise of the fight away from him. He noticed nothing now as I lugged my burden of M16s and grenades and laden bandoliers cautiously back along the edge of the jungle the way Frances and I had come. I made my way up the rubble slope to the far end of the Nunnery, reflecting unchivalrously as I passed downwind of it that the ladies' john smelled just as bad as the gents'.

I cached the armaments and took out a knife I had liberated from dead Eugenio. An improvement over the little buckle-knife that was again helping to hold up my pants, it was one of the commando-type daggers shaped somewhat like the old Arkansas toothpick—not to be confused with Jim Bowie's lethal blade, which had been a different breed of edged weapon altogether, long and heavy enough to decapitate a man instead of merely stabbing or slicing him to death. But this was a sticker, not a chopper; and I reminded myself that rumor in the trade said that a lot of knives of this pattern had been manufactured that, while deadly-looking enough, were either so soft they wouldn't hold an edge, or so hard and brittle that they snapped when too much was asked of them.

With this in mind, I dealt with the Nunnery sentry very gently after first luring him around the corner of the building with a couple of tossed pebbles—I told myself that I seemed to be getting into a rock-throwing rut, but it still worked. He came in to investigate the faint clattering sounds like a mallard to the decoys; and I got an arm around his head from behind to prevent an outcry, and slipped the dagger into him without any fuss, and held him while he died. The rattle of his dropped rifle, and the scuffle of his last convulsive thrashings, were blown away by that blessed night wind out of the jungle.

The camp remained dark and silent. The only movement I could see when I looked around the corner of the Nunnery was the steady marching of the conscientious sentry up by the high Citadel. After retrieving my arsenal, and adding the contribution of the recently deceased, I waited for the man up there to start the back portion of his beat, behind the ruin. Then I staggered with my burden along the patio to the fourth little corbeled doorway from the other end and stumbled inside.

"Guns, anyone?" I asked breathlessly.

There was a startled gasp from Gloria Jean and a rustle of movement from her husband—I noted that they were sleeping unsociably on opposite sides of the little chamber, as Frances and I had done. When they sat up, I saw that Putnam seemed to be in underwear shorts; his wife had on some kind of dark pajamas.

"Sam? What have you got?" Jim Putnam asked, instantly awake and reaching for his pants.

"Three M16s and enough fodder to nourish them for a while. Six or seven grenades, I lost count somewhere along the line. Two handguns and three knives. Can you block the entrance and have you got a light?"

"We've tried the mattress pads; they'll cover the doorway if we rig them right. There's a flashlight and a penlight. Glory, why don't you slip out and tell Paul and the general that we're in business. . . ."

I said, "You do it. You don't have to worry about our local guard, but watch out for the guy up on the pyramid." When Putnam hesitated, clearly annoyed at having his orders countermanded, I said, "Excuse me, but I've got kind of a hole in my back and I'd rather have it tended by a pretty girl."

"Serious?"

I didn't flatter myself that the quick concern in his voice was due to affection for me. He had plans for using me in the approaching campaign and didn't want me disabled.

"I don't think so," I said. "It happened almost an hour ago and it hasn't killed me yet, but it's still bleeding."

"I'll get out the first-aid stuff, what little we've got," Gloria Jean said. I felt her pull my blood-soaked shirt out of my pants, behind. "Sam, turn a little, please. . . . It isn't very big, but you'd better ask if any of the others have a sterile dressing, say four by four, and some peroxide, Jim. Bring it back with you. We do have some tape." Then Putnam was gone and she was rummaging in a suitcase behind me. Her soft voice reached me. "Was it bad, Sam?"

I said, "Like the flyboys say, you never really mind the ones you can walk away from. But the weather got kind of gory out for a while, I will admit."

"Tell me if I'm hurting you. I think even without a light I can see it well enough to clean it up a little, if you keep your back to the doorway. I've got some water in a bottle if I can find . . . Ah." I felt the water cool against my skin.

Presently she spoke again. "It's not a hole, really. Just a kind of furrow about three inches long, but it seems to have got burned. . . ."

"The muzzle blast did that," I said. "Probably cauterized it nicely. Ouch!"

"Sorry . . . I won't even ask how you got yourself shot with the gun poking into your side like that."

"It's just as well. It's nothing you want to hear about."

"Sam." Her voice was hesitant.

"Yes?"

"Can I ask you to look after him? Please. He's in a crazy mood; please try not to let him get hurt. Maybe . . . maybe some day everything will be all right with us again, but it won't ever happen if he gets himself killed trying to prove something to me, something I don't give a damn about, but I can't make him see that."

"I'll try if I get the chance," I said. I glanced around, but I couldn't read her expression in the dark. I said, "So the problem isn't on your side? If you don't mind talking about it."

She said, "Oh, I feel a little . . . tarnished, of course, a little . . . used; but I can live with it if he can. But he feels that he failed me. He thinks I feel that he failed me. My God, all I wanted was for him not to do anything stupid and protective that would get him shot! I *wanted* him to do just what he did. Hell, I'm not made of glass, Sam, I don't break that easily. But now he's made such a big thing of it, and we can't seem to talk about it sensibly. I don't know what to do, Sam. Well, it's not your problem, but please, please, do what you can tonight to keep him from doing something brave and glorious and . . . and fatal to justify himself in my eyes. Who the hell needs his lousy justification? All I need is him. Alive!" Then she said, "I'm sorry. I just haven't been able to talk with anybody else about it; I didn't mean to pour it all out like a hysterical little—Oh, here they come."

There was a scuffling sound outside, and Olcott slipped in, and after a minute or two, Henderson and his wife. It seemed unlikely that Mrs. Henderson had received an official invitation to our council of war, but she came anyway. Jim Putnam joined us, and we passed him the mattresses, and he secured them across the opening. Gloria Jean was handed some sterile gauze pads and a bottle of peroxide.

With Mrs. Henderson holding the penlight for her, she did a quick and competent job of patching me up.

I said, as I tucked my shirt back in, "Jim, if you don't mind, I have a suggestion to make. We need time, and that guy up at the Citadel may get a little nervous if hours pass and he sees no sign of his buddy down here, who happens to be dead."

"What's your idea?" Putnam asked.

I spoke to his wife. "How strong a stomach have you got, Gloria Jean? He was a smallish man and you're about the right size. He's lying in the entrance to the men's john. Can you strip him and get into his clothes and take one of these M16s and bandoliers to complete the costume? Be sure to tuck all that hair into the cap. But before you answer, let me remind you that he didn't die a natural death. It'll be a little messy."

She hesitated, and spoke very carefully. "Is it all right if I throw up?"

I grinned. "Puke all you want, as long as you do it where the Citadel boy can't see you."

"Glory . . ." That was her husband.

She said quietly. "It's all right, Jim. I can't be much help with the fighting; but this is something I can do. I'll be all right."

Somebody handed her the necessary props, and the doorway was cleared enough for her to slip out into the night, after waiting for the sentry on the pyramid to make his turn.

After a little pause, I said, "I don't want to hog the floor, Jim, but I've just been out there and maybe you'd like my report. You now have eight men to worry about. One whom you don't have to worry about is Col. Ramiro Sanchez. You can plan accordingly."

There was a lengthy silence. We were on a military footing now, I realized, with Olcott the lone civilian—Mrs. Henderson would have been the first to say that she was as military as anybody. Only Olcott regarded me a bit strangely, therefore, as he made the subtraction in his head: Eight live men from twelve live men was four dead men. General Henderson nodded slowly, and his wife inclined her head in royal approval. Putnam whistled softly.

"You've been a busy little fella, fella."

"You have no idea," I said. "Now, you'll want the layout

of their headquarters down there. I got it from Frances. . . ."

"Where is Frances?" Putnam asked.

"She's . . . waiting down by the Arch of the Emperors where we had a little hassle with Sanchez, never mind the details right now. I saw no sense in her coming back here to get shot at." I still hadn't decided exactly what to tell them about her; but at least now they'd know where to look for her if I fell in battle. I went on: "Anyway, according to her, that temple they're using, the Chapel, is divided by a heavy masonry wall, no connecting doorway, making one large room at the end where they make their cook-fire, and one small one at the end where they park the Jeep. The small one is officers' country. There's a tarp hung to give a little privacy to Sanchez's cot; Barbera sleeps in the other half of the room. A folding table and a couple of chairs. A rack of machetes. Some spare weapons and ammo. So much for the colonels and lieutenants. The men all sleep on the floor of the larger room, the barracks room. Frances couldn't tell me much about that; she was never inside."

"Nice clear report just the same," Putnam said approvingly. "Carry on."

"That's headquarters," I said. "As for the rest, well, you can see that our major problem is the Citadel sentry with a bird's-eye view of everything from the top of his pyramid. We're lucky that he's up there not only for prison-guard purposes, but also for military purposes—to spot any rescue teams or Costa Verde army patrols heading this way— so that he needs a three-hundred-and-sixty-degree view. If he stayed entirely on this side of the temple, we'd have real trouble. We're unlucky, however, in that we seem to have got us an Eagle Scout up there tonight; that boy takes his duties seriously. The other remaining sentry, when last seen, was parked by a big tree with a kind of whitish trunk where the Copalque road enters the clearing. He's a sleepy and unobservant chap. I've passed within fifty yards of him twice and he's failed to spot me. He should be easy to sneak up on. Any questions, Jim?"

"There will definitely be no interference by any of the four you've dealt with?"

"Not unless they've learned the secret of instant resurrection," I said. "Which brings me to a final point I'd like to make, if I may, Captain Putnam, sir. Let's keep in mind that what we have to have here is, not just victory, but total annihilation. No crips, no captives. Don't you agree?"

I saw him start to nod, but Olcott said quickly, "But we can't just massacre . . ."

It was Henderson who spoke, in a crisp, cold voice I'd never heard him use before. "If you can't, you're in the wrong church pew, son."

I explained what was self-evident to everybody but Olcott: "We not only have to win here, Paul, we have to get clear away before Montano hears about it and sends a couple of hundred of his guerilla fighters to round us up. We can't afford to let a single one of these men get away to spread the word. And the catch is, we have a bunch of sentimentalists in the party who'll be bound to scream cruelty if we tie up a prisoner too tightly or tie up a wounded man at all. I wouldn't put it past some of them to speak up and loosen the bonds in the name of humanitarianism—oops, there goes one prisoner and fourteen lives, our fourteen lives. I'm not kidding one little bit. Some people do think like that, and we've simply got to avoid giving them a chance to louse us up. Pat Tolson, for instance, has already betrayed us once for undoubtedly very idealistic reasons of her own; she came damn close to getting me killed tonight."

"Oh, my God!" Olcott's voice sounded sick. "Elspeth said she was asking a lot of questions. Is that how she learned? . . ."

"I'm afraid your wife is a bit too trusting, but it doesn't matter now. The point is, if those men are all dead, there's no problem, right? So if you can't bear to finish one off, call one of us homicidal characters and we'll be happy to do the job for you. But don't for Christ's sake let any of them get away. There's plenty of ammunition. Use it." I drew a long breath. "Okay. Over to you, Jim."

Putnam said, "Paul, you heard the man. Are you in or out?"

Olcott swallowed. "Sorry if I seem naive. I've never done anything like this before. But I'm in if you'll have me."

Jim Putnam said, "We're not only happy to have you, we're going to hand you the toughest assignment of the lot. As Sam said, our big problem is the man up by the Citadel. Not only can he spot everything that goes on down here; with his assault rifle he can raise hell with anything we try.

It's long range for an M16, but if he knows how to use it, and we've got to assume he does, he can make life damned uncomfortable, and probably very short, for anybody he catches out in the open. Ideally, he should be taken out before we even start operations. However, our one professional take-out specialist—I used to know something about it myself, but I'm way out of practice—is wounded and doesn't much like climbing pyramids anyway, as we've all seen." There was a ripple of laughter at my expense. Jim went on: "So that alternative is out. Which means it's up to you, Paul. You're the stalker and mountain climber and you've been up that pyramid once. Can you get into position up there without being spotted, and nail him when the action starts, before he has a chance to zero in on us?"

Olcott nodded slowly. "Yes. I should be able to manage that."

"Remember, this M16 isn't designed for the kind of one-shot kills you probably like to try for, hunting. You've got fifty-five grains of bullet instead of a hundred-and-eighty or whatever you're used to. So use it on automatic and keep pumping lead into him; and if he should manage to crawl into cover anyway, don't feel too bad about it. Just slap in a fresh magazine and give him a burst every time he sticks his nose out. Keep him pinned down, keep him busy, don't let him get to where he can shoot at us, don't let him get away, and you'll be doing fine. And if he does hole up, don't try to go in after him. You don't know how. Wait until we've cleaned up down here, and yell for reinforcements. Sam and I will come up and ferret him out for you. Questions?"

"Somebody's going to have to show me the buttons and levers; I've never used an M16."

General Henderson said, "Yes, I think a little demonstration is in order, Captain. It's not a weapon with which I'm familiar, either."

Putnam nodded. "Wait until I check the doorway. . . . All right, if you'll hold this flashlight, sir. This is the charging handle. Pull it straight back until it locks, but it won't pull unless you hold it so you're depressing this catch, here. The weapon also remains open after the last round is fired. Bolt release here. Magazine release here. Three-position safety here: SAFE, SINGLE, AUTO. Questions?"

Olcott and Henderson each checked out a weapon with

the aid of the flashlight. Both knew firearms and needed no further instruction. No questions.

Jim Putnam said, "General, the low-level sentry over by the Copalque road is yours. Find yourself a spot over there from which you can nail him no matter where he goes. Your signal is gunfire up at the Citadel. The minute Paul opens up or his man does, you wipe out your target. And Paul opens up the minute his target spots Sam and me as we go for the Headquarters temple." He looked at me. "There's no cover at all between the Nunnery and HQ, Sam, so there's no sense in us trying any sneaky belly-crawling. We have to make it while old Eagle-Eye up there is on the far side of the Citadel. I suggest that we make a straight run for it, hoping that even if he does spot us, we can get a grenade or two into each end of the building before the shooting wakes them and they come boiling out like hornets. I think we can make it if Paul can keep us from getting clobbered from above."

I realized that this was why Putnam had chosen me for his partner here. The old general could have done as well, or maybe even better, once he reached the target area, but at his age he couldn't be expected to manage a hundred-yard dash. I hoped I could.

"You call it," I said.

"I'm going to have to shortchange you," he said. "You'll be hitting the officers' end of the temple, and you can have half the grenades, but I'll have to ask you to use either your revolver or the Browning for the clean-up work. You're not likely to have more than one or two to deal with and if you get a grenade in there right away, they shouldn't cause you too much trouble. I'm sorry I can't tell you if Lieutenant Barbera is in his quarters. They were kind of milling around earlier, and I lost track of who was going in and out. Sometimes an enlisted man stands guard over the stuff in there when both officers are out. Hell, for all I know Barbera sleeps with a kid soldier when his commanding officer's away and other men's wives aren't handy." His voice was totally without expression. "But I should say that the most you'll have to handle is two, and the place may even be empty. The other room is larger, I'll be dealing with more men, and the grenades may not be as effective in the larger space, so I'd better have the remaining M16 to handle the overflow. And whichever pistol you take, Mrs. Henderson should have the other, just in case somebody slips by us and heads this way."

"Sure," I said.

I freed the Smith and Wesson, holster and all, and handed it over to the general's lady. I preferred it as a weapon—I was brought up on revolvers—but with its sawed-off barrel it was strictly a short-range proposition, and it only held five cartridges against the thirteen that still remained in Sanchez's automatic. (I had no trouble at all in remembering where the fourteenth round had gone.) I tucked the big Browning under my waistband after rechecking the loads. I saw Jim Putnam glance at his luminous watch dial.

"Paul, how much time will you need?"

"I'll have to go around the south end of the clearing so I can approach the pyramid from the jungle side. Can you give me an hour?"

"Just about. We want to get it over with before they start stirring around to change the guards at midnight. Very well, at twenty-three-oh-five Sam and I will assume you're in position and stage our heroic attack against fearful odds. Ready? It is now twenty-two-oh-five. . . . Mark!"

"I might as well go now, too," General Henderson said. "I don't move as fast as you young sprouts these days, and I don't mind sitting under a tree until the action starts. Captain, it is a pleasure to serve under you. I'll deal with my man and then wait at that end of the field to shortstop anything that gets loose and comes my way. . . ."

Then they were gone. In the silence, we could hear the footsteps of Gloria Jean outside, pacing her beat—well, it was hers now. Jim Putnam let out a long breath.

"It's not the fighting that gets you, it's the goddamn briefing," he said. "And the goddamn waiting. No sense in our getting out there yet, Sam. We can be at our jump-off position in five minutes." He hesitated. "I'm rather curious about how you and Frances cleaned up on Colonel Sanchez and his cohorts."

Mrs. Henderson said placidly, "Yes, I've been wondering about that, myself."

I said, "Well, you see, I had that .38 hid out. . . ."

They appreciated the story I told them just as much as if it had been the truth.

CHAPTER 27

THE path seemed longer this time, which was odd. Usually a trail you've traveled a few times and got to know after a fashion goes by faster than it did when you were exploring it for the first time and didn't know how much of a hike it was going to be. However, I'd experienced a certain amount of blood loss earlier; and since then, I'd done some more fighting and my ears were still ringing with grenade blasts and gunfire. I was only carrying one M16 on this trip, plus my little revolver, returned unused by Mrs. Henderson; but I also had a machete, a full canteen, and a haversack.

On the plus side was the fact that I was reasonably clean and presentable for a change, having been sponged off and rebandaged by the general's formidable spouse; I'd even got to exchange my bloodstained clothes for fresh ones. Nevertheless it seemed to take me a long time to raise the loom of the Monastery against the sky, and longer still before I found myself on the cleared Melmec road with the Arch of the Emperors darkly visible ahead.

A sudden rustling and scurrying noise had me unslinging the assault rifle hastily, ready to hit the ground; then I heard the low, snarling sound of a four-footed scavenger standing its ground against the two-footed predator approaching. Clearly the bodies had already been found by the Eaters of the Dead, as the Melmecs had called them.

I made a cautious detour, not knowing what the hell was there, only that it sounded sizable and brave; it could be anything from a coatamundi to *El Tigre* himself—or maybe just a pack of dogs from a native village. In any case, I wasn't looking for more combat; but the encounter put a sudden fear into my mind. I hurried on and was relieved to find Frances lying at the side of the arch where I'd left her, alone and apparently unharmed.

She didn't speak. I got rid of my load and knelt beside her. "Roll over a bit so I can get at your wrists," I said, and cut them free. "All right, now the ankles."

She sat up, rubbing her wrists. Rising, I helped her to her feet.

She looked at me for a moment and spoke without expression: "Teacher, may I leave the room?"

"Yes, Frances," I said. "You may leave the room."

She disappeared around a corner of the arch, moving a little uncertainly after the long hours of immobility. Presently she returned, buckling the belt of her jeans. She smoothed down her shirt and brushed herself off a bit and pushed her hair back from her face with both hands, standing in front of me.

"It's a funny thing," she said in an odd, thoughtful voice. "It's a very funny thing. I've probably lost a husband I loved very much. When all this comes out, I'll probably lose a university position I worked very hard to get. I've probably wrecked a very promising academic career. It's quite possible that I'll be sued for every cent I own and wind up penniless, jobless, disgraced, and ruined. If a certain individual cares to press charges, I may even wind up in prison for attempted murder. And as if all that was not enough to think about, I could hear the carrion-eaters working out in the dark, and I wondered when they'd get around to ripping me into little bloody pieces, and eating the pieces. But what was I *really* worrying about, lying here helpless, Mr. Helm? I'll tell you, the only thing on my mind for the last hour or so has been whether I should urinate in my clothes immediately or hold out a little longer. Silly, isn't it?"

I wasn't going to apologize for leaving her here so long, if that was what she was hinting at. I said, "I have water and beer. And some soggy crackers."

She said, "Warm beer at three o'clock in the morning is positively indecent, isn't it?"

I said, "Actually, it's closer to four, but there's no sense in trying to move until it gets light. They won't start from Labal until they can see. When we hear the Jeep we can cut straight across to the road and join them. It can't be more than a quarter of a mile through the jungle, and I brought a machete."

I gestured toward the steps of the arch, and we sat down

209

side by side. I opened the haversack, set the carton of crackers between us, and got the caps off two bottles of beer. She picked hers up and drank thirstily.

"Like I said, indecent," she said. She threw me a sideways glance. "I suppose you killed them all, just as you did here."

"Of course," I said. "Where Helm has been, no living thing remains."

She shivered. "Do you want to tell me about it?"

"Do you want to hear about it?"

She nodded. "In a way I'm responsible, so I should know about it, shouldn't I?"

"It was a very professional operation," I said. "Jim Putnam and I went for different ends of the headquarters temple. We were almost there when we were spotted by the sentry up on the Citadel. He got off a hasty burst that missed; but Paul Olcott was in position and cut him down. At the same time I heard the old general open up at the far end of the clearing and I knew he had his man. Then I pitched a grenade into the officers' end of the building, and Jim got two into the barracks end, and nailed a man who came staggering out, but another got around the corner. I heard him coming my way and dropped him with my Browning. Jim stepped out into the clear and finished him off with his .223; but in the meantime another had stumbled out and was limping down the field toward the escape road. We didn't dare fire that way because we didn't know where Henderson had taken cover over there. Then we saw something flicker among the trees—those flash-hiders leave something to be desired—and heard the general's careful five-shot burst. The running man went down, and that was just about it. Except that later we had to climb the pyramid and dig out Paul's man, who'd managed to crawl into a hole up there. But he'd lost too much blood to present a problem. No casualties among the good guys."

It hadn't been quite that simple, of course. There had been the inspection of the blasted headquarters temple afterward, and the discovery that my grenade had been wasted on an empty room but Jim's double explosive present had done a thorough and very messy job on three of the occupants of the barracks, no coups de grace required. Jim had sent me up to see if Paul Olcott needed any help at the Citadel while he reassured the rest of the party and got them started on preparations for pulling out.

I'd found an undamaged M16 in the wreckage of the officers' room. Climbing the pyramid with it slung across my back, in the dark, hadn't been my idea of recreation, particularly since no matter how I hung it the damn gun kept bumping me where I hurt. Paul Olcott signaled me over to a mass of unassembled masonry that was presumably awaiting further restoration. They put those old fallen-down buildings back together like jigsaw puzzles.

"I'm sorry; I goofed," Olcott said when I reached him, panting. "I hit him a couple of times, I'm sure, but I guess I was a bit nervous, and I didn't know the gun, and the shots went low. He managed to find cover over there in the corner behind the fallen pillar. He did a little shooting earlier, and I fired back; but there's been no sign of life for a while. I didn't want to go in after him until somebody else got here, for fear he was playing possum; but if you'll cover me . . ."

I shook my head. "Let's not be hasty. I'll take a look; you stay here and watch the rat hole."

He said stiffly, "It's my job, Sam. You don't . . . wound a lion and let somebody else go into the brush after it, dammit!"

I said, "Any lions you wound you can have, with my compliments. This is a man; and men are my business. You did your job, you kept him off our backs when it counted, now let me do mine, okay?"

But after all the heroic arguments, there was nothing to it. Approaching cautiously, I found an angle from which I could see the dark shape of the wounded man behind the pillar, lying belly-down, unmoving. He seemed to have a smashed thigh. There was a black pool of blood beneath it, and the leg lay at an angle that was just slightly wrong. There was an assault rifle on the ancient stone paving by his right hand.

I could have made sure of him from where I was crouching, of course; but something made me close in warily, watching the hand. At the last moment, it moved to grasp the M16, and the prone man tried to roll over to shoot me, but he was too weak and slow. I stepped in quickly and kicked the gun away. He sank back with a groan. When I turned him over with my foot, he choked back a scream of pain. I reached down and added another Browning, and another knife, to our arms collection.

I called, "It's okay, Paul, but get Jim up here, will you?" Putnam had apparently been coming to join us, anyway; he appeared almost immediately. I said, "I thought you might like to have this one for your very own, amigo."

We stood regarding the overly conscientious sentry who'd been so much trouble to us. Then Jim Putnam looked down at his M16 and set the selector very carefully to single fire. I touched his arm. He glanced around quickly, annoyed by the distraction.

I said, "You know her better than I do. But some women are kind of unreasonable about being raped. I knew one who bought a little knife and, with some help, personally castrated both characters who'd done it to her. Really kind of a nice girl, too."

He hesitated, and turned his head. "Paul. Would you go on down and ask Gloria Jean to come up here, please?"

Lt. Julio Barbera lay looking up at us with hating eyes, saying nothing. At last we heard footsteps and the girl appeared. She'd shed her borrowed sentry costume; and she was wearing a short-sleeved black knitted shirt and snug jeans tucked into her boots. The boots did not seem as big and clumsy with pants as they had with skirts. Even in the dim light I could see that she looked sturdy and attractive and very durable; a girl designed to last the right man a lifetime. She stepped forward and looked down at the wounded officer. I couldn't make out her expression. Perhaps it was just as well.

I turned and walked away, but I heard her voice behind me speaking softly but quite clearly: "No, I've never used one. You do it for me, please, darling. You know how." A weapon offered and refused. And the crack of a single shot. . . .

But there was no need for Frances to know these details. We sat under the massive arch, listening to the ugly noises of the scavengers feeding back along the ancient road. I thought the sky was getting faintly lighter in the east, but it was hard to be sure.

"Yes," I said, "a very neat and professional operation."

"Modesty is clearly not one of your many virtues."

I said, "It wasn't my operation. I asked Jim Putnam to run it. Big military maneuvers are out of my line."

She glanced at me. "I rather doubt that you felt incapable; it doesn't seem like you. What was your real reason for turning it over to Jim?"

I said, "Clever women make me sick. All right. He needed it. I didn't." When she didn't speak, I went on: "It was kind of pitiful, a good man, a good fighting man with a fine record, running around in a ridiculous hippie suit because, goddamn it, if they disapproved of him because of what he'd done in the army—in Vietnam—he'd give them a life-style to *really* disapprove of, and fuck them all. I had to remind him who he really was. What he really was."

"And what was he?"

"Basically he was, and is, a killer, just as I am. Very handy fellows to have around, we killers. You can feel fine and self-righteous about disapproving of us when you don't need us; and you can feel fine and self-righteous about handing us medals when you do. And in the meantime we keep you safe and do your dirty work for you; and you keep your hands clean and nobody ever, ever shoots at you."

"You sound bitter. And are you sure you've done Jim Putnam a favor, reminding him of his true nature, if that's what it really is. I doubt Gloria Jean will love you for it."

"No bitterness, but perhaps a slight touch of cynicism," I said. "And Gloria Jean is a very smart girl who will love anybody who'll give her back a live proud man for a husband instead of a brooding zombie. I think she's been waiting for years for something to shake him up. Wake him up. Well, he came awake tonight and did a good job, a very good job indeed. I think with her help he'll make it from here."

"As a killer?"

I grinned. "You don't like that word, do you? A colleague of mine once pointed out that the Victorians had a thing about sex but we have a thing about death. But let's note that when the lady got real upset she gripped a revolver very hard and emptied it, the whole damn cylinder, at a gent who'd annoyed her. Where do you get off sneering at killers, Dillman? If you weren't such a lousy shot, you'd be one yourself right now."

There was a lengthy silence. After a little I heard her

voice: "Yes. I deserved that." After a little, she asked, "Why didn't you shoot me?"

"After your gun was empty? What would that have accomplished? And before, I had to make a choice: Who was more likely to hit me, you or Eugenio? I didn't have time to deal with both. Well, that's a hard little revolver to shoot straight, particularly for a self-righteous female individual who makes a big thing of being scared of nasty firearms, as if it were something to be proud of. So I took the gamble of ignoring you and concentrating on Eugenio, and my hunch paid off."

"You forget the unarmed boy you deliberately shot to death first."

"Unarmed, hell. There was a nice big 9 mm Browning lying within ten feet of him somewhere. Two people shooting at me was quite enough; I didn't need three." After a little, I said. "I told you, Frances. I warned you. I tried my damndest to explain it to you so there would be no misunderstandings; I even described the *El Fuerte* job so you'd get the idea. And what do you do? You ignore every word I've said and send against me three silly little tin soldiers complete with their handy-dandy dimestore popguns! Jesus Christ, don't you *ever* listen to anything anybody tells you? What the hell did you think I was talking about, anyway? Do you think I'd have lasted as long in this business as I have if I could be wiped out so easily by a lousy little bunch of half-ass revolutionaries?"

She licked her lips. "I . . . thought I had to do it. To save Archie. Maybe I was wrong. Anyway, he'll die now, when Lupe Montano hears about this, won't he?"

"It's possible, but I couldn't sacrifice a dozen people for your Archie even if you could. And I don't want to get your hopes up, but there's still a chance, although I'm afraid it's getting slimmer with every day that passes. That's one reason I held off so long, almost too long as it turned out; I was waiting for something to happen. It could still happen. Keep your fingers crossed."

"I don't know what you're talking about," she said. After a moment, she went on: "Look, it's getting light over the trees. I guess we'll be joining the others soon." She hesitated. "I can't say I'm exactly looking forward to it, Matt. What will they do to me? I suppose they all hate me.

214

Not that I blame them. They have every right after the way I betrayed them."

"Have another beer," I said. "Save me from having to carry them." When she nodded, I distributed the two remaining bottles, open, and said, "You're a lousy liar, Dillman, remember that. And a terrible actress." I mimicked her cruelly: *"Don't touch me, I'm dirty. . . . I just couldn't let you be killed, my darling!* Jesus! Amateur night in the jungle!"

There was no resentment in her voice: "Is that how you knew it was a trap?"

"That, and other things. Like the sentries all carefully looking the wrong way or snoring blissfully. And before that, the way you tasted kind of sweet instead of salty when I kissed you chastely on the forehead. Not at all the way you'd expect a girl to taste who claimed to have recently been engaged in perspiring sexual activities. And not to be indelicate or anything, but even the daintiest and most fastidious ladies tend to exude at least a faint special aroma after indulging in vigorous copulation in a tropical climate. All I could smell on you was good soap. Obviously, you'd just mussed your hair a bit and pulled out your shirttail to support your touching story of how you'd grimly sacrificed your precious virtue for my sweet sake. And if you were lying about that, what else were you lying about?"

"Sherlock Holmes returns," she murmured.

I said, "But of course I knew right along, ever since we came to Labal, that you were expecting to set me up."

She glanced at me sharply. "Knew? How?"

I drew a long breath. "You said there wasn't anything you wouldn't do to get your Archie back safely, but you were wrong, weren't you, Dillman? You learned there was one thing, something you were completely incapable of doing, Archie or no Archie. You couldn't sleep with a man you knew you might soon have to lure to his death." I grinned. "You even felt obliged to make his last days pleasant by washing his clothes for him."

After a long time she whispered, "Damn you, Matt, how do you know so much about me?"

I said, "You could sleep with me to keep an eye on me. You could sleep with me for information. But you couldn't

215

sleep with me after you learned you might have to help them kill me, even though, as it turned out, you were quite capable of shooting me yourself, or trying to. But use sex for that purpose, no. I'm afraid you're really rather a nice girl, Dillman, hard though you try to conceal it."

She said softly, "It *is* getting light. We'll have to be going soon."

"We'll hear the Jeep," I said. "And the point of this whole discussion is that you can't lie worth a damn or act worth a shit. That's where we started from. So you're going to have to be careful to say as little as possible. Tell them how terrible it was. Tell them how scared you were, so scared you don't really remember what happened; and if anybody wants the whole story he'd better consult Mr. Felton. . . ."

"What——"

"Shut up and listen," I said. "We were working together. I had you get next to Colonel Sanchez deliberately and pretend to work for him, more or less, so you could obtain information from him. You did. You gave me a good description of the temple they were using. You kept me posted on how the negotiations were progressing. And last night you learned that Sanchez, tipped off by Pat Tolson, was going to make an example of me to forestall our camp mutiny. You hurried to warn me as soon as you could. You told me of a possible escape trail; and we decided to make a run for it together. We got this far when Sanchez and two men caught up with us—but what they didn't know was that I was carrying a little knife that had escaped their search, and that I'd also, anticipating trouble, hidden a revolver I'd been carrying, near the Monastery. We'd retrieved the gun as we fled, and I'd let you pack it, figuring that if they caught us, they'd search me first. When they did, and gave me an opening, I knifed Sanchez and you shot the boy soldier, whose gun I then managed to grab and turn on Eugenio. It was awful. Blood all over the place. It was terrible. You simply can't remember clearly and you're rather glad you can't. You don't want to believe you really killed a man; you just remember being dreadfully sick afterward. . . ."

"Matt," she said.

"No, don't talk, listen! We don't have to worry about bullets and ballistics; the scavengers out there are busily

216

destroying the evidence. By the time they're through, nobody'll be able to tell who shot whom with what; and I doubt that there are many forensic or ballistic experts in Costa Verde anyway. So just be the modest, inarticulate, reluctant heroine and you'll be all right. Remember, the others don't know a damn thing. I've told them nothing but the yarn you just heard. They don't suspect a thing, so don't arouse their suspicions by talking too much. If you just stick to this one story and don't try to embroider it, you'll be in the clear. . . ."

"Matt" she said. "Matt, I tried to *kill* you."

I looked at her for a moment, rather a long moment. "Yes, you tried to kill me," I said at last, "and I'll admit it kind of upset me, but I've had time to cool off and remember . . ." I cleared my throat. "Remember that I don't like cautious, careful ladies who hedge their bets. You didn't, Dillman. You had to make a choice. You had to choose between me and your goddamn Archie and you chose him. All the way. And how the hell can I hate a woman, hurt a woman, destroy a woman, for doing for another man what I'd have been very proud to have her do for me?"

She hesitated. A little time passed. At last she reached out to cover my hand with hers, and started to speak, and stopped. We sat like that for a while; then she turned her head, listening.

"There's the Jeep," she said. "We'd better go. Thank you, Matt."

CHAPTER 28

AT ten in the morning I was playing rear guard to our straggling safari, a very unmilitary procession that stumbled along the Jeep track between the vine-entangled trees, mostly fairly low, but with an occasional jungle giant among them—gigantic for that scrubby jungle at least—generally decorated with a ragged bird's nest or some wild orchids. When the road ran straight for a while I could see the whole party strung out ahead of me except for Jim Putnam and Paul Olcott, who were scouting far out in front of the slow procession.

Gen. Austin Henderson was driving the Jeep we'd liberated from the late Colonel Sanchez. It was loaded with weapons and ammunition, food and water—our luggage had been left behind, since there wasn't room for it all in the little vehicle. Ahead of the Jeep I could see Frances in her red shirt and Gloria Jean in her black one. The two schoolteachers, in similar dusty black slacks, marched side by side up there. Behind the vehicle stalked Mrs. Wilder in white pants that had got smudged in the seat, staying close to her damaged but healing husband, who was wearing wine-colored slacks and a red-checked sports shirt. The Gardenschwartzes trudged along together, and handsome blond Mrs. Olcott, deserted by her husband, kept company with Mrs. Henderson, whose wilted blue pantsuit did nothing to conceal the ample dimensions of her figure. Presently the younger woman said something to her companion and lengthened her stride to pull ahead, while the older woman paused at the roadside to rest, mopping her face. When I came up she fell in beside me.

"Thanks for asking Jim to let the old man drive," she said. "His heart really isn't very good."

"I didn't notice much wrong with his heart last night," I said. "At least it didn't interfere noticeably with his shooting eye."

"He didn't do too badly back there, did he?" She smiled fondly and glanced at me. "You know, in all these years, Sam, that's the first time I ever got to see him in action. Oh, on the drill field, of course; but always before when it was for real he'd go away and be gone for weeks or months, sometimes years, and come back all shot up or at least so tired he could hardly stand, and they'd hang another pretty on him and tell me what a hero he was; and I'd have to settle for what I could find to read about it because he'd never tell me how it had been." She hesitated. "I suppose it's heartless of me, but I can't help being glad about the way this has turned out. He's having himself a hell of a time, the old warhorse; and there aren't going to be too many more for him. We were figuring this was probably the last trip we'd get to make together."

I looked at her quickly. "That bad?"

She nodded and said quietly, "They gave him one year five years ago. He fooled them, but it's catching up with him now. I don't know what the hell I'm going to do with myself when he's gone. We women just live too damn long." She found a Kleenex in her capacious purse and blew her nose. "Pay no attention to the mushy old lady. She always gets depressed when her feet hurt."

Later, Patricia Tolson fell back to keep me company briefly. "I suppose you think you're pretty brave," she said. "Killing all those men."

I said, "I don't think I want to discuss it with you, Miss Tolson. I find it very difficult to be polite to people who've conspired to have me murdered. Go fink on somebody else, lady."

Her face turned pale and grim, and she turned and marched away, holding herself very straight. Her plump sidekick, McElder, started after her, but turned back to me fiercely.

"You don't all have to be so mean to her! She was only doing what she thought was best for all of us, trying to prevent the terrible violence you were planning. She hates violence!"

They all hate violence and cancer, but they never seem to come up with a cure. Later it was Howard Gardenschwartz, in faded khaki pants and an old white shirt, looking as if he were heading out into the garden to prune the roses or spray the delphiniums, or whatever you do to delphiniums. He walked along beside me in silence for a while. When he spoke, his voice was diffident.

"I don't suppose it matters," he said, "and I'm not complaining, you understand, but I am rather curious. I did wear a uniform once, you know, even though I didn't often wear it where I could get shot at. I had a little military training, although I don't suppose I remember much of it now. But I think I have a right to know: When you selected your . . . your team, you didn't even approach me. Why?"

He had a certain dignity, and I gave him a straight answer: "CHC."

He frowned. "CHC. What? . . . Oh."

I said, "In the course of this mission, as a matter of routine, I got thumbnail sketches of just about everybody involved, including one Gardenschwartz, Howard W.,

Ph.D., etc., etc., secretary of his local chapter of the Citizens for Handgun Control, also member of at least one other antifirearms group. Well, I'm not going to argue the principle with you, Dr. Gardenschwartz, we wouldn't get anywhere, but if I have an appendix to be removed, I don't need a surgeon who's rabidly opposed to knives. Or even an operating-room nurse: 'I'm sorry, doctor, I can't hand you that scalpel; my principles won't let me handle edged weapons.' Well, I had some people to be removed, so I didn't call on a man who hates guns. Okay?"

After a little, he nodded slowly. "I suppose that's reasonable," he said. He cleared his throat. "However, theory is one thing and practice seems to be another. If you can use another recruit, I think I could overcome my theoretical objections to firearms long enough to help you get my wife out of here."

I said, "Hell, grab a bandolier and an M16 out of the Jeep if you want. Just let me show you how it works; it's considerably different from the old M1 you were probably checked out on."

Toward noon, I made a scout back along the road and climbed a little man-made knoll surmounted by a brush-covered ruin of some kind. I sat on a dressed limestone block up there watching the road and the jungle stretching behind us back toward Labal, but nothing moved. The strong winds of the night were dying, and it was quiet and pleasant up there.

I thought about the ancients who had once populated this area. I thought about a girl who was dead. I thought about one who wasn't, but might as well be, as far as I was concerned; I hoped her goddamn Archie knew what he had there. I thought about a retribution still to be exacted. I found myself nodding and realized that I was very sleepy. . . .

Suddenly I was awake and alert. My unfocused eyes, scanning the jungle idly, had caught a tiny flash of light in the distance that didn't belong there. As I watched it came again, and I knew it for what it was: the reflection of sunlight on metal, probably the metal of a machete being used to cut trail for someone disinclined to expose himself on the lone road through this area. I waited a little, but the flash did not come again; I must have been lucky enough to catch it just right through a hole in the brush and trees way off there. I made my way down to the road and headed after the party at a lope, but found they'd made it easy for me to catch up by stopping for lunch. Jim Putnam had come back to join them.

"Trouble?" he asked as I hurried up to him.

"Company," I said. "Coming up astern, say two miles back. Not too fast; they're breaking trail instead of using the road."

"Numbers?"

I shook my head. "All I saw was a reflection off something, probably a machete. Of course it could be a lone Indian out hunting."

"It's a nice thought, but we can't gamble on—Marshall!"

"Yesh, shir, Captain Putnam, shir!"

"While Sam grabs something to eat, you take a hike back to the bend in the road beyond that one you can see, take cover, and listen. Listen hard. If you hear anything at all, come running."

Marshall Wilder still didn't like me very much. His mouth was less swollen than it had been, but the scabs where the split lips were healing were not attractive, and the missing teeth still prevented him from talking clearly. Obviously whether I starved or not was the least of his worries, but he jogged off without protest, with an assault rifle at the ready.

Jim Putnam glanced at me, with a brief grin. "He saw Howie Gardenschwartz with a toy and couldn't bear not to have one like it. I just hope I'm behind them and not in front of them when they open up. Mrs. Henderson's got one of the Brownings in that big shoulder bag of hers, and Paul's wife's got the other. He says she can shoot pretty well even if she talks a little too much sometimes—he was kidding her when he said it. They're okay." He was just rambling along while he considered his decision. "Not much choice, is there, Sam?"

"Not much," I said. "Even if we stick the worst slow-pokes in the Jeep, and there's not room for many, we'll never outrun a bunch of healthy, jungle-wise characters who are probably about half the average age of this party." I found a sandwich and a bottle of beer being thrust into my hands by General Henderson. It had been a long time since that morning snack at the Arch of the Emperors; and the big hunks of local bread with some kind of tinned meat

221

between them tasted very good. "Thank you, sir," I said belatedly.

"Never mind the sirs, son; I'm just the chauffeur around here." The old man glanced at Jim Putnam. "I gather we have problems."

Putnam grimaced. "Sam made the mistake of looking back, like the man said not to, and something is gaining on us."

"Well, we're in no shape to outrun it, whatever it is, that's for sure. With your permission, Captain, I'll get the Jeep under cover."

"Permission granted. Grab anybody you need to help." Jim looked around. "Thank God for those indefatigable old pyramid-builders. How about that big one over there, with all the rocks on top? We can hold out up there for a while at least and hope that somebody with a white hat hears the shooting. . . . Oh, Christ, here comes more trouble!"

Elspeth Olcott, who'd apparently been keeping her husband company up ahead, was approaching at a tired run, her blond hair damp around her shiny face. She had to keep holding onto the big 9 mm pistol thrust into the waistband of her smart but rather dusty green slacks. A bunch of middle-aged, inexperienced folks playing jungle fighters; but I had nothing but respect for them now. They hadn't all endured captivity well; but now they were mostly doing the best they could. Jim Putnam went to meet the breathless woman, listened to the report she gasped out, and came back.

"Motors ahead," he said. "More than one vehicle approaching, Paul says. It looks as if they've got us whipsawed." He shook his head quickly. "Well, there's no choice now. We'll take cover up there. Glory, run and get Marshall back here on the double, please. Howie, jog on up and ask Paul to come in, fast. Everybody else start climbing. . . . To hell with outposts. If we have to shoot, with the amateur talent we've got, we want to be able to let them fire at anything that moves in this lousy brush without worrying about whether or not it's one of ours. Come on, Sam, let's give Austin a hand. . . ."

Shortly, the Jeep was out of sight, well back in the jungle, covered with brush. The vegetation damaged in getting it there had been hastily replaced or repaired. The noncombatant ladies were safely hidden in the rocks of the fallen temple—if it was a temple—on top of the artificial hill. Unrestored, this pyramid exhibited no steps, just steep rubble slopes covered with scraggly vegetation. The combatant ladies—including Gloria Jean who, at her insistence, had been given a spare M16 and a thirty-second course in how to use it—were stationed around the defensive perimeter with their husbands.

I'd been assigned to help Henderson direct the defense of the rear of our position once things got really tough and we were surrounded up there; in the meantime I crouched behind some tumbled masonry beside the Putnams wondering how, in the rush of events, they'd managed to find time to resolve their personal problem, but it was quite evident that they had: The girl was looking so pretty you could hardly stand it. I reflected upon the fact that love merely turns men unbearably smug, while it turns women beautiful, which doesn't seem quite fair. We watched the road, since nothing had shown in the jungle behind us since those telltale machete flashes. The sound of the approaching motorized force was quite loud now; and presently the lead Jeep came into sight filled with armed men who looked dangerously tense and alert.

"It's Montano's bunch, all right," Jim Putnam whispered. His face was grim. "No army insignia; and I recognize that bent fender. That's one of the Jeeps they used to transport us to Labal." He glanced at me and grinned tightly. "George Armstrong Custer, where are you now that we really need you? Any brilliant suggestions, Mr. Government Agent?"

I said, "Hell, man, why do you think I dumped it all in your lap? You get to make all the fun decisions. Fight and die, or surrender and die."

"Yes, if we do surrender, I don't suppose Mr. Montano will be very nice to us after he finds all those dead men. We'd better make as much of a fight of it as we can, and hope for the best."

I said, "Agency policy has always been to take as many of the bastards with you as you can, when you go. If you simply have to go. But let's not rush it, they haven't spotted us yet. . . . Whoa, wait a minute! Let me have those toy binoculars, please."

The lead Jeep had gone by without seeing us or our

hidden vehicle. Now, after a considerable interval, the second Jeep was coming into sight at the end of the straight stretch of road below us. I focused on it with the expensive little folding glasses belonging to Elspeth Olcott, which had been overlooked when our captors relieved our luggage of all other negotiable valuables. Occasional trees and branches intervened—we didn't have a totally unobstructed view of the road—but I saw that there were three men in the second vehicle and that there was something lashed to the rear of it that reflected silvery glints in the sunlight.

The driver was a small dark man I didn't know. The man in the rear was, rather to my surprise, an Anglo—as we call the non-Spanish up in my home state of New Mexico. Gringo, if you prefer. I didn't know him, either. I tried to see the man up front beside the driver, but a tree got in the way, so I swung the glasses onto the car behind. This was a beat-up old armored personnel carrier of some kind, full of lower-class manpower just as the first Jeep had been. The one between the two vehicles was, as I'd thought, the command car. The face of the man in the forward passenger seat came into clear focus. . . .

"Don't shoot!" I whispered urgently to Jim Putnam. "Don't let anybody shoot. Slip around quickly and tell them all to keep their heads down and hold their fire no matter what happens. . . . Here, take these."

He took the glasses and the assault rifle I handed him. "What are you going to . . ."

I said softly, "Take a quick look at that Jeep and you'll understand. Just for God's sake keep everybody from getting trigger-happy. I've got to get down there before they get clear past us."

I went out of there low, keeping cover between me and the road and angling right to cut off the slow-moving Jeep below; also to draw attention away from our hiding place, if I were spotted. I found a solid slab of limestone that had slid down from the ruins on top, and rose up behind it.

"Hey, Dick Anderson!" I shouted. "Hey, Ricardo Jimenez!"

I threw myself flat behind my protecting slab just in time. As I'd expected, the crowded vehicles exploded like damaged hornets' nests, men diving for cover in all directions, hosing down the surrounding jungle as they ran: the good old if-it-moves-or-talks-shoot-it syndrome characteristic of green troops under heavy stress. All we needed to have a firefight nobody could stop was a couple of shots from our pyramid fortress; but Jim Putnam had them under control up there and nobody fired back.

As the shooting petered out, I heard orders being snapped below. I raised my head cautiously and shouted, "Tell them to cut it out, amigo, or I won't push your damn wheelchair any more."

After a moment, young Jimenez's voice called back, "Come on down, Matt."

I drew a long breath and stood up slowly and made my way down the slope to the road, which was now full of revolutionary manpower more or less in uniform. Another vehicle had appeared around the curve to my left; and I thought I could see more behind that. The members of the Army of Liberation seemed a little abashed at the way they'd made fools of themselves, which was a hopeful sign, much better than if they'd been mad at me for being the cause of it.

Ricardo Jimenez was standing beside his Jeep, holding onto it for support, while the driver unstrapped the shiny wheelchair secured behind. He was in a khaki uniform with an officer's cap more or less concealing his bleached hair, and a big automatic pistol at his hip—a .45 Colt, I noted, rather than the locally popular 9 mm Brownings. Fewer shots, but more authority per shot.

Ricardo made an apologetic gesture. "Sorry about that. They're a bit keyed up."

"A bit," I said. "Tell them to relax, if it's Colonel Sanchez they're worrying about."

Ricardo studied me for a moment. "I see. That is how you come to be free. So Sanchez got careless? We were not informed."

"We didn't leave anybody to inform, amigo. That would have been stupid, wouldn't it? You'll see the *zopilotes* when you get down the road a ways." I looked at his military column. "Do I gather there has been a change of command?"

Ricardo nodded. "I . . . took your advice."

"Kind of slow about it, weren't you?" I said. "I waited damn near ten days, until Sanchez forced my hand. I was beginning to think you'd let that two-gun *bandido* beat you to the draw."

He shook his head. "The situation was never right. I could not, after all, fight with him for the kidnaping he'd used to force Señora Dillman to help me into the country, which I had not known about—I was naive enough to think that she was simply an idealistic and freedom-loving lady—but it had been done for me. It would have seemed ungrateful of me to quarrel with him over that. It was not until I saw your camera case and the Putnams' jewelry in his quarters, and learned how he was using our revolution for his own profit, shaming and defiling our cause with his cheap thievery and his million-dollar extortion plot. . . ."

Ricardo smiled thinly. "Your advice was very useful, Matt. My men were ready when he lost his temper at my accusations and reached for one of his big pistols. They took care of his bodyguards; but it was my shot that took care of him."

"You're improving," I said. "But you've got a ways to go, Generalissimo."

"What do you mean?"

"Shouldn't that armored job be out front? And what the hell are you doing making a target of yourself in an open car? Well, military techniques aren't my bag; all I know is that right now you've got half a dozen *fusilitas automaticas* or whatever the Spanish for M16 is, looking down your throat. If we'd been Sanchez, you'd be dead, and a lot of your expeditionary force with you." I glanced at him sharply. "You figured if he'd heard about Montano's death and your takeover, he'd be laying for you?"

"It was a possibility. Or he would have taken his place quietly enough as my second-in-command and then plotted to displace me. You have done me a favor by removing him. He was an ambitious man, with strong overseas connections; and there are, I'm afraid, some in our ranks who find the Marxist doctrine attractive. There are also some who would prefer as their leader a seasoned military man rather than a crippled boy, even if the boy's name is Jimenez. They could be right." He grimaced and looked up at the pyramid. "Up there? Yes, even a group of tourists, properly armed, could have done us much damage from up there. I do have things to learn, I am afraid. But tell them to come down. It is safe now."

I hesitated. "How about the gang you've got coming up behind us? I'd hate to have them blundering in here with their safeties off and their fingers on their triggers, if they're as nervous as . . . What's the matter?"

Ricardo was frowning. "Somebody is following you? I have nobody out there, Matt. You did say you wiped out *all* of Sanchez's unit?"

"Sanchez, Barbera, and ten men. All we ever saw. I guarantee they're following nobody. You'd better throw out some scouts between here and Labal and see who the hell is sneaking around out there. . . . Just a minute. I've got an idea. How proud are you, Generalissimo?"

"What do you mean?"

"Are you too proud to take advice? I don't know a damn thing about this kind of an operation; but we've got a resident expert up in those rocks, if you're willing to ask him for help." When he nodded without hesitation, I raised my voice: "Hey, Jim, tell them peace has been declared. And haul your ass down here, please, we need you."

A few minutes later, certain orders had been given and men had hurried off to execute them. I left Ricardo and Jim Putnam in earnest consultation about further tactical matters outside my experience—I remembered that Ricardo's father had, after all, been a very competent army officer before he became a less competent president; some military knowledge had apparently rubbed off on the son.

I turned to the unidentified gringo who was still sitting in the rear of the Jeep. He was a handsome man in his thirties with a sensitive intellectual face made more sensitive and intellectual by big horn-rimmed glasses. His dark hair was cut too long and wavy for my taste, and he was wearing one of those expensive poplin safari suits, all loops and straps and bellows-type pockets, that make them look like ersatz Great White Hunters—but then I'd known before I saw him that there was no way I was ever going to like this man. His left earlobe was missing, but the injury was healing well.

"Dr. Archibald Dillman, I presume," I said.

CHAPTER 29

I awoke in sunshine to see Frances Dillman standing over me. "It must be nice to be able to sleep anywhere," she said.

"All it takes is years of practice," I said. I sat up and yawned and brushed myself off a little. "Is the war over? Can we go home now?"

She smiled. "Great military maneuvers seem to be taking place out there. We've heard a little shooting, but none in the last half hour." She looked down at me curiously. "I'm surprised you're not out there with them."

"Whatever the hell for?" I asked. "They don't need my help. A soldier I'm not."

There was a little silence. I was sitting on a small shelf or bench about halfway up the side of the pyramid we'd chosen for our gallant last stand. Originally it had probably been a paved ceremonial terrace of some kind. I'd had a patch of shade when I first started to nap, but since then, the sun had moved westward around my chosen bush to get a clear shot at me. Some members of our party were chatting on a larger terrace above us; and above them Ricardo, or Jim Putnam, had stationed half a dozen armed men in the temple ruins we'd vacated. From my lower viewpoint I couldn't see the road clearly, but I could make out through the trees the silhouettes of a couple of parked vehicles and catch occasional glimpses of moving men with guns. It was all very warlike, and very peaceful, at the same time.

I looked up at Frances standing there, still faintly elegant-looking despite the dust on her expensive jeans and the rather wilted condition of her red silk shirt—the same clothes, I remembered, in which she'd once watched a human sacrifice with me. It seemed a long time ago, so long ago that the memory was losing reality. (I didn't *really* believe in ancient blood rites and telepathic communication, did I?)

Frances crouched down beside me. "Don't tell me what you're not, Matt," she said softly. "Tell me what you are. Even after all this, I still don't know."

"It's none of your damned business what I am, married lady," I said. "How was the sentimental reunion?"

But I didn't have to ask; I could see how it had been. She was a tall and dignified and handsome adult woman; but at the moment she had a young-girl glow about her that was a dead giveaway, very much like Gloria Jean Putnam. Her interest in me was obviously only a momentary female curiosity about a man with whom she'd shared some mildly intriguing experiences, now ended.

"It was . . . sentimental," she said cautiously. Then she went on in a breathless way: "Oh, God, Matt, I'd given him up! After last night I was sure Montano was going to kill him and I'd never see him again. I was trying to understand how I could possibly endure a whole lifetime without him. And then I saw him in that Jeep!" She swallowed hard.

I told myself that it wasn't that I had anything against undying marital devotion; but why did they have to keep waving it under my nose? The loving young Putnams, Mrs. Henderson and her old-soldier husband, and now this woman with whom I'd slept more than once and her intellectual spouse in his safari suit with his intellectual eyeglasses and his soulful eyes—why the hell didn't they just save it for the bedroom and keep it decently concealed in public?

"Sure," I said. "It's great, but did he get my message? He didn't seem to be paying a great deal of attention when I laid it out for him. If he doesn't play this right, you can still be in considerable trouble."

She actually blushed a little. "I'm afraid we didn't get around to discussing any practical matters like that. He just mentioned that you'd been trying to tell him something, but he'd been too eager to see me to listen closely. That's why I climbed down here to find you."

I said, "Okay, it goes like this. He was never kidnaped— make sure he understand that. He was never kidnaped, because if he was kidnaped, people will start wondering what you were supposed to do to get him back—did to get him back—and that's the one question you don't want anybody asking."

"But——"

I said, "It will work, if you play it right. If he plays it right. Ricardo already has too many abductions credited to his Costa Verde liberation movement to make him happy. He'll be delighted to do without this one; he'll see that it's kept quiet at his end. I'll talk to him. Nobody's going to be too damn interested in your husband, as long as he keeps a low profile. We're the real story—big semiscientific expedition held for ransom—particularly the Putnams, since they're the beautiful people who were being taken for a million bucks. Nobody's going to give a hoot about Professor Archibald Dillman, who was just kind of looking around for his wife after coming to Copalque to give her a nice surprise by joining the tour unexpectedly. Only, when he got to the site, no wife. So he poked around and questioned his contacts among the local population and learned who was responsible for the disappearance. He had a native guide lead him to Montano's camp, where he almost got into trouble, since Lupe didn't appreciate his snooping. But fortunately there was a fight among the revolutionary leaders, and the survivor, Ricardo Jimenez, didn't believe in kidnaping and extortion as part of his national liberation program. Once he had control, he hurried off to Labal to set us free, bringing your husband with him. Okay? Do you think you can sell that to your Archie?"

She didn't answer my question immediately. Instead she said, "You don't like him, do you?"

I looked at her and said, "If you were to think very hard, use all those trained brains you're supposed to have, you might be able to come up with a reason why I wouldn't be too fond of any guy you were married to."

She put her hand on mine lightly. "Matt, I'm sorry."

I said dryly, "This is the place where you say you never meant to hurt me—even when you were emptying a .38 Special at my back."

Stung, she took her hand away; then I heard her laugh. "Chalk up a point for the tall man with the overnight whiskers. And in answer to your question, yes, I'm sure Archie will agree it's the sensible thing to do. And we both thank you." She looked at a piece of paper I held out, a sheet torn out of my little photo-notebook. "What's that?"

230

"Memorize and destroy," I said. "If there should be any repercussions after we get out of here, and you think I can help, that number will reach me, although perhaps not right away. Or . . ." I hesitated. "Or if you should ever get into any other trouble where my special talents might prove useful."

She shook her head quickly. "Matt, I couldn't ask you for any more help, ever, you must know that. Not after what you've already . . ."

I said, "Hell, you might misplace that guy again and want him retrieved. Would you jeopardize his precious life because of some silly qualms about asking favors of the one man you know who might be able to get him back for you?"

She laughed once more. "You really are prickly today, aren't you? All right, I'll memorize your number gratefully, my dear, and thank you again."

I said, "You probably don't want advice, nobody wants advice, but I'll give it to you anyway. Don't tell your Archie anything he doesn't have to know if you haven't already." Her slightly guilty look told me that she hadn't yet found the right moment for the great confession-session and she wasn't looking forward to it. I went on, "Sure, he should know the general outlines of what happened, so he can help protect you from damaging publicity. But certain demands were made of you that nobody needs to know about, particularly not your husband, if you know what I mean. Confession may be good for the soul, but it can play hell with a marriage."

"Says that old married man, Matthew Helm!" Her voice was suddenly sharp.

"Precisely," I said. "As it happens, that's just the reason I'm no longer married. My wife had learned something I'd have kept from her, for her sake, but she did go looking where I'd asked her not to. One of our children was involved, and I'd had to do some rather unpleasant things to save the little monster. The knowledge that her husband was capable of such acts—even with the best motive in the world—was more than my tender bride could bear. Once our baby was safe she started brooding about it. End of marriage."

There was a long silence. At last Frances licked her lips and said, "I'm sorry, I didn't know. You never told me you'd been . . . I shouldn't have said that. I'm sorry."

"It was a long time ago," I said. "And you're sorry, but you're still going to babble like a brook in spite of all my brotherly advice, aren't you?"

She hesitated; then she nodded. "I have to. Don't you see that I have to? I can't . . . can't soil our marriage with that kind of a lie, that kind of concealment. . . ."

She was interrupted by the snapping sound of gunfire not too far away out in the jungle. I pulled her quickly down beside me, listening. At last I sat up.

"Go get your husband and get behind a rock. Tell the others. It isn't very close, but those little bullets travel a long way; it would be very dumb to get killed now by a wandering slug. . . . Go on, run!"

On her feet, she hesitated. "Matt, I———"

"Beat it," I said. "See you in a nice, dark sacrificial cave some time, Dillman."

I got to my feet and watched her reach safety up there before I turned away. I was heading down the slope toward the road when a guerilla fighter, junior grade, came running up to me.

"Señor Helm?"

"*Si, yo soy Helm.*"

He informed me that *El Jefe Menor* desired my presence, and I indicated that I would be delighted to grant such a reasonable wish. I followed him at a brisk pace, noting that the shooting had stopped. We found Ricardo about a quarter of a mile down the road in the direction of Labal, sitting in his wheelchair in the dubious shade of a Jeep.

I raised my hand, movie-Indian-fashion, and said, "How, Minor Chief."

He wasn't amused at first; they tend to take themselves a little seriously down here. Then he grinned and said, "My father—the former president of this country, as you'll recall—was *El Jefe Mayor*, or Big Chief. Clearly that makes me *El Jefe Menor*, or Little Chief." He stopped grinning and looked at me narrowly. "Are you sure you have no idea who was following you, Matt?"

I shook my head. "None whatever. Why?"

"Jim has them pinned down out there, whoever they are," he said. "There are only about a dozen of them, he thinks. They have sent a messenger; they are willing to parley; but they will speak only to Señor Matthias Helm." He was still watching me closely. "That is your real name, is it not? Who would be out there in the jungle who would ask for you, Matt? Or Matthew/Matthias, as the case may be?"

"I have friends in strange places," I said. "And enemies. But what one of them is doing out there I have no idea. Make up your mind, Ricardo."

"The messenger was in civilian clothes, but he had carelessly forgotten to remove his Costa Verde army dog tags. And I do not forget that there could still be a matter between us of a lady who was murdered in Chicago, even though you so generously claim to have absolved me of the guilt incurred by other members of my family."

I said, "You're in a tough spot, Little Chief. You're going to have to either trust me or shoot me. As I said, make up your cotton-picking mind."

He smiled thinly. "Oh, I wouldn't dare to shoot you, Señor Helm. Sanchez tried it and died with all his men— but now I am wondering if you accomplished that feat entirely without outside assistance."

"And then called your attention to my invisible allies out in the jungle so you could make trouble for them?" I shook my head. "Well, it's a natural doubt, I suppose, but you'll have to resolve it for yourself."

He looked at me for a moment longer and smiled slowly. "*Bueno, amigo.* It is resolved. I am foolish enough to think that you are an honest man in your way; such naivete will probably destroy me eventually. But go put an end to this stupid shooting before some of my men are killed."

I looked at him sitting there; and for the first time I found myself wondering if perhaps his crazy revolution stood a chance. There was more to this wheelchair-bound young man than I'd thought.

"Any restrictions?"

He shook his head. "Use your judgment. Execute them or let them go, as you wish. It is up to you."

Another young revolutionary in a sweaty uniform guided me along a hastily cleared trail through the dry forest to where Jim Putnam had set up a little field headquarters of sorts.

"Goddamn shoestring operation," he grumbled when I came up. "Half the communications gear doesn't work worth a shit. And the only English-speaking noncom I've got I had to send off to straighten out a mess. . . . Well, never mind that. You got the message?"

I nodded. "Who do you think you've got in the bag?" I asked.

"Hell, there's no telling in this stuff. Nobody's had a good look at them." He slapped an insect that landed on his neck. "They're about three hundred yards off thataway, in another of those lousy ruins," he said, pointing through the tangled brush in a southerly direction. "Instant pillboxes. We've got a good knot tied around them, and we could clean them out, but they know what they're doing and we'd take some losses. These are good boys, but they're awfully damn green. Does Bullet mean anything to you besides what comes out of a gun. Or Metal Pee?"

"Sounds like a serious urinary problem," I said.

"Come over here." He led me behind a tree to where a wounded man was lying, wearing a loose dirty-white cotton shirt and tattered denim pants. There was a considerable amount of blood. Jim Putnam glanced at me and said, a little defiantly, "Hell, nobody ever told these boys about a white flag. Anyway, it wasn't until we picked him up that we saw what he was holding."

That must have been the shooting we'd just heard. I said, "Well, you're damn well going to personally unload every gun along your line of battle before I get out in front of your trigger-happy heroes. They've had their crack at me for the day."

He spread his hands a little. "Okay, okay, they're a bit wild, I admit it. But you don't know what a relief it is to have troops that'll actually pull their goddamn triggers, instead of the tender mama's boys we used to be sent as replacements over there, who'd let themselves be killed and a lot of good men with them, rather than fire their nasty weapons at precious human targets. At least you know these tough little bastards are going to defend themselves if you give them half a chance; you're not just sending them out to be helpless dead meat."

I looked at him for a moment and realized that he, like Ricardo, had changed considerably in a very short time. Already he was identifying with the inexperienced guerilla fighters he'd had command of for only a couple of hours.

Then I looked down as the man at our feet tried to speak.

Jim said, "see if you can get some sense out of him. Find out who sent him. I hate to let you go out there not knowing who's there."

I crouched beside the wounded man. *"Como se llama su jefe?"* I asked in my horrible Spanish. "What is the name of your leader?"

The man seemed to be muttering something about a bullet, using the English word, not the Spanish. Then, realizing he wasn't getting through to me, he said desperately: *"Pie de metall!"*

"There's your metal pee," Jim Putnam said.

The man said very clearly, "Bullet Man."

I straightened up. "Okay, that takes care of it," I said. "Incidentally, *pie* means foot in Spanish. Why don't you get this poor bastard back to the road? Mrs. Henderson and your wife both know some first aid; maybe they can do something for him. And tell me when you've got those guns unloaded. I'm going in. Where's that white flag? For what little it seems to be worth around here . . ."

A few minutes later I was making my way through the organic barbed-wire entanglement that surrounded us, clearing the way with a machete, my only weapon, unless you call a stick with a soiled white hanky a weapon. The bandaged groove in my back didn't make my progress any easier, or less painful. When I'd gone about a hundred and fifty yards in the general direction Jim Putnam had indicated, making plenty of noise so as not to catch anybody by surprise, I stopped. There was nothing in sight now but trees and brush and thorny vines. Some of the bushes had thorns on them, too. There were no pretty jungle flowers in sight, or gaudy jungle birds. I wondered why the hell I seemed to be the one who got elected, every time, to risk my vulnerable hide between the hostile armies.

I drew a long breath and shouted, "Hey, Mr. Metal-foot. Hey, Señor Bullet Man."

A voice behind me, quite close, said, *"Bitte,* lay down the machete, Herr Helm. It is said that you are with it quite skillful. . . . So. Now you may turn. Where is Gregorio?"

I said, "Hell, you heard the shooting. Sorry. These aren't the best-trained troops in the world. They even let off a few rounds at me earlier in the day. Your man is alive and being taken care of, but I wouldn't want to make an optimistic prognosis."

I had turned upon being given permission. Now Bultman came toward me cautiously, holding a well-worn P38 automatic pistol, the weapon that might be considered the Germanic successor to the Luger of romantic memory. Actually, it's a better weapon than the Luger, with its atrocious trigger mechanism, ever was.

The Kraut looked just like his fuzzy pictures in the dossier I'd studied: the typical tall lean super-Aryan of the old Nazi movies, not the thick-necked Prussian-type villain, but the storm trooper with a conscience, perhaps, who was revolted by the atrocities committed by his comrades, and let the pretty Jewish heroine escape, and finally blew out his brains to resolve the terrible conflict between good and evil within him. He was a rather handsome fellow, not young, but well preserved and in good condition, with a blond, cropped, dolichocephalic head. He was wearing stained khakis, but, like Frances Dillman, he was the kind of person who'd look elegant in rags.

I said, "I thought you'd be in Chicago by this time."

"You know about Chicago?"

"What else would Rael hire you for? He's got Echeverria to handle his local assassinations."

"Is that why you have been looking for me, *hein?* Oh, yes, your inquiries have not gone unnoticed. You wish to prevent me from my work accomplishing in Chicago?"

I said, "Hell, no. I'm all for your Chicago caper; in fact, for personal as well as official reasons I'd like to give you a discreet hand there. But we don't have time to go into that now. No, the guiding geniuses of a certain well-known undercover organization instructed us to save them from possible public embarrassment by insuring your permanent silence—I think you can guess who gave us those instructions. What the hell made you accept that idiot contract? From those people? You know how they are."

The P38 was steady. "You speak so of your own government colleagues?" Then Bultman shrugged his shoulders and spoke wryly: "You know how it is, Helm. One wonders if one could do it. Then one is offered very much money to do it, and it is a great challenge, *nicht wahr?* To be the one who accomplished it, who actually removed the bearded one at last, after so many had failed . . ."

"So you joined the ranks of the failures and wound up with a tin foot and the little publicity-shy lads from Virginia running scared along your trail."

"So frightened, apparently, that they did not dare to catch up with me, but sent you instead."

I grinned. "Hell, that's what we're for. Every so often they remember it. Very reluctantly."

"And what do you plan now, Helm?"

"Why," I said, "I am going to complete my assignment according to my own best judgment, as my chief instructed me to. Raise your right hand . . . Oh, for Christ's sake! I'm unarmed and I'm sure you've got a couple of guns covering me besides your own."

Bultman hesitated. "I do not understand. . . . Ah, very well." He switched the automatic to his left hand and held up the other.

"Good," I said. "Now swear to me on whatever you hold sacred that you will never, under any circumstances, reveal the identity of the organization for which you were working on that ill-fated mission on which you lost your foot."

"*Ach*, this is stupid!" he said irritably. "I do not betray the names of my principals——"

I said, "I know that. And you know it. So what harm does it do to swear it?"

After a moment, he smiled thinly. "Very well. I do so swear."

"*Danke schön*," I said. "I have now insured your permanent silence as my orders required. There's my official assignment in Costa Verde, all taken care of. What's yours? The last I heard, you were in Mexico City, recruiting."

"You are well informed. But some of the specialists I needed were not immediately available, so I called my principal here and asked if delay was permissible. I was told that it was; but I was asked if I would be willing to perform a small additional task while I was waiting. At a price, of course."

"Of course," I said.

"This mass kidnaping has come to the attention of my principal. He fears that if the hostages are harmed he will face strong disapproval in the United States on the grounds that he is no longer able to maintain order in his country; he may even lose the American support he requires to stay in power. On the other hand, he cannot afford to allow the prisoners to be ransomed. He cannot let one million dollars fall into the hands of the rebels."

"So he's making it as tough as he can for them to transfer the money; and meanwhile he's hired you to pick a small task force from some crack units of the Costa Verde army and slip in and blast the hostages out."

Bultman nodded. "With a generous bonus to be paid if I could manage to eliminate a certain Lupe de Montano in the process. However, when we located the rebel camp the prisoners were not there, and Montano had already been shot to death by one of his associates. We ascertained that the hostages were actually being held by a small guerilla unit at a place called Labal, and hastened there, and found nothing but dead men. That must have been an interesting fight in the place of the arch, Helm."

"It was a busy evening," I said. "So you came after us——"

"To place you under my protection, ja. When you met this force of rebels I assumed that you had simply recaptured been. I moved in to see if I could take them by surprise and rescue you—only to run into a very skillful ambush here."

"Yes," I said. "You're on kind of a spot, aren't you?"

"You should know; you are responsible." He grimaced. "I was aware that you were considered expert with edged weapons and very good with long-range firearms; but I had not been told that you had experience in handling troops in this kind of terrain. I thought I was dealing merely with a crippled boy who knows only the textbooks he read in his military school; but suddenly these clumsy guerillas started behaving like jungle-trained veterans. My congratulations."

"Wrong man," I said. "You had the bad luck to tangle with a very experienced graduate of Vietnam. You admit that he's got you trapped, and that he's got enough manpower to wipe you out?"

Bultman said stiffly, "It will not be so easy. We will give a good account of ourselves."

I said, "Fuck the heroics. You're a pro. You don't want to die bravely, you want to live profitably. Suppose I were to get you out of here, and maybe even arrange it so you

238

get a little credit for bringing us poor hostages out unharmed, would you be willing to cooperate with me on a
project I have in mind?"

CHAPTER 30

Two days later I was sitting in my hotel room in
Santa Rosalia waiting, like the others, for Latin-American
bureaucracy and international diplomacy to cope with the
perplexing problem we'd handed them. The phone rang and
I listened to the voice of our current man in Costa Verde,
never mind his name, reporting that our eager researchers
back in the States had made the startling discovery that Dr.
Archibald Dillman was not attending the archaeological
conference he was supposed to be attending. He also said
he'd received some information I'd asked for, and would
send it right over.

"And you wanted to know if Bultman showed up at *El
Palacio de los Gobernadores*," the voice said. "He was seen
leaving there this morning after having had appointments
with Enrique Echeverria and *El Presidente* himself."

I grimaced at the sunlit window. "It could be good; or it
could be the biggest double-cross since the tenth disciple
played his dirty trick. Keep an eye on him. Thanks."

With nothing better to do, I went downstairs to have a
drink by the pool. Some of our people were there in swimming attire, reminding me of another pool we'd frequented,
actually in prettier surroundings than this tiled patio. I'd
just settled down in a metal chair beside a glass-topped
table when one of the swimmers came up dripping, drying
her hair on a big towel.

"What in the world do you call that?" Gloria Jean Putnam asked. "It's positively gigantic."

"Let me introduce you to the local banana daiquiri, Mrs.
Putnam," I said. "Cocktails, dinner, dessert, and after-
dinner drink, all in one."

"I'll have one, if you don't mind." She was in a snug and

239

quite plain black tank suit that did nice things for her well-developed young body. She gave me a straight and steady look. "I need some advice. Please?"

"Sure," I said. "It's what we've got most of. Make yourself comfortable."

When I returned with her drink, she'd pulled a chair close to the one in which I'd been sitting. "Thanks," she said, and then: "I feel kind of weird, don't you? I mean, I feel that any minute now I'll wake up and discover that I've been dreaming, I've just been taking a nap up in our little private temple, or whatever it was, and it's time to grab the dirty clothes and give them a good scrubbing in the *cenote*."

"I know what you mean."

She said abruptly, "I'm not really a vengeful person, Sam. It gave me no satisfaction to see that man wounded and in pain. But I had to know that he was dead with . . . with what he'd learned about me. As long as he was alive, I knew I'd never quite be able to make myself forget it, and neither would Jim." She shook her head abruptly. "But that's not what I wanted to talk with you about." She moved a little, and her towel dropped onto the tiled patio floor. "Pick it up for me, please," she said. A little surprised at the direct order, I did as she'd asked, bringing my head close to her chair as I bent over. I heard her ask softly, "Is it safe to . . . to discuss things here, Sam?"

I picked up the towel and gave it to her. "There you are, ma'am." After a moment, not looking around but considering the surroundings—the nearby bar, the noisy pool, the high wall surrounding the whole patio—I nodded. "I think it should be reasonably safe."

She said, "I know your real name is Matt, but I still think of you as Sam." She hesitated. "Does that revolution of Ricardo's really have a chance, Sam?"

"Not much at the moment, I'd say." I frowned thoughtfully. "Oh, they can probably hang on out there in the jungle and make themselves obnoxious almost indefinitely, but as far as breaking out and taking over the country is concerned, I wouldn't put much money on them."

"Do you mind telling me why you think so?"

"Ricardo," I said. "Let's face it, Lupe Montano may have been strictly a robber chief, but he was a seasoned fighter. Ricardo's heart is very much in the right place, but the poor guy doesn't get around very well and he doesn't really know what he's doing in a military way—hell, look at the way he ran that scouting party right under our guns, a bunch of tourists like us."

She gave me a level glance. "You know why I'm asking this, don't you?"

"I can guess," I said. "Your husband can't bear to think of those trigger-happy guerillas of his—well, they were his for an afternoon—taking orders from anybody else."

"Ricardo has offered him a rather high commission in the Army of Costa Verde Liberation."

"And with that and twenty cents he can make a phone call, except where it costs a quarter."

Gloria Jean shook her head quickly. "No, you mustn't make fun of it. It's very serious for me, Sam. For both of us. Because I can make it go either way. If I ridicule it as you just did, if I kick and scream and say I can't stand having him do this crazy thing doesn't he love me any more, he'll refuse it and forget it, I'm afraid. Well, not forget it, he'll never forget it, but he'll resign himself to——"

"Afraid?" I interrupted, looking at her curiously. "You're *afraid* that he'll do what you want him to?"

She gave me that straight look of hers again. "Of course. Because he shouldn't, should he? If it's what he really wants, really needs, should he give it up because his stupid wife throws a stupid tantrum?" She made a wry face. "I mean, it isn't as if he'd ever lied to me or deceived me. I knew I was getting a soldier when I married him, didn't I? We made our . . . our deal on that basis; and he'd be perfectly justified on booting me to hell out of his life if I started having second thoughts and trying to interfere with his chosen career. And before Vietnam he'd have done it, too. But they took such a lot out of him in that war and afterward, they took such a lot away from him, including the work he was trained for; and I'm afraid that the bitter way he feels now I really could influence him against his better judgment. That's why I need your advice. If this revolution is a lost cause, should I let him accept that commission anyway? Can I let him go and maybe be killed, when I know I can stop him if I really try?"

I said, "That's kind of up to you, isn't it, Gloria Jean? Do you want a safe half man or an unsafe whole one?"

She drew a ragged breath. "I guess that's about it. It's been so wonderful seeing him come back to life, so to speak; but is it worth his life to keep him that way?"

I said, "According to Bultman, who should know, Jim had those clumsy, inexperienced revolutionaries behaving like seasoned jungle fighters in a mere couple of hours. Your man is good at what he does."

"Of course he is," she said calmly. "But that doesn't solve my problem, does it?"

"Don't be too sure," I said. "Because with Jim in the picture, the picture could change considerably. With Ricardo and his well-known name for the country to rally to, and his crippled body to remind everybody of the brutal oppression they're fighting; and with Jim whipping those wild-eyed liberators into a disciplined fighting force and handling them expertly, there could be a significant shift in the odds. I'm sticking my neck out saying it—I'm no military expert—but they could make it. Indications are that Rael's army isn't very loyal. If they get hit hard once or twice, they may start coming over in droves with all their U.S.-made equipment, flocking to the Jimenez name they remember from the time of his soldier daddy, forgetting that old Hector wasn't the greatest president they ever had —just as Montano hoped when he got Ricardo sprung out of La Fortaleza. Remembering *El Jefe Mayor,* they may even adopt *El Jefe Menor* as a mascot and carry him on their shoulders right into the Palace of the Governors. It's a wild scenario, but it could happen—*if* somebody with military brains is handling the fighting end of it. Somebody like Jim Putnam."

There was a long silence. At last Gloria Jean shook her head minutely. "I'm a bitch. I'm discovering that wasn't the answer I wanted to hear."

"I know."

"But . . . but you can't keep a man around for a pet if he's worth anything, can you? Anyway, I had that, years of that, and it wasn't so great."

After a little, I said, "There's something Jim should know if he takes the job. There are a lot of munitions hidden away in that cave we were all going to see at Copalque, that we never got around to exploring as a party. Montano hid them there. They're booby-trapped, so anybody who goes in after them had better know what he's doing, but I can't imagine Lupe being too fancy with his explosives and detonators."

Gloria Jean frowned. "I'll tell Jim, of course; but isn't it likely that Ricardo already knows——"

"That's not my point," I said. "The point is, if he takes charge, Jim should make a special effort to get that stuff out of there immediately. The cave is sacred to the local people, they employ it for . . . certain ceremonies, and they're not going to be fond of anybody who blasphemes against the old gods by using it as an arsenal. Tell Jim to look up a gent called Cortez, rather an impressive old character, you may have seen him around when we were there. He's the local high priest. Tell Jim to apologize in the name of the liberation movement for the acts of Montano, defunct; tell him to ask Cortez how he can best atone for the desecration committed by Lupe; tell him to inform Cortez he will cooperate to the best of his ability in any purification ceremonies required. Ricardo will probably understand; but be sure Jim makes him understand."

Gloria Jean looked at me searchingly. "Of course I'll do what you ask, but . . . do you really feel it's that important, Sam?"

I said, "Let's put it this way: If I were running a revolution based in old Cortez's jungle, I'd make damned sure he was on my side and not the other. I'd want all the help I could get, and I'd much rather have his ancient gods fighting with me instead of against me. You never know about those old gods. Me, I'm not about to make them mad if I can help it." I laughed, a little embarrassed; I hadn't meant to say quite so much. "And hell, if all Jim gets out of it is a few local recruits, he's still ahead of the game. Ricardo himself told me they're the best jungle scouts in the business."

She smiled, and drained the last of her big daiquiri. "I'll pass the word, Sam. And thank you. For everything."

"*De nada.* Good luck, Gloria Jean."

I watched her move away, a brave and very bright young woman; and I reflected that Jim Putnam was a lucky man. I finished my drink and headed for the stairs, since my room was only one floor up and the single small elevator was an exercise in slow motion. Halfway up, I met Frances Dillman and her husband descending.

She was in a simple white dress, presumably purchased

locally, since we'd never got back our luggage (or my cameras). For the wicked bandits to return our belongings politely after our dramatic escape from their clutches might have aroused a certain amount of suspicion. Dillman was wearing slacks and a bright sports shirt. I noticed that his hair was long enough to cover his damaged ear, carefully combed as he had it now. They made a handsome couple, but I couldn't help thinking that he wasn't really quite tall enough for her and I knew somebody who was.

"I think we're gaining on it," Frances said, pausing. "I've talked to the embassy and the Minister of Tourism. They should be letting us go home pretty soon."

I said, politely, "I really regret the part of the tour we missed. Even though I wasn't exactly along for sight-seeing —I'll apologize once more for my duplicity—I was enjoying it very much."

She smiled, also politely. "It's very nice of you to say so, Mr. . . . Helm."

Her husband was only mildly interested in me, so I knew she hadn't got around to telling him everything yet. I hoped for her own sake she would continue to keep her mouth shut. Dr. Archibald Dillman didn't look like a very understanding or forgiving husband to me.

My room was in a corner of the building over one of the busiest intersections in the city of Santa Rosalia, subjected to the constant racketing sound of cars and trucks and buses stopping for the traffic light right under my window and starting up again. I drew the heavy curtains to diminish the decibels slightly. The phone started ringing. I picked it up.

"Bultman here," said a voice in my ear. "We have an appointment with His Presidential Excellency at three o'clock three days from now, Thursday, the earliest I could arrange. I will pick you up in a taxi. Echeverria will be there. Bultman pays his debts, *nicht whar?*"

CHAPTER 31

THEY used to design their mansions and palaces on the railroad-car principle down here, long and narrow—actually just one room wide with each room leading into the next. This guaranteed cross-ventilation in that tropical climate but left something to be desired as far as privacy was concerned. However, the great houses were generally built to encircle a central patio onto which the large, luxurious rooms opened, so you could avoid marching through an occupied chamber by taking a trip outdoors to reach the one beyond.

Air-conditioning has, of course, rendered this arrangement obsolete. A room with two exposures has no advantages, quite the contrary, when all windows are tightly sealed against the outside heat. We'd had this pointed out to us when our group had visited *El Palacio de los Gobernadores* during our previous stay in the city; also the fact that the building was an anachronism in another respect. It still retained the name given to it in the bad old days when this area had been ruled by Spanish governors, not always the nicest fellows imaginable. It was surprising that this reminder of European domination had been allowed to survive, but apparently nostalgia had prevailed over nationalism. It had always been the Palace of the Governors; and the Palace of the Governors it remained.

Bultman's taxi dropped us off in front of the iron gates facing the city's tree-shaded central plaza. Not knowing what languages the driver understood, or whom he might be working for besides us, we hadn't spoken beyond the normal greetings. I followed Bultman out of the battered vehicle. He stopped to smooth down his white linen suit and settle his necktie. He was looking very sharp today, the true tropical gentleman, very different from the stained and sweaty character I'd dealt with in the jungle. As for me, I'd managed to pick up a navy blue suit of a tropical material

245

resembling light sailcloth that fit after a fashion, and shoes, socks, shirt, and tie to go with it; so I wasn't too much of a disgrace to my country or my sinister profession.

The sentries at the gate were armed with the familiar M16s. They let us pass unchallenged, since part of the palace was open to the public. We marched side by side across the wide flagstone space between the gate and the arched doorway. I noted that Bultman managed his artificial foot very well.

"What do I call Rael?" I asked.

"Excelentisimo Señor Presidente," he said. "Or Honorable Presidente, or *Su Excelencia,* or Your Excellency."

"And Echeverria?"

"As director of the SSN, he is called Honorable Director, or Señor Director, or Señor Honorable Director. You are aware that he is actually a military man, currently holding the rank of colonel? As a matter of fact he was the military brain behind Rael's coup d'etat."

"Yes, I'd heard that."

"Nowadays there seems to be some friction between him and the army generals who outrank him. He could probably persuade his president to elevate him a few grades in rank, but he has chosen instead to make a point of dressing as a civilian and emphasizing that his service is a civilian organization wholly outside military control. . . . There he is now. A great honor, for him to meet us so, Herr Helm."

"He probably wants to give himself plenty of time to make sure we're not armed before he admits us to the august presence, Herr Bultman; two dangerous characters like us."

The dapper figure of Señor Honorable Director Enrique Echeverria awaited us in the archway ahead, beyond which I could see the interior courtyard of the palace, rather attractive with colorful, well-tended flowerbeds. Echeverria was wearing a dark suit, the snowy white shirt required of any Latin-American gentleman appearing in public during business hours, and a dark tie. The reflections off his highly polished shoes were blinding. His neatly trimmed red beard looked quite devilish—using the word in its sinister, not its jaunty, meaning. His cold brown eyes made a cursory inspection of Bultman, whom he knew; then for a moment they gave their full attention to me, whom he didn't.

Then there were the obligatory fulsome greetings between him and Bultman, with Bultman indicating his Germanic respect for the other's high official rank without going as far as actual subservience; after all, he was a professional man of some standing, also. At last he indicated me with a flourish.

"Herr Director, this is the man calling himself Samuel Felton, of whom I have told you. Matthew Helm."

Echeverria bowed coolly. "Señor Helm. We do not usually approve of visitors who enter our country with false passports."

"Señor Director," I said, also bowing. "Is a passport really false when it is prepared by a legitimate agency of my government for purposes of which I am sure you will approve?"

"I will be very interested to learn about those purposes, and so, I am sure, will His Excellency, President Rael. Come. This way."

He indicated the door to our right, marked NO ENTRADA—the wing to the left was the part of the palace open to tourists, which our group had visited a few weeks earlier. A sentry stepped forward smartly to open the door for us. As we entered the cool dusk of the small room beyond, I was aware that a gent back in a dark corner was monitoring an instrument of some kind; and I knew that we'd just been screened by a metal detector. No sweat. I'd disposed of my revolver back in the jungle with some regrets—it wasn't a bad little gun, but with the publicity that would undoubtedly be generated by our kidnaping and rescue, and the official attention that would result, I'd figured I'd be better off without an illegal firearm.

Today I'd even left the trick belt behind. Even though it was unlikely to be discovered, I preferred not to bring any weapon into the presence of an undoubtedly paranoid dictator-type politician. They're all very assassination-conscious, with some justification. After all, Ricardo had already taken a crack at this one. Anyway, I had no designs upon the life of Armando Rael, and he was, after all, Washington's fair-haired boy in these parts—a condition I did hope to be able to do something about eventually. . . .

We proceeded from the anteroom into a large room with a very fine carved ceiling. A man was working at a large desk, and a woman was working at a smaller one. The woman picked up the phone, spoke into it briefly, and nodded to Echeverria. Another armed sentry opened the door as we approached; then we were entering the presence of the President of Costa Verde. It occurred to me that I would really much rather have been stalking him with a gun, not because he was such a bad man—although on the record he was—but because, while I'm always fairly confident of my ability with firearms, I wasn't a bit certain that I was clever enough with words to pull off what I planned here.

It was another fine light room with a high carved ceiling and windows on two sides. There was a maroon carpet on the floor, the modern wall-to-wall stuff seeming a little out of place in that old-fashioned atmosphere. There was a big shiny desk of antique design. I wasn't good enough at antiques to determine if it was genuinely old or a modern replica. There were several large chairs of a similar pattern; but the president's own piece of sitting-furniture was of thronelike proportions, with a back that kind of enveloped the smallish plump figure in bemedaled army uniform that occupied it.

It would have been very unwise to crack a smile, of course. I put from my mind, very firmly, the thought of a certain small, round, crowned cartoon character who appears daily in my hometown newspaper, and kept my face very polite and sober.

President Rael looked at us for a moment and spoke in English: "Señor Bultman we know, Señor Director. Be so kind as to introduce to us this other gentleman."

"He is an American government agent named Matthew Helm, Your Excellency. However, he is traveling under the false name and passport of one Samuel Felton and pretending to be a magazine photographer. He says we will approve of his reasons for breaking our laws in this manner."

Rael turned to my companion. "Do you vouch for this man, Señor Bultman?"

Bultman threw me a slightly apologetic glance and shook his head. He said, "By no means, *Excelentisimo*. How can I? I only met him a few days ago, although I had heard of him previously. But he seems to have useful information in his possession; and I thought you should hear what he has to say. If he should be telling the truth, he could make easier the task for which you have employed me—the primary task for which you have employed me."

"Yes, the secondary task was executed in a highly satisfactory manner, as we have already informed you."

They were presumably discussing the release of our group of kidnapees, which had, as I'd promised, been credited largely to Bultman. He was the one who in the end had escorted us out of the jungle and summoned transportation to take us to Santa Rosalia.

Since there were several in the party who would have taken pleasure in doing exactly the opposite to what I asked them, even if I begged them not to jump off a cliff, I'd got hold of General Henderson and explained that, both for Ricardo Jimenez's sake and our own, it would be better if Ricardo's name did not figure in the stories we gave to the press. We should agree to say only that we had escaped Labal through our own efforts, but we had been about to be recaptured by the wicked *bandidos* when Bultman and his little force had appeared in the nick of time to drive them off and bring us to safety. Rather to my surprise, even the most obstructionist members of the group had gone along with Henderson's suggestions, putting Bultman into my debt, not only for his life, but for whatever bonus Rael had promised him for getting us released.

Bultman bowed in acknowledgment of the president's complimentary words. "Your Excellency is too kind."

Rael stared at us across the table. He was not as small as the big chair made him look. His solid stoutness made him appear to be a very short man; actually he was a rounded individual of only a little less than average height for that part of the world. He had a thin black moustache that reminded me unpleasantly of the late Lieutenant Barbera's hirsute decoration. His eyes were small and brown and not unintelligent, but they did hold a rooster arrogance— not a man to whom you'd offer any slight or insult, at least not as long as he was in a position of power.

"Be seated, gentlemen," he said at last. I had a hunch he'd have kept us standing to inflate his ego, except that his ego could not bear to look up at taller men. "Now, Señor Helm, or whatever your name is, let us hear your reasons for breaking the laws of our country."

"It is a rather long story, Your Excellency," I said. "May I tell it from the beginning?"

"Pray do."

I spoke without expression: "A few weeks ago I was

asked to assassinate the President of Costa Verde." This created a certain sensation. I waited until the stir had subsided. I went on smoothly: "The request was made, indirectly, by a gentleman with whom I had once operated in this country, when he was a member of your armed forces: Colonel Hector Jimenez."

"We are acquainted with the name." Rael's voice was cold. "Why should this exile Jimenez approach you on such a matter?"

"Because, as I said, we worked together once, and he knows I'm good, Your Excellency," I said.

Echeverria said tartly, "Hardly a matter of pride, I should think, to be a skillful murderer."

I took a chance and said with a shrug, "Some people take pride in skillful assassination, some in skillful, cr, interrogation. As we say in my country, it takes all kinds." Anger showed in Echeverria's face. I spoke respectfully to Rael: "Do you wish me to continue with my story, Your Excellency, or should we debate the subject of self-esteem?"

"Continue," Rael said, but I'd seen a flicker of pleasure in his small eyes. He had not been unhappy to see the powerful head of his secret police slightly discomfited, a good sign.

I went on, "You are aware, of course, that Jimenez had organized a previous attempt upon your life that failed miserably, using an amateur marksman, a member of his own family. Stubbornly intent upon his purpose even after this disaster, he apparently remembered me. It may be that time had left him with a rather glorified memory of my abilities; at any rate he seems to have convinced himself that I was the man for the job, the only man for the job."

"Even though he knew you to be still an employee of the United States Government?"

"He took care of that, *Excelentisimo,* or thought he did. He abducted—or had abducted—and threatened the life of a lady who meant a great deal to me."

Rael watched me closely. "A dreadful predicament for you, Señor Helm."

"Dreadful," I said, "but hardly a predicament. A predicament is a trap without an exit. We have standing orders governing such situations. It was, of course, a ridiculous demand anyway, Your Excellency, considering the high regard in which you are held by the government I serve. I informed the go-between, another of Jimenez's offspring, that I could not possibly comply with the request." I cleared my throat. "Shortly thereafter the dead body of the kidnaped young lady was delivered to my doorstep."

There was a little silence. Echeverria broke it, with a sneer in his voice. "You are a strong-minded man, to make such a sacrifice."

I ignored him and continued to speak to the elaborately uniformed little man on the far side of the big desk. "Naturally, Your Excellency, I requested permission to punish those who had done this. The permission was refused, in a qualified way. I was told that for an agent of the U.S. government to indulge in private retribution *within the borders of our country* was unthinkable; there was too great a chance of the agency being compromised. However, my chief does not like us to be subjected to this form of coercion. He therefore left the door open for me to deal with any Jimenez or guilty associate I could catch abroad. He even authorized light surveillance of their Chicago establishment so I could be alerted if any of them should leave for foreign parts." I paused and smiled thinly. "I'm afraid I exceeded my orders slightly there, *Excelentisimo*. I arranged to have a close watch kept on the Jimenez household. Then, having learned that one of the sons was leaving the U.S. and heading this way, I joined the same tour, made his acquaintance, and worked hard to gain his confidence."

"That was the escaped assassin, Ricardo Jimenez?" When I nodded, Rael went on: "You intended to kill him?"

"Of course, Your Excellency. Let the murdering parent sit safe in Chicago. I would bring him the news of his firstborn's death. A small compensation for what he had done to me."

"But you did not carry out your intentions."

"That is correct, Your Excellency. Acting as a friend to Ricardo Jimenez, managing his wheelchair, drinking with him as I laid my plans to deal with him, I happened to obtain from him some information that, as an agent, I felt duty-bound to transmit to Washington. I felt obliged to ask for official instructions, even though they might conflict with my private plans."

I was conscious of Bultman, on my right, listening carefully and saying nothing. He was aware, of course, that I was bending the truth slightly here and there, but his face remained impassive. Echeverria, beyond him, leaned forward impatiently.

"Well, what was this invaluable information?"

I addressed Rael: "One evening after I'd got him slightly drunk, Your Excellency, young Jimenez boasted to me that he planned to pick a fight with Lupe Montano, kill him, and take over control of that ragtag rebel movement of Lupe's." It seemed diplomatic to describe the revolutionary movement in derogatory terms whenever possible. I went on: "I guessed that the young man was acting on behalf of his father, an experienced army officer, since Ricardo himself knows nothing of soldiering beyond what he learned as a boy in some military school or other. I assumed that if the murder attempt was successful, Hector Jimenez himself would then try to slip into the country and take command of the so-called Army of Liberation from his son."

That should do it, I thought. Never try to sell a simple homicide if you can make it into a complicated conspiracy; everybody loves a conspiracy. And the thought of this one should reinforce Rael's already strong motive for desiring the death of Hector Jimenez.

"This is what you reported to your superiors in Washington?" Rael was still watching my face closely; I saw that I had his interest, if not his trust. When I nodded, he asked, "What orders did they give you?"

I said, "I was informed, Your Excellency, of Señor Bultman's visit to the Costa Verde capital. I was told that there were indications that you had probably hired him to dispose of the elder Jimenez in Chicago. I was ordered to forget my revenge. I was instructed to let the younger Jimenez live and proceed with his plan to eliminate Lupe de Montano. I was also ordered to give Señor Bultman every assistance with his Chicago project, except that of course our agency must still not be known to have been involved. If things went as planned, I was told, a valuable ally of the United States"—I bowed respectfully toward the man behind the desk—"would have been relieved of two adult and experienced enemies, Lupe Montano and Hector Jimenez, and would face only a ragged bunch of self-styled revolutionaries led by an inexperienced and crippled boy. It

252

was thought, Your Excellency, that you would find this solution to the problem satisfactory."

Rael frowned judiciously. "It certainly has a great deal to recommend it, wouldn't you say, Señor Echeverria? And we are informed that the bandit Montano is already dead at the hands of the young Jimenez, confirming at least part of Señor Helm's story." When Echeverria did not speak, clearly reluctant to approve of me in any way, Rael made a small gesture of impatience and turned back to me. "What assistance can you offer in the Chicago matter, señor?"

I said, "As I said, *Excelentisimo,* I have had the Jimenez menage there under close observation for several weeks. I have some reports here that may interest Your Excellency. *Con permiso?*" When he nodded, I took out the envelope I'd asked our man to get me. I said, "Señor Bultman may like to examine these also. Here is the current composition of the household. There is the family: Hector himself, the daughter Dolores, and the younger son Emilio. There is also a close friend of these young people named Manuel Santos Cordoba." I saw Echeverria glance at me sharply, and I knew that my voice had changed a bit, but I'd been unable to help it, pronouncing the names of Leona the Lioness and Lobo the Wolf, and what I now knew to be the name of Oso the Bear. I cleared my throat and went on: "Then there are six other men on the grounds who pose as servants, ostensibly a chauffeur, a valet, a butler, a gardener, a yard man, and a male cook. The names and dossiers are here."

I paused to give Rael time to catch up. He looked through the papers and slid them across the desk to Bultman, and nodded to me to go on.

"Here is the latest watch schedule maintained on the premises," I said. "Here is an aerial photo of the grounds, which, Your Excellency will note, are quite extensive and well fenced. A detailed drawing of the house interior. A diagram of the alarm system. Positions of the yard lights; locations of the switches. An estimate of available weapons. There are two guard dogs kept in kennels when they are not on duty. Here." I pointed to the aerial photo. "They are cared for, and largely handled, by Manuel Cordoba. Names. Breeds. Duty schedules. Feeding time and type of food. Commands." I straightened up from the papers on the desk and sat back in my chair. "That's all I have for now, Your Excellency, but if other information is required by Señor Bultman, it can probably be obtained. My observers are still in position."

Rael glanced at Bultman, who said, "All this could not have been obtained without alerting the subjects to the fact of surveillance."

"Of course they're alert," I said. "They have been alert for almost a month; I have deliberately kept them so. My people were instructed not to be too inconspicuous. If I am not allowed to attack the murderers directly, I can at least make them sweat as they huddle inside their suburban fortress, knowing that they are being watched every minute of the day and night. They think I will be coming for them eventually—I made some loud threatening noises before I left Chicago—they just don't know when."

"That does not for me an easy operation make, to have them warned," Bultman said.

"On the contrary," I said, "they should be nicely worn down for you by now, after being kept so long in a state of siege. And remember, you have a definite advantage: They are not expecting your kind of assault. They know me. That is, they know me as a long-range rifle specialist; they even know that I've had a suitable weapon made ready and ammunition loaded especially for it. I said I wanted them to sweat; and there's nothing that generates perspiration quite as well as the thought that any high window in any tall building behind you may hold an accurate rifle with a telescopic sight aimed at your back. That's what they're really awaiting, not your type of operation, amigo. So the defenses you'll meet at ground level shouldn't be insurmountable. They're expecting death to come from above, from afar."

"Yes, that is an interesting thought," Bultman said. "I will keep it in mind."

There was a little silence; then Echeverria said in his contemptuous way: "One assumes this assistance is not offered, as you say in your country, entirely without attached strings, Señor Helm."

I glanced at him briefly and looked at Rael. "Your Excellency, the information is yours, to do with as you wish. There are no strings, as the Honorable Director calls them. However, there are two favors I would like to ask, one for myself, one for a person of some importance whose name I can reveal only to you, in private."

Echeverria snorted. "Favors!"

Rael's eyes had narrowed slightly. "We will consider your requests, Señor Helm."

I said, "For myself I ask only that the Jimenez family be wiped out; and in addition the man Cordoba, who was an accomplice in my . . . lady's murder. I would like her to be able to sleep peacefully, knowing that this debt has been paid."

Rael smiled thinly. "It seems like a reasonable request. Señor Bultman, what is your opinion?"

"I do not make a habit of leaving any live witnesses behind me, Your Excellency."

I was reminded that, although we were getting along well together, he was not really a very nice man; but then, who was?

"And we will soon have this young cripple by the heels, Señor Helm. I think we can promise that your vengeance will be fulfilled." As I'd hoped, Rael was now looking at me with greater approval. My first request had tickled his Latin fancy. They know how to hate down here; they can appreciate a kindred spirit. "Proceed. The second favor?"

"For that, I must request a private audience with Your Excellency, so that I may reveal the identity of the man for whom I am speaking."

Echeverria said quickly, *"Excelentisimo! . . ."*

Rael waved him into silence. "I appreciate your concern, Enrique; but I do not think we have anything to fear here. You may leave us. Señor Bultman also." There was a pause while they obeyed, Echeverria hesitating in the doorway as if to make a final protest, then thinking better of it and marching out angrily. The door closed behind him. Rael leaned forward to study me across the desk. "Very well, señor. You have your audience. Now, who is this mysterious person on whose behalf you wish to ask a favor?"

I said, "You are that person, Your Excellency."

He frowned quickly. "I do not understand!"

I said, "You are highly regarded in Washington, *Excelentisimo*. It is considered of vital importance that you and your administration be safeguarded against all threats."

255

"Washington's concern is appreciated. But what further steps can be taken in this particular situation?"

I looked at him for a moment. I hoped it was a significant look. "This man Bultman," I said deliberately. "Are you certain he is capable?"

Rael frowned again. "He comes well recommended. What are you suggesting?"

"I have a personal, vengeful interest in his success, of course," I said. "But as a representative of my government, I feel also that it is of extreme importance that Hector Jimenez be eliminated before he can put his military experience to use here. I have fought beside Jimenez, Your Excellency. Whatever his failings in other respects, he is a good soldier. If he should be permitted to live, if he should manage to join forces with his older son, he could become a serious menace to Your Excellency." I was, I decided, becoming a truly accomplished liar, in my flowery way.

"We are well aware of this," Rael said. "Do you contend that Señor Bultman is not competent to carry out this mission? His record is excellent."

"His record *was* excellent," I said. "But he led a raid into Cuba not too long ago that was a complete failure, and he received a crippling wound in the course of it. Such a thing has been known to affect a man's courage and interfere with his efficiency. And in confidence, Your Excellency, I must tell you that the 'rescue' he is supposed to have performed a few days ago did not happen in quite the heroic way he doubtless reported it. Let us say that he required a little help. He would have been in a bad spot without it."

Rael's little eyes were narrow. "You mean he lied?"

I spread my hands in a soothing gesture. "Please, Your Excellency, such ugly words are inappropriate. Was there ever a military commander who diminished his achievements in his report of an engagement? Señor Bultman's arrival was truly very welcome. Nobody in our party begrudges him his reward for the services he performed for us, even if those services were perhaps not quite as great as he may have claimed. I am merely suggesting that it might be well to let a competent observer go along with him on this Chicago mission; a man capable of giving advice and, perhaps, correcting errors before they are made; perhaps even taking charge, if the situation should call for it."

Rael was frowning at me. "You are asking our permission to accompany and assist Señor Bultman? But——"

I shook my head quickly. "Not I, Your Excellency. I repeat that my agency cannot afford to become openly involved. But you have a trained and experienced man quite close to you." I paused, and spoke carefully: "He should be quite capable of steadying Señor Bultman's hand if it should falter on a simple job like this, since I have heard that he claims to be the man whose genius was largely responsible for bringing Your Excellency to power."

"That is an untruth!" Rael's face was suddenly dark with anger so strong that he forgot to employ his customary royal plural. "*I* planned and executed the campaign that overthrew the corrupt Jimenez. I had many loyal allies and assistants, to be sure, but they operated to *my* orders!"

The fact was that before his political elevation, Armando Rael had been a fairly prominent Santa Rosalia attorney with no military experience whatever; his present rank and medals were self-bestowed. But by this time he had undoubtedly convinced himself that he had conquered his country practically single-handed. They always do.

I shrugged apologetically. "You know how these rumors get started, *Excelentisimo*. I beg your pardon if I have said anything wrong."

A mean little smile twitched the thin black moustache. "But you are correct, of course. Much as we will regret having the so-efficient Señor Echeverria absent from his post, he is the logical man for this task. We will issue the orders immediately. . . ."

CHAPTER 32

It was snowing in Chicago. I didn't get there until well after dark the following day, a little surprised to find myself back in winter again. You tend to think that the weather you've got, wherever you are, is a worldwide phenomenon. As we drove away from O'Hare I sat in the

257

passenger seat beside the man who'd come to meet me, shivering with my thin tropical blood in my thin tropical clothes until the heater got the situation under some kind of control.

Already, I found, after a day of fighting airline schedules to which the airlines didn't seem to pay much attention, Costa Verde seemed a long way off; and so did the people I'd known there. This had its advantages in certain instances, such as the case of Frances Dillman.

We'd said our polite good-byes that morning in the hotel lobby with Dr. Archibald Dillman standing by looking very bored by his handsome wife's dull tour companion, me; so that I knew she was still keeping our guilty secret. Now I was careful not to bring her too clearly to mind, because I knew pain was there waiting to be exposed and awakened. To hell with it, I told myself firmly; you can't have all the girls in the world, and what would you do with them if you did get them?

I allowed myself to think, instead, of the Señor Honorable Director Enrique Echeverria. When I'd seen him waiting for me at the airport with an SSN escort, I'd thought something must have slipped badly and it was my turn for La Fortaleza, which was, of course, exactly what I was supposed to think.

"Señor Helm?" There were two of them, obviously SSN thugs, obviously armed, obviously hoping for some kind of resistance. The taller one spoke. "Señor Echeverria sends his compliments and wonders if you would spare him a moment of your time, señor. This way, *por favor.*"

Down there, I'm sure, when they lead you up to the scaffold, they say they're very sorry to inconvenience the gracious señor, but if he would be so kind as to incline his head slightly to facilitate the placement of the noose, his cooperation would be greatly appreciated. I was marched over to where Enrique Rojo was waiting. He regarded me coldly for a long moment, letting me sweat, knowing exactly what I was thinking because so many others had thought it before me when confronted by the red-bearded director of the infamous *Servicio Seguridad Nacional.* Then he smiled thinly.

"I am instructed by His Excellency, President Armando Rael, to give you His Excellency's best wishes for a pleasant journey, and to tell you that His Excellency hopes you will again honor our country with your presence in the near future."

I bowed. "Please inform His Excellency that his gracious words are greatly appreciated."

Echeverria said, unsmiling. "That is my president's message, Señor Helm. Now hear mine: Please do not take that return invitation too seriously. If you are as intelligent as I think, you will give Costa Verde a wide berth in the future."

I regarded him for a moment. He was really a very good-looking chap, in his sinister way. I remembered Ricardo Jimenez's brutally crippled body confined to the wheel-chair; but that was not really my concern and I put the memory away. There was no need to let this man know what I felt about him beyond what he doubtless guessed already.

"The warning is noted, Honorable Director," I said.

A flicker of something that might have been uneasiness showed in his brown eyes for a moment. I knew that he was receiving certain messages about me despite my poker face—and poker mind—and that they were telling him that it was not wise for him to let me leave this country alive. But he had definite instructions, and his president was already displeased with him; he could not take the risk of incurring further displeasure.

He said, "Very well. You may go."

Then I was on board the plane; and shortly the roaring jets were shoving us up into the blue tropical sky. For once, smoggy, snowy Chicago looked very good to me when I finally arrived there. It was great to hear people talking crude *Ingles* for a change instead of flowery *español*. Even the black, glistening streets along which we drove looked attractive and friendly, now that I was safely out of the Costa Verde trap. The snow was melting where it hit the pavement, but it left a sugary frosting on the parked cars that glittered under the street lights.

I looked at the man behind the wheel, who'd been in charge of our local arrangements ever since Eleanor Brand's kidnaping and death had caused Mac to throw an abnormally large task group, for us, into the Chicago area. My driver was thin and wiry, with a lined farmer's face and very pale blue eyes. I knew him only as Jackson. I wondered idly, as you always do, where Mac had got this one and what kind of training he'd had. It couldn't have been my kind of training or he wouldn't be running surveillance errands—well, not unless he'd hit, or been hit by, something very bad in the line of duty, bad enough to disqualify him from the heavy work of the agency.

"Thawed out?" he asked, sensing from my glance that I was not ready for conversation. "There's a flask in the glove compartment, if a little antifreeze . . . No? All right. We've put you in the Allmand Hotel. It's about a twenty-minute drive from Lake Park, less at the time of night you'll probably be heading out that way. We retrieved your suitcase—your other suitcase, the one you brought with you from Europe—from the Brand apartment right after you left town, so you won't have to go shopping for warm clothes. It should be in your room by this time. You've got a car in the hotel garage, a little Datsun. All you have to do is call and they'll bring it up front for you."

"Any word yet from our super-Aryan friend?"

"Yes. The word. Bultman goes in at oh two hundred in the morning, day after tomorrow."

I grimaced. "The Kraut moves fast, once he gets going, damn him. He's not leaving me much time. Weather report?"

"Clearing. Winds ten to fifteen southwest tomorrow, easing toward nightfall. Calm tomorrow night."

I grimaced. "Well, they've got to be right some time. Let's hope this is the time."

"Instructions?"

"Get everybody to hell out of Lake Park; tell them to take their cigarette butts and bobby pins with them. Make sure there's no sign of us out there. It's Bultman's baby now. We don't want to be involved in what happens next, in any way. . . . Well, just one way, but I'll take care of that."

"Yes, we managed to get you a spot up in the new Park Towers, but it wasn't easy. Fortunately somebody knew somebody who knew somebody who was willing to take a little trip, for a consideration, and keep his mouth shut."

"How safe?" I asked.

Jackson shrugged. "Only one way is really safe."

I shook my head. "It's not that important; leave the poor guy alone. If he's got any brains at all, he'll keep his mouth shut when he figures out how his apartment was used, if he ever does. It may not ever come out, if we're lucky."

Jackson nodded. "Here's the key. It's a dupe, just ditch it in a safe place when you're through with it. You'll have an observer and a helper. I'll let you know the routine tomorrow night after I've checked with them again."

"What about a range?"

"There's a shooting club south of town where they play the silhouette-target game. It's very popular these days, it seems: using high-powered rifles to knock down metal silhouettes of rabbits, turkeys, deer, moose. Well, I may not have quite the right tin animals, but they shoot them at fairly long distances and have a safe backstop area. You ought to be able to take care of your business there. I've made the arrangements."

"And the rifle?"

"I'll drive you out in the morning. I'll bring the gun. And get it to the apartment afterward." He gave me a quick glance and grinned. "Don't say it. Yes, sir, I will treat it as if it were made of glass after you've got it sighted in. Like as if it were a bottle of nitro ready to blow at a jiggle. I know how you long-range boys are about your precious guns. . . ."

I slept well that night. The chore ahead of me didn't worry me greatly—you learn not to let them—and you don't louse up your internal clock flying north and south the way you do flying east and west. In the morning I was informed that the Chicago satellite community of Lake Park had been totally cleared of our people, but not before reports had come in to the effect that the Jimenez establishment out there was now under surveillance by others. Bultman was moving his forces into position, presumably employing the information I'd given him—after doing a little careful checking of his own, no doubt.

I took a ride into the country with Jackson and got bounced around a bit by the big rifle—that .300 Holland and Holland Magnum is considered small stuff by the rugged gents who fire enormous double-barreled guns at elephants in Africa; but it's still a very potent firearm with plenty of authority at the butt as well as at the muzzle. It took me a full box of cartridges to get it zeroed in properly, since the original telescopic sight, designed for daylight sniping, had been replaced at the last minute by a tricky optical device more suitable for night work. I returned to the Allmand Hotel with my shoulder sore and my ears bruised by the hearing protector I'd worn that Jackson must have borrowed from somebody with a noisy job and a small head. .

After a somewhat belated lunch I crawled into one of the big double beds in my room for a nap, since there was a long wakeful night ahead. Around five I was aroused by the telephone and listened to Jackson telling me that Bultman had just confirmed date and time. The Kraut was going in tonight. Well, at oh two hundred; which made it technically tomorrow morning. . . .

CHAPTER 33

I tried very hard to think about Gloria Jean Putnam as I drove the little Datsun in the dark toward the Chicago suburb where the big rifle awaited me. Why Gloria Jean? Well, she was one of the least disturbing subjects I could dredge up, and I tried to visualize her now, wondering whether or not she really had sent her man off to war.

Of course I could have occupied my mind, but not so safely, with thoughts of Frances Dillman, wondering if she was still keeping our adulterous secret or if she had succumbed to the terrible wifely urge to confess all.

Eleanor Brand would not have been a safe subject for reflection; there was too much disturbing guilt associated with her death to make her good thinking material for a man who'd need to be totally relaxed quite soon. However, even Elly was safer to think about than the shot I'd have to make shortly.

The best way to fluff a difficult shot is to think too much about it. Oh, advance planning and preparation are necessary, of course: The gun must be properly tuned and sighted, and the ammunition must be carefully loaded unless you're willing to settle for the lesser accuracy of the factory product—perfectly reliable, of course, but in the nature of things it can never be tailored to the characteristics of your particular rifle. The target area must be inspected to make certain that no twigs or branches will intervene to deflect the bullet. The firing point must be selected with care, and a steady rest provided. The probable wind conditions must be studied; and a table of allowances must be prepared for various wind velocities. The range must, of course, be determined with care although, with a powerful, flat-shooting weapon like the .300 H. and H., you do have some leeway.

But once all this has been done, the thinking must stop. In particular, all clever last-minute brainstorms, adjustments, inspirations, and corrective impulses must be strangled at birth.

I could still remember, very clearly, my first shot at an antelope. I was a boy, hunting with my father; and there was the dream buck we'd been looking for. But he looked so *small* compared to the mule deer I'd already hunted successfully! The mental computer went into action unbidden: Looking so small, he must be very far away, best to hold over a bit to allow for the drop of the bullet at that great range. So I shot high, and missed high; and it was another two years before I finally bagged an antelope, not nearly as spectacular as that one. Actually, the target had looked small simply because the pronghorn is a small animal. A dead-center hold such as Dad had carefully instructed me to use would have got me that trophy—the first one lost to me by excessive cerebration, but not the last.

Tonight I knew that I had a particularly dangerous trap to look out for. I'd be shooting from the eighth floor of an apartment building into the front yard of a house four hundred and twenty yards away. It was a downhill shot in a sense; and everyone knows that the tendency is to shoot high downhill, and that therefore you must always hold low under such conditions. Well, this is perfectly true on a steep mountainside where you're estimating the range along the precipitously sloping ground between you and the target. Gravity does not operate in a slanting direction; bullet drop does not depend upon the slant distance to the target but only upon the horizontal component thereof; so on long shots you have to hold under to allow for this.

But here the range figure I'd been given, and for which

I'd sighted the rifle, *was* the horizontal distance from the base of the selected condominium to the Jimenez garage doors. As a matter of fact, the difference between the range measured from the base of the building, and that measured from my eighth-story-window firing point, was insignificant. (I'd actually punched it out on a pocket calculator: 420.0 yards versus 421.3 yards.) So I reminded myself firmly as I drove that when I got up there I must not, repeat, *not,* think of it as a downhill shot even though I was fairly high in the air. In fact I must not think of it at all. The thinking had all been done. All that was required now was the shooting. . . .

There had once been many large estates out in the Chicago suburb known as Lake Park, perhaps even before it was known as Lake Park; but a significant percentage of them had gone for apartments and developments now. The Park Towers occupied, I'd been told, part of what was formerly a model horse-breeding establishment owned by a gent who'd made his money selling some kind of pain-killer pills. The adjacent property was still intact, however. It had been owned by a soft-drink king and was now the retreat-in-exile of the former president of Costa Verde, along with his daughter, his younger son, and their well-armed entourage.

I stopped well away from the three tall condominium buildings, first, and got out of the car and walked a small distance up the road. It was a clear night for Chicago, but the stars were dim and distant; we put on a better celestial show out in my home state of New Mexico. I stood quite still for a minute or two, listening to the wind. Well, "listening" is perhaps not quite the right word; but I've always found my ears to be most sensitive to air movements, even when the zephyrs are too weak to make a real sound. Now in winter there were no leaves on the trees to respond to wandering breezes; and any pools or ponds that I might have used to get an estimate of wind speed and direction were either drained or frozen. I felt a slight chill on my left ear as I stood there, but it wasn't strong enough to be significant. The weather boys had got it right for a change: a nice calm night.

I got back into the Datsun and drove around to the parking lot behind the apartment building to the right. I flashed the lights twice before cutting them entirely. Locking the little car, I walked up to a metal service door in the rear of the building, as instructed. It was opened by a husky dark-haired young man in white coveralls, not clean. Whether he actually had a janitorial job there, or was just depending on the fact that nobody pays any attention to a workman around a building like that, I didn't know.

"Go on up the stairs," he said. "It's a climb, but you'll have plenty of time to catch your breath. I'll be along as soon as I've checked to see if you brought any company with you."

I climbed the seven flights of concrete stairs, making some use of the tubular iron railings—as I'd been told, it was a climb, but at least the steps were engineered for ordinary human beings, not like some steps I'd climbed recently, which had been designed for priests and gods. A heavy fire door let me into a carpeted hallway on the eighth floor; the key I'd been given let me into the apartment with the proper number. I proceeded through the place without turning on the lights.

In the dining room I found what I was looking for. The dining table, a fairly husky piece of modern furniture, had been pulled over to the window. On it lay the long gun case, a respectable piece of luggage constructed like a good attache case but several times as long. There were also two black binocular cases, some small sandbags, and a couple of little items that turned out to be penlights. Well, all that could wait. As the man had said, there was plenty of time, two hours and twenty minutes to be precise—assuming that Bultman actually hit at the hour he'd specified of the night he'd specified and didn't get cute and tricky.

I moved to the window. It was a country view, night version, with the landscaping, tennis courts, empty swimming pool, and lighted drives of the condominium complex spread out below me. Beyond them, across the main road, was the businesslike chain-link fence topped with barbed wire guarding the Jimenez property, more rustic and less manicured. A goodly distance behind the fence—four hundred yards is a lot of yards—was the rather elaborate dwelling, with the grounds around it brightly floodlit.

The house had been built in an era when stately country homes, or replicas thereof, were the in thing; it was a two-story manor house in the British tradition. Constructed of stone, it was blocky and impressive. The adjacent swimming pool with its green corrugated plastic windbreak did not really go with the original architect's design; it had obviously been added later, as had the garage wing with its three blank doors that faced the paved parking area at the end of the drive curving in from the elaborate front gate of the estate, which was complete with a little gatehouse. There was a light inside this, and a man.

I was aware that my colleague of the evening—observer, Jackson had called him—had entered the apartment and come to stand behind me.

"Four-hour shifts at night," he said. "Two on at a time. Everybody takes turns except the daughter and Jimenez the Elder. That's Arturo Valdez, the cook, holding down the gatehouse now. Manuel Cordoba is working the perimeter with one of his dogs; the other cut a foot and is kenneled tonight." He glanced at the glowing display of his digital watch. "We should see Cordoba over by that big pine tree inside the fence, in just a minute. . . . There he comes."

I reached for one of the binocular cases, got out the big night glasses, and focused them on the distant figure that had just appeared. The dog, walking at heel, was a black Doberman with brown edges, quite a handsome fellow. The man was tall for the country from which he had come, and quite broad; he had a big black piratical moustache. It was a face I'd seen once before in a stolen car from which a dead girl had just been thrown. Oso the Bear. We'd come the long way around, at least I had, but here we both were, although he didn't know it. Strangely, I found no hatred now. Well, there seldom is any, when the time comes. It's generally enough just to know that they'll be dead shortly.

The glasses were heavy 7 x 50s, a Japanese brand with which I was not familiar, but sharp and clear. I watched man and dog disappear again into a thicket of leafless trees.

I said, "Hell, the way the place is lighted, we didn't really need to go for that crazy night-fighting gadget. A good bright four-power scope with fairly heavy crosshairs would have done the job."

He thought I was criticizing him and said quickly, "I had to consider the possibility that Bultman would wipe out the lights somehow, or that we might get a night with poor visibility."

I said, "I wasn't complaining, just commenting. You're the one who set it up?"

"Yes, I've done more long-distance sniping than Jackson. I'm Marty."

We shook hands. "I'm Eric," I said.

He grinned. "Well, if you're not, I'm in big trouble."

But I could sense a certain amount of resentment. There always is some, when they have to do all the dirty work and are then asked to roll out the red carpet for the big-shot prima donna marksman who'll march in at the last moment and take all the credit for making a perfectly easy shot they could have managed perfectly well by themselves. There was also some curiosity. He wasn't quite sure whom I was here to shoot, although he was guessing hard.

I said, "It's a good setup. Let me check out the placement of those sandbags—I think I have bigger hands and longer arms than you do—and then I guess I'll lie down and rest a bit. Wake me if you see anything unusual; if not, kick me in the ass at one-thirty."

I actually did go to sleep; which I think impressed young Marty more than my gaudy reputation as a hot-shot senior operative. Aroused at last, I yawned and stretched and pulled myself together and went into the bathroom and took care of that, no bladder distractions tonight. I wondered idly how many important shots, and great opportunities, had been missed in the course of world history because somebody had to go at the wrong time. It was better than wondering just what the wind was doing out there now, and whether or not the damn gun was going to fire at all. Some haven't.

Then it was only to wait by the open window, with the big rifle resting on the sandbags, muzzle well inside the room to contain the blast a bit. Cartridge in chamber. Safety off and to hell with the conventional safety rules. The piece wasn't going to fire itself lying there, and nervous thumbs have been known not to get that lever all the way to "off" when shooting time came around. Night sight on, and what a Mickey-Mouse gadget that was: our own long-range adaptation of a military gizmo that wasn't too pretty a design to start with. I'd been assured that the battery was good for hours, even days; and that as a matter of fact the thing should be switched on well ahead of use to make sure the circuits had time to stabilize—well, if you

267

don't like my scientific terminology, make up your own. Anyway, everything was ready that could be readied; and I was pleased to discover that Marty was smart enough to know this was no time for idle chatter. He busied himself with his binoculars and kept his mouth shut as we waited.

Suddenly he poked my arm. "That man in the gatehouse. I think he's dead."

I picked up my own glasses and studied the small, distant, illuminated house. The head of the man inside had fallen over at an odd angle. A very neat and sneaky piece of work. I glanced at my watch. Two o'clock.

I asked, "What about the dog patrol?"

Marty glanced at his own watch. "We'll know in . . . three minutes. He should appear by that . . . There he is, a little ahead of . . . Christ!"

I had just spotted the man with the dog far off along the perimeter to the right, when the dog fell down. The man started instinctively to bend over the animal, but realized his mistake and whirled, unslinging the machine pistol he carried; but he never got it into firing position. He seemed to flinch and freeze; then he fell down beside the dog. Scratch Oso the Bear. I felt no great triumph. He was merely dead, as he should be; and I always hate to see a dog killed, even a savage guard dog that's hardly more than an animated weapon. But the dog has no choice. He can't help it if his fierce loyalty is employed in the service of a bunch of bastards. He can't resign his job and go find some nice people to work for.

"What the hell are they using?" I asked.

"Arrows," Marty said, squinting through his binoculars. "For God's sake, real Robin Hood arrows with feathers on!"

"Probably with poison pods attached, to work so fast," I said. "They made succinylcholine pods legal for bow-and-arrow deer hunting once, somewhere. Don't ask me where, and don't ask me to spell it for you; but you'll be happy to know that the meat remains perfectly edible. . . . Ah, here comes the main attack! Can't say the Kraut doesn't have discipline!"

With the guards out of the way, black-clad shadows were filtering in from the fences they must have cut or climbed, and converging on the big house. The doors delayed them only briefly; then they were disappearing inside.

I heard a faint distant tinkling sound: the alarm bells. Then there was a mild rattle of sound like popcorn popping in a skillet several rooms away as the guns went into action. I remembered a tough little brown man, a good soldier, with whom I'd once done a difficult job in the Costa Verde jungle. Well, if they will go the terrorist route because it looks easy, the only answer is to show them how hard it really is.

Hector Jimenez was getting his hard answer now. I felt a little cheap, and a little relieved, because I wasn't delivering it personally.

Meanwhile the estate gates had opened. Two vehicles entered and moved into the parking area before the garage doors. One was a big Lincoln, the luxurious semilimousine size that's slightly out of fashion now; the other was a long Ford van. In addition to the driver in front, the Lincoln had a passenger in the rear. I tried to make out his face with the binoculars—I thought it was a man—but you can't see much through that damn tinted glass.

But it was getting toward time for me to make my contribution to the evening's performance. I laid the glasses aside and hunched over the big .300 Magnum in the benchrest shooting position, right hand closed around the pistol grip of the stock to steady the weapon, left hand brought around under the butt in such a way that I could make fine adjustments in elevation simply by clenching or relaxing my fist. The fore-end of the rifle was, of course, solidly supported by the sandbags.

I squinted through the trick electronic scope and saw the idiotic little red dot glowing in the center of a field that looked a bit like a camera ground-glass except that, thank God, the image was at least right side up. The colors were all screwed up. I wondered if perhaps I shouldn't focus the intense aiming dot a little more sharply. Then I told myself to stop that, leave it alone, cut it out! No final fiddling, dammit! And don't hold low, you stupid jerk! Stop thinking. . . .

"Oh, Jesus!"

I glanced quickly at Marty. He was staring through his binoculars, fascinated and aghast. Moving carefully so as not to disturb the gun too much, I reached for my nightglasses left-handed and put them to my eyes, and winced. A small pretty figure, elflike and unreal in a single long loose white garment, was stumbling through the gap in the swimming-pool windbreak: a slim young girl with long black hair whose bare arms and feet looked unbearably cold, and whose thin fluttering nightgown was darkly stained. She stopped and turned, waiting for someone, and he came: a young man bare to the waist and barefoot, wearing nothing but a hastily-pulled-on pair of trousers. Well, there they were, I told myself grimly. Leona the Lioness, and Lobo the Wolf.

He was carrying a submachine gun of some kind. As he turned to fire it behind him, he was hit hard and dropped the weapon. He went to his knees. The wounded girl staggered back to him and tried to lift him and lead him away, but her own strength was fading and his weight pulled her down. She managed only to pull him aside a little before she collapsed against the plastic windbreak, sliding down to a graceless sitting position—the girl who'd passed the sentence of death on Elly Brand. Okay, she had it coming, I told myself firmly. So she was a pretty young girl, so what? She still had it coming. I watched her find enough strength to lift her brother's head into her lap.

The rear door of the limousine opened. Enrique Echeverria got out. There was no mistaking the red beard, even at night at that distance. As befitted his status as observer, he was in ordinary street clothes covered by a sharp-looking gray overcoat. But he was clearly unable to pass up the opportunity to make his own little contribution to the night's proceedings. He stopped to take out an automatic pistol and haul back the slide to chamber a round; then he walked over to where Dolores Jimenez sat in her bloody nightgown, weakly stroking the unconscious face of her brother Emilio.

I laid the binoculars aside and bent over the big rifle once more. In the weird field of the image-intensifying gadget, as if on a TV screen that badly needed its colors adjusted, I saw Echeverria standing over brother and sister. The girl looked up at him dully, perhaps hoping for help. Echeverria took careful aim and put a bullet into Emilio's head. He turned to Dolores. I had a strong urge to shoot, to hell with vengeance; but there were bushes along the windbreak and I could not be certain that a branch was not in the way. Anyway, the damn girl had made her choice, and I hadn't come all this way to make a sentimental gesture on behalf of someone who wouldn't survive the night anyway. Bultman would take care of her if Echeverria didn't. No witnesses.

I waited and saw the man's gun-hand jump with the recoil. Echeverria backed away and stood looking down at his handiwork with satisfaction. Bultman was inside dealing with the old wolf, but he, Enrique Rojo, had made sure of the cubs out here, with pleasure. The floodlight on the nearby roof shone brightly on the back of the natty overcoat, no branches intervened now, and the silly little red aiming dot looked very good, very steady, where I placed it carefully. . . .

The Magnum fired. It made a fearful roar. It slammed back against my shoulder and reared up off its sandbags like an old-time artillery piece lifting its wheels off the ground in recoil. Then it fell back, leaving a ringing silence.

"Call it!" I said.

"Got him!" Marty said. "Dead center. I think you got the spine, the way he fell. Good shot, sir!"

It was the first time he'd called me sir, and he had no business doing it. There's only one sir in our outfit.

I said, "Start putting this stuff away while I watch what's happening."

"Yes, sir. Greg should be along any minute to give us a hand cleaning up."

I was watching through the binoculars. It had worked out better than we'd hoped, planning it. We'd expected that Bultman would have to coax the man out of the car with some excuse and set him up for me. Of course Bultman could not actually dispose of Echeverria, the representative of his client, himself. That would have been unethical—and if you feel like laughing, I suggest you do it where Bultman can't hear you. He's a very ethical guy according to his lights.

But now he could with a clear conscience remind President Armando Rael that he, Bultman, had protested vigorously against having a babysitter inflicted upon him; and if the guy wouldn't stay in the car as he'd been told but wandered around in the middle of the firefight to exercise his silly little pistol, and stopped a stray slug, it could hardly be called his, Bultman's, fault or sufficient reason for withholding the balance of his fee.

The withdrawal was a very quick and neat operation.

271

They came running from the house and filed into the long van rapidly. I could see only one casualty that had to be helped. Bultman came last, in black like the rest, limping a little on his artificial foot and carrying a machine pistol that looked like an Uzi. He paused briefly to glance at the two dead young people, and bent for a moment over Echeverria's body where it lay in a spreading pool of blood. He straightened up, looking in my direction, nodding. Bull's-eye.

You had to hand it to the guy. For all he knew I was watching him through the night-sight of the Magnum rifle; and as he was well aware, there were people in my government who wouldn't mind a bit hearing that he was dead. But he was a pro, and I was a pro, and he stood there for a moment allowing himself to be a perfect target; then he turned deliberately and got into the Lincoln. The big car rolled away in the wake of the van.

There was no sign that the single shot had aroused anybody in our building—one shot at that time of night generally just wakes them up confused wondering if they actually heard anything. But I heard a long, wild howl in the distance. The remaining Doberman, that had survived in its kennel because of a hurt foot, was mourning its dead.

CHAPTER 34

MAC thought he was entitled to an explanation. It was morning, and I was sitting on one of the big beds in my big double room in the Allmand Hotel, listening to the familiar voice in the telephone.

"I think I'm entitled to an explanation, Eric." The voice was stiff and reproving. "Your mission—one of your missions—was to deal with a professional killer named Bultman. I am informed that, after expertly disposing of a fairly prominent Latin-American politician for reasons known only to yourself, you then passed up a very good shot at your assigned target; and that as far as is known,

Bultman is still quite healthy except for the foot he lost in Cuba."

I said, "Sir, if you'll review my orders, you'll find that in the Bultman matter I was instructed to use my own judgment. I made contact with the Kraut down in Costa Verde. I assured myself that there is no way in the world he'll ever reveal who hired him for his disastrous Cuban venture. That's what our friends over in Virginia are really concerned about, isn't it?"

"Do I get the impression that you like the man?"

"Like, no," I said. "Respect, yes. And without direct orders—none of this use-your-judgment stuff—I'm not going to make a needless touch on a guy who's done us no harm just because those clowns down there across the Potomac are so blabber-mouthed themselves that they can't conceive of anybody else keeping quiet about anything. Furthermore, I had a use for Bultman, so I made a deal with him; and I saw no reason to go back on it last night. That was my second mission, wasn't it, to stage an object lesson for the benefit of anybody else who might try to influence us by kidnaping and intimidation, call it Operation Jimenez?"

"An object lesson hardly serves its purpose if nobody gets the point. That paramilitary attack was very obviously not our kind of operation."

I said, "People aren't stupid, sir. At least the people we want to impress aren't. By now the word has got around that the Jimenez outfit pulled the old hostage routine on us and, when their demands were refused, killed the hostage. Pretty soon the word will go around that a month afterward, the Jimenez outfit was totally annihilated. No matter who actually pulled the trigger, or triggers, nobody who's thinking of tackling us by that method is going to dismiss it as coincidence, sir, remembering a few other folks who tried to blackmail us like that who didn't get what they wanted, either, and who are no longer around."

There was a pause. At last Mac said grudgingly, "Very well, let's say that you have accomplished your objectives in a reasonably satisfactory manner. However, I still think I'm entitled to an explanation of why the resources of this agency were employed to help you in the quite unauthorized removal of a stray Costa Verde police functionary."

"Stray, hell," I said. "That's an insult, sir. Echeverria didn't stray one little bit. He came right under my gun because I talked his president and Bultman into putting him there. Incidentally, the bullet seems to have achieved total penetration and nobody seems to be interested in hunting for it. With so many dead bodies on their hands, the authorities are apparently cutting a few corners and attributing them all to submachine gun fire, except the bow-and-arrow jobs of course. But you might tell the armorer we may not have got as much expansion with that new bullet as we should have. If the slug had mushroomed properly, it would have met enough resistance to stay in the body at that range. As it turned out, of course, it was all for the best; but normally I hate to waste bullet energy drilling holes in the scenery behind the target."

"I will transmit the message." Mac's voice was chilly once more. "Was this a personal vendetta, Eric?"

"Not at all," I said. "The guy was a bastard, but he never did anything to me, to amount to anything." I stopped, but Mac was silent, refusing to help me out with leading questions. I said, "Would you agree that, in a sense, Elly Brand died for us, sir? Would you agree that the outfit owes her a memorial gesture of some kind? Of course we could pass the hat for flowers for the grave, although it's a litttle late now, or make a contribution in her name to a suitable charity. However, it occurred to me that there was something we could do that would have pleased her more. You may remember that she was always a great girl for human rights and democracy."

"Go on, Eric." His expressionless voice gave me no help at all.

I said, "I went down there, as you'll recall, partly to check up on whether or not Hector Jimenez was expendable, as far as his country was concerned. I learned that he was, in the sense that when he was in power he let his old army buddies practically rape the country, financially speaking. On the other hand, there seems to have been none of the brutality and oppression that Rael brought to the office. Jimenez's regime was corrupt, but it wasn't vicious. In fact, after all these years of Rael, the people are looking back rather fondly at his kindly, if slightly crooked, predecessor. The Jimenez name is quite popular in liberation circles. They're remembering the good soldier and forgetting the bad president. And now the older son is trying to follow in his papa's political footsteps. He's a bright and conscientious and concerned young man with a lot going for him. He may be able to do something for his country— if certain people in Washington don't keep supplying his opponent, Rael, with endless quantities of arms, munitions, and just plain old Yankee money."

Mac said, "I'm not certain I want to hear this, Eric. International politics are not our concern."

I said, "Hell, all I did was put President Armando Rael's signature on that slaughter out in Lake Park. He can't very well deny responsibility with the chief of his own secret police force lying dead on the premises holding the gun with which he personally disposed of two of the victims. . . . I hadn't hoped for that, but it's working beautifully. Have you seen the Chicago newspapers?"

"No, but I have seen the television news."

I looked at the paper on my bed. It had a photo of the English-style mansion house, and a formal publicity portrait of Enrique Echeverria in Costa Verde army uniform; but the place of honor belonged to a rather distressing photograph, brutally illuminated by the electronic flash that had been used, of a lovely young girl in a bloodstained nightgown sitting against a swimming-pool windbreak with the head of a handsome young man in her lap. The obvious resemblance between the two dead faces made the picture very poignant; it was clear that brother and sister had died trying to help each other flee the terrible massacre taking place inside their house. The fact that they were both cold-blooded murderers in my book was, of course, quite irrelevant.

I said, "It's working. Already there are loud editorial outcries against our policy of supporting a regime that sends important government officials at the head of ruthless commandos to massacre political refugees living peacefully in this country. I think it's going to be a long time before Armando Rael gets another shipment of M16s. Or dollars. Elly was always very upset about the way this country of ours always seemed to back the most repressive regime it could find. I think she'd have liked knowing that, because of her, Ricardo Jimenez has been given just a bit of a chance to overthrow the current dictatorship down there. What he does with that chance is, of course, up to him."

There was a brief silence; then Mac said, "There seems to be something wrong with this connection. I didn't hear any of that, Eric. I prefer not to hear it; it's a totally indefensible perversion of the functions of this agency. Furthermore it shows regrettable sentimentality on the part of one of my senior operatives." He paused, and went on: "Have you completed your period of mourning now, or can I expect further Machiavellian gestures of atonement?"

I thought of a small girl lying dead in a dark street. I said, "I think it's taken care of now. As much as it will ever be."

"I certainly hope so," Mac said. "Get to Washington as fast as you can, please. Now that these minor matters have been dealt with, we have work to do."

That should have been the end of it, of course; and I had a very busy spring and summer by the end of which I couldn't have told you the names of all the people with whom I'd shared a brief imprisonment in an odd place called Labal. Only one reminder reached me during those months: an envelope containing a brief note signed Emily, and a newspaper clipping concerning the death, after a brief illness, of General Austin Henderson, U.S.A. (ret).

But one night between forays abroad, resting in my small Washington apartment, I turned on the television for the news and found a very familiar building dominating the screen. As I watched, the charges went off and the massive limestone walls collapsed into piles of rubble while the smoke and dust rose high into the blue Costa Verde sky. Very dramatic. The unctuous voice of the anchorman informed me that I was watching the ceremonial destruction of the infamous prison known as La Fortaleza by elite demolition units of the victorious Costa Verde Army of Liberation.

We heard a few words from the Commander in Chief of that army, General Jaime Putnam, observing the event with his attractive young wife. The general said that mopping-up operations should be no problem now that Armando Rael had deserted his trapped remnant of an army and fled the country. The youthful political leader of the liberation movement, Ricardo Jimenez, gave an interview from his wheelchair, stating that La Fortaleza had been a symbol of oppression to his country as the Bastille had once been to France; and that he intended its destruction to inaugurate a better and freer life for his people.

For months I had carefully avoided thinking of Costa Verde. Perhaps it was being involuntarily reminded of everything that had happened down there that made it difficult for me to go to sleep that night. Then I had a violent dream. It was a savage battle in the jungle; and the spearmen had fled as the Spears always do, and the great stone axes were doing their work as we held the causeway by the Arch of the Emperors giving the king and his entourage time to withdraw. Somehow I knew perfectly well, with part of my mind, that it was a phony vision sent to me by an old master showman who could have made his fortune in Hollywood. It had never happened, and if it had happened, it hadn't happened with those weapons, but it was a hell of a good fight anyway and we Axes made an orderly withdrawal down the fine stone road, the King's Road, making them pay us high for every inch of it, until somebody kicked some courage into the Spears and sent them in from the flanks. . . .

ADIOSGUERREROGOODBYE

The message blasted through, wiping out the dream and bringing me upright in the bed. I reached for the light switch but took back my hand. I wasn't quite ready to return to Washington, D.C.

"Adios, Cortez," I said aloud.

Then I felt foolish sitting in a dark apartment with traffic rolling by beneath the windows, talking to a primitive old character in a foreign country without benefit of telephone or radio. I mean, who believes that stuff?

But the believing part of my mind knew what it had heard, if you want to call it hearing. It knew something else, too. There had been another message sent, and the receiver was not far away. I could feel it. I got up and turned on the lights and debated getting dressed, but at one-thirty in the morning there was no sense in that. I just put on dressing gown and slippers, set out a couple of glasses on the little corner bar, got some ice out, and waited. Presently the front door buzzer sounded. I hit the button to release the latch downstairs. Shortly the knock came on the door. I opened it.

She said a little breathlessly, "I've been staying in a hotel a few blocks away trying to make up my mind. Anybody would think I was timid or something. I guess I was afraid of making a fool of myself. I didn't know if you'd really want to see me after all these months. Then I had a dream and I knew you were having one very much like it, and I knew that I had to . . . that I was supposed to . . . Tell me if you want me to go away."

I said, "Frances, stop talking nonsense and come inside."

She was wearing a light-brown fall coat over a tailored beige dress with buttons down the front—as I learned upon helping her off with the coat. She was wearing heels and nylons, and her legs were as slim and lovely as ever. Her crisp brown hair was very smooth and her lipstick was very neatly applied and she didn't look a bit as if she'd just tumbled out of a strange hotel bed after a disturbing dream. I made drinks for us and put hers into her hand.

"What was your dream, Sam?" she asked.

"A battle in the jungle," I said. "Actually, it took place by a certain ancient arch I think you remember."

She grimaced. "I ought to. I spent enough time there, brutally tied hand and foot. Well, I deserved it."

"What was your dream?" I asked.

"It was . . ." She stopped, and her eyes avoided me suddenly; and I saw my tall, handsome lady blushing like a young girl. "I don't think I'll tell you what it was," she said a bit stiffly. "Of course I don't believe a word of it; but he was dying, wasn't he? Saying good-bye like that?"

I said, "Me, I don't take no stock in any of that extra-sensory crap either, ma'am; but I wouldn't want to bet any important money that if we hopped a jet this minute and got ourselves down there, we wouldn't reach Copalque just about right to find the old High Priest being buried and the new one, Epifanio, performing the ceremony. Cortez took a pretty bad beating that night in the cave; I guess he never really recovered. And Epifanio gets the nice job of doing whatever has to be done, High-Priest-wise, when the three sacred calendars come into conjunction some time in the not too distant future."

Frances was silent for a moment; then she asked, "Do you really think he'll call his people together and pass out the poison as in that other dream we had? And does the prophecy, or whatever you want to call it, apply only to the descendants of the ancient Melmecs, or to the rest of the world as well?"

I said, "Hell, we don't need any high priests to order us to poison ourselves. We're doing it quite voluntarily, using every poison from auto pollution to radioactive junk of one kind or another. And of course we're all very civilized people and don't need any old doomsday calendars to tell us when to kill ourselves—and if it should all happen according to that big stone wheel beside the sacred *cenote* down in the sacred cave of Copalque, it'll all be just a crazy coincidence, right?"

She smiled faintly. "Right on, man. Science pays no attention to such foolishness and there's undoubtedly a simple scientific explanation for everything we've seen and heard. . . . Matt."

"Yes?" I said.

"Just Matt," she said softly, watching me. "Just getting used to it. I guess it's all right. But I kind of liked Sam, too."

There was a little silence. I stepped forward and gently turned her face toward the light. It was the face I remembered very well, even though I'd expended considerable effort trying not to remember it at all; but there were faint marks of pain I hadn't seen before.

"What have you been doing to yourself, Dillman?" I asked; and then I understood and said, "I told you not to tell him."

"And I told you I had to. I couldn't live like that. Not with a secret like that between us. I thought he loved me enough. . . ." She stopped and drew a long ragged breath and said quite without expression, "Matt, he was very big about it. Very big. He was willing to *forgive* me. Wasn't that sweet of him?"

I said angrily, "What the hell did he have to forgive? He as much as told you to do anything you had to in order to save him, didn't he?"

She didn't seem to hear me. She swayed a little, standing there. When I stepped forward to steady her, she made a quick little please-don't-touch-me gesture and turned sharply away from me. Her voice was harsh when she spoke again.

"Yes, he was very sweet and noble, Matt; but he said I really shouldn't have taken him so *literally*. He said he certainly hadn't meant for me to do anything like *that,* and naturally he'd expected me to use a little *judgment;* and if I

279

wanted to fuck stray government agents, he couldn't stop me, but I certainly had no right to put the blame on *him*. . . . But of course, since I was his wife, although I seemed to have forgotten it temporarily, he thought he might be able to forgive me in time, since I'd been honest enough to make a clean breast of my transgression." She turned back to face me and made a helpless gesture of despair. "Oh, God, darling, I loved him. I would have killed for him and died for him—I almost did both—and I had to stand there watching him turn himself into a cheap, cowardly, sneering, pompous little man right in front of my eyes. And afterward I . . . I stood it for months, my dear, but at last I couldn't live with that awful condescending forgiveness any more. So I used the number you gave me and got your address and here I am. If you want me."

There were things unsaid that didn't need to be said. We both knew that if one day her husband managed to swallow his pride and jealousy and begged her to come back, she would probably go, even though he'd revealed himself to be something less than the shining knightly figure she had thought she'd married. But that was in the future. This was tonight.

"Need you ask?" I said.

She smiled slowly. "A woman always likes to be told."

I took her into my arms and told her.

ABOUT THE AUTHOR

Donald Hamilton has been writing Matt Helm novels for over 20 years. An expert yachtsman, he has also written nonfiction books and articles on sailing. He and his wife live aboard their yacht, *Kathleen,* and in Santa Fe, New Mexico.